The Pulp Adventure
MEGAPACK®

H. Bedford-Jones
W.C. Tuttle
Murray Leinster
Raymond S. Spears
Ray Cummings
Roy Norton
Frederick C. Davis
Andrew A. Caffrey
A. DeHerries Smith
Alma and Paul Ellerbe
Richard Howells Watkins
L. Paul
H.P.S. Greene

The Pulp Adventure MEGAPACK®

Edited by
John Betancourt

WILDSIDE PRESS

CONTENTS

INTRODUCTION

When you think of the pulp magazines that flourished in the first half of the 20th century, it's hard not to think of adventure—the term "pulp fiction" these days has come to mean slam-bang action. That's what this volume of our MEGAPACK® is here to celebrate: great adventure stories.

Although the pulps published every type of fiction imaginable, from romance to mystery to science fiction to westerns to horror, I have focused this volume on tales of heroes—both small and larger-than-life—with a special emphasis on stories from *Adventure* magazine. It's an eclectic mix, with westerns, sea stories, air stories (pilots were heroes in the early days of aviation, especially during and after World War I), mysteries, and more. It surprises many who aren't familiar with pulps that the quality of fiction they published—especially in the leading magazines, whose circulations often topped a million copies per issue—was quite high. They paid substantial money for the stories they published, and successful writers earned good livings. Some transitioned to movies; others moved on to the "slick" magazines (which paid substantially more). But many, especially those who enjoyed working in specific genres like mystery and science fiction, were content to write just for the pulps.

Among the notable names in this volume are W.C. Tuttle (who was quite prolific and one of the top western authors of the era); H. Bedford-Jones (the self-proclaimed "king of the pulps," who published millions of words of fiction every year and became a favorite of many for his tales of adventure, often in exotic lands); Murray Leinster (still remembered for his classic science fiction—though he wrote in every genre, from romance to mystery to mainstream); and Ray Cummings (who wrote classic science fiction before the term was invented, and went on to have a decades-long career in the science fiction magazines and comic books). Also check out Raymond S. Spears, who is one of my favorite pulp writers—I don't know much about him, but he never fails to entertain.

Enjoy!

—John Betancourt

HE SWALLOWS GOLD,
by H. Bedford-Jones

Originally published in Argosy and Railroad Man's Magazine, May 3, 1919.

I

"We, all of us," said Huber Davis reflectively, "like to show off *how* we do things; we like to tell people about our methods; we like to exposit our particular way of managing affairs. Each of us thinks he is a little tin god in that respect, Carefrew. That's the way of a white man. A Chinaman, however, is just the opposite. He does *not* want to show his methods. He does things in a damned mysterious way—and he never tells."

Carefrew sucked at his cigarette and eyed his brother-in-law with a sneer beneath his eyelids. Only a few hours previously Carefrew had landed from the coasting steamer, very glad indeed to get out of Batavia and parts adjacent with a whole skin. His wife was coming later, after she had straightened up his affairs, and he would then hop aboard the Royal Mail liner with her, and voyage on to Colombo and Europe. Ruth Carefrew, however, knew little about the deal which had sent Carefrew himself up to Sabang in a hurry.

"You seem to know a lot about Chinese ways," said Carefrew.

"I ought to," admitted Huber Davis placidly. "I've been dealing with 'em here for the past ten years, and I've built up a whale of a business with their help. You, on the other hand, got into a whale of a mess through swindling the innocent Oriental—"

"Oh, cut out the abuse!" broke in Carefrew nastily. "What are you driving at with your drivel about Chinese methods? I suppose you're insinuating that they'll try to get after me away up here at Sabang?"

"More than likely," assented Huber Davis. "They have fairly close connections, what with business tongs and the Heaven-and-Earth Society, which has a lodge here. They'll know that the clever chap who carried out that swindling game in Singapore, and then managed to put it over the second time in Batavia, is named Reginald Carefrew. They'll have relatives in both places; probably you ruined a good many of their relatives—"

"Look here!" snapped Carefrew nastily. "Let me impress on you that there was no swindle! The Chinese love to gamble, and I gave 'em a run for their money—that's all."

Huber Davis eyed his brother-in-law with a trace of cynicism in his wide-eyed, poised features.

"Never mind lying about it, Reggy," he said coolly. "You'll be here until the next boat to Colombo, which is five days. In those five days you take my advice and stick close to this house; you'll be absolutely safe here. I'm not helping and protecting you, mind, because I love you—it's for Ruth's sake. Somehow, Ruth would be sorry if you got bumped off. No one else would be sorry that I know of, but Ruth's my sister, and I'd like to oblige her. I don't order you to stay here, mind that! It's merely advice."

Under this lash of cool, unimpassioned truths Carefrew reddened and then paled again. He did not display any resentment, however. He was a little afraid of Huber Davis.

"You're away off color," he said carelessly. "Think I'm going to be a prisoner here? No. Besides, I honestly think there's no danger, in spite of your apprehension. The yellow boys have nothing to be revengeful over, you see."

"Oh," said Huber Davis mildly. "I understood that several had committed suicide back in Batavia. That makes you their murderer, according to the old beliefs."

Carefrew laughed; his laugh was not very good to hear, either.

"Bosh!" he exclaimed. "Those old superstitions are discarded in these days of New China. You'll be saying next that the ghosts of the dead will haunt me!"

"They ought to," retorted Huber Davis. "So you think the old beliefs are gone, do you? Well, we're not in China, my excellent Reggy. We're in Sabang, and the Straits Chinese have a way of clinging to the beliefs of their ancestors. You stick close to the house."

"You go to the devil!" snapped Carefrew.

Huber Davis merely shrugged his shoulders, as though he had received all the consideration which he had expected.

"Li Mow Gee," he observed, "is the biggest trader in these parts, and I know he has a raft of relatives back your way. I'd avoid his store."

Carefrew, uttering an impatient oath, got up and left the veranda.

Huber Davis glanced after his brother-in-law, a sleepy, cynical laziness in his gaze. One gathered that he would not care a whit how soon Carefrew died, except possibly that his sister Ruth still loved Carefrew—a little. And except, of course, that the man was his own brother-in-law, and at the ends of the earth a white man upholds certain ideas about caste and the duty of white to white, and so forth.

II

Singapore is called the gateway of the Far East, but the real portal is the free-trade island harbor of Sabang, at the northern end of Sumatra.

At Sabang even the mail-steamers stop, coming and going. From England and India, coal is dumped at Sabang; the wharves and floating docks are many and busy; the cables extend from Sabang to all parts of the globe.

From the harbor heads runs brilliant blue water up to the brilliant green shores, and under the hill is snugly nestled a city whose Chinese streets convey a dull-red impression. Here, as elsewhere, the Chinese are the ganglia of trade and activity. The Dutch government likes them and profits by them, and they profit likewise.

One of the narrow Chinese streets turns sharply, almost at right angles, and is called the Street of the Heavenly Elbow for this reason. At the outside corner of the elbow is a door and shop sign, opening upon a narrow room little wider than the door; but behind this is another room, widening as one goes farther from the elbow, and behind this yet another room which broadens into a suite of apartments.

Such was the shop of Li Mow Gee. As is well known, Li is one of the Four Hundred surnames, and betokens that its owner is at least of good family, also widely connected. Li Mow Gee was both; to boot, he was very rich, considerably dissipated, and his private affairs were exactly like his shop—they began at a small and obscure point, which was himself, and they widened and widened beyond the ken of passersby until they comprised an extent which would have been incredible to any chance beholder. But Li Mow Gee saw to it that there were no chance beholders of his private affairs or shop either.

Li Mow Gee was not the type of inscrutable, omnipotent gambler who somehow manages to control fate and carry out the purposes of destiny, such as appear to be many of his race. He prided himself upon being a "son of T'ang"—that is, a man of the old southern empire whose ancestry was quite clear and unblemished through about nine centuries.

He was a slant-eyed, yellow-skinned, wrinkled little man of fifty. He had a bad digestion and an irritable temper, he was much given to rice-wine and wives, and he possessed an uncanny knowledge of the code of Confucius, by which he ruled his life—sometimes.

Upon the day after Reginald Carefrew arrived in Sabang the estimable Li Mow Gee sat in his private back room, which was hung with Chien Lung paintings, whose subjects would have scandalized Sodom and Gomorrah. Li Mow Gee sucked a three-foot pipe of bamboo and steel, and watched a kettle of water bubbling over a charcoal brazier. At the proper moment he took a pewter insert from its stand, slipped it into its niche inside the kettle, and watched the water boil until the pewter vessel was well heated. Then he poured hot rice-wine into the thimble-cup of porcelain at his elbow, sipped it with satisfaction, and clapped his hands four times.

One of the numerous doors of the room opened to admit a spectacled old man who was a junior partner of Li Mow Gee in business, but who was also Venerable Master of the local lodge of the Heaven-and-Earth Society. As etiquette demanded, the junior partner removed his spectacles and stood blinking, being blind as a bat without them.

"As you are aware, worshipful Chang," said Li Mow Gee after some preliminary discourse, "my father's younger brother has become an ancient."

Mr. Chang bowed respectfully. A son of T'ang never says of his family that they are dead. But Mr. Chang had heard that Li Mow Gee's father's younger brother had committed suicide, with the intent of sending his avenging ghost after one Reginald Carefrew.

"You are also aware," pursued Li Mow Gee, refilling the steel bowl of his pipe, "that the brother-in-law of my friend Huber Davis has arrived in Sabang for a short visit. As a man of learning, you will comprehend that I have certain duties to perform."

Mr. Chang blinked, and promptly took his cue.

"You doubtless recall certain canons of the law which bear upon the situation," he squeaked blandly. "It would give me infinite pleasure to hear them from your lips."

Li Mow Gee had been waiting for this. He exhaled a thin cloud of smoke, and quoted from his exact memory of the writings of the Confucian canon:

"With the slayer of his father, a man may not live under the same sky; against the slayer of his brother, a man must never have to go home to seek a weapon; with the slayer of his friend, a man may not live in the same state."

Li Mow Gee smoked for a moment in silence, then continued:

"Thus reads the Book of Rites, most venerable Chang. And yet our friend Huber Davis is our friend."

"If the tiger and the ox are in company," quoth Mr. Chang squeakily, "let the ox die with the tiger."

"Not at all to the point," said Li Mow Gee in irritated accents. "Do not be a venerable fool, my father! I desire that a messenger be sent to my bazaar."

"Speak the message, beloved of heaven," responded the elder.

"In our safe," said Li Mow Gee slowly, "is a three-armed candlestick of white jade, bound in brass and having upon its three arms the characters signifying chalk, charcoal, and water. It is my wish that this precious object be taken to my bazaar and placed there near the door, with a sign upon it putting the price at nine florins; also, that our clerks be severely instructed to sell this object to no one except Mr. Carefrew."

Mr. Chang wet his lips.

"But, dear brother," he expostulated, "this is one of the precious objects of the Heaven-and-Earth Society."

"That is why I desire your permission to make use of it," said Li Mow Gee. "Am I to be trusted or not? Is my sacred honor of no worth in your eyes?"

"But, to be sold to a foreign devil!" the junior partner exclaimed.

"That is my wish."

Mr. Chang threw up his hands, not without a smothered oath.

"Very well!" he squeaked angrily. "But when this swindler, this murderer of honest folk, sees it for sale in your bazaar at so ridiculous a price, he will buy it and take it away, and laugh at Li Mow Gee for a fool!"

"If he did not," said Li Mow Gee, pouring himself another thimble-cup of wine, "I should be a most wretched and unhappy man!"

III

A Chinese candlestick is meant to hold, upon a long, upright prong, a candle painted with very soft red wax, so soft that the finger cannot touch the paint without blurring and marring it. Otherwise, it is like Occidental candlesticks in general respects.

Reginald Carefrew, who had plenty of money in his pocket, but who had left Singapore in something of a real hurry, walked into the Benevolent Brethren Bazaar in search of silks and pongees to take home to Europe. The bazaar, which bore no other name, confined itself almost exclusively to such goods. In the front of the shop, which was upon one of the half-Dutch streets overlooking the harbor, were strewn about a few objects of brass, bronze, and the cheap champlevé cloisonné which are made for tourists.

Almost as he entered the place, however, the vigilant eye of Carefrew discovered a very different object, placed in a niche which concealed it from view of the street. It was no less than a candlestick of three arms, a most unusual thing; also, it was made chiefly from jade, highly carven, while the upright prongs and the trimmings were of brass. Altogether, a most extraordinary and wonderful candlestick—priced at nine florins.

Carefrew, naturally, thought that his eyes lied to him about the price. With excitement twitching at his nerves, he walked back and bought several bolts of silk, ordering them sent to him at the residence of Huber Davis.

Then, casually, he inquired about the candlestick of the smiling clerk.

It was, he learned, a worthless object, left here for sale long years ago by some now forgotten Hindu native, or maybe Arab; one could not be certain where years had elapsed and the insignificance of the object was great, but of course the books would show, should it be desired that the affair be looked into.

Naturally, Carefrew did not desire the affair looked into, because some one was then sure to discover that the candlestick was real jade. There was no doubt about that fact, and he was too shrewd to be deceived. A passing wonder did enter his mind as to how yellow men, especially men of T'ang from the middle provinces, could have supposed the candlestick to be worthless; but, after all, mistakes happen to all men—and other men profit by them. The candlestick was not a wonder of the world, but was worth a few hundred dollars at least.

So Carefrew laid down his nine florins, and carried his purchase away with him, wrapped in paper.

Carefrew found the bungalow deserted except for the native boys; the siesta hour was over, and Huber Davis had departed to his office. After a critical inspection of his purchase, resulting in a complete vindication of his former judgment, Carefrew set the triple candlestick on the dining-table and swung off to Chinatown again.

It was the most natural desire in the world to want to complete that princely candlestick with appropriate candles; particularly as Carefrew was now on his way to Europe and would have little further chance to get hold of the real articles.

Being downtown, Carefrew dropped into the office of Huber Davis, and found a letter which had come in that morning by the coast steamer from Batavia. The letter was from Ruth, confirming her passage on the next fast Royal Mail boat. Upon the fourth day from this she would be at Sabang, having taken passage as far as Colombo for herself and Carefrew, whose loose business ends she was arranging.

"I suppose," inquired Huber Davis in his cool, semi-interested fashion, "you did not take her into your confidence regarding your late financial ventures?"

"Why in hell would I want to bother her about finances?" retorted Carefrew, with his bold-eyed look. "She doesn't understand such things."

"Damned good thing she doesn't, perhaps," reflected the other. "Well, see you later! By the way, here's the receipt for that thirty thousand you laid in my safe."

"I don't want receipts from you." protested Carefrew virtuously.

"Maybe not, but I want to give 'em to you," and Huber Davis smiled.

"Damned rotter!" reflected Carefrew as he passed on his way.

He was not acquainted in or with Sabang. It was not hard to see what he desired, however, and presently he succeeded beyond his expectations. A dirty window filled with dried oysters and strings of fish and other things, after the Chinese fashion, carried also a display of temple candles. They had only appeared in the window that morning, but Carefrew did not know it, and would not have cared had he known it.

Carefrew stopped and inspected the candles, which were exactly what he wanted. There was a half-inch wick of twisted cotton, around which was built the candle, two inches thick. The outside was gaudy red and blue with sticky greasepaint, and at the lower end was a protruding reed four inches long.

By this reed one might handle the affair without marring the paint, and into this reed fitted the upright prong of a candlestick. The whole candle was bound inside a big joint of bamboo, which held it without harm.

Noting that there was one candle on display, and that there seemed to be but two more with it, Carefrew entered the shop, found the proprietor, and priced the candles. The proprietor had brought them from Singapore ten years previously and did not want to sell them. However, Carefrew offered a ten-florin note, and carried them home.

He was, for the moment, a child with a new toy, completely absorbed in it, and utterly heedless of all the rest of the world. Another man might have had weights upon his conscience, but Reginald Carefrew was not bothered by any such.

He laid the three bamboo cylinders upon the dining-table, after it had been laid for dinner, and opened them, cutting the shrunken withes that held them securely. The glaring red candles lay before him, and for a moment he pulled at his cigarette and studied them. Knowing what sort of candles they were, he tentatively touched them with his forefinger. The touch left a red blotch at the end of his finger, so soft was the greasepaint.

One by one he set them carefully upon the three prongs of his jade candlestick. One could not blame his ardent admiration. Even to an eye which knew nothing of Chinese art, the picture was exquisite; to one who could appreciate fully, it was marvelous. Candles and candlestick blended into a perfect thing, a creation.

"And to think that it cost me," said Carefrew to his brother-in-law, when Huber Davis appeared, "exactly nineteen florins—ten of which were for the candles!"

Huber Davis gazed at the outfit appraisingly, a slight frown creasing his brow.

"If I were you," he said after a moment, "I'd get rid of it, Reggy. You certainly picked up something there—but it doesn't look right to me. You don't catch John Chinaman handing out stuff like that at a bargain price, not these days!"

"Bosh!" ejaculated Carefrew. "A pickup, that's all—one of the things that comes the way of any man who keeps his eyes open."

Huber Davis shrugged his shoulders.

"Got the red stuff on your hands, eh?"

Carefrew smiled vaguely—his smile was always vague and disagreeable—and glanced at his hands. He rubbed them, and the red spots became a fine pink rouge.

"I'll light 'em up," he said, "and then wash for dinner, eh?"

Huber Davis said nothing, but watched with cold-growing eyes as Carefrew lighted the three wicks. He was somewhat long in doing this, for they were slow to catch. When they did flare, it was with a yellow, smoky light that sent a black trail to the ceiling. Carefrew turned to leave the room, but the voice of his brother-in-law brought him about quickly.

"Wait! I had a letter today from my agent in Batavia, Reggy. He said that Ruth had been in the office—he was helping her straighten up some of your affairs."

A subtle alarm crept into the narrow eyes of Carefrew as he met the cold, passionless gaze of Huber Davis.

"Well?" he demanded suddenly. "What is the idea?"

"You didn't say anything was wrong with Ruth," said Huber Davis calmly. "But my agent mentioned that her right arm looked badly bruised—her sleeve fell away, I imagine—and she said it had been a slight accident. What was it?"

Carefrew's brows lifted. "Damned if I know! Must have hurt herself after I left, eh? Too bad, now—"

He turned and left the room, whistling. Huber Davis gazed after him; one would have said that the man's cold eyes suddenly glowed and smoldered, as a shaft of sunlight suddenly strikes fire into cold amethyst.

"Ah!" he muttered. "You damned blackguard—it goes with the rest, it does! You've laid hands on her, and yet she sticks by you; some women are like that. You've laid hands on her, all right. If I could prove it, by the Lord I'd let out your rotten soul! But she'll never tell."

Presently Carefrew's gay whistle sounded, and he sauntered back into the dining-room.

"That's queer!" he observed lightly. "The red ink wouldn't come off. I'll get some of your cocoa butter after dinner and try it on. Hello! Real steamed rice, eh? Say, that's a treat! I despise this Dutch stuff."

17

IV

Huber Davis, who had an excellent general agency, always dealt with Li Mow Gee in silks and fabrics—that is, he dealt with Li Mow Gee direct, which meant that he was one of a circle of half a dozen men who did this. Not more than half a dozen knew that Li Mow Gee had any particular interest in the silk trade.

Two days after Carefrew had brought home the candlestick and appurtenances thereof, Huber Davis sought the Street of the Heavenly Elbow, and entered the dingy cubby-hole which opened upon the widening shop of Li Mow Gee. That morning Carefrew had carefully tied up his temple candles again and was preparing to pack his purchases of silk.

After a very short wait Huber Davis was ushered through the fan-shaped apartments to the hub and kernel of Li Mow Gee's enterprises, where the owner sat before his charcoal brazier, heated his rice-wine, and gazed upon his nudes—to call them by a polite name—with never-flagging appreciation.

Li Mow Gee greeted him cordially and ordered tea brought in. Huber Davis said nothing of business until the tea had been poured, and then he did not make the usual foreigner's mistake of drinking his tea. He knew better, for Li Mow Gee followed the tea ceremony implicitly.

When he had concluded his business in silk Huber Davis took from his pocket a sheet of note-paper upon which were inscribed three ideographs.

"I wish you would do me a favor, Mr. Li," he said. "My brother-in-law is visiting me, and the other day he picked up a candlestick bearing these characters. For the sake of satisfying my own curiosity, I copied the characters and put 'em up to my clerk, but he said they were very old writing, and that only a university man like yourself could decipher them correctly. So, if you would oblige me—"

Li Mow Gee took the paper and glanced at the three ideographs. He wrinkled up his dissipated eyes and gazed at Huber Davis. Then he picked up his pipe and began to smoke.

"Your clerk was a wise man, Mr. Davis," he said quietly. "You have heard of the Heaven-and-Earth Society, no doubt?"

Huber Davis started. "You mean—"

"Exactly, my friend. How your esteemed brother-in-law picked up this candlestick I cannot imagine; but it is marked with the emblems of that society, of which I am a member."

Huber Davis whistled. He knew that not all the power of the Manchu emperors had availed to stifle that secret fraternity, and he knew that Reggy Carefrew was playing with hot coals. But he kept silence, and presently he had his reward.

"If we were not friends," said Li Mow Gee reflectively, "and if the ties of friendship were not sacred and honorable things, I would say nothing to you. Even now it may be too late; as to that I cannot say, for others may know that your brother-in-law made this purchase. But, because we are friends, for your sake I shall try to help you."

"I appreciate it," said Huber Davis, not without anxiety. His anxiety was warranted. "If you will give me advice it shall be followed implicitly, I assure you."

Li Mow Gee smoked until his long pipe sucked dry.

"Well, then, bring to me that candlestick and whatever else was with it—candles, perhaps. I will make good whatever sum your honorable relative expended, and I will see to it that the matter is adjusted in the right quarters in case trouble has arisen. But, remember, time is an element of importance."

"In half an hour," said Huber Davis earnestly, "I shall return with the things."

Li Mow Gee picked up his cup of tea, signaling that the interview was ended.

Huber Davis dropped business and hurried home. If he could have reconciled it with his conscience, he would have let matters alone in the confidence that before a great while Reginald Carefrew would be removed from this mortal sphere; but Huber Davis had a stiff conscience. Besides, there was Ruth. If Ruth still loved this swindler, Huber Davis intended to protect and further him—for her sake. There was a good deal of the old conventional spirit in Huber Davis.

He expected trouble, and was prepared to handle it firmly; but he wanted to avoid a scene if possible. So, finding Carefrew engaged in packing, he lighted his pipe and watched for a few moments without broaching the subject on his mind.

"How much," he said at last, "do you expect to get for that candlestick if you sell it?"

Carefrew looked at him in surprise.

"Eh? Think I have some judgment, after all, do you? Oh, I ought to get a hundred easily."

"Well, see here," proposed Huber Davis, "I do like the thing, Reggy. Tell you what: I'll give a hundred and twenty-five, cash down, if you'll turn it over. Eh?"

Carefrew grinned. "Hundred and fifty takes it," he said.

"You nasty son of—" thought Huber Davis. With an effort he controlled himself and produced his check-book. By the time he had written the check Carefrew had unpacked the candlestick. Huber Davis remembered the negligible remark which Li Mow Gee had made about the candles.

"Throw in the candles," he said, waving the check to dry it. "I want 'em."

Carefrew assented with a laugh. "You are welcome, old boy! I've never yet got that damned red stuff off my hands; nothing touches it. It'll have to wear off. And it itches!"

Huber Davis paid little attention to him, but picked up the wrapped candlestick, took the two-foot bamboo sections, and started off down the hill.

"Now, you dirty whelp," he mentally apostrophized his relative, "I've got you out of a cursed bad situation, only you don't know it and would never believe it!"

Upon reaching the funny-bone in the Street of the Heavenly Elbow, he sent in his name and was ushered quickly to the presence of Li Mow Gee.

"There's the stuff," he said, with a deep breath of relief. "And I'm in your debt, Li. I'll remember it."

Li Mow Gee smiled slightly, ironically, as though Huber Davis might stand more in his debt than was known or dreamed of.

"Don't forget the price," he said quietly. "Accounts must be kept straight, my friend. What was the cost of this thing?"

"Nineteen florins, but don't bother about that," returned the other, saying nothing of his payment to Carefrew.

"Pardon me, but it must be made all straight." Li Mow Gee counted out nineteen florins from his pocketbook, which Huber Davis accepted. "Now a little wine to our friendship, eh?"

Huber Davis drank a thimble-cup of hot wine and took his departure, feeling that his hundred and fifty dollars had been well spent, having pulled Carefrew out of a bad situation, and thereby benefited Ruth.

Li Mow Gee, alone with his charcoal brazier and his pictures and his pipe, left the wrapped candlestick as it was, but took the three candles in their bamboo wrappings and opened a door in the wall where no door appeared to sight. He entered a long, narrow room which contained a great many queer little bottles, many of them old Chinese flasks carved from agate or amethyst, and a long table; the room did not appear in the least like a laboratory.

When he had laid the candles upon the table Li Mow Gee carefully cut the wrappings, but left each candle lying in its cradle of bamboo. Then he took a large glass bottle from the corner, and poured oil over each candle until the bamboo cradles were filled. When he lighted a match and ignited the oil one realized that the table was of ironwood.

Li Mow Gee stood placidly watching while the three candles became reduced to scorched and smoking masses of black grease, then blew out the lingering flames, cleaned the débris from the table into a brass jar, and returned to his own apartment.

When he had emptied six cups of wine he clapped his hands four times, and promptly the venerable Mr. Chang appeared, removing his spectacles and blinking.

"I return to your keeping the honorable candlestick of our lodge," said Li Mow Gee, "and I thank you for the loan, venerable master."

"Are the spirits of the dead satisfied?" queried Mr. Chang.

Li Mow Gee poured himself another cup of wine and positively grinned.

"If they are not," he said, this time in English, "they are damned hard to please!"

It will be observed that Li Mow Gee was out nothing whatever—except certain obscure labors—for while he had paid Huber Davis nineteen florins, Carefrew had paid nineteen florins to agents of Li Mow Gee. And this, according to Oriental notions, was the acme of honor and propriety.

V

The Royal Mail boat, the "through packet" on which Ruth Carefrew was coming, held due for Sabang late in the afternoon. Upon the morning of that day Huber Davis went to the wireless station and sent a message to Ruth, aboard the steamer, to prepare to leave ship at Saban and cancel passage.

Then Huber Davis returned to his own bungalow, and met Dr. Brossot as the latter was leaving.

"Well," inquired Huber Davis quickly, "what's the trouble?"

The physician shrugged his shoulders.

"It has come, that's all. Java has been swept, the west coast of Sumatra has seen them die by thousands, and now—it is here."

"The influenza?" said Huber Davis.

"It can be nothing else. High temperature, and you say he had chills yesterday; much pain, everything according to the ritual. I am sorry, Mynheer Davis; his room had better be quarantined, of course."

"You think it is dangerous?"

"No. The danger, of course, lies in the pneumonia afterward. We must wait and see?"

After this, events moved fast. At noon the doctor arrived again, in response to a hurried message from Huber Davis. An hour later the two men sat in the study of Davis.

"But, Brossot," said the latter, staring at the doctor, "what the devil was it, then? You say there was no pneumenia—"

The honest Dutchman shook his head. "Mynheer, upon my word of honor, I don't know! I shall call it heart-failure; that's what we all say, you know, to conceal our ignorance. The Chinese would say that he had swallowed gold, another polite way of saying the same thing. If you want an autopsy—"

Huber Davis rose, paced up and down the room, his brow furrowed.

"That's not half bad, that Chinese saying," he muttered. "No, Brossot, no autopsy. His wife arrives this afternoon, you know; my sister Ruth. Swallowed gold, did he? I believe it's the truth, at that!"

But he never thought again about the red grease-paint on those candles, and he did not know anything about Li Mow Gee having a little laboratory—in the Chinese style—opening off his apartments. Nobody knew about that laboratory, except Li Mow Gee; and Mr. Li never boasted of his methods.

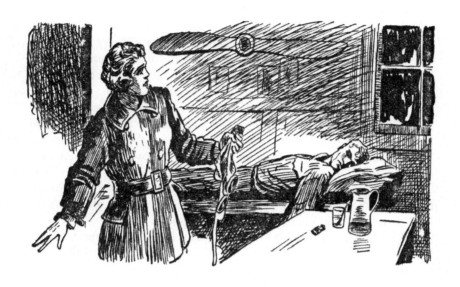

PLANE JANE
by Frederick C. Davis

Originally published in Adventure, August 1928.

Don't go wonderin' if I'm a expert on the subject, but ain't there a
kind of girl that looks her prettiest when she's wearin' a kitchen dress
and rollin' out biscuits? And ain't there another sort of girl who trans-
forms herself into the most beautiful when she appears in a filmy
evenin' gown and waits for you to waft her out into the moonlight?
Then there's another that becomes the one and only when she is wool
from head to toe and cuddlin' beside you on a toboggan. And there's
one who is a shade above Venus when she comes slashin' out of the
surf glistenin' and lithe and fresh.

Jane Alton wasn't any of these kinds, but, oh, what a dream she was in a flyin' suit! Jane was born to ornament the air. With a stick in her hand and flyin' joy in her eyes, she was an angel—and, of course, bein' an angel, she belonged in the sky. She put herself there every chance she got!

It was a mornin' full of smooth air and high visibility when Jane came rompin' around the hangars, shinin' leather all over and, seein' us, smiled brighter 'n the sun and ran straight for our plane.

Ned Knight was in the fore cubby, jazzin' the motor, ready for a take-off. He grinned and remarked over his shoulder:

"Benny, ol' nut-twister, here's where you lose your seat, back there. Jane's all set to take another trip to her home port, Heaven, and there's no use tryin' to stop her. Better start gettin' out."

I'd already begun startin', and I was all the way out when Jane came up laughin'.

"Thank you, you ol' darlin'," she said to me, and I ain't so old, either. "I can't wait another minute to get up into all that glorious sky. Ned, would you mind changin' back to Benny's seat?"

"What!" barked Ned. "Listen, Jane. I'm takin' this little Alton up for a check-ride. Your Dad is waitin' for the data on it. Just this time won't you ride in back, just this once, and lemme—"

"Ned Knight," came back Jane, "am I not the holder of a pilot's license?"

"Yes, but—"

"Haven't you, my only instructor, pronounced me to be a flyer equal to any other you know?"

"You sure are, Jane, but—"

"Can't I handle that stick and do a good job of gatherin' data myself?"

"I'm not sayin' you can't, but—"

"Do you want me to go up in another plane, *without you*, Ned Knight?"

"No!" said Ned, and so he began gettin' out!

Me, I couldn't 've held out half that long against Jane Alton. I was plenty crazy about that girl, but bein' only a grease-monkey, and havin' a map resemblin' a mauled-up bulldog's, I confined myself to bein' just her slave. Ned Knight, however, being the best flyer in the state, and the handsomest in six, got a lot of time from her. I suspected maybe that there was some kind of romance goin' on there, between the flyer and the daughter of the plant owner, 'cause they flew a lot together, those two.

So, with Ned back in the rear pit, Jane climbed into the front one, settled to the controls, jazzed the motor, and waved one tiny gloved hand to me. I socked the blocks; she stepped on the gas; and the Alton was off. It trundled to the other edge of the sand, and Jane pulled it up neatly; she circled twice, got herself a nice lot of altitude, rode a few air waves in sheer joy, and then deadheaded across the blue.

Now and then she cut the motor. Say, there wasn't any tellin' what went on between them two, all alone up there, so close to Heaven! I know they didn't exactly dislike the open solitude of that sky! I remember once, when Jane hopped out of the Alton, after a spell of hootin' with Ned, she said to him: "I *love* to be all alone with you up there!" And Ned was never quite the same when he came down from a flit with Jane, anyhow!

Well, while the Alton was banking and skimming at about a thousand, Robert Bennett Alton himself came out onto the field. He was owner of the field, and of the factory where the Altons were made. He was manufacturing a sturdy, speedy, almost foolproof plane that was just about the ultimate in aviation on a small scale. A man dissatisfied with anything short of perfection—that was Alton. And a fine man, in and out from the heart. He stood beside me, watching his little moth weave across the sky.

"What a ship!" I said. "What a joy of a ship!"

"It seems to handle well, Benny," was all Alton said. "What—what's that?"

Starin', I went cold. From the front of the plane some black smoke spouted out; and then came the flashin' of fire. Fire it was! The nose of that plane was bein' licked by the flames leapin' back from the engine. One second it had been all o. k., and the next it was pushin' a bonfire through the sky! If the fire reached the gasoline lines and the tank—if it kindled the linen—it meant disaster! And I, myself, I had inspected that ship to make sure it was o. k. All but passin' out, I continued to stare, and Mr. Alton got as white as the clouds.

"Benny, who's pilotin' that ship?"

"Jane!"

"What!"

Now the plane was sideslippin' away from the flames; it tore off them, and they disappeared.

"And Jane knows her stuff!" I shouted.

Once havin' snapped away from the danger, Jane dove at full throttle, but the fire flashed out again, worse than before. As soon as it did, Jane sideslipped again, and the wind put the fire out. This time when she recovered she banked steep, gradually losin' altitude and made for the T. Mushin' out, she cut the gun, and the Alton glided for the sand. The fire popped out again, not so bad this time, but bad enough!

The burnin' ship trundled in, and before it stopped Ned Knight was out of it. Jane jumped right behind him. Ned scooped up sand and threw it on the fire, and Jane worked just as fast. Mr. Alton and me and some of the other boys ran for the ship, but by the time we got there, the fire was all out.

Ned Knight, plenty mad, stepped up to me chin first. "Benny, your job is to keep these ships in trim, ain't it—'specially this one, that's goin' to fly the race—or was! Then how come the timin' is off, and fire got sucked back into the carburetor? I'll bet my hat that the screen and drain is in bad shape, too, you—. Good gosh!"

"Well, I got it out all right, didn't I?" inquired Jane, who seemed to think that any scrape wasn't very bad if she got out of it alive.

"You sure did! You got us out like a veteran. Jane, you're all right. Benny, dang you—"

I wasn't wastin' time standin' there and bein' bawled out. I put my head into that motor, and it took only a minute for me to find out that some monkey business had been goin on—grease-monkey business! The engine had been tampered with. Our pet Alton! The ship we were dressin' for the race! And with Jane in it! Lord!

I whirled around and barked out my troubles. And then there was plenty of quiet for a minute.

* * * *

Ned Knight moved first. Some other members of the hangar crew had come out to share the excitement. He singled out a pilot named Stud Walker, and stepped right up to him. Ugly eyes that man had, and an ugly face, and an ugly heart—Walker. His eyes sort of flashed with fear, and he tried to back away, but Ned had him nailed.

"Walker, lemme ask you some questions! Last night, while I was fussin' around the field, I heard somebody inside this Alton's hangar. That was strange. By the time I got it unlocked, and went inside, the noises stopped, and the hangar was empty. But I found a hole in the sand, under the tin wall, that was fresh dug, and that hole was hid by two empty oil barrels. You know anything about that? I'll answer for you. You know *all* about it. You're the man that tampered with the plane!"

"You can't prove—" Walker gulped.

"Your guilty face proves it for me! I'm goin' to smash—"

Ned began to sail in with both hands and feet, but I grabbed him. While he was talkin', two other greaseballs had got behind Walker, and blocked his retreat. Also, they kept Ned from killin' him. And right then Mr. Robert Bennett Alton himself stepped up and spoke.

"Ned, if you're accusin' this man of tamperin' with that plane, I hope you can prove what you say."

"Mr. Alton," Ned came back, "some time ago I caught Walker tappin' a gin bottle on the field, and ever since then I've been watchin' him. A few days ago he acted funny. I watched closer. After dark a sedan drew up, and Walker got in. The car stayed, and I watched it. Inside it was Gifford, at the wheel—Gifford, of the Stormbird people. He and Walker were talkin' low. Then I saw Gifford pass money to Walker. That is proof enough for me that he's in Gifford's pay, working against us. He was clever enough to jim the plane so I couldn't find the trouble last night, but he's got now!"

Walker looked plenty sick. Alton looked at him, and he couldn't look back. He might 've killed Ned Knight and Jane—Jane!—with his trick, done for pay. He couldn't face the man that had hired him out of good faith.

"Walker, you look guilty!" Alton spoke up. "You've tried to cripple us in favor of the Stormbird people—so they can win over us, of course, in the air derby tomorrow. Thank the Lord you won't have a chance to get in any more of your dirty work! The Stormbirds are so afraid that we'll outfly them that they have to hire crooks to beat us, eh? Do you know, Walker, that you could be jailed for what you've done?"

Walker was white around the gills.

"Walker, I don't want to bother with you. I think too little of you and what you've done to prefer charges against you. Now, Walker, get off this field. Get off! If you show your face on it again, man, I'll break you with my bare hands!"

Alton didn't usually say much, but this was plenty for the occasion, and he meant every word. Alton's contempt was worse than a lickin' for Walker to take. Let loose, he shambled away, looks of disgust and hate followin' him. When he disappeared around the hangars, the field seemed like a better place to stay.

Mr. Alton spoke quietly now to the boys, askin' 'em to look over the planes careful, suggestin' that a guard be put around the hangars tonight so that nothin' could happen to the planes before the start of the air race the next day; and they'd better keep a gun handy; and—

"Ned!" Jane called out, not bein' able to hold herself in any longer. "Please, let's get another plane out and go right back up!"

* * * *

27

"Jane," Mr. Alton said, "I want to talk with Ned a little, so you'd better let the flyin' go a while. Benny, is that ship damaged much?"

"No, sir," I answered. "By adjusting the timer and putting in a screen, and some new ignition wires—they're burned off—she'll be shipshape again."

"Start on it right away," Mr. Alton told me. "Ned, how did the ship feel today?"

"Better than ever before," Knight answered. "Jane was at the stick, but I could feel the pull of the new prop. We get the proper revs now when we're climbing."

"The stabilizer?"

"Works like a dream. The ship's as steady as a Rolls Royce on Fifth Avenue and she stays that way. Also, it's easier to hold her head up. And the ailerons can be used when she's throttled way down—that's somethin' that's improved with the new prop and stabilizer. She's ready for any race now, Mr. Alton."

"Good!" said the Boss.

The boys'd been helpin' me to roll the plane tail-to into the hangar, and then, leavin' Mr. Alton, Jane, Ned and me in there alone, they went back to work. I tore off the old ignition wires while Mr. Alton talked.

"Ned, are you ready to fly your best tomorrow? Goin' to reach Curtiss ahead of all the other entries, are you?"

"Sure he is!" spoke up Jane. "I'm his mascot!"

"I think your plane is a better flyer than any other in the line-up, Mr. Alton," Ned answered. "The Stormbird will tail us, but we'll win."

"I hope so!" Mr. Alton came back, sighin'. "Ned, I'm goin' to take you into my confidence. You're goin' to pilot that ship tomorrow, and Benny will be along with you, and you both ought to know that I'm bankin' on you boys heavily. Aside from the purse—which, of course, the pilot is goin' to keep, for he's the man that is goin' to earn it—the reputation of the Alton is at stake. The number of accidents that have happened recently in Altons has given us a black-eye, Ned—you know that."

"People'll forget that when we zip across the finish field first," Ned answered.

"They will—if we win," Mr. Alton answered. "That will help. But that's not all. That ill will has hurt our business. We have been runnin' on a shoestring—and we've just about reached the end of it. We need the winnin' place in this race because of the good it will do our business. If we don't come in number one, Ned, I'm afraid that we'll have to be closing up the plant soon."

Ned got pale, and I forgot work, and Jane listened plumb excited. Mr. Alton was talkin' in a low, serious tone. Since the Alton plant was all any of us had in life right then, it was serious. We knew business had been bad, but we never suspected it was that bad—never suspected that this air derby was becomin' a life and death matter for Alton planes.

"I'll explain a little more," Mr. Alton went on, solemn and quiet. "You know that the United Airways is holding up a large order of planes—enough to keep us busy for the better part of a year—and will place its order dependin' on the outcome of the race tomorrow. They're lookin' for speed and stamina, and they think they'll find it in the winnin' ship. I had a talk with Finley, the manager, last night. 'Win the race, and I'll place my order with you,' he said. That's how the matter stands. And that United order, if we get it, will save our lives."

Lord!

"There are other orders in the balance, too," Mr. Alton went on. "The government is going to give the winner some places in the air mail and border patrol fleets, to replace the antiquated DeHavilands. There's a passenger airport in Texas that I've been tryin' to land, that's waitin' for the winner to take the order away from it. I could name half a dozen more such examples; but it isn't necessary.

"You understand, Ned, that when you fly tomorrow, you'll be flyin' to win—win not only the purse for yourself, but a new life for us. And if you lose—but we won't think about that now. You're goin' to win."

"Yes, sir," said Ned. "We're goin' to win!" He gave a look at Jane, and Jane's eyes sparkled. "There's still another reason why I'm goin' to win, Mr. Alton!"

"There is?"

"A pilot that ain't married usually hasn't got a habit of savin' his money—and I've spent all mine, till lately. But if I had to buy a house and a lot of furniture, right now, I couldn't do it. But with that purse in my pocket—five thousand dollars—it wouldn't be so hard! I want to do that, Mr. Alton. I want to win that race, and then step up to you, and say, 'Sir, I want to marry your daughter!'"

Mr. Alton smiled. "From Jane's conversation at home, which has just two subjects—flyin' and Ned—I'd suspected the situation." He chuckled. "I'd rather have a pilot for a son-in-law than anybody else, and of all the pilots I know, you rate highest with me, Ned. Well, after you win that race, and step up to me, and say your say, I'll talk with you about it!"

"Thanks!"

Mr. Alton walked out of the hangar, havin' said *his* say to us—which was plenty. For a few minutes I was stunned. Things was comin' too fast for me. That whole big plant, out there, was in danger of vanishin'. Those peppy little Altons were in danger of eventually droppin' out of the air. Altons had been the subject of our talk and dreams for years, and if they went—it would be worse than a death in the family. And yet, there the whole matter was, flat up and lookin' us in the face—and all of us swore, right then, that this Alton *had* to win that race!

I turned and got to work on it—and how I began to work!

Somethin' that happened behind me sounded a whole lot like a kiss.

"So!" said Jane Alton. "You think, do you, Ned Knight, that you're goin' to win me in a race as though I was a kewpie doll on a rack?"

"Why—"

"And if you don't win the race, you won't ask me to marry you at all?"

"Well, gosh!"

"Young man," said Jane in her most business-like manner, "I have somethin' to say to you—in private!"

She tugged him out of the hangar. Beyond the doors I could hear 'em whisperin'. Then they moved away, and I didn't see either of 'em again that day—because I wasn't lookin' at anythin' but that plane.

I worked on her like a maniac. I forgot lunch and dinner and kept workin' on her till my arms were about ready to drop off. I wouldn't let anybody else touch her. I tested her everywhere, tuned her to the prettiest pitch she could give, tightened her everywhere she would tighten. There wasn't any dingus on that plane that I overlooked. When I called a halt it was after midnight.

Then I put blankets beside her, and tried to go to sleep; but I couldn't sleep. I had to get up and look her over again. Every half hour after that I was up, to make sure I'd tested somethin' that I thought I *might* have overlooked. I couldn't stay away from that plane. Too much was dependin' on it and the shape it was in.

And at last, as I was for the tenth time feelin' over the control wires, I saw light comin' through the cracks of the door, and I knew it was tomorrow.

The day of the Trans-state Air Derby had come!

* * * *

It was the day of days. All over the country, airplane makers had been lookin' forward to this day, and preparin' for it. Every maker of light planes was goin' to be represented with the best job they could turn out. A string of single-motored planes was goin' to line up, every one ready to do its best, and compete for the championship—and the competition was goin' to be murder! A big Commission was behind the project, directin' it. Newspapers all over the world were runnin' notices of it, 'cause the results were goin' to be official; and the winner's name was goin' to be written right into air history in big red letters.

There'd been guards outside the hangar all night; and when a knock came, I opened the doors. Ned Knight, fresh and dapper, came in, bringin' a early mornin' paper. He showed it to me. Splashed all over the front page was big headlines: *Planes Ready For Big Cross Country Race!* There below was the list of makers: Alton, Stormbird, Zephyr, Lightning, Ranbros, Impco, and all of 'em. And then the pilot's name: Alton carryin' Ben Benson and piloted by Ned Knight. Stormbird carryin' William Carson and piloted by—

"Good gosh, Ned!" I busted out. "That must be a misprint!"

"Nope, Benny; it must be true. Stormbird's made a change in pilots at the last minute."

Right there in black and white it said that the pilot of the Stormbird entry was goin' to be Stud Walker! Stud Walker, the self-same crook that we'd fired off the field—who had been in Stormbird pay, and jimmed our plane! It was easy to see that Stormbird was usin' him because Walker would be hell-bent to beat us out, for our handlin' of him. We were goin' to have a real enemy flyin' against us!

"Gosh!" I croaked. "Ned, we can sure count on Walker's beatin' us if he possibly can. He'll fly like a wild man to beat us!"

"I'm goin' to do some flyin' myself," Ned came back. "Is the plane ready, Benny? If it is, we'd better be gettin' over the field. We've got to check in and get lined up. Mr. Alton has drawn third place for us."

"Third? Who's second and first?"

"Impco is second."

"And—?"

"Stormbird is first."

"Hang it all! They're gettin' the breaks all around. I suppose it figures out all right in the end, but— I hate to have 'em leadin' us at the very start!"

"Benny, aren't you goin to dress up? Those overalls of yours 're dirty enough to walk around by themselves."

"I wouldn't change 'em for a suit of ermine, Ned," I answered. "They may be dirty as mud, but I love 'em!"

Then, Ned tells me, we should be on our way. We roll the plane out, and block her; Ned gets in, contacts her, and we pump the prop. She roars off, higher and higher, and the engine begins to warm and sing a sweet song. When she's hot, she's the sweetest soundin' motor I ever heard. Grinnin' all over our faces, Ned and I get set. She steps off down the field, swings into the air, and away we go, for the startin' field, as full of hope as any man could be without bustin'.

Pretty soon the field slides into view. There's a crowd pushin' around on it, and lined up, staggered in back of each other, are planes. We circle and come down, and taxi smoothly across the field. Then we ground-loop neatly, and come amblin' back. Ned cuts the motor, and we hop out. For a minute we're busy registerin', and then official greaseballs push the plane into place, third in the line.

And there's the Stormbird, our deadly opponent, with its nose 'way out in front. As we come past it, the pilot comes away from it. It is Walker, lookin' uglier 'n ever, with gloatin' eyes and crooked sneer. We give him hard looks and want to go on, but he has somethin' to say.

"Yesterday was your innin', you hooters. Today is mine. I'm goin' to fly you off the map!"

"Not in that wash-tub!" I come back.

"Hush up, Benny!" Ned nudges me. "Walker, you're takin' all the joy out of this race. We want to fly with real flyers, not with crooks. Depend on it, man, we don't intend to be beaten by dirty play. And if you fly square, Walker—you've only primed yourself for the lickin' of your life!"

Walker glares a killin' look at us, and cusses us out as we pass on.

Then there's a squeal, and Jane Alton comes rushin' around the line of officials, followed by her Dad. She runs up to Ned and, right out in public, gives him a big kiss. She talks fast as a whirlwind, bein' all jazzed up with excitement and hope. Her Dad just shakes us by the hand and says:

"In a few minutes you'll be off, boys. Remember—we're goin' to win."

We promise him—our hearts in our throats. That big Stormbird looks like a flyin' devil to us and winnin' won't be a cinch for anybody.

Jane asks, breathless: "Ned, won't you *please* take me along?"

Ned laughs. "No, Jane. It can't be done. I'm sorry."

"Oh, please!" she begs.

And he chuckles again, "No!"

Mr. Alton closes in then for a confidential talk with Ned; and Jane, in a minute, grabs my sleeve and pulls me a little bit aside.

"Benny, will you do somethin' for me?"

"Jane," I says, "All you've got to do is ask."

She pulls me aside a little farther. "Would you do it for me, even if it meant a lot to you?"

"Well, Jane," I say, "I guess I can equal anybody so far as doin' things for you is concerned. You know that."

She tugs me still farther, and we're gettin' close to the locker room.

"Benny," she says then, "I want to fly in this race with Ned."

I choke up at that unexpected request, but I might 'a' known Jane would 've been dyin' to get up in the air on this big occasion.

"Gosh, Jane!" I say. "We couldn't stow you away. It'd overweight the plane and hurt our chances to—"

"Oh, I don't want to stowaway!" she says. "I want you to let me take your place!"

Oh, boy! She was askin' the impossible. There she was, with her implorin' blue eyes close to mine, eyes shinin' with hope and fire, and beggin' me, beggin' me. No, sir, I couldn't let her do that—but there she was, a girl I just couldn't refuse if she'd asked for my life. Lettin' her go up in my place would be a crazy thing to do, but she kept beggin' me with little pleases and won't-yous, and Bennies, spoken soft like, and—Lord!

"If you let me get into your coveralls, and helmet and goggles, nobody'll ever know the diff'rence!" she said.

"Jane, please don't go beggin' me!" I begged her. "It ain't fair to me. I can't resist you any more 'n the tail of a plane can resist the prop. You know Ned would blow up if he heard of it, and your Dad—and Lord!"

"Benny, it's the only thing I've ever asked of you; and it means more to me than anything else in the world right now. I've *got* to fly in that race—*got* to. Benny—Benny—please!"

"Oh, Lord!"

"All you'd have to do is slip into that private locker and take off those overalls, and then stay out of sight. I'd just get in 'em, and climb into the plane, and stay there. Benny—please?"

"You can't do any good up there—"

"Don't you know that Ned will fly worlds better if I'm along with him? And you want us to win, don't you?"

"Oh, Lord!" I said. "Well—here goes!"

Right then she flung her arms around my neck, hugged me close, and kissed me one, two, three times right on the lips, and said, "Oh, Benny!" And after that I wasn't nearly in my right mind. I dived into the locker, shed my overalls, and eased out again. With one last look at her, I dived into the crowd and lost myself.

Jane hurried into the locker, and in a minute she was out, in my coveralls and helmet and goggles. I could hardly believe my eyes, she looked so much like me! It was sure astonishin'. She eased back toward the planes, just when a guy in a megaphone was shoutin' the last warnin'. Jane walked right past Ned and Mr. Alton and made for the plane.

"I've got to get into the ship!" Ned said. "Say, where's Jane? Ain't she goin' to wish me good luck?"

They looked around for her, while she was within ten feet of 'em.

"Say, Benny, have you seen Jane?" Ned hollered at her; and she wags her head: no!

The last minute is gone; and Ned is forced to his plane. Jane was already in when he got there; he climbs in, not givin' her any special notice. There is a poppin' and roarin' of motors all around, up and down the line. Greaseballs turn the Alton over, and she sings a sweet tune. The whole line-up is stirrin' up a tornado when *bang!* a shotgun goes off—which means the race is started!

The Stormbird tears off like a maniac, lifts, climbs steady, and then deadheads on. Thirty seconds pass, forty, fifty, sixty. Then, *bango!* the gun goes off again, and the Imp plane stretches itself out across the sand. It lifts, roars, pulls on, and flies in the wake of the Stormbird.

Ned Knight bends to his stick and glues his eyes to the instrument. The seconds are tickin' off. Forty—fifty—sixty! *Whacko!* The gun! Ned stomps on the gas. Away goes the Alton. It takes off quick, climbs fast and, roarin' high, plows into the sky.

And I, back on the field, watch it go with tears in my eyes!

One by one, at sixty-second intervals, the planes take off, and soon they're parading along the sky, and trailin' out of sight. Once they're gone, there is nothin' to do but wait for reports along the way. The crowd lingers, and I avoid Mr. Alton. He goes to his car; I just float around. What's happenin' to Ned and Jane now, I wonder? What's goin to happen to 'em as they drive across half a dozen states. Are they goin' to pull onto Long Island and get down to Curtiss first? Oh, Lord!

Well, plenty happened in that plane on the way, and this is what!

Ned Knight concentrated on his controls as he had never concentrated before. In the back seat Jane just sat and enjoyed herself. Little by little the Alton went up to her top speed. With the throttle gradually opened, she tore through the sky screaming. With the wires shrieking, the struts rattling, the whole plane trembling and throbbing, it roared on its way, hell-bent for victory.

The string of planes kept goin' across the sky spaced like they were at the take off for a while. At the Ohio line one of them began to drop, and took to the ground, disabled, and disqualified, 'cause the race was a non-stop affair. Another one soon followed. Others began to draw back a little, and still others drove ahead a little. And while Ned was strivin' to pass the Impco and reach the Stormbird, Jane removed her helmet and goggles, and then reached forward and gently tapped his shoulder.

Ned looked back; for a minute he thought he was dreamin'. Then he shouted something that was lost in the thunder of the motors, and bored on. He couldn't snap off the ignition a minute; 't would slow the plane. Jane smiled at him, still enjoyin' every minute; and then he looked back again, and grinned. He'd caught onto the joy of the thing and then Jane was satisfied.

Ned bent to his controls again, for the Impco was slippin' closer. It wasn't bearin' up under the continued, terrific strain. Ned grasped the opportunity and kept the throttle wide open. Bit by bit the Impco slid back, and Ned gave it a wide berth. Slowly, but surely, the Alton advanced. For miles the planes bobbed side by side; and then the Alton crept forward, inch by inch, until it was leadin'.

Jane gaily waved at the Impco pilot and threw him a couple of kisses!

The Alton bored on, and Ned concentrated on the Stormbird. It was still thundering on, a strong ship, much better than the Imp, perhaps equal to ours—perhaps even better! Ned kept the throttle wide; and Jane settled down to the serious business of takin' the lead.

The earth was bobbin' below the planes, slidin' by gentle but fast; one town and another came into view and disappeared. And then the Alton began to wobble. The motor roared up and down. Ned was actin' funny with the controls. Jane watched him close; and then she saw Ned's head bob, and his shoulders slide forward. Just then the ship began to dive and lose speed.

"Ned!" Jane screeched, grabbing his shoulder and shakin' him. "What's the matter?"

He pulled himself together some, looked around; and in his eyes was a dreamy, sick look. Jane shook him again; but he acted almost drunk. His lips mumbled words that were lost in the motor's roar; but

Jane knew that something was very much wrong with him.

The ship was losin' speed; the Stormbird was leading by a long distance; and even the Imp was drawing close again. Jane didn't wait for any more trouble. She unsnapped her safety belt and, calm as you please, put one leg across and into the fore pit. Then she pulled forward, and came into the pit with Ned. She crammed herself down into and on him, and grabbed the stick. Ned's feet were loose on the rudder-bars, but the stabilizer kept the plane on an even keel without much help from the controls.

Jane shook Ned again; and he was conkin' out fast. He pulled off one glove and looked at his right hand. It was red and swole up, and across it was a red streak, a scratch. He looked up with eyes full of pitiful request for help, and tried to talk. Jane was desperate; she cut the switch to hear him.

"Sick," he mumbled. "Scratch—somebody on field. Bumped against me. Must be—poisoned. Oh,—I can't—go on—"

And he slumped forward in the pit. Jane snapped on the ignition, kept the stick steady, pulled Ned back up, and pleaded in his ear.

"Try, Ned! Try to get up! Try to get back into the other pit. I'll handle the stick. You get back—try! Please try!"

Sick as he was, he tried. He dragged himself up and tottered in the air, while Jane assisted all she could. Then Ned tumbled into the rear pit, half on the seat, and without makin' a move to get up, passed out completely.

Jane settled to the controls with all the fire she had—which was plenty! She snapped on the ignition and opened the throttle wide as she could. The motor blasted. The plane almost jumped ahead. The Imp, which was almost nose to nose with the Alton again, gradually dropped back. There was the Stormbird, far ahead. Jane fixed her blue eyes on that plane, and kept the throttle open, and prayed.

She didn't understand perfectly then what had happened to Ned. It was this: while he was on the field, talkin' with Alton—while Jane was talkin' with me, private!—somebody brushed past him, and then Ned discovered a scratch on his hand, lookin' like it was made by a pin. He thought nothin' of it, but that scratch was full of a drug. What it was we don't know yet, but it was powerful, and without the shadow of a doubt it had been used by somebody in the Stormbird people's pay—somebody, probably at Stud Walker's behest. The object was to put the Alton out of the race by cripplin' its pilot—and, if it hadn't been for Jane, the trick would have succeeded! But with Jane at the stick, it was far from succeedin'!

Jane stretched that ship to the limit. The Imp bobbed far behind.

Territory unreeled under her. The Stormbird loomed large again. Both ships were goin' their limit. The race settled down to a question of which ship had the more speed and power and stamina, and the victor would be decided by a very narrow margin. Jane kept the throttle wide, and waited for the Alton to do its stuff—and it did.

Slowly she drew up. She kept the Alton on a level with the Stormbird's tail for a hundred miles. Then slowly the differences in the ships began to tell. The Alton crept up. An inch. Another inch. Another inch—forward always, at a mad airspeed, the motor blasting like a demon loose out of hell, the whole ship shaking, the wires screaming. The earth spun and veered. Another inch—another. Little by little the Alton crept up on the Stormbird until, prop even with prop, they drove ahead without either gainin' a mite.

Once again the Stormbird began to slip back; and Jane—yes!—tossed Mr. Stud Walker an ironic kiss!

Jane kept that ship howlin'. On she went. On. The skies began to darken. The air got a little bumpy. The visibility dropped. The exhaust tubes of the planes, white-hot, spouted orange fire. And Jane drove on. Little by little, again, the Alton took its margin of lead.

What was that? Water! Long Island Sound! Only a few miles away was the finish field!

Jane kept the plane drivin'. The Stormbird howled on the Alton's tail. Both planes were crazy flyin' things—crazy.

Then the field, the big square! Closer and closer! Jane stepped down to it, slowin' as little as possible. Down she swooped, and the ground swung up at her. She felt the trucks touch. She zipped across the sand; she ground looped; she trundled back. And as she came to a stop, and the crowd started for her, the Stormbird dropped out of the sky.

Jane jumped out of her plane. She knew Ned wasn't seriously hurt, but he needed help, and to the first man she saw she shouted: "Get a doctor!" Then, with reporters mobbin' her, she just smiled, gave her name and that of the plane, and waited until a fat man with an official badge, head of the Committee, came up to her. Then she said pertly:

"Well, I guess I won, didn't I?"

The Committeeman was flabbergasted. He hadn't expected to see a girl. Reporters were yowlin' for Jane's name, and facts about her, knowin' that a girl hadn't been scheduled to pilot the Alton, and sensin' a big story. The Committeeman muffed a few words, not knowin' what to do or say, but seein' plain enough that she had got to the field first.

Then a man in leather tunic and with goggle-prints around his eyes came pushin' through the crowd, with four other Committeemen, all lookin' indignant and outraged. That guy was Walker—Walker was howlin'.

"There she is!" he yelped. "This race is bein' run on the square, ain't it? Well, you can't rate her winner. She isn't the pilot that belongs to that ship. Her name is Alton—the pilot registered for this plane is named Knight!"

The Committeeman got red-faced and mad and still more dignified. They waved a hand for silence and bellowed to the reporters, after a hot and fast conference among themselves:

"The Alton is not the winner of this race. The Alton is not the winner! It is disqualified because of irregularities. The official winner of the race is the Stormbird, with Walker pilotin'!"

"Just a minute!" Jane spoke up, pert and clear. "Where are the irregularities? The Alton has come through clean, without any. The pilot of this ship is supposed to be Knight, and it wins the race because *my name is* Knight!"

That's a poser.

"I intended to fly this ship all along!" Jane declared. "And I win the race—"

"Your name is Knight?" the Committeemen demanded in one big voice.

"Yes, indeed," said Jane. "Mrs. Ned Knight. It has been that since last evenin'. So there!"

* * * *

Whenever I see Jane comin' onto the testin' field of the big, boomin', prosperous Alton factory, to take a little sky-spin with her husband, I size her up and sigh and tell myself all over again that that girl sure looks right in a flyin' suit!

ARCTIC ANGELS,
by A. DeHerries Smith

Originally published in Adventure, Nov. 15, 1928.

Howls floated out on the thin Arctic air, filling rock-walled Kan-nequoq Inlet with dirge-like notes. A dozen gaunt huskies padded to and fro near the red boulders to which they were tied; they eyed one another in murderous speculation, straining uselessly at the tethering sticks fastened to their shaggy necks.

Occasionally one of the animals halted its ceaseless trotting, squatted and, elevating a long wolf snout, sent out another wail to echo and re-echo back from the granite cliffs.

"Rotten! Rotten! Rotten!" Sergeant Richard Cleaver muttered to himself, striding up and down the narrow confines of the Mounted Police detachment building. "That brute Scarth is torturing those dogs just for pure devilment; can't be any other reason that I can see. For five cents I'd go down there and shoot up the whole works."

Peering through one of the little windows, he gazed down at the trader's roof, set on a lower rock ledge, and then at the whimpering blurs beyond. A moon faced halfbreed, lounging in the post doorway, glanced up at the huskies and spat contemptuously. Apparently the man saw something humorous in the situation. Yellow teeth showed momentarily when the native tore off another mouthful of tobacco from a black plug.

Thin columns of smoke continued to well up undisturbed from the huddle of skin *tupiks*, sheltering beneath the cliffs from the ever present winds. But beyond the curling smoke there was no movement; none of the Eskimo inhabitants took any notice of the starving animals' plea for food.

With a curse, the sergeant swung away from the window to glare at Constable Timothy Noonan's thick frame stretched on his bunk.

"Helluva lot you care, you fat lobster!" Cleaver threw out at the slumbering man's round, freckled face. "You don't give a hoot about the prestige of the service, do you? Said you'd never make a dog man, and that goes! Blah!"

An angelic smile stole across the sleeper's features. He rolled over lazily, grunting his contentment. Sergeant Cleaver snorted and stamped out of the cabin, crashing the door behind him.

* * * *

Sergeant Cleaver shrugged his khaki service tunic up on wide shoulders, staring across the inlet at the precipitous coastline beyond. Already the brown hillsides were showing red where the lichens were commencing to take on their summer hue. There was a faint hint of green at the blue white glacier's foot. A brilliant sun shone down out of an amazingly blue sky.

"Spring, all right," he mumbled to himself as gray eyes roved over the ice pans and bergs tinkling together in the bay. "Another eight months' winter over, and I ought to be tickled pink. Damn Scarth and his dogs, anyhow!"

The supply ship would probably be coming in another month or so, but he couldn't go out on leave with all these sick and starving Eskimos on his hands, the sergeant ruminated, when his gaze swung about to the huddle of *tupiks*. Had to look after the poor devils somehow.

40

"I'll make him feed those dogs, at any rate," he said with sudden decision.

Quick fingers fastened the glinting brass buttons of the faded tunic, as soft stepping sealskin boots carried him downward in long strides.

A sudden chorus of expectant howls broke out from the watching huskies when Cleaver passed Scarth's fish cache, and swung in at the trader's open door.

The sergeant's keen ears picked up a low whistle when he stepped into the post's dim interior and stood, motionless, waiting for his eyes to become accustomed to the gloom.

"That you, Uluk?" he queried, blundering forward.

Twin grunts answered and, following the direction, he made out two lounging blurs behind the wood heater's rounded shape.

"Look here, Scarth, you'll have to feed those dogs," Cleaver announced, pushing forward until he was looking down at the trader's narrow face and flickering eyes.

"Huh—huh," Scarth grunted, giving the faintly grinning Uluk a soft kick on the leg with his sealskin mukluks. "What the heck am I goin' to feed 'em on, eh? You Arctic angels goin' to tumble down a bunch of manna, eh?"

The trader's narrow shoulders quivered slightly. To cover the motion he jumped erect, pulling up his ever slipping and dirty mackinaw shirt. A yellow hand waved toward his empty shelves.

"Yes, I know you're traded out," Sergeant Cleaver agreed, ignoring the tone as he followed the gesture. "No grub left. You can fish though, can't you?"

"Nothin' doin'," Scarth laughed. "That's a native's job. Think I'm goin' to have the Esks see me an' lose my white man's rep? Not so's you'd notice it."

"Well, what about Uluk?"

"Uluk?" Scarth replied, a note of feigned astonishment in his tone. "Why, the lad's half white, ain't he? Got to look after his rep too. Don't want to have the Esks see him workin'. No, sir."

The halfbreed grinned faintly in response to the trader's nudge.

"Well if it wasn't for the fact that you'd report it and I'd be replying to fool questions from headquarters for the next two years, I'd shoot your blasted huskies," Cleaver rumbled.

He wheeled away, pacing up and down the post's earthen floor, followed by two pairs of amused eyes. Only just enough dog feed left to keep the police huskies going until the supply ship got in, the Mountie reflected. Out of the question to feed Scarth's animals on his team rations. And the hungry Eskimos had eaten their sled dogs long since.

"Hey!" Scarth's thin voice came suddenly. "Lookit, Cleaver. That skin boat of your'n is the only thing left in Kannequoq that'll float. There's walrus out there on the floes. Red meat. Why don't you go out an' belt one down for the Esks? I'll buy the scraps for the dogs. How's that?"

Again Cleaver sensed thinly covered insult in the little man's tones and again he ignored it. Under other conditions he would have quickly removed the sneer from that weasel face, but now only one thought pulsed through his brain—how to feed the Eskimos and those yowling brutes up on the rocks.

* * * *

Followed by twin grins of satisfaction, the Mountie padded to the door to stare out across the ice filled inlet. Yes, there were walrus out on the float ice; he had seen them through the glasses. It was as much as a man's life was worth, though, to venture out among those razor edged pans in a frail skin boat.

Cleaver clenched brown fists, swung away from the post and, padding across the ice polished rocks, reached the first of the *tupiks*.

For a moment he stood with one hand on the caribou skin that served for a door, his sunburned face wrinkled in disgust. Abominable odors floated out on the crisp air from the *tupik*; the stench of unwashed humans, half tanned deerskins, moldy furs.

Cleaver pulled out a handkerchief and, holding it across his mouth and nostrils, ducked his long body and came upright in the *tupik*. The foul smelling interior was littered with the Eskimos' priceless possessions; they were too far gone now with the coast sickness to care. Wooden pans sewn with rawhide, and stone cooking pots were thrown about in confusion. The floor was a wild jumble of feverish natives rolling about on bearskins, sealing spears, snowshoes and mukluks.

"By Christopher, they've got to have red meat or they'll all kick out," the Mountie said to himself, staring down on the emaciated, yellow faces. "Guess I've got to do it."

"Oh, Kanneyok," Cleaver called in the Innuit tongue. "I come bearing a message. Listen well, O you people of the ice."

Three tousled heads were elevated for a moment above the skins; a thin arm waved to signify that the message had been heard.

"Thus and thus," the sergeant called in Innuit through his handkerchief. "There must be red meat or you will all pass to the shadow hills. Therefore, because the great white king does not forget his people, I and the fat one go to hunt walrus. With the new sun we bring meat. I have spoken."

Faint clucking sounded when the Eskimos passed this satisfying information along. A chorus of grunts.

"That's the way to shoot it to 'em," Scarth's nasal tones came suddenly from the doorway. "You police sure knows your onions. Fall for this white king stuff, don't they? But, by cripes, you'd better make good, Cleaver, or the Esks'll give you the hee-haw from Alaska to Greenland—"

"*Anumlatciaq tamna oomiak!*" a laughing voice broke in on Scarth in the Eskimo tongue.

There followed a crisp oath from the trader, the sound of a blow, and a yelp from Uluk.

"*Anumlatciaq tamna oomiak!* The skin boat it never goes out!"

Cleaver translated the halfbreed's phrase slowly, subconsciously aware that the sick Eskimos had heard and understood the words. Several of them were sitting upright, bony faces staring over at the door flap.

"By God, I've stood all I'm going to take from you and that grinning breed of yours!" the Mountie roared, gripped by long suppressed passion.

One leap carried him across the littered *tupik*. Two hard hands fastened on Scarth's scrawny throat. The sergeant dragged the little man out into the glaring sunshine, shook him viciously for a long moment, and then sent him spinning with a well placed kick.

The trader was on his feet again in a moment, close set eyes darting fire. He opened his slit of a mouth; then thinking better of it, he wheeled away and padded off for the post, mumbling to himself.

Cleaver watched him pass out of sight; then once more he ducked back into the *tupik*, calling:

"Oh, Kanneyok, I have made a true talk; I am a redcoat and you are the children of the great white king. The skin boat goes out. There will be red meat before the sun comes again. I have spoken."

"*Ai! Ai!*"

A chorus of grunts answered him, but Cleaver sensed that the natives' tones lacked conviction. Swearing softly to himself, the Mountie plunged out into the clean air and made his way up to the detachment building.

* * * *

"Ain't no way for a buck to talk to his superior, but that was a

43

damn' fool play," Constable Noonan offered from his perch on the bunk. "You got us in dutch, Sergeant dear. We'll never be able to handle the Esks again if we falls down on this job, an' I got a hunch that's what Mr. Scarth is after. Suit his tradin' fine if the natives go wild an' woolly. I ain't no Sherlock Holmes, but if this ain't a plant I'm a Hindoo philosopher."

"Oh, shut up!" Cleaver put in irritably. "I've got enough on my hands without scrapping with you. We're going out in the skin boat in the morning, ice or no ice, and we're going to bring back a walrus. I've given the king's word for that. It's getting dark. Any intention of feeding the dogs tonight?"

"Thought you said I weren't no dog man—"

"You've got enough brains to feed them some tallow, at any rate," the sergeant cut in on him. "Go out, Timothy Noonan, or I'll throw you out!"

Constable Noonan dodged about the heater, grabbed his parka off a peg and slid through the door. Once outside he listened for a moment to the ice pans' tinkling and the mournful wailing of Scarth's huskies. Then with an expressive shoulder shrug, Noonan made his way up to the little storehouse.

The key grated in the lock, and with that well known sound eager whines burst from the dogs penned in the corral. Scarth's starving brutes heard those expectant whimpers and filled the night air with agonized howling.

It was a good three hours later when Noonan pushed in the door of the detachment building and grinned over at his chief. Cleaver was stretched on his bunk, khaki shirted, body bathed in yellow lamp-light, and deep in "Soldiers Three". The sergeant threw the book down and glared at the rubicund face.

"Look here, you nighthawk," he called. "Haven't you got any savvy at all? You stay away from that girl, or I'll—"

"Nix on the gentle sentiment tonight," the constable broke in. "Love's off; murder's on. Been prowlin'. We won't possess any skin boat in the mornin'; the Esks will have it that the great white king ain't the caribou's chin whiskers no longer, an' Scarth will be known as the very strong man from here to Hoboken."

"What's the matter with you?" Cleaver boomed, jerking bolt upright. "Scarth wouldn't dare break up that boat; not after that three months I got him for monkeying with our schooner last year."

"Oh, you'd be surprised!" Noonan mocked his superior. "There's more ways of killin' a polar bear than choking it with chocolate eclairs. Climb into your parka an' mukluks an' we'll take in the movie. It's a real fifty cent show. Come on."

* * * *

Mumbling uncomplimentary things regarding his companion's mentality, Cleaver vaulted off the bunk, pulled on his sealskin boots and parka, and followed Noonan's squat figure out into the night.

A bright moon bathed Kannequoq Inlet, flooding the open spaces with soft radiance, softening the rugged coast's raw contours. The two men stood motionless, ears filled with the subdued tinkling of the ice pans and the distant honking of some migrant geese seeking open water.

Noonan caught the other man's sleeve and pointed down to Scarth's trading post. Cleaver nodded. Yes, the lights were out—and for the first time in a month the unfortunate huskies had ceased howling. He turned to peer down at the constable, but Tim avoided the glance, padding off and beckoning his comrade to follow.

Swinging wide of the settlement below, the little man made his way over the moonlight bathed ridges until at length he arrived at one of the giant boulders that studded the beach. Beyond him, and less than a dozen yards away, the police skin boat lay overturned on the white sands.

"Well?" the sergeant's glance read as he lowered himself to the cold shingle alongside his comrade.

Noonan made no offer to enlighten him, signaling for silence.

The sergeant and the constable lay motionless, staring up at the stars.

All at once the constable twisted over on his face, when Cleaver's hard hand gripped his thick arm.

A new sound had been added to the faint night noises. Both Mounties knew what it was; the soft slithering of sealskin boots over the rocks.

Then suddenly two upright figures were blurred against the ice filled waters when Scarth and the halfbreed stepped down from the rocks and padded over to the skin boat. Each man was leading a number of the trader's huskies.

"*Pst!*"

Noonan pulled Cleaver's head down to him, whispering:

"You've seen hungry dogs up here chewin' the rawhide lashings off sleds, ain't you? You've seen 'em eatin' the sides outa skin houses, an' gnawin' old sealskin boots? Sure. Well, now they're changin' the diet; goin' to scoff our old skin boat."

Cleaver's right hand jerked back toward his revolver holster, but before it reached the weapon Tim's fingers fastened on his wrist.

"Not yet! Not yet!" Tim Noonan urged. "See the whole show. Comic's comin'. Savvy what it is, Dick? We've given the king's word that there'll be red meat for the sick Esks in the mornin' an' Scarth has passed the talk around that there won't be any. If there ain't no meat our name is mud, frozen mud at that. An' how the heck can we get walrus without a boat?"

Cleaver glared down at the constable's grinning face. What was he repeating that for, and why the blazes was he so happy about it?

The sergeant wrenched his hand free, thrusting the revolver forward. At the same moment a low oath sounded from one of the two men, and Cleaver's trigger finger relaxed.

* * * *

Scarth tugged the lines off the dogs he was leading, kicking one of the starving brutes toward the walrus hide covering the *oomiak*. But instead of rushing forward and tearing at the skin the dog squatted on the shingle, staring up at its master. Three more of the released huskies lay down and curled up for immediate sleep. Some of the others commenced to wander along the beach. None of the animals took the least notice of the skin boat.

Scarth's rumbled cursing and the halfbreed's clucking sounded dimly in the sergeant's ears as he rolled over to stare in amazement at the bursting Noonan.

"Oh, my fat sides," Tim groaned. "Seventeen dried fish, eleven tins of bully beef, five lumps of tallow, an' a chunk of pemmican as big as a battleship. An' they polished off the whole works. An' now Scarth's offerin' 'em a dried up old walrus skin for dessert. A dog's life, that's what it is."

Sudden realization stabbed Cleaver's mind. Tim had sneaked out and fed Scarth's starving huskies so that they would not attack the skin boat!

"Listen," Noonan's voice came again. "Yesterday a big floe grounded beyond the point. There was a walrus on it as big as the side of a house. Uluk shot it. Get the idea? With the skin boat gone we couldn't pull the Arctic angel stuff, and when we fell down on the job Scarth would lug in his walrus an' get the glad hand from the Esks. Cripes, you're in a hurry, eh?"

Cleaver had vaulted from the icy ground with a catlike leap. As Noonan lumbered to his feet he heard Scarth's surprised cry and the halfbreed's yelp of dismay.

The trader threw himself face down on the beach when the white

46

faced sergeant raced across the slippery shingle. A single lunge brought Scarth to his feet.

Then sounded the slithering of Noonan's mukluks on the shingle as the little man raced after the grunting halfbreed.

"I take it all back about the dogs, Timsy," Cleaver yelled at the flying figure. "Damn it, I'll recommend you for corporal's stripes for this!"

"Keep 'em!" Noonan's voice panted. "I'm the detective sergeant of this man's army, an' that's good enough for me. All right, you blubber chewer, try a taste of that!"

Whug! Whug!

Cleaver laughed softly, turning back to the squirming Scarth.

"Look here, you insignificant fragment of decayed whale meat," he growled at the trader. "You're too small to pound, but I have something nice in store for you. It'll be daylight in an hour. You and the breed will cut up that walrus and bring it down here. Then you'll keep on making soup for the Esks until they're well again. On top of that you're going to wash all their clothes and clean up the *tupiks*. That's slow motion death, if you ask me. Not a word, you rat. Move!"

As he shoved Scarth forward, Cleaver saw his comrade come upright and fan himself vigorously. Surrounding him were four of the satiated huskies. They sniffed gratefully at Noonan's legs.

THE TAKING OF CLOUDY McGEE, *by* W.C. Tuttle

Originally published in Short Stories, Feb. 10, 1926.

It was easy to see that fate had been kind to Ferdinand P. Putney, because he was not in jail. In fact, he never had been in jail. But he was comparatively a young man yet. He was six feet three inches tall, would weigh about a hundred and forty, and wore a size eleven shoe.

His face was very long, his eyes pouched, rather inclined to redness, which gave him the mien of a very old and very wise bloodhound. His almost yellow hair grew without much opposition from the barber, and he wore a derby hat of a decided green tinge.

Ferdinand P. Putney was the lawyer of Lost Hills town. The folks of Lost Hills were not given to carrying their troubles to the law; so one lawyer was enough. Ferdinand had been many things in his forty years of life, but that has nothing to do with the fact that he had studied law—a little.

And there was another rather prominent man in Lost Hills, whose name was Amos K. Weed. Amos was the cashier of the Lost Hills bank, mate of his own soul, (Ferdinand P. Putney was the captain) and a bottle-drinker after working hours.

Amos was a scrawny individual, five feet six inches tall, with a high, wide forehead, pinched nose, beady eyes and long, slender fingers. His shoulders were slightly stooped and he shuffled when he walked. Amos' life consisted mostly of looking up and down a column of figures.

But for many years Amos had dreamed of being a great criminal, a master mind; of smashing through things like a Springfield bullet. But his .22 caliber soul had held him back. Amos usually figured out a perfect crime, dreamed that he was about to be hung, and discarded the plan.

On this certain day Amos closed the bank at a few minutes after three o'clock. He carried his hat in his hand, and his breathing was slightly irregular. He fairly slunk away from the bank, shuffling his feet softly, as though afraid his departure might be heard.

He covered the half-block to Ferdinand P. Putney's office in record time, and found the lawyer at his desk, tilted back in a chair, his big feet atop a pile of dusty books on the desk. Amos slammed the door behind him and stood there, panting heavily. Ferdinand shifted his gaze from the book, which he had been reading, and looked reprovingly upon Amos.

"Well?" queried Ferdinand softly.

"Well!" squeaked Amos. It is likely he intended to thunder, but Amos' vocal cords were all of the E-string variety. He came closer to the lawyer, his Adam's-apple doing a series of convulsive leaps, as though trying to break its bounds.

Ferdinand closed the book and waited expectantly for Amos to go further in his conversation, which he did as soon as he had calmed his jerking throat.

"Putney!" he squeaked. "We're ruined!"

Ferdinand Putney slowly lowered his big feet, placed the book on the table and stood up.

"This?" he said huskily, "is terrible. Just how are we ruined,

Amos?"

"They—they didn't strike oil!"

"Oh!" Ferdinand stared at Amos.

"You mean—*you* didn't strike oil?"

"Us! You got me into it, Putney! You know darn well you did. You advised me to soak every cent I could get my hands onto in that Panhandle oil field. You did! You did! You did! You——"

Ferdinand got into the spirit of the chant and began beating time on the desk-top.

"And so you did, eh?" said Ferdinand. "How much, Amos?"

"Fuf—forty thousand dollars!"

"I didn't know you had that much."

"I—I didn't!" Amos' voice went so high it almost failed to register. Then he whispered, running back down the scale. "It was the bank money."

"Mm-m-m-hah," Ferdinand nodded slowly, wisely. "I'm going to have a hell of a time keeping you out of jail, Amos."

"You're as guilty as I am," shrilled Amos.

Ferdinand shook his head. "No lawyer was ever put in jail for giving wrong advice, Amos. But I'll do my best to defend you as soon as they put you in jail."

"You—you wanted your cut out of it," choked Amos. "That was the agreement. You hinted that I might take a few dollars from the bank. I bought a third interest in a well, and they never struck oil. I'll tell 'em—the law—that you helped me; that you advised me to steal from the bank; that you—you——"

"If you keep on talking that way, Amos, I won't defend you."

"Defend me? You talk like I was already arrested."

"It probably won't be long, Amos. Are you sure they'll miss it?"

"Miss it? There's only ten thousand in the bank right now, and the bank examiner is due almost any day."

"'We are lost, the captain shouted, as he staggered down the stairs,'" quoted Ferdinand. "That's worse than I anticipated, Amos. You have practically looted the organization, and the Lost Hills depositors are not the kind that——"

"I know that all by heart!" wailed Amos. "They'll hang me."

"But there is still ten thousand dollars in the bank," mused Ferdinand. "Does Jim Eyton suspect you?"

Eyton was the president of the bank, a big, bluff sort of a person, who trusted Amos implicitly.

"Not yet," moaned Amos.

"Hm-m-m-m," said Ferdinand judiciously. He rested his head on one hand, thinking deeply.

And as he racked his brain for a solution out of the difficulty, a man came down the wooden sidewalk, bareheaded, his sleeves rolled to his elbow. It was Miles Rooney, the editor of the Lost Hills *Clarion*, a weekly effort, seven-eighths syndicate matter and one-eighth sarcastic editorial.

He was a living example of the fact that the Lost Hills *Clarion* was not a paying proposition. His sparse hair stood straight up in the breeze and in one bony hand he clutched a piece of paper.

"What am I going to do?" he demanded, handing the paper to Ferdinand. "I ask you, Putney."

Putney read the paper slowly. It said:

Editor of Clarion:

I ben redin what you sed about me and i want you to no your a lier and it aint so ive all way had a firs clas repitashun amung men and i aint no menis to no budy and nothin like it and im goin to maik you wish you keep your damn nose out of my bisnes.

y'rs respy
Cloudy McGee.

Putney placed the paper on his desk and squinted at the editor.

"You wrote an editorial on Cloudy McGee, eh?"

"Yes."

"Do you know him, Mr. Rooney?"

"I do not," Mr. Rooney flapped his arms dismally. "I don't need to know a man of his reputation in order to flay him in print, Mr. Putney."

"He's a bad egg," put in Amos.

"Bad?" Putney lifted his brows. "He'd just as soon kill you as to look at you. If I was running a newspaper, I'd either say nice things about a killer, or I'd say nothing."

"What satisfaction is your opinion to me?" demanded the harassed editor. "How can we stop him from coming here?"

"We?" Putney shook his head. "He has nothing against me. I have never seen the man in my life. This is a case for the sheriff—not an attorney."

"Sheriff!" The editor spat angrily. "He and I do not speak. I wrote an editorial about the inefficiency of our sheriff's office, and——"

"Now he won't help you save your life, eh?"

"It amounts to that, Mr. Putney."

"You might apologize to Cloudy McGee, Mr. Rooney."

"I might!" snapped Mr. Rooney. "But when Cloudy McGee meets me, will he wait long enough to let me do it? The man has a terrible reputation. Why, there's a thousand dollars reward for him. Will a man of his type be satisfied with an apology?"

"It would establish a precedent," murmured Putney. "Still, there is only one thing for you to do and that is to wait and see. McGee is a bank robber, I believe."

"Exactly."

"According to that letter, he will be here soon. If I were in your place, I would shut up shop and go away for a vacation."

"Couldn't we get out a restraining order, Mr. Putney?"

"Yes, we could do that. But it is not likely that the sheriff would serve it. Would you know Cloudy McGee if you saw him?"

"Not at all. No one in Lost Hills has ever seen him."

"McGee is a gambler," remarked Amos Weed, who remembered seeing a general description of McGee on a reward notice. "They say he'll bet on anything. You might make him a gambling proposition, Rooney."

"Bet him that he can't hit me three times out of four eh?" retorted Rooney, as he picked up his letter and went away. Putney knitted his brows, as in deep thought, while Amos Weed gnawed a finger-nail. Suddenly the lawyer got an inspiration. He leaned across the desk so suddenly that Amos almost bit his entire nail off.

"Watch for McGee!" snapped Putney. "You're in a bad fix, Amos. You might as well die for a goat as a lamb. You say there is ten thousand dollars left in the bank—in cash. All right. What do I get for my scheme?"

"For your scheme? Tell it to me, Putney."

"On a fifty-fifty basis, Amos. If you win, I get half."

"And if I lose?"

"You've already lost, you poor egg."

"All right," eagerly. "Fifty-fifty, Putney."

"That's a bet, Amos. How soon will the bank examiner come?"

"I don't know. He's due any old time."

"All right. Cloudy McGee is also coming—to kill Miles Rooney. You see McGee before he kills Rooney. Not that we care what he does to Rooney, you understand; but he must postpone it.

"McGee is our meat. Watch for him, Amos. And as soon as you see him, bring him to me. But do this secretly. If there's any killing going on—remember I'm a lawyer, not a target."

"I'm no target either," declared Amos. "I don't know Cloudy McGee, but I'll do my best. You've got to get me out of this. I took your advice once—and lost."

"This is a cinch," assured Putney. "Just let me get at McGee."

Twenty miles south of Lost Hills was the town of Salt Wells, from which place a stage line ran to Lost Hills. In a dingy little room at Salt Wells' only hotel, two men sat at a table playing poker. It was early in the evening, and both men were too interested in the game to light a lamp.

One man was tall and lean, with deep-set eyes and a long, damp-looking nose. He breathed through his mouth, and regularly he wiped a long, gnarled finger across his nose, in lieu of a handkerchief.

The other man was also fairly tall, but not so thin. His face was also tanned, but his fingers were more nimble with the cards. He seemed greatly amused over his good luck. On the table between them was a cartridge-belt and holstered Colt six-shooter, and a scattering of currency.

The man with the bothersome nose spread his hand, his watery eyes triumphant. But the other man spread his hand, and without a word he picked up the belt, gun and money.

"Anything else?" asked the winner.

"Nobe," The other man got heavily to his feet. "I'be cleaged."

"All right, pardner. It was a good game eh?"

"Good gabe for you."

The winner smiled and left the room, a huge sombrero, with an ornate silver band, tilted rakishly over one eye. The loser looked gloomily after him, flirting a forefinger across his nose. He dug in a pocket and took out several little bottles and boxes, which he studied closely. Each and every one was a guaranteed cure for colds.

He selected a tablet from each receptacle, put them in his big mouth and took a big drink from a broken-handle pitcher. Then he put on a derby hat, yanked it down around his ears, and went heavily down the hall and into the street.

For several moments he stood on the wooden sidewalk, looking up and down the street, before crossing to the Road Runner saloon, where he leaned against the bar. The sleepy-eyed bartender shuffled around behind the bar and waited for the order.

"Rog and rye," thickly.

The bartender placed the bottle and glasses on the bar and watched the man toss off a full glass of the sweet whisky.

"Yo're the only man I ever seen that drank rock and rye all the time," observed the bartender. "Got a cold?"

"I hab. It's killid be by idches—dab id!"

He sneezed violently, clinging to the bar with both hands. When he looked up there was a great fear in his eyes.

"Why don'tcha take somethin' for it?" asked the bartender.

"Take sobedig? I've tried id all." He shivered, and poured out another drink.

"Had it long?"

"Nod this wod. Sobe day I'll ged pneumodia and die—dab id."

"A feller don't last long when he gets that," declared the bartender hollowly. The sufferer shook his head, shivered and sneezed.

"You ought to take care of yourself, pardner."

"No use," wearily. "I'be fought id all by life. It'll ged be sobe day—dab it."

"It kinda takes the joy out of life, when yuh know darn well it'll get yuh in the end," sympathized the bartender.

"Pneumodia is bad," nodded the man tearfully. "Shuds off your wid."

"Why don'tcha see a doctor?"

"Nobe."

"Scared?"

"Whad you don't know won't hurd yuh." He poured out another drink of sweet whisky, shuddered violently, ran a finger across his nose and buttoned up his collar.

"How far is id to Lost Hills?"

"About twenty miles north of here."

"Thang yuh."

The man with the pneumonia complex went out into the night and approached a hitch-rack, where several riding horse-were tied. After looking them over he selected a tall sorrel. Loosening the cinch, he removed the blanket, mounted and rode north, wearing the blanket around his shoulders, holding it tightly around his throat. He sneezed several limes, as though bidding Salt Wells good-bye, and faded away in the darkness.

Amos Weed was not to be caught napping. There were not many strangers ever seen in Lost Hills, but Amos spotted one that night. He was rather tall, slender, but was not dressed conspicuously. Amos dogged him from place to place, wondering if this could possibly be Cloudy McGee.

The stranger went from game to game in the War Path saloon, showing only a mild interest in the gambling. He picked up a billiard cue and spent an hour or so knocking the balls about the old pool table, paying no attention to anyone, while Amos humped in a chair, watching him closely.

He followed the stranger to the Chinese restaurant and watched him. This man wore no gun in sight. He seemed of a serious disposition, ate heartily, which was something Amos had been unable to do since he had heard of the well failure. He knew it must be a failure, when they did not strike oil within the four thousand foot depth.

The stranger left the restaurant and sauntered around the street, with Amos following him at a distance. Miles Rooney was getting out his weekly edition, and several interested folks were watching the flat printing press through the *Clarion* window. The stranger stopped and watched the operation.

Amos came in beside him, also watching the operation.

"Pretty slick, the way it prints 'em, eh?" said the cashier. The stranger nodded.

"Stranger in Lost Hills?" asked Amos.

The man nodded quickly. "Just came in today."

"Going to stay with us a while?"

"No, I don't think so. At least, not long."

"Drummer?"

"No-o-o-o. Bank examiner."

"Oh." Amos dropped the subject and got away as fast as possible. This was terrible, he thought. If the bank examiner was in town, tomorrow his theft would be discovered. Amos felt of the knot which was already galling his left ear.

Then he galloped down to Putney's house, almost fell in through the front door, and blurted out the news.

"I tell you, we're sunk, Putney!"

"You are, you mean," indignantly.

"O-o-o-o-oh, hell!" wailed Amos. "I might as well blow out my brains, I suppose."

"Well," said Putney judiciously, "it might save complications. Might be safer to shoot the examiner."

"But I can't shoot straight, Put! You sure advised me into a lot of misery. What'll I do?"

"Give yourself up."

"And get hung?"

"Start running."

"Run where? I haven't got enough money to make a getaway."

"Well, you can shoot straight enough to kill yourself, can't you?"

"Oh, you're a hell of a lawyer! Didn't you ever give any good advice to anybody?"

"This ain't a point of law, Amos—this is emergency."

"Uh-huh. You sure are good in emergencies. Give up, run, or shoot myself. Any damn fool could give that advice."

"Then keep on looking for Cloudy McGee. That's your last chance. He might show up, you know."

"Where there's life there's hope," sighed Amos. "I'll do it. In the meantime, you think of something, Put." Amos went back to the street, hoping against hope.

Amos Weed was the first one to spot the stranger with the big hat and the silver-studded hat-band. He remembered that the reward notice had mentioned the fact that Cloudy McGee wore that kind of a hat. Amos was both frightened and thrilled. He saw the stranger go into the War Path saloon; so he went to the hitch-rack and looked at the stranger's horse.

On the back of the saddle cantle was the single initial M, in a silver letter. M must stand for McGee, reasoned Amos. He rather thrilled at the thoughts of meeting a man like Cloudy McGee, who flaunted his big hat and an initialed saddle before all the sheriffs, who would be only too glad of a chance to gather him in and collect the thousand dollar reward.

Amos sauntered back to the saloon door, and met the stranger, who was just coming out. He glanced sharply at Amos and started across the street, with Amos trotting at his heels. The man stopped and looked at Amos. It was dark out there, and Amos' knees smote together, but he summoned up his remaining nerve.

"Mr. McGee, can I talk with you for a minute?" he said.

The tall stranger started slightly. "What about?"

"Business," Amos swallowed heavily. "But not here in the street," he hastened to say. "Nobody knows who you are, except me. But you shouldn't wear that big hat, you know." It pleased Amos to give advice to Cloudy McGee.

But McGee didn't seem to mind. He waited for Amos Weed to continue.

"You follow me," said Amos. "I want you to meet a friend of mine."

"Just a moment," said Cloudy McGee. "What's the game?"

"The game," said Amos nervously, "is to make some easy money for you."

"Easy money, eh? Say, I don't believe I know you."

"I'm all right," quavered Amos. "I'm cashier of the Lost Hills bank."

"I see. All right."

They went to the sidewalk and headed down the street to where Ferdinand P. Putney kept bachelor hall in a little two-room building, just off the street, on the south end of town.

It was a great thrill for Amos, to walk with Cloudy McGee, on whose head was a thousand dollars reward. Cloudy stopped to light a cigarette, and Amos shivered as the match illuminated McGee's ornate sombrero. Amos was afraid that Jim Potter, the sheriff, might see him.

A man was coming up the street toward them, but Amos did not know who it was. The man watched Amos and Cloudy McGee go in the front door of Ferdinand P. Putney's home. Against the lamplight it was easy for this man to see the huge sombrero.

The man sneezed several times, cleared his throat raspingly and walked over toward Putney's front door. It was the man who had stolen the horse in Salt Wells. He had ridden almost to Lost Hills and turned the horse loose, not wishing to be arrested for horse stealing.

Ferdinand P. Putney drew up three chairs, after shaking hands with Cloudy McGee.

"I—we were looking for you, Mr. McGee," said Putney. "Mr. Rooney, the editor of the Lost Hills *Clarion*, said you were coming to—er—see him soon."

Cloudy McGee nodded indifferently, and Amos mentally decided that the killing of an editor was merely an incident in the life of such a man as Cloudy McGee.

"You are a man of action," said Putney, looking upon McGee with considerable favor. "What would you do for a thousand dollars?"

McGee grinned. "All depends."

"I'm going to lay my cards on the table," said Putney. "A man of your caliber appreciates honesty."

"Such is my reputation," nodded McGee.

"All right." Putney stretched out his legs and squinted at Amos, who was not at ease. "Our friend here, is cashier of the Lost Hills bank. Some time ago he stumbled upon a flattering oil proposition."

"Now, don't lie about it, Put," wailed Amos. "You advised me to put every cent——"

"If you will pardon me, I will tell Mr. McGee the story, Amos."

"Well, don't leave yourself out, Putney."

"As I said before, Mr. Weed saw the possibilities of this investment, and, not having sufficient funds of his own, he took forty thousand of the bank money, in order to take a third interest in the Panhandle Number 7 well, a Texas oil company. It promised enormous returns. Today he received a communication to the effect that at a depth of four thousand feet, they have struck nothing. The average depth of that field is much less.

"It puts my friend in a bad position. The depositors of this bank are not of a forgiving nature, and in the event of an embezzlement it is doubtful whether the law would ever have a chance to pronounce sentence upon Amos Weed."

"They'd lynch him, eh?" asked Cloudy McGee heartlessly.

Amos shivered.

"I am doing my best to save my friend's life," continued Putney. "The forty thousand is gone. And the only way we can explain the loss is to have the bank robbed. You know how to do things like that, Mr. McGee. There is already a thousand dollar reward for your arrest; so another robbery won't make much difference to you one way or the other."

"Well?" queried McGee thoughtfully. "How much do I get?"

Ferdinand P. Putney did some mental arithmetic. He knew there was ten thousand dollars in the bank. It would be just as simple to make this a fifty thousand dollar robbery as a forty thousand dollar robbery—and there would be ten thousand to split between himself and Amos.

"Suppose," he said, "that we give you a thousand dollars. You don't need to pull off a regular robbery; just come in the front door, fire a few shots, run out the back door, get on your horse and beat it. As you go through we'll hand you the one thousand."

McGee shook his head quickly. "You might hand me a package of nails."

"Oh, I see. You think we might not hand you the money."

"Be a fool if you did, Putney."

Putney turned his head and considered Amos.

"Don't look at me," wailed Amos. "I've got no thousand."

"I guess that's no lie," Putney turned again to McGee.

"How do I know you'd do the job?"

"You don't. But you've got to take some risk."

"How about you?"

"I take plenty, don't you think? I've got to outrun the sheriff."

"That's true," nodded Putney. He turned to Amos. "If I give Mr. McGee a thousand dollars, you've got to make good with me, Amos."

"I will," whispered Amos. "All I want is to get out of this mess."

Ferdinand P. Putney went into the next room. He did not trust the bank, because he knew Amos Weed too well. In a few moments he came back, carrying a thousand dollars in currency, which he counted out to Cloudy McGee.

"I'm banking on your honesty," said Putney. McGee pocketed the bills.

"No one can ever say I was crooked in business," he said. "When is this deal to be pulled off?"

"Tomorrow morning at exactly ten o'clock. There hasn't been a customer in that bank at ten o'clock for months. Am I right, Amos?"

"You're right," whined Amos. "Nobody ever comes in that early."

Cloudy McGee shook hands with them on the deal and left the house, promising Amos Weed to keep his big sombrero out of sight.

"Well," sighed Amos, "that's settled. If the sheriff does kill Cloudy McGee, he won't squeal on us, Putney."

"He better not," grinned Putney. "But the deal ain't all finished, Amos. You go down to the bank and take out every cent of that ten thousand dollars. Nobody is goin' to wonder if you go in there this time of night, because you often work late."

"You—you mean I'm to swipe that money, Putney?"

"Sure thing. We split it two ways—I take six thousand and you take four."

"Aw-w-w-w-w, what kind of a split is that? We were to go fifty-fifty."

"That's all right. I get a commission for putting the deal over, don't I? That thousand I gave him, I gave for you. It was just a loan, Amos. Take it or leave it."

"Aw, I'll take it, Putney. I hope he don't fall down on the job."

"He's a heaven-sent angel, Amos. Now, you go and get that money and bring it up here."

Amos went, but he went reluctantly. As he left the house he did not know he was being followed by the wet-nosed stranger, who had listened, with an ear glued to one of Putney's window panes.

It was not difficult for Amos to enter the bank and come out with the money. At that time of night there were very few people on the streets of Lost Hills. He had the money in a gunnysack and carried it concealed as much as possible with his coat.

He came down the sidewalk, past the doorway of an old shack, when a big man pounced upon him, forcibly took the sack away from him, and sent him spinning with a punch on the jaw. Amos saw stars that the Lick Observatory had never dreamed of seeing, and when he awoke he was all alone and very sad.

Conscious of the fact that he had been robbed and knocked out, he staggered to Putney's place, fell inside the house and gasped out his story. Putney's consternation and wrath knew no bounds.

He fairly danced in his anger, while little Amos held his jaw and stared red-eyed at the wall.

"Cloudy McGee double-crossed us!" swore Putney. "He knew

59

we'd do this, the dirty pup. Well," Putney waved his arms in desperation, "we'll have to kill McGee and get that money."

"You do it," said Amos wearily. "You can have my part of it. My Lord, that man is strong!"

"But don't you see where it puts us?" wailed Putney. "He's got all the money—eleven thousand. He don't have to rob the bank now."

"But he swore he'd do it, Putney," Amos grasped at any old straw. "He didn't promise not to rob us."

"Well, if you can get any satisfaction out of that," said Putney. "Anyway, it leaves me holding the sack. I've got nothing to gain, even if he keeps his word. I'm out a thousand. All it'll do is to save your hide."

"Well, isn't that enough, Putney?"

"I wouldn't give a thousand dollars for you, guts, feathers and all. I've sure bought something—I have."

"Aw-w-w-w, it may turn out all right, Putney. Look at the jaw I've got on me, will you?"

"I don't care anything about your jaw Go on home. When he robs that bank. I'm going to—" Putney hesitated.

"What are you going to do?"

"That's my business. Now go home." Amos went. And as he hurried home he noticed a light in the living-room of the sheriff's home.

Perhaps at any other time Amos would not have given this a thought, but just now his nerves were in such a state that everything looked suspicious.

The big stranger with the damp nose had engaged a room at a little hotel, left his bundle there and gone to the War Path saloon, where he got into a poker game. In a little while Cloudy McGee came in, bought a drink and tackled the roulette wheel.

Several times the damp-nosed stranger glanced at Cloudy and found him looking. The first time they nodded, but the other glances were of suspicion instead of friendship.

"You've got a bad cold, stranger," observed the dealer.

"Yea-a-ah—dab id."

"You ought to take something for it."

"I hab," the stranger swallowed heavily.

"'F I was you I'd see a doctor," declared one of the players. "I had a friend that died from pneumonia. Started just like your cold."

"I thig I'll see a doctor in the mornig—dab id."

Amos Weed slept little that night, and he got up in the morning with his nerves all frazzled out. He did not eat any breakfast. He had heard of condemned criminals eating a hearty breakfast just before their walk to the gallows, and the very thought of food sickened him.

As he walked toward the bank he met the damp-nosed stranger, with the derby hat crushed down over his head. He sneezed just before they met, and Amos jerked as though someone had fired a gun.

"I'm lookig for the doctor," said the big man thickly.

Amos sighed visibly and audibly, as he pointed out the doctor's residence.

"Thag yuh," nodded the sufferer, and went on. Amos looked after him, wondering who he was, and then went on to the bank. It was about ten minutes of ten, when Amos opened the doors and went in, closing them behind him. The bank did not open until ten o'clock.

Amos looked out the front windows, his heart pounding against his ribs. It was within ten minutes of the time that would see him saved or sunk. He went to the rear door, throwing back the heavy bolts, which would give Cloudy McGee a chance to make his getaway, if he were still going to carry out his plan.

A glance showed that McGee's horse was behind the bank. Amos Weed's hopes arose like a well-filled balloon. At least Cloudy McGee was shooting square. Then he saw Ferdinand P. Putney coming down the alley behind the street, carrying a double-barrel shotgun. Amos closed the door, peeking through a crack, watching Putney, who came in behind the bank.

He looked all around. A huge packing case and several smaller boxes gave him a hiding place, into which he crawled. Amos drew away from the door, his eyes squinting painfully. It was evident to him that Ferdinand P. intended to intercept Cloudy McGee and try to get back his money.

And Amos realized that Putney was going to ruin the whole scheme. If Cloudy was forced to stop and argue the case with Putney, it would give the sheriff time to catch him, and then there would be no chance to prove that McGee had stolen the fifty thousand.

Someone was knocking on the front door! Amos trotted to the front. It was the depot agent. He showed Amos a telegraph envelope through the glass of the door.

Amos went to the door, shaking like a Hula dancer, and got the message. It was for him. He jigged back to the rear door and looked out. Then he almost swooned. Seated on the boxes, where Ferdinand P. Putney was concealed, was the sheriff, Big Jim Potter, smoking his pipe.

Amos staggered back to the front door. Seated on the sidewalk across the street was "Slim" Caldwell, the deputy sheriff, watching the bank front. Amos reeled. The clock was striking the hour, and at every chime Amos Weed jerked inside his clothes.

Then he unlocked the door and went drunkenly toward his desk, where he slumped in a chair, staring with unseeing eyes. The door opened and a man came toward him. He opened his eyes. It was the man he had directed to the doctor's office. Amos shook his head wearily. Nothing mattered now. He was still holding the telegram, and now he opened it mechanically, his eyes scanning it quickly. It read:

PANHANDLE NUMBER SEVEN BRINGS IN GUSHER AT FORTY TWENTY FIVE STOP CONGRATULATIONS

GRIMES SUPERINTENDENT.

Amos fell back in his chair, the world reeling around him. He opened his eyes. The stranger with the cold had crouched back against the wall, a gun in his hand, as Cloudy McGee came in through the doorway. Slim Caldwell, the deputy sheriff, was running across the street, almost to the door, when the stranger behind it flung up his gun, covering McGee.

"Put 'em up, McGee!" he snapped, and McGee's hands went up, a look of wonder on his face.

Slim Caldwell ran in behind him, and the gun covered both of them.

"Who are you?" asked the damp-nosed stranger of Caldwell.

"Deputy sheriff," blurted Caldwell.

"All right. Handcuff that man."

"But—but—" stammered the deputy.

The sheriff was coming in the back door, herding Ferdinand P. Putney ahead of him. He stared at the tableau. The damp-nosed stranger swung his back against the wall, half-facing the sheriff. For several moments things were rather deadlocked.

"Who are you?" asked the stranger with the cold.

"I'm the sheriff!" snapped Jim Potter.

"And I've got you, Cloudy McGee!" snorted Caldwell addressing the damp-nosed stranger, and covering him. "Drop that gun!"

The man addressed dropped his gun and Caldwell picked it up, but before anyone could stop him, the damp-nosed man had made a sudden dive and knocked the original McGee off his feet, and was sitting on him.

"For heck's sake, what's this all about?" demanded the sheriff, coming toward them, still clinging to Ferdinand P. Putney.

"Pud ha'd-cuffs on him, I tell you!" snapped the damp-nosed man. "This is Cloudy McGee."

"Yo're crazy!" roared the sheriff. "Yo're McGee yourself."

"You thig so?" The damp-nosed man turned back the lapel of his soiled vest and showed them the badge of a deputy U. S. marshal. "By nabe is Morton," he said thickly. "I hobe you're sadisfied."

"U. S. marshal?" blurted the sheriff.

"Yeah. I be been looking for Cloudy McGee, bud I didn't hab much of a describtion, excebt that he gambles quite a lot and is about my size. I heard he was in Salt Wells, or aroud that part of the country.

"I med this sud-of-a-gud and he wod my horse, saddle, hat and my gud. I thought he'd stay there bud he left; so I stole a horse and followed him. I heard hib frame up to rob this bank. They called hib McGee. That feller over there," pointing at Amos, who was almost in a state of collapse, "took ted thousad from the bank last night; so I toog it away frob him. It's ub in by roob."

"Well, for the land's sake!" blurted the man upon whom the deputy marshal sat. "They mistook me for Cloudy McGee, and I let the sheriff in on the deal. I thought you was McGee, because they recognized me by that big hat which I won away from you at Salt Wells, and we framed it to get Putney, Weed and you this morning."

"Is thad so?" The marshal wiped his nose and stared down at the man under him. "Who in hell are you?"

"Me? I'm the bank examiner."

"Huh! Loogs like a mistage—dab id."

The officer got to his feet, grinning widely.

Amos was coming toward them, holding out the telegram.

"I'll deed it to the bank," he quavered. "It's a gusher, and they're worth more than fifty thousand dollars. Just so they don't hang me, I'll agree to anything."

The bank examiner shook his head. "That's between you and the bank officials, you cheap little crook."

"Cheap?" muttered Ferdinand P. Putney. "That man must deal in big money, if he calls a fifty-thousand steal cheap."

The bank examiner took a roll of bills from his pocket and handed them to the sheriff.

"Here's the retaining fee I got from Putney last night. If you want to prosecute him, that is evidence."

"I dunno what I want to do," said the sheriff blankly.

An apparition was coming in through the back door; a gobby-black sort of a person, painted up like a war-path Indian in reds, greens, blues, purples and black. They watched him come toward them.

"My Gawd!" blurted the sheriff. "It's Miles Rooney!"

"It is," wailed the editor. "Look at me! He tied me to my own press and painted me with my own inks. I've been like this all night. I just got loose!"

"Who painted you?" whispered Amos.

Miles Rooney turned his ink smeared countenance upon the luckless cashier, pointing a gobby finger at him accusingly.

"Your friend. The man I seen you standing outside my window with last night. The man you were talking to, darn you! Cloudy McGee!"

"The bank examiner!" exploded Amos. "He—he said he was."

"He is," said the sheriff. "He's examined a lot of 'em."

The real bank examiner and the marshal walked outside, halting on the edge of the sidewalk, where they grinned at each other.

"You ought to take something for that cold," said the examiner. "The first thing you know you'll be having pneumonia."

"Dod be." The officer shook his head. "You can't scare be do more. All by life I'be been scared of pneumonia. Never had the nerve to visit a doctor. Bud I seen one today. Ha, ha, ha, ha! Fuddy, ain't id? I feel twedy years you'ger."

"What did he say was the matter with you?"

"Hay fever."

ESPECIALLY DANCE HALL WOMEN
by Alma and Paul Ellerbe

Originally published in Adventure, July 1, 1928.

Long J im Briggs wandered into Al's Dance Hall one night when "Captain Mac" was drunk and throwing things.

She had splendid deep red hair and a skin as white as blanched almonds, and he admired her extravagantly. As a child admires a Christmas tree. And differently, too—very differently. He had even given up prospecting now and then and made good money as a carpenter so that he could spend it on her. He had spent it all, and he knew her very well, but he had never seen her drunk before. He had been in such places a good deal, but he hadn't got used to seeing women drunk. It hurt him.

He was about to wander on out again when he heard one of the other girls say:

"She's gonna pay for this all right! Al will make 'er come acrost with the expenses of the whole damn' place for a month for that big mirror she broke!"

Long Jim hesitated and then started toward her. She took a saucer from one of the little tables and sailed it like a clay pigeon. It curved and hit him over the eye. The blood ran down his cheek and everybody laughed. He wiped it away with his handkerchief and put his hand on her arm just as she was going to throw another saucer.

"Why, Rosie—" he said reproachfully, in his soft, rumbling bass, and stopped helplessly. His soft black eyes looked out kindly above his soft brown mustache and his great soft brown beard, and said what his tongue couldn't find the words for.

Captain Mac was madder than she was drunk. All her sensations and her thoughts were combined in one ache, like the ache in a tooth, and she was biting upon it savagely and taking a kind of satisfaction in the keen shoots of her pain. She could have knifed Al that night out of hand and seen through stoically whatever might have come of it, but Jim Briggs' voice and his eyes were the kind of things she had forgotten the existence of, and they slipped in under her guard and pierced the quick of her.

She didn't throw the other saucer, but suddenly Rosie Ellen McCarthy, a decent Irish girl, looked out of her eyes and said with a flash of passionate appeal—

"For God's sake, Jim, take me out o' this!"

Jim didn't expect it. It touched him so deeply that he could only gulp and nod his head. With his great height and bent shoulders and baggy clothes he looked uncouth and awkward, standing beside painted, half nude Captain Mac in her spangled dress. He looked around helplessly for something to cover her shoulders with.

"This'll do," she said, stretching out her hand for a yellow scarf on the top of a gilded upright piano.

She took it with one strong pull, slinging heedlessly along the floor in a rain of broken bits half a dozen pieces of bric-a-brac that had rested upon it.

Jim folded the gaudy stuff clumsily about her and took her by the arm and started to go out, when Al came up and stood in front of him, dapper, suave and touched with cynicism.

"There's money owing me," he said politely, "and she ain't going nowhere till it's paid, see?"

The red surged into Jim's cheeks, pale from working underground, and his voice rose dangerously out of its soft rumble.

"There's a hell of a lot more than money owing you, you God-forgotten little skunk, and if you don't get out o' my way I'm liable to pay you the part of it you ain't lookin' for!"

He kept his eye on the other's hands and his muscles braced. If you started things in Al's place you finished them swiftly, or they finished you.

The white hairy fingers twitched into the expected signal and Jim swung the bony mass of his fist against Al's ear as he would have swung a pick into a stubborn conglomeration of quartz. But that was incidental. He didn't even notice where the little man rolled. Jerked forward by Al's signal, a very different antagonist was coming on the jump—Hard Pan Schmitz, the dance hall bouncer.

Jim Briggs was no match for him and knew it. Almost as if he had followed through the blow that sent Al spinning, he snatched up a heavy lighted lamp, whirled it above his head and flung it. It struck Schmitz's raised forearm, smashed down his guard and covered him with broken glass and burning oil.

In the stunned second before the racket began Jim took Rosie by the wrist and broke through to the street. Behind them the place seethed like an ants' nest laid open by a spade.

He pulled her around the first corner. They pelted through the snow as fast as she could run. He zigzagged his way through the town, taking alleys when he could. They came at length to the door of a wooden shack below the level of the sidewalk, on an unlighted street. Its unpainted boards were warped, it listed heavily and, in common with all the other houses in the block, it looked deserted. But Jim jumped down to it, key in hand, and by the time Rosie had descended the rickety steps that led from the sidewalk he had opened the door.

He shut it behind her, struck a match and led the way into a room furnished with a stove, a camp cot, a chair and a small pine table with a smoke blackened lamp on it. He lighted the lamp. Rosie fell into the chair, breathing in big painful gulps. She wasn't used to running. The great altitude—ten thousand feet—had played havoc with her breath. Jim had swung a pick there too long to be much affected. They looked at each other in the dim light.

"It's jest a place to sleep," he said awkwardly. "Nobody knows I own it. Feller gave it to me that struck it rich an' went away. Mostly

I'm in the hills anyhow. So wouldn't anybody look for us here."

And then:

"The sheriff and the marshal's both down on Al. If we can get away without bein' noticed, it ain't likely anybody'll foller."

"Maybe it'd be safe for you to stay, then," said Rosie, when she had breath enough to say anything.

"Maybe. But I was aimin' to go anyhow. Why don't you go with me, an'—an' stay with me?"

She looked at him steadily.

"I ain't fit."

"You're as fit as I am," he said quietly, in the soft, rumbling, reas-suring bass that seemed kin to rivers and winds. "What d'you say to a clean break an' a new start together?" He lingered on the last word wistfully. "I've been pretty lonesome, you know, a-knockin' round from one prospect hole to another an' livin' like a pack rat."

She got up and came close and looked at him intently. The yellow piano scarf that covered her befrizzled red head like an incongruous cowl and clashed crudely with her red dress; her silver slippers, her spangles, the bunch of cotton roses at her waist, her rouged cheeks and scarlet lips and half-bared heaving breasts contrasted strangely with her honest eyes.

"Do you want it for yourself, Jim?"

"For myself—more'n anything."

"You're not lying to me?"

"So help me God."

He had expected her arms about his neck, but she gave him her hand like a man.

"I'll never let you down," she said shortly. "Let's go."

They went out under a sky of faint, clean blue, where a frosty moon queened it amidst a scattering of small pale stars, and found a man who was driving out of town in a wagon and went with him.

By one means and another they made their way into the Gray Dome country and Jim built a cabin there.

* * * *

Fifteen years later, Rosie Briggs stood in the door of it and watched Jim climb down the steep trail toward his latest prospect hole.

There was a fresh sprinkling of snow, so light and dry that the faint wind started bits of it to rolling like feathers. Beneath it the smells of spruce and pine and juniper and little silver mountain sage were dormant. The cold, clean, thin air of early morning was stripped for the odor of Long Jim's pipe, and it drifted up, rank and acrid. Rosie liked it, at that hour and in that place.

She watched him until he waved his hand far below like a tiny marionette before he took the fork of the trail under the big Engelmann spruce and disappeared for the day. She waved back and turned to her tubs. Every week she washed the clothes of four families in Gray Dome, the mining town down the main road just around the next bend. It was hard work, but she didn't mind it much.

She didn't think about it. Besides, she only worked four days a week. The other three she rested—sewed a little, crocheted a little, knit a little—sweaters and stockings and mittens for Jim and herself, and kept her diminutive house as clean as a chemist's scales; or sat quietly out in front in summer or inside by the stove in winter and let the long waves of peace wash deeper and deeper in. Peace is good after a life like Rosie's. She lay in it thankfully, as in a bath, and soaked old stains away.

On the side of Gray Dome Mountain, with the sheer drop of the cañon at her feet and the range spread out beyond; in the midst of cleanness and silence unbroken since that old rocky backbone of the continent thrust itself up into the sun, she had risen slowly out of the shards of the life of Captain Mac and come, late but surely, into her heritage of womanliness and dignity. The years had chipped away her prettiness, but in its place was beauty for those who could see it. The smooth face had been sculptured into something fine and strong and self-directed, something steadfast and serene. She wasn't blown about by tantrums any more.

She had a stake in the game of life now, and she played to hold it. She had steadied to meet the responsibilities thrust upon her by Jim. He was as kind and patient as the seasons, and as unreliable. And she was like a cottonwood tree; she put out the leaves of her affection and confidence surely and abundantly, but with tireless caution and she rarely got nipped. She controlled him where he could be controlled, and where he couldn't she accepted him as she did the weather. Her knowledge of men was empirical, unhampered by theories.

Jim would give anybody anything she had—he possessed nothing himself—and be perennially surprised if she objected. Usually she didn't, but if it was something she wanted she went after it and got it back if she could. Any bum or crook or sharper could win his friendship and pick his mind or his pocket if either happened to have anything in it.

But Rosie's mind was her own, and instead of a pocket she used the Conifer County Savings Bank. She met him at all points as shrewdly as if he had been an opponent—which in a sense he was—but she loved him. And she knew that he loved her, and counted on it, but only for what it was worth.

She put more trust in his poverty. Every day, of course, he expected to strike it. And for a while she had thought he might. But gradually as the days lay themselves down in long, pleasantly monotonous rows until the sum of them made many years, she came to know that he wouldn't. And that, far more than his love, was the foundation of her content. While he was poor he was hers—wholly, unqualifiedly, unthinkingly hers.

Poor was scarcely the word, though. Jim lived in a moneyless world. Out of the little she made she supplied the simple necessities of both of them, and he was willing to wait for everything else until he struck it. "Then—! Then—!" was what he thought of as he made his slow way up and down the mountainside. To him the thought was roseate, luminous, rejuvenescent.

But Rosie hated it. If for nothing else, because it held the seeds of possible change. After a chancy life, she valued most, of things attainable by human beings, a life that was free from chances.

On this morning in spring an eagle slanted down the sky on wide, still wings; the ice broke up and tinkled in Little Cub Creek in the cañon; the orange and yellow shoots of the willows swelled toward catkins; and Rosie washed her clothes contentedly, secure in the knowledge that there was no "then"; while over in his hole in the side of Old Baldy Jim broke up her world with quick excited blows of a short-handled miner's pick.

She was hanging out the clothes on the squawberry bushes at the back when she heard the impatient crash of his elk hide boots. She went quickly through the house and stopped in the front door at sight of him.

When he swung up his heavy bag of samples for a signal, she knew. Knew before she heard his whoop. And when it cut across the stillness like the whistle of a locomotive it struck her cold. It chilled the core of her spirit, as an icy wind loosed in the tropics would chill a naked native.

"Struck it, by thunder! Two hundred dollars to the ton, if it's worth a cent! An' the vein as plain as a layer 'o choc'late in a cake!"

He fell into a chair on the porch. Rosie stood and stared at him. The one thing he knew was ore. He had the kind of knowledge that men had been willing to pay for when he'd sell it. His "then" had come. The realization went through her consciousness in widening rings. Whatever else it meant, it meant the end of this; the beginning of uncertainty.

He caught her in his arms and swept her into the cabin and danced her about until the place shook.

"Didn't I tell you? Didn't I say you'd ride in your own auto yet? It had to come, old lady, it jest nacherally had to come!"

He gave her a hug and turned her loose.

"I knowed it," he said solemnly. "I've allus knowed it. Away down deep in there—" he tapped his breast—"I've had a hunch."

He flung himself into a chair and looked at her hard. "Ain't you glad?" he said suddenly.

She was like a boat that has luffed into the wind. For a moment her mental sails hung flapping. Then they filled and strained and she set out before this new cold breeze. She told him as best she could that she was glad.

"To look at you a feller might think you was kinder sorry like," he said quizzically. "What's the matter?"

"I was thinkin' a little about how happy we'd been right here—just you and me and the house you made yourself."

"'Twarn't a patch on what it's gonna be," he said, and jumped up and was off with his samples to the assayer's in Gray Dome. He stepped strongly, as a young man does. Half the stoop was gone from his shoulders.

Rosie turned back slowly and sat down heavily at the kitchen table, her occupation gone. Jim didn't need a grubstaker now. She sat there a long time, while memories of other miners who had got rich swarmed in her brain like little devils that fell over each other in their eagerness to stab her: Senator Sherrill, and Tom Potts, the hotel man, and Hooker Bates, who took his flier in Wall Street; and Mike Watson, who divorced his wife for Dora Schoonmaker, and a dozen others. They made their money and then were gathered in by women like the Schoonmakers. She had seen so many of them. They always left the women they had picked up when they were poor. Especially dance hall women. Even when they were their wives.

And she and Jim had never been married.

* * * *

But Rosie Briggs wasn't a quitter. Little in her life had gone by default. When the terms of the sale of the mine had been arranged and everybody in Conifer County knew that Jim was going to be a rich man, she capped his plans with hers and squared about to meet what was coming. She went over her clothes and spruced up as much as she could to match her new station. And very carefully she laid down a program of buying to be carried out as soon as the money came in.

Among her things she found a picture that she had clipped from a fashion magazine twelve years ago—a colored picture of an electric-blue plush dress of a style that she had admired. She felt a twinge of sadness as she wondered how many other things that she had wanted and gone without would look as queer as that now.

The dress she had worn when Jim took her out of the dance hall—the red dress with the spangles on it—looked queerer, but that night while Jim was in the village on an errand after supper she put it on and sat waiting for him by the fire, determined to play such cards as she had.

When he came in he stopped at the door of the little sitting room with a whistle of surprize.

"I ain't seen that for ten years. Didn't know you had it."

"It isn't much—" she said, smoothing the skirt.

She had lengthened and renovated it as best she could. It was the only piece of finery she owned.

"It's all right. Lord, how purty I uster think it was!"

The windows were open to the night. The weather had turned suddenly warm that day, as if the old earth had decided to start life all over again with the Briggses. There was a moon, and the new tender leaves of the aspens about the cabin made patterns on it that twinkled. You could almost feel the soft wooly anemones thrusting up their oval spear points outside.

The feel of it all had got into Rosie's heart and driven out some of her fears. She even had her old banjo in her lap. She wanted to prove to him that she meant to help him to be happy. She touched the strings and began to sing.

She knew only the songs that had been popular a good while ago—"Daisy", "Two Little Girls in Blue", "Sweet Rosie O'Grady" and one or two more of the same sort. These, to her, were "music"—all there was of it. She sang:

> "Daisy, Daisy, give me your answer true.
> I'm half crazy, just for the love of you..."

and felt a load slipping from her heart as the snow slips from the summit of Gray Dome Mountain when warm weather comes.

"Gosh!" Jim murmured. "You ain't sung that sence—"

He let the sentence die. His eyes smiled above his grizzling brown mustache and beard. She wanted to put down the banjo and go to him and touch his hand. But she went on singing, pleased that she remembered the tune so well, that her voice rang out so clear and true, and

Jim came and sat close beside her.

A strange, deliciously sweet odor crept in under the smells of growing things and wet earth out there on the dripping mountainside. She felt just then that Jim was as steadfast and as sure to stand by as the huge silver spruce that the cabin was built against. She let her cheek rest on the shoulder of his coat.

> *"It won't be a stylish marriage,*
> *For I can't afford a carriage..."*

The odor came more strongly. It was like orange flowers. She smiled at the sentimental notion. Orange flowers on the side of Gray Dome—

> *"But you'd look sweet—upon the seat*
> *Of a bicycle built—"*

The odor came from Jim's coat.

It said suddenly, "Lorraine Schoonmaker," as plainly as Jim's lips could have said it. To smell it was to see the girl standing behind the counter in the Gray Dome Dry Goods Company's store. Probably there was no one in town who would have failed to connect her with that perfume.

A knife seemed to unfold inside of Rosie. It cut her song off in the middle of the line and brought her upright in her chair with a gasp.

"What's the matter?" Jim said, startled.

She got to her feet. She almost came straight out with it. That would have been like her. It was what she wanted to do. But for the first time in many years she was afraid. She stared at Jim with deep revulsion. Suddenly he was part of an elemental horror that she had climbed out of long ago and that now was closing around her again.

"I—I hadn't ought to've sung that," she said thickly. "It—makes me think too much of the old days," and went stumbling off to the bedroom.

He followed her and stood around, saying things to comfort her, and finally she pretended that her mood had passed. But when she lay still at last by his side and thought about Lorraine Schoonmaker, hard lines pulled at the corners of her mouth that hadn't been there for fifteen years. Long after all traces of it had vanished, she fancied that the air was faintly touched with the perfume of orange flowers.

"Women" would have been bad enough, but he would have tired of them and come back. There'd be no coming back from this girl of twenty-one, clever and hard of mind and soft and pink of body, with the first taste of what money could do fresh in her mouth.

Men didn't come back from the Schoonmaker women. Behind Lorraine, with her sleek black pomaded hair, her short tight pussy-willow taffeta one piece gown, her chiffon stockings and high-heeled satin pumps with rhinestone buckles, her vanity case almost as big as a traveling bag, her jeweled wrist watch and swinging bead girdle, Rosie saw Ally Schoonmaker, her older sister, who had married Timothy Bund practically on his death-bed for his house and his shares in the North Star Mine. And behind Ally, up the ladder of the years a rung or two, Dora Schoonmaker, breaking up the Watson home when Mike Watson's mine began to pay, and somehow juggling him into a divorce from the woman who had seen him through the lean grim years of penury and into marriage with her and then carrying him off East. And Effie, the oldest of the four, who had run away with Perce Williams, nearly two decades her junior, when he came into his father's money, and held him grimly to her side ever since.

Yes, and even Bertha Schoonmaker, the mother, with her wig and her dirty chiffon blouses and her painted cheeks and brown teeth and pink-lined hats with floating pink veils, playing the man-game still, at sixty-four. Their lean, rapacious Schoonmaker hands were all alike. If Lorraine took Jim, she'd take him to keep. At the altar. For very definite financial ends of her own.

The tacit bargain between Long Jim and Rosie had never got itself into words; they hadn't felt the need of them. He had pulled her out of hell. The strength of her allegiance to him couldn't be increased by the mere saying of words, however sacred, or the giving of a ring. Marriage would have added nothing to her side of it. Nor, she had thought, to his. She wished now that she had it, but it had not occurred to her to wish it before. She had had something so much solider in poverty. Marriage might hold and it might not, but while he had been dependent upon her for his food and clothes, there had been no doubt.

She went back to that over and over that night, seeing the placid years in the little house as very beautiful through a mist of pain. She had a feeling that, pulling at the almost forgotten cadences of the song, she had brought the past down about her ears. She felt the old trapped fatalistic despair and sick rage, without the old vigor. Something began banking up inside of her, steadily, relentlessly. She was terribly afraid of it. It seemed to her that it was a great bubble of black blood in her brain, and that when it burst— She tried to keep from thinking to ease the strain on it, but her thoughts streamed out swiftly from oubliettes in obscure corners of her mind.

They were hideous thoughts and really not hers at all. It seemed that some devil sent them to torture her. The unfairness of it gagged in her throat. She had fought her way out of filth and blackness to cleanness and the sun, and now, without volition, the old horror came on her again from within—clicked through her brain like yards and yards of cinema film. The current of her life had swept past its one clean tranquil place and was swirling along muddied and normal. The familiar ache was in her heart, and Rosie was herself again—Captain Mac, of Al's Dance Hall. You didn't get away from things like that.

Well, there were things that Captain Mac knew how to do that Rosie Briggs had forgotten. She had whipped a can along the street once with revolver bullets as a child whips a hoop to the admiration of every idle man in town, and ended the demonstration by shooting a stranger's plug hat off his head without disturbing his hair. Her whirling thoughts showed her Jim's old .44 in the left-hand end of the bottom drawer of the dresser.

She must wait, she told herself—and her heart gave a great bound—she must wait until she had them together! She laughed out with sudden raucous cruelty in the still cool night. Jim stirred in his sleep but didn't waken. She raised herself on one elbow and looked down at him, while her thoughts raced and danced, piling themselves into the bubble.

And then it burst and left her weak with compassion, seeing them together in her mind's eye; seeing them as clearly as the daylight that was climbing over Gray Dome Mountain. That fragile, empty, smart little thing and Long Jim Briggs! Gaunt, weathered, grizzled old Jim—and her! She'd no more be able to shoot than to enter into her dead mother's womb and be born again.

Feeling as old as the granite hills that ramparted the cañon, and with something too of their plain ineluctable dignity, she arose and dressed herself and built the breakfast fire in the stove.

When Jim came out to her she got slowly to her feet, closed the damper and faced him.

"Jim," she said, "that girl don't want you. Take a good look at yourself in the mirror over there, and then think of her. She'll throw you away like a sucked orange when the money's gone."

Long Jim Briggs stood up with his head in the rafters of the tiny room and stared like an idiot.

"I smelled her perfumery on your coat," said Rosie shortly, and comprehension dawned slowly in his face.

"Holy jumping June bugs!" he said from somewhere down in his boots. "So that's what you thought! Wait a minute. I was hidin' it in the wood house. I wanted to surprize you."

In a moment he returned with a package. With awkward swift movements he ripped off the wrapping paper and shook out the folds of a brilliant electric blue plush dress of a fashion fallen into forgotten desuetude ten years before.

He displayed it pridefully down the front of his long person, head a-cock and a twinkle in his eye.

"That's all there was between us! Smell it!" The room reeked of orange blossoms. "She made it for me nights, to make some extra money. It's the kind you kep' a picture of from a fashion book. I got it off your dresser. Do you—do you like it, Rosie?"

She tried to speak, but could only nod her head. He patted her shoulder awkwardly. The dress swam before her eyes like a pane of blue glass in the rain.

"It's goin' to be the swellest weddin'," he said huskily, "that little old Gray Dome ever seen. An' then—" he cleared his throat with a rumble like summer thunder—"we're goin' to Denver an' buy a house on Capitol Hill an' the finest auto in town, an' hire a man to run it an' drive around an' tell 'em all to go to hell!"

ISLAND HONOR,
by Murray Leinster

Originally published in Short Stories, Feb. 10, 1926.

Quite miraculously, there was an opening in the mangrove swamps and what looked like a river or harbor beyond. Such things are not to be expected when you have been very much bored by two days of unvaried contemplation of mangrove swamps on the one hand, and totally empty sea on the other. So we on the *Shikar*—most promising name for a devilish slow and unexciting tub—tacked in. There were three of us and two native boys and we thought we were being very daring and reckless, coasting down the China Sea in a fifty-footer.

The miracle continued. We did not ground on a bar. It was a river of sorts. A kite rose heavily from something unpleasant on a sand-bank and soared away. And then we saw a white man's house with a flag floating from a flagpole before it, which was most miraculous of all. And that was where we found Vetter.

I don't know what nationality he was, though this part of the world was French. He wasn't that, I'm sure. We went ashore and met him and found that he considered himself lord of all creation, and wasn't at all averse to converting us to his own belief. Technically, he was political agent for Kuramonga. None of us envied him the job. Neither did we feel called upon to console him with an extended visit. But the hunting looked promising and we dropped anchor for the night at least. And then when the soft tropic night had fallen we were too lazy to be polite and call on him.

"I want to kick him," said Cary, puffing smoke at the stars. "I haven't any reason, but I want to kick him. So for my manner's sake, if you chaps go ashore tell him I'm dead or something and couldn't come."

There was a jungle off to the right somewhere and we could hear the night noises coming from it over the water. Little squeakings, and once a scream like a human being's, which was probably a monkey, and once, very far away indeed, a snarl that would have made your blood run cold if it hadn't been muted by the distance.

"Tiger, that," said Cary hopefully. "Maybe we can get Vetter to let us have some beaters tomorrow and take a shot at him."

The doctor grunted.

"Breeding season," he said. "Why not play leap-frog with a locomotive? More healthy. And no beaters will tackle them now."

"If Vetter tells them to go, they will," insisted Cary. "He's got those natives under his thumb. They're scared to death of him."

"Paranoiac," grunted the doctor. "He thinks he's lord of creation."

It was curious. You saw that about Vetter the minute you met him. Perhaps he was a little mad on the subject of himself. Perhaps it was Kuramonga that did it, because Kuramonga is the last place on earth that God made, and it was finished up with swamps and malaria and jungles and bad water that couldn't be worked in anywhere else. They used to send men somebody had a grudge against, to Kuramonga, to drink themselves to death for the glory of *la belle France*. But Vetter liked it. He was the only white man in a hundred miles, and he had twenty little Annamite soldiers to keep his district in order with. He'd seemed much more anxious to impress us with his wonderful hold over the natives than to talk about anything else. He had said more or less flatly that he was the law and the prophets and most of the religion in Kuramonga. And he gloried in it.

Cary, in white duck trousers and nothing else, reached out of his hammock and gave himself a push to swing a little for a breeze.

"Damned luxurious beggar," said the doctor enviously. "Get out of that hammock and let somebody else have a chance."

I rose to tilt him amiably on the deck when I heard a little noise above the lapping of the river waves. Somehow, it sounded furtive, and so it wasn't a time for fooling.

"Listen!" I said sharply. There was a splash of a paddle.

"Dacoits?" asked Cary hopefully. "Thinking maybe they can slip over the side and rush us?"

He beamed and slung his feet out of the hammock, to get some guns from below. Cary was always hopeful of trouble.

"We're right in front of the Residency," said the doctor dryly, "and Vetter has a steam launch. They know it. Don't be an ass. Dacoits? No!"

Cary hesitated. Then somebody called to us across the water. Very softly, in Malay, as if they didn't want to be heard on shore.

"They want to come aboard," grunted the doctor. "Get your guns if you like, Cary, but you might want to put on a shirt, too. There's a girl with them."

Cary swung down the companionway and the doctor stretched himself luxuriously in the hammock. A dark shape took form in the moonlight. It was a regular Malay dugout with three natives in it. A man in the bow and another in the stern, with a girl between them. They came on the *Shikar's* deck as Cary reappeared with both arms full of guns.

Cary got the first look at the girl, and he dropped the guns and looked foolish. The doctor grunted and offered to get lights, but the two men protested politely but very sincerely against it. They sat down and exchanged polite phrases with the doctor, who was the only one of us who could talk decent Malay.

I sat back and wondered, feasting my eyes on the girl. Sixteen—seventeen—eighteen? I don't know. I do know she was at the prettiest age any girl could be. Malay all through, yes. But her skin was fair as mine and her eyes were wonders. There was grace and pride and blood and breeding in every move she made. She looked at the doctor mostly, quietly and composedly, but her eyes alternately flamed and brooded. Now and then she glanced at the two men.

And one of them was an old chap, white haired and stately, with a ceremonious looking kris on one side of his sash and an old percussion pistol on the other side. In the moonlight you could see his clothes were all of silk, and mighty fine quality, too. Not at all the sort of thing a man would wear who made a habit of paddling himself around. The other man was a well-set-up young chap with eyes like a hawk who looked like a young prince out of the Arabian nights. Somehow, you'd take to those two.

You just imagine it. Us three white men, disheveled and half-dressed, on the deck of a fifty-foot schooner in an unmapped harbor with the furtive jungle noises a hundred yards away. Talking to these three who'd come out of nowhere, dressed like princes and a princess in a dream. Off on the other side of the river there was Vetter's house with a light burning somewhere and his toy soldiers standing guard while he slept. And those three silk-clad figures sitting on our deck, regarding us with a poise and courtesy that made me feel like a clumsy fool.

The old chap twisted his mustache gently and looked at us. He was the picture of an honorable gentleman, somehow. Brown skinned, but you liked him. He asked quietly if he might ask advice for his daughter, without Vetter hearing that he had asked.

"You understand," said the doctor, "if there's anything we ought to repeat to him—anything political——"

"No, *Tuan*," said the old chap gravely. "I am Buro Sitt."

The doctor sat up at that, and so did I. I'd heard a yarn or so about him. He'd fought the French to a standstill, years back, and he'd been licked. But he'd fought like a gentleman and when it was over he took his medicine like a man. One or two old-time Colonials had yarned to us in Saigon about the fighting in times past and an ancient colonel had sworn that Buro Sitt was the finest fighter and the most chivalrous opponent that ever gladdened the heart of his enemy.

"Go ahead," said the doctor. "I know you. I'd like to shake hands."

Buro Sitt did not move, but he bowed very politely.

"It may be, *Tuan*," he said, "that you understand the ways of we *Orang Malagi*." He talked quite impersonally. "You know that our ways are not as your ways. But you know that we have our honor, also."

"Yes," grunted the doctor. "Especially Buro Sitt."

Buro Sitt's face did not change.

"My daughter desires to go to the house of the *Tuan* Vetter," he said without an inflection in his voice. "She loves him. But I would ask your advice before she goes."

Cary moved abruptly. The younger of our two visitors caressed the handle of his kris with fingers that quivered suddenly. The girl stared at us defiantly—and then her eyes clouded with abysmal shame. But a moment later they were flaming.

"Well?" asked the doctor. His face did not even move a muscle.

"There is another woman in the *Tuan* Vetter's house," said Buro Sitt. "Who also loves him. Will it be the custom of the white men to send her away when my daughter goes to him?"

"He might," said the doctor tonelessly, "and he might not. It would be considered disgraceful to him among other white men to have one woman living in his house if he were not married to her. It would be doubly disgraceful to have two. And of course it would be called disgraceful in the women. They would be scorned by all white men. Not scorned—despised."

The girl's face did not change. She was staring defiantly at the three of us. The younger man caressed the handle of his kris.

"Would you, then," asked Buro Sitt woodenly, "point out to him that he should send away this other woman when my daughter comes to him?"

The doctor held up his hand. He looked grim, all of a sudden.

"Buro Sitt," he said quietly, "you are lying."

Buro Sitt's hand dropped to his sash with a sudden movement. Then he bit his lip.

"Royal blood," said the doctor, "does not speak as you are speaking. Royal blood does not send royal blood to be a white man's mistress. And especially, royal blood does not speak of its disgraces. What's back of this, Buro Sitt?"

There was sheer agony in Buro Sitt's eyes.

"*Tuan*," he said, as if the words were wrenched from him, "if you were a man and a *raja*, and your honor as a man were against your honor as a king, what could you do?"

It might seem funny to think of a petty princeling—Buro Sitt could not be more—speaking of his honor as a king, but it wasn't funny then.

"Once," he said fiercely, "I led a thousand fighting men. I fought against the French. When it was ended, there were fifty left. Now there are six hundred men again who follow me. Their lives are in my hands, and their women, and their children also. And the *Tuan* Vetter has demanded my daughter."

He was telling the truth this time.

"You're going to fight?" demanded the doctor. "It's folly; suicide!"

Buro Sitt's hands clenched.

"Suicide?" he echoed bitterly. "If that were all! I am *raja* of my people. If I die, they fight—and are killed. All of them. And enough men have died for me before, Allah knoweth. Speak to him,"—he pointed to the young chap who was caressing his kris. "My daughter was to have been his wife. There are two hundred swords that follow him. And yet, if we rise——"

He was shaking all over.

"If we rise—ruin," he said bitterly. "My people slain, my villages burned, my children slaughtered! That is the price of the honor of a man, *Tuan*. And for their lives, Vetter demands my daughter. Which"—he clenched his teeth in the quintessence of bitterness—"is the price of the honor of a king."

Cary moved. He was listening to the old chap now, looking from him to the girl and back again.

"You mean," said the doctor slowly, "Vetter will set a gunboat on your people if you keep your daughter from him, no matter how?"

"If she stabs herself!" said Buro Sitt, his voice breaking. He looked swiftly at the younger Malay and then his eyes went suddenly blank again as he got control of himself once more. "So she will go to him, *Tuan*. As the ransom for my villages, and the ransom for my people's lives."

Cary began to talk angrily, spouting what Malay he knew with his whole vocabulary of Chinese thrown in to make his meaning clear. The main point of his speech was that he'd like to wring Vetter's neck and would do so at the first favorable opportunity. Buro Sitt listened without a flicker of expression on his face. He had himself in hand again.

"*Tuan*," he said evenly, to the doctor, "will you speak to him, and urge that he sends away this other woman? It will not even be safe for my daughter. There is always poison——"

"I'll remember," said the doctor, not quite directly.

"The blessing of Allah be upon you," said Buro Sitt evenly.

He swung down into the canoe. The girl and the young man followed him. They drifted off into the darkness, where the jungle noises began at the water's edge. For a little while there was no sound but the lapping of the river waves and the furtive noises that came out of the squirming mass of vegetation.

Then the doctor said thoughtfully, "I wonder what he's really up to."

"It isn't what he's going to do," said Cary angrily. "It's what I'm——"

"You're going to do nothing," said the doctor calmly. "Vetter thinks he is lord of creation, which he isn't, but he is the lord of Kuramonga. Also he has some little tin soldiers. You can't do anything direct, and as for reporting him—Well, we're civilians and foreigners to boot. The powers that be would pay absolutely no attention to us. We'd better leave it up to Buro Sitt."

"But he can't do anything," protested Cary angrily, "and I can kick Vetter, anyhow."

"Buro Sitt," said the doctor, "can't kill Vetter, because Vetter's doubtless arranged that if he's scragged Buro Sitt will get the blame. And he can't kill the girl, because Vetter would trump up a rebellion on him if he did, and his record is bad. His villages would be wiped out at once. But——"

"Do you mean you're going to stand by and watch?" demanded Cary furiously. "Let that beast Vetter——"

"I'm going to do what Buro Sitt wants me to do," said the doctor. "I'm going to do nothing whatever but sit still and look on. And, of course, remember what Buro Sitt told us. I don't like Vetter. He's a paranoiac. And it's always unhealthy to have even an ordinary swelled head. Anywhere, Cary," he added kindly, "Anywhere at all. So I just wonder what Buro Sitt is going to do."

Cary and I wrangled for an hour about it. The thing did look cold-blooded. A white man in a position where he could demand Buro Sitt's daughter—which would cost him his honor as a man—on penalty of ravaging his people and destroying them—which would certainly compromise his honor as a king. A *raja* counts himself the equal of any king, anywhere. And Buro Sitt had led his people to disaster once before. He'd taken out a thousand men and brought back just fifty. He'd feel now as if he had to make up for that.

Then the doctor shut us up and turned in. Cary woke everybody up in the middle of the night to suggest that we kidnap the girl by arrangement and let the young chap who wanted to marry her know where to find her. The doctor threw a shoe at him and went back to sleep.

"Son," he told Cary, "you forget two things. Buro Sitt did not come out here to ask us to lecture Vetter. He did have a reason for coming out here. And Vetter has a swelled head. Go to sleep."

A minute later he was snoring.

I woke at sunrise, listening to noise of the surf down at the sea splashing and roaring among the mangrove roots. It's always strangely loud at daybreak. And the jungle was making noises as the night things went to their hiding places and the day things came out again. And presently a boat came out from Vetter, asking us not to go away because he'd have something amusing to show us that night.

We guessed more or less what it was, from our opinion of Vetter and Buro Sitt's call. But we didn't leave. We loafed on the boat all day and Cary talked morosely about how pretty the girl was and wondered what her name was and how old she was. And the doctor fished.

Meanwhile I wondered how Buro Sitt, who was obviously Malay, could be a *raja* up on the China Sea, and learned that about one in four people up there are Malays, the other three-fourths being Chinese and so on.

And then night came on and the jungle that had looked very tropic and pleasant during the day began to make unpleasant noises. And Vetter sent his steam launch for us to come and see what he had to show.

The doctor had it right when he said Vetter thought he was lord of creation. Political agent over a district nobody else wanted, with a gunboat coming in every six months or so. Twenty little soldiers to back him up. Not even a telegraph line to connect him with the outside world. But in his own district he was the Almighty.

Vetter's soldiers were stiff as ramrods. They saluted when we came ashore and took us into a room to wait for him. He kept us waiting, like an emperor. When he came in he was strutting. Oh, he thought he was the great old Bhud, all right. He clapped his hands for drinks, and his servants served him with exquisite haste. Then he flung himself into a chair and grinned at us.

"You've come from the north," he reminded us. "Japan, and China, and so on. Not very respectful to white men, these Asiatics, eh?"

We agreed politely.

"I will show you," he said, showing his teeth in a grin, "how a strong man treats these swine. *I* keep them under."

He held out his open hand and clenched it like he was crushing something. He didn't wait for us to say anything. We weren't important except as an audience. But he wasn't crazy. He just had a case of swelled head that had been aggravated by authority, and he wanted to show off. He was feverishly anxious to show off. He believed he was lord of creation, and some people with that belief are pitiful, and some are amusing, but Vetter managed to be unpleasant.

"There's a *raja* here," he told us, grinning, "traces back his ancestry to the *rajas* of Malacca, in the thirteenth century. Proud as hell. Royal to his fingertips. Now watch!"

Big, and beefy, and dark, with the close-shaved hairs showing through his skin. He lay back in his chair and grinned at us.

"I'm a white man," said Vetter, "so I demand royal honors, no less. Once Buro Sitt—this *raja*—refused his taxes. He said he would appeal to Saigon. And the gunboat came in the harbor two days later. Buro Sitt came down with his retinue to meet it. Very much armed. He was going to complain of me. Of me! Only the marines from the gunboat and my men were on their way to his village. My men opened fire at sight of the guns his men carried. Like any Malays, they fired back. He lost fifteen men and we burned one of his villages."

He winked at us, and laughed. I don't think he was French. Not all French, anyway.

"The gunboat *capitaine*, he reported Buro Sitt in a revolt, and that I had him well under control. Buro Sitt paid the tax—twice over," he added significantly. "That's the way to treat these swine."

Cary scowled. I began to understand that Buro Sitt was right when he said Vetter would ruin his people if he weren't obeyed. I began to get very unfond of Vetter.

"Indeed?" the doctor grunted.

Vetter took it for admiration. He was crazy with self-applause anyhow. Ordinarily, admiration of one's self isn't a very healthy occupation, but Vetter thrived on it. He went on to explain further.

"Royal honors I demand," he grinned. "I am a white man, and a white man is royal, while I'm the white man. You'd think Buro Sitt had had enough of a lesson, eh? But no. Two weeks ago I marched through his chief village. I looked for royal honors. He did not offer them. I was patient. I asked him why he did not receive me as a *raja*—a sultan and his overlord. He said I was only a Frenchman, so——"

A sort of hubbub started off in the jungle somewhere. Vetter grinned nastily.

"This is the result." He waved toward the window. "I thought I'd show you how I treat these swine. I told Buro Sitt his impertinence meant he meant to revolt. He'd have to give me a hostage for good behavior. His daughter." Vetter laughed exuberantly. "A hostage, you understand. And she will taste every particle of food I eat, so Buro Sitt will not dare poison me."

The doctor grunted again.

"He won't?"

"Not he," Vetter nodded wisely, and grinned again. "I shall make love to her, of course. One does. I shall be to her as a god—a kindly god. But to her father I——"

The noise in the jungle drew nearer and louder. Then one of the sentries challenged sharply. There was an answer, and then the shrill and nasal reply of the sentry to the corporal of the guard.

Vetter waited, grinning. Presently two soldiers escorted Buro Sitt and the girl into the room. The young chap with the hawk-like eyes was nowhere about. Buro Sitt looked absolutely impassive, though his nostrils were distended a little. The girl—well, she was white and queerly silent.

Vetter looked Buro Sitt up and down.

"Since when," he asked in Malay, without any polite prefix, "are you permitted to wear arms into my presence?"

Buro Sitt, without a word, handed over his kris to one of the soldiers. His antiquated pistol followed. Vetter snapped at his soldiers and they went out. Buro Sitt was like a stone image. Vetter looked at us out of the corner of his eye. Then he laughed.

"Your daughter," he said insolently to Buro Sitt, "will taste all my food hereafter, lest there be poison in it."

"I understand, *Tuan*," said Buro Sitt evenly.

"And she will share my room," added Vetter grinning, "lest a snake be placed in that."

"I understand, *Tuan*," said Buro Sitt.

His nostrils looked white, somehow. It was a pretty horrible thing to watch, Buro Sitt handing over his daughter—sacrificing his honor as a man to keep faith with his people as a king.

"Then," said Vetter insolently, "you may go."

Buro Sitt bowed. Then he said, "But I beg, *Tuan*, that you send away that other woman, lest she poison both you and my daughter. Women are jealous, *Tuan*."

Vetter looked at him for an instant through half-closed eyes.

"I'll have a drink." He clapped his hands and ordered a siphon and a glass. When the servant brought it in he ordered the girl to mix him a drink.

Then he got up and walked over to Buro Sitt and laughed in his face. It was just showing off, you know, making a *raja* of the best blood in the East watch his daughter perform a servant's work for a white.

She brought the glass, deathly white and with flaming eyes. Vetter took it, then laughed.

"She will taste all I eat and drink," he reminded Buro Sitt. He motioned to her to taste it.

Staring at him defiantly, she raised it to her lips, and Vetter snatched it away and threw it on the floor.

"So soon?" he laughed. "And willing to drink too! But there is a mirror on the wall, my dear. I saw you drop a little white powder in it. We would have died together, eh? But it is much better to live."

He sat down and laughed while I saw Buro Sitt quivering and almost—almost leaping for him. But two soldiers came rushing in. They'd heard the crashing glass. And they led Buro Sitt away, with more despair on his face than I thought any human being could show.

I waited for a signal from the doctor, but he looked on composedly. Vetter turned to us, laughing.

"One needs to be omniscient, eh? To know their secret thoughts. There is no other woman. That was for you. So that when I died of poison you would report that I and—she"—he jerked his thumb negligently at the white-faced girl—"were poisoned by a jealous woman."

"I see," said the doctor dryly. So did I. It fitted in nicely. Buro Sitt's call of the night before and his talk of another woman would make us into witnesses that Vetter had been poisoned through jealousy. And it was quite clear that Buro Sitt was ready to see his daughter die too if it were any way necessary.

But Vetter believed he was all powerful, and the events of the last five minutes had given him extra proof. So he grinned and nodded a farewell and pushed the girl—shaken and shivering now—before him and left us. For all the world it was like a king or something dismissing his attendants. Vetter'd only wanted us for an audience, and now the show was over.

But Cary was raving. He turned to the doctor, his fists doubled, wanting to go and half kill Vetter. And I wasn't any too peaceable myself. Not heroism, you know. Just ingrowing dislike of Vetter. He didn't act like a white man should.

"We can't interfere," said the doctor coolly, "only when we've got proof that will stick in the teeth of Vetter's say-so. And we haven't."

There was a little noise. A queer little noise, like a sick man coughing. Then a little thud. Then nothing. The doctor looked grim.

"I think we've got it now," he said, with his mouth twisted wryly.

He put his hand in his pocket and went streaking to where Vetter had gone. I thought I heard the murmur of his voice. Then he came back. He was smiling, but most unpleasantly.

"You were mistaken," he said pleasantly, "if you thought you heard me talking to anybody. Vetter is sick. Very sick. Cary, go to the boat and get my medicine-case. And you," he said to me, "you tell the sergeant in command of the soldiers that Vetter is sick with fever brought on by excitement, and there mustn't be any noise. Not even challenges. And certainly no shooting. Not under any circumstances."

We went. The doctor's face was curious; grim and queerly

amused. But I knew he hadn't found exactly what he expected when he chased Vetter. I knew just what had happened the minute he let me in the room. There was nobody in the room but Vetter. The girl had disappeared. The doctor made me help him, and it was an unpleasant job.

When Cary came back, the doctor kept him busy on errands to the soldiers. He kept the soldiers busy, getting hot water hotter and cold water colder and generally occupied with duties that certainly weren't guard-duty. And bringing sheets and pillows and one thing and another. Cary, at the door, always growled that he'd no taste for trying to keep Vetter alive. Cary was sentimental about a pretty girl.

The sun had just risen when the doctor stopped. We came out of the sick-room and he told me to tell the sergeant the news. I went and broke it as positively as I knew how. Vetter was dead, of fever with complications. And the sergeant shuffled uneasily and said that the gunboat would be due in a week more.

I went back, and Cary was staring at the figure on the bed that we'd drawn a sheet over. There were one or two suspiciously wet spots on the floor, but Cary didn't notice them, or think that they looked as if we had been scrubbing there.

He stared at the figure. Then he tiptoed over and drew back the sheet from the face. Curious to look at a man you cordially disliked, when he's past being disliked any more.

"What was the matter with him?" asked Cary.

"Fever," said the doctor.

I felt very weak and sick from the reaction from what we'd had to do, but I grinned feebly.

The doctor handed Cary a package that was wrapped up in part of a sheet; he wanted it dropped overboard in deep water. The handle stuck out of it, and the handle was that of the kris the young Malay with the hawk-like eyes had been caressing while he sat with Buro Sitt on our boat deck.

"M-my God!" said Cary, shaken and sick. "He—he——"

"He died," said the doctor firmly, "of fever. A special sort that always follows paranoia. I'm a doctor and my report will stand, if we get him buried before the gunboat gets here. Fever, Cary, fever."

And his report did stand. I heard later that the next Political to take Vetter's post made shocked reports of how Vetter had been mistreating the natives. He had Grossly Exceeded his Authority, and all that sort of thing. Every effort would have to be made to restore the loyalty to *la belle France* that Vetter's actions would have undermined. That meant, of course, scrupulously fair treatment thereafter.

But it struck me as rather humorous that the doctor met Vetter's successor later on and listened for half an hour to hair-raising accounts of the evil deeds Vetter had done.

"*M'sieur*," said the new Political, excitedly, "it is incredible that he was not *assassiné*! That he died naturally, of fever, *c'est incroyable!*"

"Oh, not at all," said the doctor. "That's the price one pays for not taking things in time. Vetter had paranoia, and he didn't do anything to cure himself. His 'fever' was the inevitable price of his neglect."

In my mind I was contrasting Buro Sitt, with the price that had been set on his honor as a man, and the greater price set on his faith with his people. But just then a young doctor laughed at the doctor's ignorance in speaking of Vetter's death as the price he paid for not trying to cure his paranoia—which is usually nothing more or less than a swelled head, or the belief that one is lord of creation.

NERVE ENOUGH,
by Richard Howells Watkins

Originally published in Adventure, Dec. 30, 1925.

The time was when the T. M. O. Transportation Co. occupied a proud position in the latest infant industry—aerial passenger carrying.

The T., who was Jim Tyler; the M., Burt Minster; and the O., Delevan O'Connell, each had a plane of his own. The company leased a field on the edge of a sizable little city and erected hangars. No less than three mechanics labored to keep the ships in the air.

The three partners had a bank account and a growing clientele among the more progressive members of the community. They had carried doctors to patients, ministers to congregations and judges to court. Yes, undoubtedly the T. M. O. Transportation Co. was the peer of any aeronautical outfit in the country.

As Del O'Connell put it, in one of his prophetic moods—

"The day will come when T. M. O. means as much in this country as C. O. D."

That was rather strong, perhaps too strong, for not three days later, quite without reason, Del's motor threw a connecting rod clean through the crankcase. In the consequent forced landing in a pasture some distance from the field, he cracked two struts of his landing carriage in a successful effort to save the wings.

FALLS THREE THOUSAND FEET;
LIVES

was what the morning paper shouted to the city at large, and the growing clientele shriveled like a violet on a griddle, and the bank account was not slow in following it. Of course Del O'Connell hadn't fallen an inch; he had merely glided down without motor; but how are you going to explain that to a headline-reading public. It worried him, however, that the cracking of two struts should split their little business to its foundations. And he prophesied no more.

At last the T. M. O. Transportation Co. loaded itself into the two good ships remaining, left two of the mechanics behind and departed for fresh fields.

At another town, smaller than the first, they had pitched their tents and taken a field—by the month. The hard work of building up reputation in a business generally considered the apex of the risky was begun again. They carried hundreds of passengers in safety. Not once did one of the pilots yield to the desire for a jazz ride and tailspin a ship or even roll it over once or twice. The strict aeronautical aristocrats consider such antics in commercial flying equivalent to the employment of a puller-in outside the store in the retail clothing business.

Prospects were good, though the company was not yet prosperous. Then, one morning when Burt Minster took off alone to test-hop his ship, he banked a bit too much just after leaving the ground and came down in a side-slip that completely washed out his plane and left him in the wreckage with a split ear and a bad headache.

That reduced the T. M. O. Transportation Co.'s assets to Jim Tyler's ancient training-ship. They moved on, minus the last mechanic. They were no longer an organization with a fixed base, a reputation and a bank. They had descended in the world to the low estate of gipsy fliers, winging hither and yon, picking up such business as presented itself and landing in more cornfields than in airdromes.

Yes, they learned about flying from those cornfields—more than a pilot will ever know who always has four hundred yards or so of neatly groomed turf in front of him to set his ship down on, but it didn't help their self-esteem any.

And in Burt Minster's big head grew the conviction that if he hadn't side-slipped his bus in that silly way, the company wouldn't have dropped so low in the scale. He had made them aeronautical hoboes.

The day arrived when an offer came from the Baychester Fair for a stunt-flying, wing-walking, parachute-dropping exhibition. The three partners grasped it eagerly. Stunting a ship, walking around on wings and fuselage with a desert of space under you and dropping overboard with only thin silk between you and the next world are all hazardous propositions, but not nearly so hazardous as consistently going without food. It was hard on their pride, of course, for they remembered the time, only days behind them, when no money would have tempted them to descend so low as to indulge in thrillers to drag a crowd into a fair grounds. They were—had been—in the transportation, not the Desperate Desmond, business.

The contract was couched in terms that permitted them to kill themselves without incurring the animosity of one Jenkins, manager of the fair, provided that they did it in a spectacular and public manner. In return for this concession, they extracted sufficient cash from Jenkins to buy two parachutes and three square meals.

And here they were, in an old shack within the mile track of the Baychester Fair Grounds on the evening before opening day, with discord rampant in their ranks, and threatening to blow the company into its three component parts.

At one end of the rickety table sat Delevan O'Connell, a slender, animated young man. His wiry body was so short that he was compelled to lean forward on his elbows in order to raise his angry blue eyes above the two brand new parachute packs on the table and focus them on the big form of Burt Minster. Burt scowled back at him.

"Oh, shut your traps, both of you," growled Jim Tyler, bestowing an impartial glare on his two partners. "What difference does it make which of you does the first jump?"

The gist of the trouble was this: Both O'Connell and Minster felt responsible for the straits in which the company found itself, and therefore each man aspired to go over the side in the new parachutes. Now a chute jump is nothing much; but when you haven't made one before, and haven't even a man alongside you who has and knows something about the sensation and the harness, it is somewhat lacking in dullness.

Delevan O'Connell was swift to answer Jim Tyler's question. Already the discussion had gotten well within the bounds of plain speaking.

"It makes this much difference," he snapped, keeping his eyes fixed on Burt, although he spoke to Jim. "The first jump must not be botched."

"And therefore you must make it!" exclaimed Burt Minster, with a great laugh.

Del O'Connell flared up.

"I can not have this outfit broken up because this great oaf lacks a little nerve at the crucial moment."

Burt Minster leaned backward in his chair to give his chest room for the discharge of another roar of mirth.

"Why, you poor insect, you, I'm only about twice your size, but I've three times your grit, at least."

Jim Tyler thumped Del O'Connell on the back in time to halt the fiery little man's response.

"It isn't nerve but nerves that both of you have," he asserted emphatically. "You're both worried about those crashed ships, and you both want to take the first risk, in consequence."

The truth does not belong in an argument. This theory of their conduct was drowned in a combined shout of protest, but Del O'Connell was a bit faster on the tongue than Burt.

* * * *

"I'll make that first jump; I've got to!" he cried, springing to his feet and thumping a quick fist on the parachute packs. "You can't trust this fellow, and if he bungles it, we're gone!"

"I'll not bungle it," retorted Burt Minster stubbornly. "And as for nerve, I've more nerve than he has language, which is some."

Jim Tyler slumped wearily against the side wall of the shack and waited for the argument to subside.

"I stand ready to prove you a liar in any way you want to pick," Del O'Connell declared heatedly.

Burt Minster did not answer at once. His face reddened at the challenge, but his eyes, as they dwelt upon the parachutes, were merely thoughtful. Jim Tyler plunged into the lull.

"Since none of us has ever gone over, perhaps we'd better rehearse a jump this evening, before we try it on the crowd," he suggested, in the hope that action would halt dissension.

But Burt Minster had by no means given up the controversy. He had merely been planning.

"This Jenkins who is running the fair intimated today that he might raise the ante if we pulled something particularly spectacular the first day," he said slowly. "And we need the money, if we're ever to get back where we started. Well, I have a scheme that'll settle this nerve question once and for all, and give us a big lift toward buying another plane as well."

"Out with it, then," snapped Del O'Connell. "I'm willin' already."

Burt Minster laid a hand on the parachute packs.

"We have two of them, and we planned that the jumper should wear both, as is customary. Well, instead of that, we'll both jump, you and I, at the same time."

"And what would that prove?" snorted Del.

"I'm not through yet," Burt rebuked him. "We'll announce the thing as a race to earth, the man landing first winning. You see, you don't have to pull the rip-cord that opens the parachute the minute you leave the ship. You can fall free—an army expert fell almost two thousand feet before he opened his 'chute—"

Del O'Connell's eyes glinted.

"'Tis not a bad idea at all," he admitted, and looked upon Burt Minster with less rancor. "I like it fine."

"Wait a minute," interposed Jim Tyler. "You mean you'll both jump, and let yourselves fall a quarter of a mile or more? Why, that's the craziest—"

"And the man who pulls his rip-cord last wins, for he'll land first," Del O'Connell explained. "As good a test of nerve as ever I heard of."

"Well, you can fly yourselves, then, for I'll not have a hand in it," Jim Tyler announced firmly. "It isn't necessary for you two to kill yourselves to prove you're fools. I'll believe it now."

His statement made no impression on his partners. This was no sudden quarrel. Each, feeling guilty, was consequently touchy, and doggedly set on doing his utmost to retrieve their misfortunes. And from this attitude it was only a short step, in the ragged state of their nerves, to an open conflict over the issue of courage—or any other issue about which they could contend.

"Well, Jim," said Burt Minster at last, as Tyler continued to stand his ground unswervingly, "there's another plane here at the fair, you know. That fellow will take us both up if you won't."

Jim Tyler gave in at that, for he saw that his opposition to the plan was only making them more eager to try it. Secretly he nursed the hope that next day would bring them back to rational behavior.

* * * *

But the opening hour of the fair found them still fixed in their resolve to carry on perhaps the strangest duel of nerve that had ever been devised. The three partners kept apart, since talk only led to acrimony, and each at his post of observation watched the crowds gathering.

They came in battered tin automobiles, and they came on foot, and they came in ancient horse-drawn vehicles, from Baychester County and from the county across the Baychester River which flowed past the Fair Grounds. Jim Tyler's airworn but still airworthy Burgess training-plane was the center of a milling mob, for Baychester was not so sophisticated as some of its neighbors, and a flying machine was still an object of doubt and an object of awe. The ropes about it strained under the pressure of the curious, and the voices of the guards who reinforced the ropes grew hoarse and querulous. And word of the race to the ground through the thin air spread through the murmuring crowds.

The time of the flight came.

"Now boys, be sure and give us a good treat," Jenkins, a stout, harassed, badge-encrusted gentleman instructed, as he bustled up to the shack wherein the partners had come together again.

"You'll get it," returned Burt Minster grimly.

"Two of them," promised Del O'Connell, buckling the harness of his 'chute about him, and taking a final glance at the dangling rip-cord and the ring attached to it.

"I'll make it worth your while," the official declared, and dashed away.

At the plane the three men waited, while space for a takeoff in the infield was cleared of spectators. Jim Tyler warmed up his motor, and then, throttling down, left the cockpit and confronted his partners.

"If you're set on going through with this fool thing I suppose I'll have to stand by," he said briefly. "Where are you jumping from—wing or cockpit?"

"Since we're not pulling the rip-cords at once we might as well jump from the cockpit," said O'Connell. "You can signal to us better from there and it will look more spectacular."

"That suits me," replied Burt Minster curtly.

"I won't be able to get this bus up over six or seven thousand feet with the weight of three men in her," Jim calculated. "Suppose we make it five thousand, to be sure?"

"A mile is plenty, since it's going to be a sprint," Del O'Connell said, with a chuckle. "Though of course," he added, looking sideways at Minster, "one of us may not do much sprinting."

"Speak for yourself," growled the other man. "You'll probably starve to death before you get to the ground."

"Remember, when I turn and put up five fingers, get ready," Tyler broke in hastily. "And when I nod, jump! One from each side. And jump hard, so you'll clear the tail."

"Right," assented Del O'Connell eagerly, and Burt Minster nodded agreement.

The infield was clear at last. With a final glance at the fastenings of their harness and the rip-cords that would release the parachutes, the two men silently climbed into the rear cockpit. They wedged themselves into the narrow seat. Then both turned automatically and studied the direction and force of the wind, as revealed by the whipping flags on the grandstand.

Jim Tyler gave the ship the throttle. Bouncing and lurching, it charged into the wind, the propeller flickering as it cut the air and flung it back upon the tense faces of pilot and 'chute jumpers. Far across the infield the plane raced. Finally the wings took the burden from the rubber-tired wheels. The ship, with a final jolt, parted company with the ground, hung poised above the grass, and began its upward climb.

Though it was an old story to them, the two men in the rear cockpit looked downward, each upon his side, and the plane climbed in great circles above the fair ground below. The green of the countryside prevailed, but the brown of the oval racetrack cut through it, and just outside this ellipse was a speckled band of many indistinguishable colors that is the indication of people in masses. Beyond that, behind the cigar-box grandstand, stretched a tightly packed section of black and gray-black, where the automobiles of the crowd were parked. Booths and buildings, gay with bunting, displayed their tiny square outlines in regular patterns around the ground.

And then, as the plane rose higher, the fair grounds contracted until they were a mere detail of the landscape below—the great green and brown squares and oblongs, with larger irregular patches of woodland, interspersed here and there by tracts of well-watered pasture land, of a lush green. Across it all, as if dividing all the world into two parts, ran the almost straight course of the Baychester river.

Del O'Connell and Burt Minster at just the same time turned their attention from the earth to the back of Jim Tyler's head. They were approaching their mark and both sensed it, although there was no altimeter in their compartment.

The motor labored on, and both men thrust feet out straight, and moved shoulders tentatively, as if to drive away any incipient stiffness that might hinder action in that one swift leap into space. Both were entirely at home in the air, as seamen are at home on the water, but neither had ever gone out, deserting their craft for the impalpable element in which it swam.

Suddenly Jim Tyler turned a grim face toward the rear cockpit and raised his left hand, with fingers outstretched. Five thousand! For an instant little Del O'Connell and big Burt Minster turned and looked at each other. Determination was imprinted in the lines of both countenances, and together they squirmed to their feet in that cramped compartment, standing full in the buffeting stream of air flung back by the whirling propeller. Del O'Connell, with an agile twist, got one foot up on the rim of the cockpit and gripped the edge with both his hands. His head turned forward, and his eyes fixed themselves on the stern face of the pilot.

* * * *

Burt, a little slower, slung a foot over his side of the machine, and with one hand fumbled for the ripcord and dangling ring at the end of it. Tyler nodded.

Del O'Connell, with a quick spring, brought his other foot up out of the cockpit and, clinging with his hands, crouched on the edge of the fuselage. His legs bent more sharply for the leap that would carry him far out into space.

But just then the eyes of Jim Tyler caught a sudden flash of white from the pack on Del's back. The next instant the great silken parachute whipped out of its confining envelop. Del's rip-cord had fouled on something inside the cockpit, and his eager jump to the rim had jerked it.

The great spread of cloth billowed open instantly and whisked backward in the grip of the wind. For just an instant Del, entirely unconscious of what had occurred, held his place on the fuselage. Then, like a stone from a catapult, he was whipped off his feet and flung toward the tail of the racing plane.

The open parachute swept into the tail assembly. The tremendous force of the wind ripped it from skirt to vent as it caught. Shroud lines parted like threads. Then the silken cloth wrapped itself about elevators, and several of the shrouds that did not snap became entangled over the point of the balance of the rudder.

O'Connell's whirling body struck the tail of the machine. Then it swept past, dropping out into space. But the remaining shroud lines were securely held by the rudder. O'Connell's fall was checked by a bone-jarring jerk. His body dangled below the tail of the plane, swaying in the rush of the wind.

The plane wavered in the air, its flying speed dropping fast under the resistance of the silken cloth whipping backward from the tail assembly, and the drag of the man's body swinging behind. Jim Tyler opened the throttle full, and thrust the stick forward for a steep glide. The elevators responded. They had been unhurt by the lashing parachute. The nose of the plane turned earthward; its speed increased.

The sudden catastrophe had come before Burt Minster had gone over the side. He drew back in the cockpit and stared over at the figure of Del O'Connell, dragging behind the plane by the precarious strength of a few unsevered shroud lines. As he watched, he caught sight of the white face of his partner, and saw that O'Connell, dazed by the suddenness of the accident and his whip-like snap from the cockpit, was just coming to a realization of what had occurred.

Jim Tyler turned and stared backward, too, and then the eyes of Jim and Burt met. Speech was impossible in the fury of the motor's roar, but their eyes appealed to each other for help—for some way out. The plane was diving sharply earthward; to check that dive meant losing control of the ship; not to check it meant to crash at terrific speed into the ground. There was no way of getting O'Connell back into the ship; that was utterly impossible.

That communion of eyes lasted but a brief second; then both men turned despairingly to the doomed man trailing behind the plunging plane. They, too, were doomed in that headlong dash, but somehow their plight seemed as nothing compared to his.

O'Connell had not lost his senses. They perceived that with both hands he was fumbling, working at his right hip. Even as they watched, his hand went to his left side in the same peculiar movement. Then they comprehended.

O'Connell was unbuckling his harness. Already he had unclasped the snap buckles that fastened the heavy webbing straps about his thighs; now but one more buckle remained—the one across his chest. He did not look toward the plane; his whole attention was absorbed in his task, exceedingly difficult in that lashing wind, dangling there in space at the end of the cords. But in an instant he would no longer be dangling. The ship would be saved—at a price.

Jim Tyler watched, paralyzed by the horrible fascination of the thing. In another instant O'Connell would have cast himself off from the plane—and from life. His dry throat framed at last an inarticulate sound of protest at the sight of that sacrifice. The wind swept it away unheard.

Burt Minster, too, was watching. The breast buckle came apart. Del O'Connell was free of the harness. He hung there by his hands, and his face turned briefly toward them. A strained, twisted grin was on it.

* * * *

A pain shot through Jim Tyler's shoulder; it was a blow from Burt Minster's heavy fist. The big man was squatting on top of the fuselage.

"Right turn!"

His voice blared in the pilot's ear, audible even above the thunder of the motor. Jim obeyed automatically. The plane swerved sharply to the right.

As the machine swung around, O'Connell's body whipped sidewise, no longer directly behind and below the tail. In that instant Burt Minster leaped out into the air, all the strength of his powerful muscles concentrated in the thrust of his legs. His body, its momentum aided by the rush of air, shot through space. He crashed like a plunging bull into the lean, small body of Del O'Connell.

The two men dropped together as the long arms of Burt wrapped themselves about his partner.

The plane disappeared instantly from their view; they plunged downward in a free drop, locked together, face to face. Air was all about them; the thunder of the machine died away in their ears. Beneath, the countryside was slowly expanding, opening up before them like a magically blossoming flower.

"R-r-r-r-rip-cord!" roared Burt Minster. His own arms tightened their clutch on Del O'Connell until the little man's breath was squeezed out of his chest. But even before Burt had spoken the quick right hand of Del was wriggling downward, between Burt's shoulder and his own, toward the release ring. He found it. He pulled.

Burt Minster's breath followed Del O'Connell's out of his body as an iron band tightened across his breast; his thighs were squeezed as if a boa had wrapped his constricting merciless folds about them. Del felt a repetition of that shock that had hurled him from the fuselage.

Burt emitted a sound, half expiration, half grunt. His parachute had opened.

It spread above them like a shield. The country below ceased its eerie expansion. Burt Minster's grip about Del O'Connell's chest relaxed slightly, and the smaller man breathed again—deep, lung-distending mouthfuls of sweet air. There was no longer any rush of wind or roar of motor; nothing but a gentle, lulling sway from side to side under that great canopy of silk.

Burt Minster spoke first.

"These things are supposed to handle up to four hundred pounds, so I guess we're all right," he remarked, with an effort at a casual tone.

Del blinked.

"If you'll loosen up on those arms of yours, I'll be able to get a grip myself," he answered. They adjusted their positions, and Del took some of his weight from his hands by fastening his belt about Burt's harness. They continued to drift downward. The sudden cessation of hubbub and speed made this gentle movement dreamlike.

Del O'Connell cleared his throat—and cleared it again. Finally he muttered:

"That stuff about nerve, Burt—I'm a liar of the first water. Nerve? You're nothing else."

"I saw what you were doing, yourself," mumbled Burt Minster, equally shamefaced and uncomfortable. "That certainly took guts, Del."

"I'm glad to be out of that mess," said Del fervently. "Look! Here comes Jim!"

Jim it was, and he was not above but below them. He was climbing fast, and it was plain to see that he had complete control of the ship. As they craned their necks toward the ascending plane he banked sharply, and went circling under them, waving his hand toward the tail. Nothing but a few tatters of silk and several shroud lines trailed from the control surfaces of the tail assembly. Jim had dived his encumbrance into ribbons.

With the plane whistling around them, they were wafted downward almost directly over the fair grounds. A gentle wind was drifting them toward it, for Jim had calculated well before signaling for the jump. The earth was coming upward now with greater speed, as their horizon drew in upon them. No longer could they survey half the county.

Legs dangling, they waited. Past the eastern end of the racetrack they drifted, and then, suddenly, the ground thudded up against their feet, and down they went in a heap together. The parachute slipped sideways, and lay billowing on the ground.

"We finished together, Del. It's a dead heat," said Burt Minster, climbing to his feet and lifting the smaller man with him.

"Dead enough," answered Del O'Connell emphatically. "But I've a hunch this last little stunt has broken our run of bad luck, Burt. See! Here comes Jenkins on the run, and I'm crashed if he hasn't got his checkbook in his hand!"

BY ORDER OF
BUCK BRADY,
by W.C. Tuttle

Originally published in Adventure, July 1, 1928.

Buck Brady was always whittling. Thin shavings were an obsession with Buck. He would sit for hours, tilted back in a broken chair against the shady side of his little office, knees almost touching his chin, his long, thin face serious over the task of reducing a piece of soft pine to thin shavings.

Buck was the sheriff of Mojave Wells, and Mojave Wells was a heat and sand scoured, false fronted town in Road Runner Valley.

The town was invisible from a distance, because even the painted signs on the business houses had been sand blasted until they were unreadable.

It was the end of the roundup in Road Runner Valley, and Buck knew that before night the town would be filled with thirsty cowboys, whose overall pockets were lined with money, and that when whisky met cowboy there might be plenty of work for the sheriff.

The first to arrive was Ben Dolan, a thin faced, gaunt sort of cowboy, astride a weary looking roan. Instead of heading for a saloon, Ben dismounted in front of the sheriff's office, dropped his reins in the dirt and sat down beside the sheriff.

"Hyah, Buck."

"Purty good," drawled Buck squinting at his handiwork. "Whatcha know, Ben?"

"Not much."

"In kinda early, ain't you?"

"Yeah."

Ben made a few marks in the sand with a lean forefinger.

"Had a reason t' come in early, Buck. Some of the boys said it wouldn't do no good, but I thought I'd tell you how it was. 'Long about an hour from now Bud Hickman will ride in. He'll have his gang with him and they'll imbibe real freely. Mebbe 'long about that same time Pete Asher'll ride in with his gang. They'll also imbibe freely, and some of 'em will likely get kinda drunk. The boys are all thirsty, you know. I expect it'll be kinda wooly around here t'night, Buck."

"Uh-huh."

Buck cut a particularly long shaving, looked at it critically and nodded with satisfaction.

"You shore rode in early to explain all this to me," he said. "If you're all through, you might tell me the rest."

"It's thisaway," explained Ben seriously. "You know what a feud is, Buck?"

"Yea-a-ah."

"Well, that's what she amounts to right now. And it's all over a danged girl!"

"I'm glad there's a reason, Ben. Mostly allus them feuds starts over nothin'. Go ahead and tell me the details."

"Rosie Smith."

"Huh?"

"That's what I said. You know how Bud and Pete kinda shined around her a month ago. I don't guess she knowed which one to pick.

Of course, Bud thinks it's him, and Pete thinks it's him. And there you are. It's been kinda achin' both of 'em, I reckon. Anyway, Chuck Lester makes a remark the other night that he supposed Bud wouldn't be with us in Mojave Wells at the finish of the roundup, 'cause he'd stop along a picket fence before he reached the main street, and head straight through the gate.

"Pete was there, and I reckon it hit him in a sore spot, cause he chips in with a remark, which didn't set well with Bud. There wasn't much said, but it took all of us to take their guns away. We didn't want no killin' in camp. Bud was reasonable. He says to Pete, 'We'll settle this in Mojave Wells.'"

"Pete was agreeable. He says, 'That suits me. We'll make a truce until sundown, both agreein' to keep away from her. When that sun goes down, all truce is off, and we shoot on sight.'"

* * * *

Buck sliced another shaving, laid the stick aside and began whetting the blade on the counter of his left boot.

"And one of them damn' fools is goin' to get killed," added Ben.

"It's kinda hard to git straight grain stuff these days," said the sheriff seriously. "I 'member when I was runnin' a tradin' post down Yuma way, I used to git the best danged boxwood for whittlin'. I don't suppose it runs so good these days."

"Ben and Pete are both friends of yours," said Ben thoughtfully.

"Uh-huh. I like 'em both."

"A killin' might start trouble. The boys has kinda took sides."

"I s'pose."

"Bud and Pete are both good shots."

"Yea-a-ah—purty good shots. Awful damn' fools in lotsa ways, but good shots. Uh-hu-u-uh. Well, I've got to write me some signs, Ben. It's two hours till sundown."

"I thought you'd like to know about it, Sheriff."

"Yeah, I do. Thank you kindly."

"You're welcome."

Ben took his horse and headed for a saloon, while more cowboys came racing in, their horses covered with lather and dust. The sheriff watched the first contingent arrive. It was Bud Hickman and his gang from the Tumbling K. Bud was a likable looking cowboy, about twenty-five years of age, tall, lithe, swarthy as an Indian, with curling black hair and a white toothed smile. His crew was a wild riding lot of hard bitted punchers, ready for fun or fight at a moment's notice.

They noted that Pete Asher and the J88 boys had not arrived yet;

so they all headed for the Desert Well Saloon, the biggest place of its kind in Mojave Wells. The sheriff stood on the edge of the sidewalk for a while, cogitating deeply. He had been sheriff of that particular county for nearly two terms, which meant that Buck Brady was pretty much of a man. Finally he went into his little office, and after a search he found an old paint brush and a few ounces of almost dried paint in a battered can. He kicked the ends out of a soap box, drew out the nails and sat down at his desk.

Pete Asher and his crew rode in from the J88, tied their horses farther up the street and entered the Prospect Saloon. Asher was a heavily built, hard faced cowboy, about the same age as Bud Hickman. His hair was almost a neutral shade, his eyes deep set and blue. There was little to choose between his gang and the one which came in with Bud Hickman, and in numbers they were about equal.

There were more outfits to come, but they were not connected with the feud. Rud and his men were at the bar when the sheriff came in, and they greeted him noisily. He was carrying a box end and a hammer, and without any leave from the proprietor he proceeded to nail his sign to one of the walls. It read:

> FROM NOW ON EVERY MAN
> MUST TURN HIS GUN OVER
> TO MY OFFICE UNTIL HE IS
> READY TO LEAVE TOWN.
> BY ORDER OF
> —BUCK BRADY.

Some of the men laughed: some swore. Bud Hickman strode over to the sheriff and glared at him belligerently.

"You tryin' to kid somebody, Buck?" he asked.

The sheriff looked steadily at Bud for several moments.

"I ain't in the habit of kiddin' anybody, am I?"

Bud flushed quickly, but he recognized the fact that Buck Brady would back up his sign. That was why Buck was their sheriff.

"Kinda sudden, ain'tcha?" asked Bud.

"No-o-o. I've been thinkin' this out quite a while, Bud."

"Is this the idea?" queried Bud. "We all turn our guns over to you, and you turn 'em back when we're ready to leave town?"

"That's what the sign says, Bud; and I wrote the sign."

Bud laughed and turned to his men.

"It's all right, boys. Shuck your guns. I reckon we can stand it, if the others can." And then to the sheriff, "You might have a little trouble with Pete and his gang."

"I hope they'll be reasonable."

The men put their guns on a poker table, and the sheriff picked them up, putting some in his pockets, some inside the waistband of his overalls.

"You'll have to remember your own guns, boys," he said.

"I reckon I can spot mine," said Bud. "I made them handles."

* * * *

The sheriff thanked them kindly and went back to his office, where he locked the guns in his desk. Then he went over to the Prospect Saloon, where he nailed up his other notice. Asher and his men didn't take so kindly to the idea. Some of them were openly belligerent, and it seemed for a few moments that the sheriff had a tough job, but Asher took the matter out of their hands.

"I suppose this thing only applies to me and my men, eh?"

"You're supposin' wrong, Pete; I've already collected from the Tumblin' K."

"You've collected from Bud Hickman?"

"Why not?"

"Oh, I jist wondered. But suppose we don't give you our guns?"

The sheriff considered Pete calmly. Then:

"I've allus liked you, Asher. You've been a damn' fool in lotsa ways, but you're jist human like the rest of us. I've posted my notice, and I wrote it myself."

"But jist suppose we refuse to give up our guns?"

"That," said the sheriff calmly, "would be jist too damn' bad."

"Oh—" softly—"and if I should happen to want to leave town, you'd give me back my gun?"

"Jist like the sign says, Pete."

"All right; here's mine. Take 'em off, boys. We don't need 'em—now."

The sheriff looked over the guns as he deposited them about his person; he walked out, swinging the hammer in his hand.

"Don't that beat hell?" laughed Pete.

"I'll betcha somebody told him somethin'," said a cowboy.

"I don't like the idea of a moth eaten old sidewinder takin' my gun away," complained a cowboy who was new to the country. "We'd 'a' had some fun, if we'd refused."

"You've got a sweet idea of fun," growled Pete. "That moth eaten old sidewinder is jist thirty-two years old, and if we hadn't turned them guns over to him he'd jist about ruined the whole gang of us with his pet Winchester. When you see 'By order of Buck Brady,' you better read the upper part of it and act accordingly."

* * * *

All the cowboys went back to their drinking, and the sheriff was forgotten, but both Bud and Pete kept track of the sun. The sheriff, humped in his chair, still whittling, saw Pete come out, saunter to the hitching rack, where he could view the sun. It was still an hour high.

Ben Dolan, fairly well filled with liquor, came over again and squatted on his heels beside the sheriff. Ben was as hard bitted as the rest of the cowboys, but he liked both Bud and Pete so well that he hated to see either of them wounded or killed. And Ben was wise enough to understand that both men would claim their guns at sundown.

They saw Bud leave the Desert Well Saloon, walk halfway across the street, as if heading for a store, stop and look toward the west. He too was keeping cases on the sun. Then he turned and went back to the saloon. Ben made meaningless marks in the sand with a forefinger, while the sheriff whittled thoughtfully.

"You shore collected a lot of guns, Sheriff."

"Yea-a-ah."

"Almost sundown."

The sheriff shut one eye and considered Ben. Then he looked toward both saloons, and went on whittling.

"The boys are gettin' nervous," said Ben.

"I notice."

Several cowboys were standing in front of the Prospect Saloon now, and one of them essayed a clog dance. His boots sounded loud on the old wooden sidewalk. Another beat time on a porch post with the end of a quirt. It was like the beating of a tomtom, and he kept it up for a time after the dancer had stopped. The beater was swarthy, with high cheek bones.

Some of Bud's gang came from the Desert Well and stood around in front of the building. One of them, a little drunker than the rest, started across the street toward the sheriff's office, but the others stopped him and, after an argument, persuaded him to desist.

"It's kinda sultry," said Ben, rubbing his forehead.

The sheriff nodded and looked at the sun, only half of which was visible now. He blinked from the strong light and cut several shavings, which did not suit him at all. A couple of dogs met in the middle of the street; town dogs, fat and with a friendship of long standing. But now they growled ominously at each other, as they circled, looking for an opening.

"Sic 'em!" hissed a cowboy from in front of the Desert Well.

"Take him, Tige! Shake his fleas loose. Four bits on the yaller one."

"You've done made a bet, cowboy. Choose him, Ponto."

But the dogs only circled and growled, and finally separated.

"Mebbe they're waitin' for the sun to go down," whispered Ben.

The sheriff shook his head.

"Got more sense than men have."

* * * *

The sun was down. Only the tip was visible, and the crests of the broken hills showed a golden highlight. It was very still in Mojave Wells. The shadows were gone now and the street glowed with a yellow light, which would not last long. Twilight was unknown in Mojave Wells. Sundown, a streak of gold, would quickly fade to blue, and then darkness.

Bud Hickman came from the Desert Well and went straight to the hitch rack, where he untied his horse and swung into the saddle. Simultaneously with Bud's move, Pete Asher came riding from the rack beside the Prospect. It was not a casual move. They intended to deceive nobody, not even the sheriff of Mojave Wells. The cowboys of both outfits were in the street, watching intently.

Bud came straight to the sheriff, and fifty feet behind him was Pete. Bud's face was grim, his mouth set in a thin line.

"I'm pullin' out, Buck," he said softly. "Would you mind handin' me my gun?"

The sheriff stopped whittling, tilted forward in his chair and got slowly to his feet. He looked closely at Bud, but said nothing, as he turned and went into the office. Pete moved in closer, but he and Bud ignored each other. Ben sighed and leaned against the wall.

The sheriff came out, carrying a gun in each hand. For several moments he looked at the two men rather sorrowfully.

"I reckon you're pullin' out, too, ain'tcha, Pete?"

Pete nodded quickly and held out his hand for the gun. They had been friends, these two, until a woman had come between them. Bud holstered his gun, swung his horse around and rode slowly down the street, looking straight ahead. Pete accepted his gun, glanced at it to see that it was fully loaded, snapped it down in his holster and swung his horse around, riding back to the center of the street.

Ben swore softly under his breath. Both of these men were good revolver shots.

"Goin' to be a funeral around here—mebbe two," he muttered.

"Why don'tcha stop it, Buck? Gawd A'mighty, this ain't right! Look at Bud—he's turnin'!"

"You didn't expect he'd run away, didja?"

The contestants in this desert town drama were two hundred feet apart, facing each other, both horses moving slowly. They had both played a square game. There was no advantage now. Two hundred feet is a long shot. Both men had drawn their guns. Bud's horse was dancing a little, and he spurred it viciously.

Pete waited.

Ben's hands were gripping the wall beside him. He had seen gun fights before, but they had all been unpremeditated affairs. This one was too much like an execution. The groups of cowboys were as immobile as dummy figures. Even the horses at the hitch racks had ceased moving.

Bud and Pete were closing the gap between them, closing it slowly, each waiting for the other to make the first move with a gun. They were only a hundred feet apart now. It was close enough. But neither of them made a move to lift his gun.

Ninety feet; thirty yards. Either of them could hit a tomato can at that distance. Eighty feet! Horses walking slowly, Seventy feet; sixty feet. Twenty yards now. They were almost in front of the sheriff's office. Ben laughed foolishly. It would be a double funeral. He had seen Bud shoot the head from a prairie dog at that distance.

"It's a nice evenin' for it," said the sheriff rather inanely.

And then it happened!

* * * *

Both guns came up at exactly the same instant. Ben's eyes snapped shut and he turned his head aside.

Came a tiny ping, hardly louder than the mere snapping of a revolver hammer. Another and another. Bud's eyes jerked open. The two riders were thirty feet apart, leaning forward in their saddles. Not a shot had been fired.

With a swift movement, Bud Hickman swung out the cylinder of his Colt and emptied the cartridges in his hand. Every primer had been dented. There were marks on the bullets, marks made by the jaws of a pair of pliers.

Pete was swearing viciously, as he drew cartridges from his belt and started to stuff them in his gun.

But the sheriff halted him with a sharp word.

"Damn you, you pulled the powder on my shells!" snarled Pete.

"Yeah; and I'll pull somethin' else out of you, if you make one more move," said the sheriff calmly. "C'mere, Bud."

Bud rode up to him, still holding the empty gun in his hand. Pete had quit trying to load his gun. They looked coldly at each other.

"You boys hadn't ort to fight," said the sheriff calmly. "Both of you goin' off kinda half cocked, as you might say."

The men from both outfits had moved in close now, trying to understand what it was all about, their enmity all but forgotten in this queer turn of events.

"I pulled them bullets," admitted the sheriff. "I don't reckon either of you showed any yaller streak. You played the game square, and I like you both for it. Personally I kinda enjoyed it. It was like lookin' at a show. I was the only one that knowed how it would turn out."

"Was it any of your damn' business how it turned out?" demanded Pete hotly.

"In a way, it was, Pete—" calmly. "Barrin' my friendship with both of you, and my position as sheriff, it still was my business, in a way. Now, you two boys was aimin' to kill each other over a woman. Yeah, Ben told me about it. You might thank Ben instead of glarin' at him.

"He liked both of you, and he didn't want no killin' done; so he told me about it. I don't think for a minute that this Smith girl would care to have you killin' each other over her. Most girls don't. Anyway, it was a sucker idea, because there ain't no Smith girl around here any more; so you was tryin' to kill each other for nothin'."

"What do you mean?" blurted Bud.

"The Smiths ain't moved away," offered a cowboy.

"If you hadn't had so much killin' on your mind, you might have found out that me and the Smith girl was married over a week ago. You boys better go back and have your spree, as soon as you give me back them guns, 'cause I've got work to do."

"Whittlin'?" asked Bud blankly.

"Lookin' for somethin' to whittle on."

CODE,
by L. Paul

Originally published in Adventure, Nov. 15, 1927.

There was a queer feeling about the ship. "Hush," thought the man who stood by the gangway. That was the apt word. A battered ship, a dirty craft, small, obscene, unseaworthy, of foreign register. And silent—hush! Grim faced men going about their business, sparing no word for him, though they might have talked, he guessed, had they cared to.

This man who watched wore soiled dungarees. There was a day's stubble of beard on his thin face. His expression, when a passing man darted a look at him, was blank. His eyes fell when other eyes probed him. He looked over his shoulder at times, at the rotting dock in the small British port of Beverstock near Liverpool, where this ship, the *Cora*, lay. He had come aboard, nobody knew how. One moment, and the ship end of the gangway, creaking as the current swayed the little tramp, was empty. The next moment he was there. Nor did these others think it strange. They looked as if this sudden yet stealthy approach was usual, an accustomed thing, an item, strange perhaps to some, yet of little moment in their full lives.

The man in dungarees stood there till the first cheerful man he had seen aboard rolled up, the stout chief engineer.

"That's him," said the chief, and tapped him on the shoulder.

The man winced, turned, and saw, climbing the steep gangway, a man.

"That's him," repeated the stout chief. "Captain Bain."

The man in dungarees saw a tall, glum seafarer, with graying hair, his frowsy shore going linen peeping from sleeves of shiny serge, his lapels greasy; his boots polished long after polish had become a mockery; and, topping all, a master's cap.

This was Captain Bain, right enough. He stopped, stared at the man in dungarees and said briefly—

"Where from?"

"American Bar," the man in dungarees replied.

"Come this way," said the captain. "My name's Bain. This is my cabin. We can talk here. Out on deck talk's barred in port. Who sent you?"

He fell silent, not because he waited for the answer, but more as if he had run down, as if this long speech had been an effort, a breaking down of his accustomed reserve. The man in dungarees waited, as if expecting him to say more, then at last replied:

"Who sent me? Dip Laplace."

He fumbled in the pocket of his dungarees and found a wad of crumpled paper.

"He sent this, too."

The captain of the *Cora* took the paper, opened it, held it up to the beam of light that stole through the grimy port. The man in dungarees sat down on a locker.

"My name's Drake," he remarked.

His eyes were fixed on the captain. He saw a wave of color sweep up over old Bain's weatherbeaten neck, into his cheeks, then recede again.

What the captain read, spelling out large printed words, was this:

Sparklers—they're wise—watch.

The captain of the *Cora* crumpled the paper in his hand.

"You read this, of course?"

"I'm no liar. I did, of course," the man in dungarees mimicked him. "As I said, my name's Drake—"

"And this paper?"

"I've forgotten what was on it," Drake told him.

"Dip gave it to you. Dip grows jocular," the captain laughed harshly. "Are you another of his jokes?"

"I am a passenger."

"I don't carry passengers."

"My kind? Dip sent me, remember."

"You know then; you have money?"

Drake spread five fifty-pound notes out on his knee.

"As bad as that?" The captain whistled. "You could swank aboard a liner for that."

"And swank off across the pond?"

The captain stroked his long jaw reflectively. His eyes wandered over Drake's face, stopped for a moment on the wall clock above his head, dropped to the pile of treasury notes and dwelt there.

"As bad as that?" said the captain of the *Cora*. "Not murder?"

"No, Dip sent me. He knows. Need you?"

"Need I? God forbid. Can you swim?"

"Yes, why?"

"You'll have to. I see you don't know the game we play. Better learn before I take your money. You find it—convenient—to travel informally, to land on the other side incognito— No, your name may be Drake, and I don't care if it is or not. Names don't count here. But you wish to land as Drake, unknown to anyone. We arrange that. No immigration folk to pester you. No police. We sail for Montreal. Below that city fifty miles or so are islands. Sometimes we go slowly through them, close to land. An active swimmer, dropping overside—you have more money, have you not?"

"Yes, Captain, a little."

"There's a man on one island, there. He has a boat. If you give him more than five pounds, he's robbing you. After that your movements are not my concern."

Again, as the captain paused, Drake had that strange feeling that here was a man talking overmuch—a man more fond of silence.

"And that's all?" Drake asked. "Simple, isn't it?"

"Why do you say that?"

"I feared I'd have to work my passage, and I'm lazy."

The captain of the *Cora* reached for the little pile of notes.

"A man must live," he growled, as if apologizing for his delinquencies. "A man must live, and there's no money in tramp shipping. You'll find a small cabin on the port side—the empty one. It's yours. We sail with the tide. If you come on deck before that and are nabbed—" he patted his pocket where he had stowed those notes—"that's your lookout, Drake."

Drake rose and crossed the little cabin. At the threshold he paused.

"Those other cabins—"

"You are three. The others, you won't meet till we are at sea."

Drake stepped out, dropped down a steep iron stair to the deck, slid into the port alley, where tiny doors formed a row, tried first one, then another, till he found one unlocked, entered, and found himself in a cabin so small that it could scarcely contain a bunk and its occupant at the same time.

Men had watched him—shadowy figures, heads out of the galley, the engine-room, the firehold. They had said nothing, betrayed no surprise at his coming. They were silent men.

"Hush!"

* * * *

The salt wind drifted across the deck of the *Cora*. She was wallowing in the Atlantic.

Drake and the fat chief sat in the lee of the funnel. They had struck up an acquaintance during the first half of the voyage. Drake had traveled; he knew things. The fat chief, a jovial rascal, had the curiosity of a child and a stout man's zest for effortless, vicarious adventure.

The two other passengers had kept apart. There was Quayle, as yet sticking close to his cabin, save at mealtimes when he joined Drake at the captain's table. He had given that name, Quayle, casually, as if it had just occurred to him, as if names were matters of only passing importance.

He was a tall, silent man, middle-aged.

The third passenger messed with the crew. He was a small Liverpool dock rat. He claimed that he had not killed his wife, but had only beaten her. The captain, after discreetly calling up a hospital, found that this was true. Because he had but twenty pounds they had taken him for that. He never came up on the boat deck; he viewed the ocean with ignorant terror and kept behind the high steel bulwarks of the well deck, when he came out for air.

114

The chief, having a romantic mind, decided that the Liverpool man's wife would probably take a turn for the worse and die. He held that the other passenger, Quayle, was a Bolshevik.

The chief and Drake sat there and yarned through the long sea morning.

"A rum ship," Drake hazarded.

"We are that," the chief grinned, "at home to rum company."

"True, but you know each other; we don't, we passengers."

"Five new faces in the ship's company," the chief laughed. "Ye see, we can't keep 'em. We ship so many passengers that it has made *their* pile easy, or on the way to make it easy. It corrupts the lads. Five new faces—five old 'uns gone to do likewise—on the trail o' easy money. Man, dear, 'tis restless labor is getting to be—"

"Eight of us, new chums, not knowing each other—for five and three is eight."

Drake stared out to sea.

"Eight souls," sighed the chief. "Where they comes from. Gawd only knows. Where they're bound, Gawd don't care; speakin' more exact, nine. For I'd forgot Sparks."

Drake glanced forward. The tall radio man was in his hencoop, a scant twenty feet away. The door was open.

"Why him?"

"Another bird o' passage. D'ye notice his duds?"

"New and fancy."

"Know what the pay is? Man, dear, if he bought them out of wages, he's never had smoke nor drink in years. Ever see a tramp's wireless wonder before? No. Know what I think? He's an absconding Scot. He figured we'd soak him hard for an unconventional passage. You know what you paid, so—"

The chief closed his eyes and gave the details of his imaginative romance in a few low words:

"Sparks gets him a uniform. Eighty bob, mebbe; or steals one. He finds out we're gettin' a new radio man this voyage. An' then, back in port some poor dub brass pounder is wakin' up, mebbe in hospital. And this sport—well, he's on the papers as Sparks, but we lose our dividend on his passage thereby."

"So you figure him, as you might say, a jailbird of passage."

Drake had raised his voice. The chief clutched his arm.

"Don't ye now; don't rile that one. Man, dear, every time that devilish contraption spits sparks I shudder. Think o' the slander yon lad could spread and nobody knowin'."

"Slander?"

115

"Slander 'bout—you—or me, M'Ginley. Oh, aye, there's tales he could tell, even if he's new. Would ye believe it?" The old chief rose. "Ye might not; but some o' the lads aboard here has loose tongues. A thing I abhor, personal." And off the old man waddled.

Drake sat there a moment. He was thinking:

"I wonder. Another little swimmer when we come to that island? Will there be four of us in the water? Will the fourth be Sparks? If so—best watch him."

Rising, he added a codicil to this conclusion.

"There's nine aboard, counting myself," he thought, "nine that may be, well, anything. Best start figuring this one out. That'll leave eight. And one of the eight is me, Drake. Wonder what I'll be, when we come to the end of the voyage?"

He glanced aft. The stout chief engineer was there, where he had paused on the stair that led below.

"Them that don't talk here," said M'Ginley, "them that don't talk on this ship—they guesses."

* * * *

Drake slipped forward till he stood by the open door of the wireless coop. The new Sparks looked up.

"Want anything?" he asked.

"Just loafing round." Drake rolled a cigarette slowly, clumsily. "Smoke?"

"Yes."

The wireless man reached for pouch and papers, twisted with swift fingers, struck a match and was exhaling smoke, almost before Drake himself had lighted up.

"You've been in the States?" Drake asked. "Learned to make a gasper there, didn't you?"

"And you're from the old country, calling a cig that?"

"A good country to come from—and the faster the coming the better," Drake drawled. "Old country's not—healthy."

"For some."

The wireless man bent over his complicated machinery, as it became alive. Drake looked on, wonder in his eyes, almost a childish wonder.

"But that's marvelous," said he. "Words coming out of the air."

"Dot dash dot dash," said the wireless man. "See that smoke yonder? The *Paladin*. She's asking the *Caradoc* if they've met ice. Bergs drifting now, you know."

Drake glanced at the wall clock, then drifted toward the door.

It was eleven o'clock. It was Wednesday—five days since they had left port. This old ruin of a ship was traveling with speed.

The voice of the wireless man followed him.

"I'm Cray; come again," he called. "This packet doesn't run to rules."

Drake turned. He seemed uneasy.

"If—" he began.

"If what?" Cray waited.

"If you hear something with that gadget about a man named Drake, the fewer know—the better. Get me?"

"Don't slip me money." Cray's hand met his, thrust it back. "You'll need all you got. A rum lot, on a rum ship."

"And you as rum as they come," thought Drake, as he walked away.

Cray watched him go.

"Wonder if he knew what was on the air just now," he scowled. "If I shove it to the Old Man will he—well, this time I'm a wireless man. Next time we'll see."

To him, too, this strange ship was saying, "Hush!" Yet his pencil slid over flimsy paper. He rose with a message, took it to the captain on the bridge.

"Rum lot aboard, sir." He handed the message over, winked.

The captain started, backed away into a wing of the bridge, scanned that message.

"You are right," he replied. "This came in code, I presume?"

"Yes, sir."

"Then why not leave it in code. We don't want the world knowing."

"Nobody's seen it, sir, but me."

"Damn you! That's an order. Anything else comes, leave it in code."

Cray went white and was about to speak. Then he checked himself. He walked away; he was thinking.

"Him, too—the Old Man. Wonder what he knows that the world don't, that he's afraid of the world learning? I'll, maybe, find out. I'll see. Tonight, maybe. He might work in. Who knows?"

The captain, staring at the retreating back was staring at words that floated before his eyes.

For that message had read:

> All ships. All ships. All ships.
> Varnavosk necklace stolen. Suspect at sea.
> Watch passengers. Stand by for more.

The urgency of the thrice repeated "All ships"—that stabbed him, made him wince. Trouble, trouble in large consignments, coming out of the air. Other messages, and the field of search might narrow, perhaps, till it centered on an old tramp wallowing across the Western Ocean; till some swift offshore craft might draw alongside, and some officious jackanapes would climb up the ladder and ask fool questions about eight new faces aboard the *Cora*.

There was trouble on the ship that said, "Hush."

The captain walked stiffly across the bridge and down to his cabin. Cray, on the boat deck, watched him go.

"Yes, we'll use you, my bucko," said Cray. "Now I wonder—" and he stared down on the well deck, forward, where the little Liverpool passenger sprawled on a hatch cover.

"You've got a shiner on your eye, my lad," thought Cray, "and you mess with the crew. They'll be eating any moment now. I think we'd better not wait. We'll begin with you."

He followed the old captain of the *Cora* to his cabin.

When the passengers who messed with the skipper came in to lunch, that worthy's chair was vacant. Cray it was who greeted them, smiling at Drake, bowing stiffly to tall Quayle.

"Old Man's busy," said Cray. "Don't wait for him, gentlemen."

* * * *

That was Wednesday. On Thursday the fat engineer M'Ginley sought the warm lee of the funnel once more. Drake was there, waiting.

"I made my peace with Cray. If he was mad about what I said, he didn't show it."

"A bad case," the fat old chief growled. "There's more in this ship than ballast. There's a mystery."

"Eight little mysteries," Drake jeered, "of which one is my humble self. Maybe nine, counting Cray. Or ten—"

"What you alludin' to now?"

"You, honest old M'Ginley."

"Me? Man could see clean through me." The chief winked at him. "But look at this code; and all that pencilin' under it is writ by the most talented engineer on the Western Ocean."

Drake glanced down at the flimsy bit of paper. He saw first a jumble of phrases and part words. But below that a penciled legend made sense.

All ships.

Varnavosk dying. Look for strong man capable killing bare-handed.

No signature this time.

"Where'd you get this?"

Drake stiffened. He glanced forward uneasily; but Cray's blind was drawn on the little window of his cabin. Cray's door was shut.

"Where'd you think? Notice the Old Man yesterday and today?" the old chief asked. "Well, he's fair wild. He come down this mornin' an' asks me to trot along, confidential. We goes to that wife beatin' runt's cabin. The runt is out on deck. Old Man and me, we rip up the floorboards, we pry apart the bunk."

"Looking for what?"

"He wouldn't tell at first. Then, when we found nothin', he begun to rave about jewelry. Him, that's carried such downan'-outs before, lookin' for jewelry in that cabin. Told me to shut up. Left me standin' on air, like. So I mooched. Half an hour ago Cray comes down with this. Old Man looks her over, puzzles her out. He was standin' by his cabin. Next he dives in, grabs somethin', pockets it—an' comes out again. Know what he grabbed?"

"No."

"His gun. Me, I grabs somethin' else. This. Now you know as much as I do, unless you know more."

Drake stared at him, then dropped his eyes.

"And if I do?"

"Cray and the Old Man know a heap. My guess is there's been robbery; and now it looks like murder. Like as not the search'll narrer down. Scotland Yard ain't manned by fools. Like as not there'll be other messages. Liverpool runt's been cleared. He don't pack no valuables. There's seven new faces aboard beside him, leavin' Cray out. If things gets hot and they start to search the lot—well—him that has them jewels is like to swing."

"Unless—" Drake seemed to be master of himself now—"unless!"

"Unless the lad slipped 'em to a good natur'd old fool of an engineer. There's places below." Old M'Ginley winked. "Well, if you meet the man aboard here, you tell him."

"Thanks, I will. Cray's blind's gone up." Drake rose. "I'm going to have a chin with him."

"If there's one thing more'n another has hanged fool men, it's words," M'Ginley warned, and left him.

* * * *

Cray grinned as Drake opened the door.

"You—you heard anything?" Drake asked, nervously.

"Nothing."

"Thought, maybe, some message might have drifted in; seen you writing a while back."

"There was," Cray laughed. "Fool operator on the *Jessamine* was askin' me if I'd bought my girl that diamond yet."

Drake stood by the table, his lean fingers clasped about its beveled edge. Cray, watching covertly, smiled. That table was shaking, though it was fastened to the floor.

"You're a strong man, ain't you?" Cray asked.

"There's stronger aboard this packet," Drake answered tonelessly. "Where'd the Old Man dig up those new sailormen? Two of them I saw this morning, ramming at that bent stanchion that supports this deck. Take four of me to make one of them."

"That's an idea," Cray smiled, as if relishing his chance to play with this man.

"What is?" Drake frowned. "Makin' one of them from four of me?"

"Then there's Quayle; he's husky, too. Well, beef don't count with me." Cray shoved a chair forward. "Want to listen in?"

He reached for an extra headset, plugged in, adjusted it for Drake, then watched him, keenly, as some faint message came.

"So that's what it sounds like?" Drake looked up. "I've often wondered."

But Cray was busy, writing. His pencil fairly shook as it sped over the paper.

"What's that?"

Drake looked over his shoulder. Too late, Cray shoved a hand over what he had written, for Drake had seen, seen plainly, the uncompleted sentences:

All ships.
Varnavosk died this morning.
Communicate with us if....

"You seen, hey?" Cray fidgeted, seemed annoyed; yet he might be pretending. He was, at any rate, ill at ease.

"You seen? Well, what's a Russky more or less to you or me? Don't tell the Old Man I showed you. The others came in code. This one's plain English. Best beat it; I've got to take this to the Old Man."

Drake got up and walked silently out. On the threshold Cray

stopped him with:

"Ever know any Russians, Drake? Some of them is big men—hard fighters. Take a powerful man to handle them."

"Meaning—" Drake spun about fiercely— "Meaning—"

"You know more'n you let on," Cray laughed. "Thought I'd catch you. You know who Varnavosk was, owner of the Varnavosk necklace? You know why he's dead—"

Drake rolled a cigaret with his usual clumsiness.

"What mobsman doesn't know?" he asked. "Come, come, Cray. You know what sort we passengers are on this dirty little ship. Know Varnavosk and his necklace? Who does not, in my walk of life? What gang but has had their eyes on him and his jewels? And now, that a cleverer man than myself has pulled the trick—"

"So you're a crook," Cray jeered. "So—"

Drake smiled pleasantly.

"Did you think me a lily?" Drake was composed now. "Imagination's a grand thing, Cray. Sometimes it leads men into trouble, though. You've been reading dime novels."

Drake walked away. Cray watched him go aft along the boat deck and down the steep stairs.

"You'll worry, my man," growled Cray. "Now, what's next. Liverpool swine is ruled out. That fool of a skipper—a child could see through him. He's ripped that dub's cabin to pieces. At this rate he'll have the whole ship torn apart, every manjack on edge. Not one'll get by him without him poking and prying. And he's fool enough to make a bad break. So, we're five days from port, and—"

He stared at that last message, which he had left incomplete. With a swift pencil he ended it.

All ships, westbound. Communicate with us if you have news. Proceed with caution.

—Scotland Yard

"And that," said Cray to himself, as he took the message to the captain of the *Cora*, "that'll hold him for a while. This ship is jammed full of *strong men*."

* * * *

"So you can't find him, the thief," Cray jeered.

There was no deference in his tone, no respect. Here he sat in the Old Man's cabin and yarned away as if such a thing as discipline had ceased to exist.

"The thief? He's been a murderer for two days." Old Bain scowled

121

at him. "You have me nigh crazy. First we rip up that little rat's cab-in—"

"That was you; I just hinted—" Cray began.

"Hinted like you did when that message came about lookin' for a strong man who could kill barehanded!"

"A strong man; you've found several," Cray retorted. "Was it me said it might be one of those two sailors? Oh, yes. I admit I didn't contradict you. I'll say I let you have your way, do your own crude sleuthing, searching that forecastle. Don't you know that sailormen are a neat lot, even such scum as this? They know this moment that you have been prodding about. And now you say—"

"You put things into my mind, damn you!" The Old Man glowered at him. "I thinks things, and says things, and there ain't no reason to them when said and thought. They ain't my thoughts; they ain't my actions, an'—"

"Mine, of course, hey? I do it all? Mebbe I did this. This came to-day." Cray shoved a sheet of paper at him. The Old Man ran his eye over a jumble of code, then reached for his book, translated.

"You know what it is?" He lifted his head and stared at Cray. "You know—"

"All ships? No, not this time. The search has narrowed down," Cray grated. "This one is:

"Ships outward bound, Beverstock. Man aboard you. Hold him."

"Which means—" The skipper of the luckless *Cora* waited.

"Us!" Cray's face was tense. "Scotland Yard—they've got a line on us; they're closing in on their man."

"And when—when some detective comes up the ladder— We're nigh into St. Lawrence Gulf—" the Old Man stared out of the grimy port—"When the showdown comes."

"Never such a ship for secrets as this," Cray said. "They'll come for one. They'll find a heap."

"You, for instance," the captain suggested.

"Sure, me an' you. Think I'm sweating over this just for fun? Think I give a damn if they get their man? Me? Hell, no! I got my reasons; so have you. They'll come aboard with the pilot, maybe. They'll begin poking round. Unless—"

"Unless what?"

"Unless the man's ready for them. Then, it's a pat on the back and a clean bill of health for you; and, 'Thanks, my noble radio man; your message was music to our honest ears,' for me." Cray stopped.

"And so—"

Cray leaned closer.

"Get this. There's two men we ain't searched yet—Drake and Quayle. Either one, mebbe—"

The old captain rose.

"We'll start with Quayle, eh?" He made for the door, but he stopped, turned. "You put that into my head, damn ye!"

"What if I did?" Cray cried. "What if I did? Since you have no detective aboard, what price Cray, hey?"

"What price Cray? I'll tell ye. I'd as soon to God we had a detective aboard," the captain growled. "That's what price Cray!" He stumped out.

The wireless man got up slowly and idled about the cabin as if it were his own. That last remark of the skipper's had hit him.

"A detective," said Cray softly. "Maybe we have, at that, my brave old sea-dog. Maybe we have, at that."

He followed the captain on deck and twitched his sleeve. He drew him into a corner.

"I'll do this next job myself," said Cray.

"You mean Quayle?"

"Him. You better stick to your knitting. Talk like a human being at lunch, keep that solemn-faced, secretive Quayle there, until— You ever figure there'll maybe be a reward for them diamonds?"

"Reward?" The old captain of the *Cora* snorted. "Reward? If I can sleep again o' nights, that'll be reward enough."

"I could do with a good sleep myself," Cray laughed. "I might sleep through lunch hour, while Quayle's cabin is empty."

* * * *

Morning again and bright sunlight on the Gulf. Tomorrow would see the pilot coming aboard at Father Point. Tomorrow would see, well, something rather ghastly to men who clutched secrets close, who feared the eye of the law.

But today the sun shone. Drake and the old engineer sat there by the funnel.

Old M'Ginley was sleepy. A bearing had been heating. He had not yet been to bed. He had come up for a whiff of fresh air. He was soon wide awake, for Drake, leaning over, whispered—

"I've been thinking what you said."

"I said a heap, laddie."

"About hiding things."

He opened his dungaree suit. The old man saw a long thin packet

123

of brown paper, sealed with wax, tied with many intricate knots.

"I've been thinking—and whispering a bit," Drake went on.

"Oh, aye, doubtless."

M'Ginley's eyes glinted. A chief engineer, he knew, could hide things, where nobody, not even the man who had trusted them to him, could find them.

"Oh, aye," he repeated, "something else has whispered, me bold lad. Fear has, I'm thinking."

Drake's face was blank.

"I told the person what you said. There's been funny work. Cray and the skipper searching yesterday, today, all cabins but mine. To-morrow—"

"Perhaps yours. Tomorrow the pilot and—"

The old man too was leaning closer. The packet passed.

"If a knot's untied, or a seal broken—my—my friend says there'll be no split," Drake grated.

"Unless he goes where splittin' is hard, save he split rocks," M'Ginley laughed, and he drew back. "That bearin'—it needs a pile o' lookin' after."

He lumbered away. Drake sat there. The man Quayle, the silent, secretive Quayle came up on deck. He walked along. He bent over Drake. He whispered something. Drake sprang to his feet. Quayle was of an age with him, taller by a head, powerfully built.

Both the captain, staring down from the bridge, and Cray, peering out of his little window, saw Drake's fist shoot out—a blow that seemed but to glance off Quayle's jaw. Yet Quayle fell, lay there, knocked out.

Drake walked forward. He beat on Cray's door with his fists, crying:

"What kind of a ship's this? What sort o' man are you? Blab-bin'—blabbin'—"

The captain, clutching the bridge rail, leaned over and bawled:

"You keep still, mister. What's wrong with ye? One more crack like that and—"

He paused. Tomorrow, when the pilot and whoever else was wait-ing came aboard, he would no longer have the power, save to stand dumbly by and watch.

But now, now Cray had his door open and was talking to the en-raged Drake. And Drake, calming himself by an effort, was being drawn inside. The captain wished that this strange man Cray would leave that door open. He hoped, at least, that afterward he would tell him frankly what now was going on.

Inside, Cray was talking swiftly:

"What'd he say? Did he tell you I was blabbing?"

"Blabbing. What talking's been done—" Drake paused, as if uncertain. "Forget it. A man don't like to be told he's like to swing. I'm hot headed. I figured mebbe you'd told him what was in that cablegram—the one about Varnavosk bein' dead—mebbe more, too. But—"

"*Forget it* is right."

Cray was acting strangely. Yesterday he had told the captain that the murderer, supposedly on their ship, must be either Quayle or Drake. Now he seemed to have shifted his views, unless he wished to lull Drake into a state of false security.

"Forget it is right," he grinned, reaching for the spare headset, already adjusted to fit Drake. "Want to listen in a spell? I'm goin' out for a breather. If you hear anything funny call me."

Drake hesitated.

"What you planning to do?"

"Nothing," Cray answered. "Be a sport. Most men'd get hot if you come ravin' at 'em; but me, I'm different. You set there. Forget it!"

"I'll try," Drake scowled. "If the Old Man says anything about that row with Quayle, you tell him it's an old score we were settling."

"Right!"

Cray crossed the threshold and slammed the door shut. Drake listened as he walked down the deck; he heard other footsteps. Out of the window he caught a glimpse of the captain's gray head, then the boatswain, supporting a limp Quayle toward the stair.

"I wonder—" Drake frowned at the wireless set—"what's their next move. And old M'Ginley—what's he doing?"

Old M'Ginley, cutting loose cord after cord, breaking through wax seals, was opening that brown paper parcel.

What he found turned him into a covetous old man, who thought furiously. Finally, one hand fondling his pocket, he climbed heavily down ladders to his own peculiar domain.

* * * *

Once more Cray faced the old skipper in his cabin.

"You saw that?" Bain was eager. He sensed, at last, the end of this mystery. "You saw that Drake and heard him howl about blabbing!"

"Yes," Cray scoffed. "Heard a heap; but I'm not taking that for gospel."

"It must be him. You found nothing in Quayle's cabin?"

"Not yet," Cray answered. "I'm figuring on looking again. Know what I think? They're both in the theft, if not the murder. Take those names. Both birds' names—Quayle and Drake—ain't they? Sort of funny, them both choosing the same sort of monikers for this trip. Like one had thought of one, and the other had followed suit. Crooks are like that."

The captain gazed at him speculatively.

"Cray—crayfish—another zoölogical name. Well, go on. You don't pass as an honest man, Cray. Lay to that. You're no better, if no worse, than the rest aboard this packet. What were you going to say?"

"I got an idea they been passing that necklace from one to t'other," Cray explained. "They had hard words. What if Quayle had it last, after I searched his dump? What if he wouldn't hand over, an' Drake—I been working on him, scaring him—if Drake, I say, figured Quayle was goin' to gyp him? How about that? Mebbe Quayle ain't scared of getting caught. I searched his dump careful. He may figure he ain't suspected no more. He may think, if he is suspected, that we don't know how to search right. And Drake, figurin' he's losin' out, gets mad."

The captain shook his head. Father Point was getting closer. Morning and the pilot would come, and with them—well, iron bars, perhaps; certainly a lost ticket and a lot of trouble. A man couldn't account for three extra men on his ship—and such men.

"I don't know. If we miss this time—" He paused.

"We'll search both cabins," Gray broke in, "and both at once. You take Quayle's; I'll go for Drake's. We'll win this time."

The captain stared at him.

"We'll do it; but how?"

"Easy," Cray smiled. "That worthless old chief engineer—let him tag on to Drake. They are thick, anyway. As for Quayle—he's battered up, ain't he? Or if he ain't exactly battered, he's shook. Take a couple of men, drag him out, say you're givin' him your room, more light an' air. Sure, he'll suspect, but what can he do? Take them two big sailormen."

"It might be; but when? Drake sticks below of afternoons."

"Tomorrow morning we got a couple of hours," Cray went on. "When we find that necklace—"

"We give it up, and get clear of—"

"Like hell! We keep it!" Cray corrected him. "Or I keep it. Never mind how. I'll pin the job on one of them. Don't you worry."

The captain stared at him, aghast.

"But they'll search the ship."

"Let 'em. They won't find it." Cray got up. "I left Drake in my monkey- house. Best get him out of there. Tomorrow morning."

"Tomorrow."

The captain looked out the door, as Cray opened it. The hills of the south shore of the Gulf stood out grim and gray, somber, all shadow. Tomorrow. Well, sooner it comes, sooner over.

* * * *

The two big sailors dragged Quayle, protesting, out of his cabin. A strangely ungrateful man he seemed. Up on the boat deck Drake heard the row.

"What's that?" he asked.

The old chief, M'Ginley, leaned closer.

"Them—them diamonds," he whispered.

"How'd you know. You've broke the seals," Drake accused.

M'Ginley shrank back.

"Me? What you think? Ain't I acted straight with you?"

"You'd better."

Drake thrust one hand inside his dungaree suit. Something bulged under his arm. M'Ginley wasn't looking at a paper packet this time.

"You go heeled; don't blame ye," he blustered. "Why pull a gun on me? They're searchin' your cabin."

He told this with the air of one revealing a previous secret.

"They won't find nothin'."

"Not in mine," Drake grated, "but elsewhere, perhaps. You sit still. We've been playing blind man's buff overlong. You sit still. This is loaded, you old fraud. You figure on holding out, hey? Look me in the eye, in ten minutes, and maybe you'll change your mind."

M'Ginley quivered. He was gross mountain of a man, and shaking like jelly.

"Ten minutes. What you mean? Why—"

Drake rose.

"If you value your health, sit tight. If you don't, I play a hard game. I've an ace in the hole. A neat little ace, isn't it, in its shoulder holster. Sit where you are."

The old man watched him as he walked, cat footed, to the stair, and as he slowly disappeared down it.

"Some one is goin' to catch plain hell," said he, "but it won't be me, M'Ginley. Mebbe, when they finish their rough stuff there'll be a nice corpse for Scotland Yard and—what's hid below for M'Ginley."

But M'Ginley was not down in the alleyway; and it was there that things were due to happen.

First the old captain's voice, as he cried through the thin partition between Drake's cabin and Quayle's:

"Come here, for God's sake, Cray! I found somethin'..."

Cray, running in from Drake's cabin, saw a velvet covered case, long, narrow, bound with precious metal.

The captain laughed in relief.

"Got our man."

"Where—where'd you find that?"

"There!" The captain kicked a disreputable handbag. "In the lining, sewn in. I felt it, first shot. Now—"

"Open it, open it," Cray urged. "Let's see."

"It's locked some way; but—"

Old Bain's strong fingers wrapped themselves about the slim thing of metal and velvet. The cords of his wrists stood out for a moment. Then the case was open, cracked like a walnut shell. It was empty. The captain glared at the fragments in his hands. Cray, leaning closer, muttered:

"Never mind. Hang on to that. It's evidence, ain't it? Quayle—he'll tell more, when them detectives get after him. He'll talk. Man can shorten his stretch that way. Unless—" he thrust his face close to the captain's—"unless we find them diamonds, ourselves. Then, this'd do for Quayle; they'd take him on the strength of this. And we'd—"

"To hell with the diamonds!" In the old skipper's voice was relief. "This'll do for me. You keep your gab shut, mister. The least you know the best, I've got Quayle locked in my cabin. He'll stay there. If trouble comes aboard, it comes for him, personal. Not me, nor you, if you're wise. You stop snooping round for them diamonds. I won't have it, I tell you. First thing there'll be a murder—another murder."

Cray, his voice edged, face pale, sneered:

"Changed your tune, hey? Now you found this useless junk, you figure you'll let them diamonds go, hey? But you figure without Cray. I'll have this ship apart, if need be, but I'll lay hands on them stones. I'll—"

"You'll go easy!" Captain Bain thundered. He was becoming himself rapidly now. "You'll keep quiet. There's others besides Quayle can be locked in their cabins, and nothing said of it. And I'm master of this ship, by God!"

"And if—" Cray smiled, though he was still under tension, although that smile was not a pleasant one. "If I told you the truth, would you sing small, I wonder?"

"Truth? My God! Truth?" the badgered skipper rasped. "You tell the truth? What in hell are you, to tell the truth?"

"A detective," said Cray softly, "a detective."

The captain stared, at first unbelieving; then he wilted. Too many little things on Cray's side. The chances were that he might be. Certainly he'd acted like one at times. And if he were, what of the *Cora*, of her secret sins?

"A detective?" he gasped.

From behind Cray came another voice; the cabin door swung open.

"A detective? That's fine; for there are two of us, then, my dear Cray."

It was Drake. He had his gun. In that tiny cabin a gun in the hand meant mastery. Drake closed the door after him. His gun covered Cray. He disregarded the old captain. Indeed, old Bain hadn't an ounce of trouble making left in him. He was a crushed man. Not one detective, but two! Not one man, who might conceivably be bribed, but two, each knowing his little immigrant game, and, what was worse, each knowing that the other knew. He slumped down on the single bunk. He stared from Cray to Drake, from Drake to Cray. He shook his gray head sadly.

Cray, snarling, turned on him.

"A hell of a captain! Don't you see his game? His turn to hang on to them diamonds. He figures we'll search his room next; likely found out I'd been searching it. He's desperate."

"And a strong man, Cray, which you are not."

Drake reached out suddenly with his left hand, caught both Cray's thin wrists, brought his hands together. Then with his right hand he laid his revolver on the bunk.

"Which you are not, Cray, my man," said Drake.

The captain heard steel jingle, then saw it flash. He heard a faint click. Drake turned to him.

"We'll adjourn to your cabin, Captain. This is a bit crowded."

Glumly the old skipper obeyed. Cray stood there, handcuffed, silent now, as if with the snapping of the steel handcuffs had gone from him his last chance.

They stumbled out into the alleyway, Drake's steady hand on Cray's elbow. As Cray walked along, men eyed him. He scowled at the first; his face was blank as he passed a second. But when the third man stared, he smiled cockily. He was on parade and would be on parade until Drake and his kind had done their best, or worst. He must act out his part, confidence in every look, every gesture. That was his code; he would follow it.

Despite the reason for his captivity, there was a certain desperate gallantry about Cray, as Drake led him off, handcuffed, to the captain's cabin. He even managed to whisper, as they climbed the steep iron stairway to the boat deck:

"A pretty job, Drake; if your feet didn't look it, nobody'd take you for a dick. Only thing is you got the wrong man."

"Have I?" Drake asked. "Have I? Maybe it's Quayle should be wearing these."

Cray kept silent at that, as if reluctant to tell; as if, now the enemy had appeared in his true form, he were changing his whole tune; as if those under the law's suspicion must close up their ranks and stick together.

"Quayle—there he is in the cabin," Drake went on. "I'll be bound, he'll be glad to see us. You see, Quayle's my partner, Cray."

* * * *

Drake and the old captain were alone. Quayle had taken Cray away, had locked him up, was keeping an eye on him. Drake had remained with Bain. He was talking jerkily, as if thinking back over this business, partly because he rather plumed himself on the way it had been managed and partly because he feared, should he stop, what would follow. Old Captain Bain, there, lips moving, eyes downcast was probably going over the sins of a long and pettily wicked life. Probably, as soon as he got the chance, he'd pour out a flood of confessions and would incriminate himself hopelessly in a dozen dark matters.

Drake, a one idea man, busy with that one idea, didn't have time, or, to do him justice, inclination for the rôle of father confessor to the captain of the *Cora*. So he talked, like a man talking against time, elliptically, as things came into his head. And the captain half listening, heard:

"Began at Dip's American Bar. Bless you, we at the Yard have known your little game for years, Captain. Began at Dip's, when this robbery thing broke, we traced a motor car within a mile of his place. From then on, well, it was chance and luck and, if I may say it, psychology. We came aboard, Quayle and I, separately. We looked about, used our eyes, wormed in where we could. We had no idea what the man was like, what he had done before. We just played a hunch that he was aboard. Began with you—

"Remember that little note I brought you, ostensibly from Dip? Well, that told me a lot. Bless you, Bain, you aren't the murdering, thieving sort. I ruled you out, right then. But, to go on. You remember

130

when the thing broke aboard? That first message?"

"Yes," the old man nodded glumly, "I won't forget. 'Twas as if some big, horrible eye was lookin' all over, slow but steady. An' I knew that sooner or later it'd stop on us; and then, o' course—"

"That," Drake laughed, hastily breaking in, "that was the intention. I arranged for that wireless. Scotland Yard? Well, we at the Yard don't broadcast what we know, unless we want it known for a damned good reason. I had that wireless sent. Fixed it up in the hour I had between trailing the car to Dip's and coming aboard here. That was my bombshell."

"But—" the captain stared at him, puzzled—"how'd you—you didn't know it was Cray you wanted?"

"What I wanted was a disturbance. If he wasn't in the business he'd perhaps talk. If he hadn't talked, I could fulfill that omission and blame it on him. I wanted every manjack aboard here to know that diamonds had been stolen, that Scotland Yard—they don't sign themselves that way, I might confess—were on the trail. The rest—well, ever throw a rock into a pool? The ripples follow each other to shore. The rest was plain Cray. I'd struck it lucky. Those other messages—he made 'em up, every one."

"But why—why?" The Old Man was incredulous.

"His game." Drake laughed. "First half of the voyage, well, Cray was lying low. He knew his job, you see. He figured on passing as the regular wireless man; but he didn't know his ship, or its company, and he didn't like that company, when he looked 'em over. So he carried the necklace in his pocket, like a pipe or a handkerchief. Well, the day after that first bombshell of a message came, he felt for the diamonds—and they were gone."

"Gone?"

"Yes, never mind how."

Drake got up, walked across to the old skipper of the *Cora*, flipped one agile hand across his vest and dangled his watch, chain and seals before his eyes.

"Like that," Drake laughed. "Well, to get on, there he was, this Cray, with those jewels gone and nothing for his pains. So he began to get mysterious messages. Bit by bit suspicion formed, centered, first on this one, then on that one. You played right into his hands, Captain. You had me worried. I was afraid you two would run out of suspects before we made our landfall."

"You mean he deliberately had me on?" The captain shook his head. "No—if 'twas just theft—but murder—You mean this man let me think we had a murderer aboard, let me know it, when he could have kept it dark—and him the guilty one? Man don't tie his own hang-man's knot, mister, not even to get back diamonds."

"There was no murder." Drake laughed, again. "That was just his artistic touch. No fool, Cray. He knew you'd rise to it. But you worried him. He wanted to search every last cabin, but he also wanted to make the job hang out till the last moment, in case you might show a rush of brain to the head and get to suspecting him. Well, you did it as he planned, between you. Until, well, there were two of us left, Quayle and myself. Cray was getting scared by now. So, when he searched Quayle's cabin yesterday, he planted the box that those diamonds had been in when he lifted them. Then he worked things so that you would find it, not him."

"But why?"

Drake stared at him. What use going on like this? How could this man, who but half listened, understand, when even he saw some things but vaguely? You threw a straw into the water, then a dozen more. If one of them taught you anything of drift or eddy, you were content. When he spoke again his voice was crisp and incisive.

"That fight. A fake of Quayle and me, in case Cray suspected us of working together, as he did, eh? Just a precaution. It bothered him, as other things did, too. His problem was twofold. Those stories, you see; the wireless messages he was making up—they worked on him in the end, as well as on you. He almost believed them, believed that they might have some accidental truth in them. And, of course, he wanted his loot back. Safety and loot; two ends to gain. If you had it, it was as good as his, for he's smooth and you—well, the thing's plain, isn't it? Notice how he gave in at the end? No gunplay. Clever men don't go in for that. Amateurish, that sort of thing. Watch the papers later on and you'll see how Cray fights through his mouthpiece. Good criminal lawyers are rich men."

"But why all this?" the captain growled. "You knew in mid-Atlantic that he was your man. You had the stuff and could have nabbed him easily then and there."

"In my game a man never stops learning," Drake told him. "You may believe me, or not. Your ship said, 'Hush.' I wanted to make her talk, and Cray did it for me, eh? I wanted to see what he'd do and how he'd do it. A clever rogue he proved, but too imaginative."

"So you raised hell with us, with me. Let me run round like a fool."

The captain of the *Cora* bit his lip, for who was he, standing in a slippery place, to antagonize this detective. Drake looked at him pityingly for a moment.

"You're worried. You're saying, 'Now Drake'll begin on me.' The answer is, of course, Drake won't. I've known and the Yard's known, for years. If we'd wanted to, we could fill a gaol with you and your like; but what's it to us if now and then some petty thief gets away? Men like that Liverpool rat. It's the big, fat, long whiskered, clever rats we're after. When they come drifting along, flying the country, we know where to look."

He turned toward the door.

"You run our rat trap, Captain. Why in the world should we spring it?"

The door opened as he put his hand on the knob. The fat engineer, M'Ginley, crowded in. He laid something that gleamed and glittered on the little table. Beside this he methodically piled brown paper, broken wax seals, bits of cut and knotted string.

"Ye'll bear witness," said M'Ginley to the captain, "ye'll bear witness, I'm an honest man. There it all is, Mr. Drake, everything ye gave me. I'm an honest man; and besides, there's a ship comin' up astern flyin' the blue ensign, with the Canadian coat-of-arms in the fly of it. I'm an honest man. When they board us, ye'll tell 'em so, doubtless?"

But Drake was not listening. Bending over the table, he was brushing coal dust from the Varnavosk necklace.

SALVAGE,
by Roy Norton

Originally published in The Popular Magazine, Feb. 4, 1928

Piræus, that historical port of Greece, lay drenched and sweltering in sunshine. Its great water front, whence galleys had sailed bravely forth in ancient days, was packed with shipping, most of it idle; for trade was in the doldrums. Docked between two big "smoke boats" lay the very trim and neat steam schooner, *Malabart*, Captain Eli Drake, owner and commander; and there was nothing in the *Malabart's* physical appearance to indicate that she, too, was yawning for a cargo of any sort, or to any port, though the charter rate might be so low as to barely pay expenses. Captain Drake, whose sobriquet of "The Old Hyena" had survived the days of sail, was ashore, harassed by cares.

He had been eating into capital to keep his ship in commission, and his crew, which he had gathered in the course of many years, from being disbanded. He prized his crew and, after his ship, they came first in his affections. In quest of cargo—any cargo—he had scoured the port, made daily trips over the short drive to Athens, and spent liberal sums on cablegrams to many agents, without avail. He felt like cursing the big steamship companies, which, with their army of organized runners, were rapidly driving the independent owners and tramps off the seas.

In a mood of sullen obstinacy he had tramped almost the length of the docks when, unexpectedly, he heard the clatter of a cargo winch; and the sound was so unusual that, like a magnet, it drew him in its direction. He found a rusty tramp that was lading.

"Now what—how did I miss getting that cargo?" he reflected. "The Rhodialim, eh?" And after a moment's thought he muttered: "Oh, yes. Belongs to that firm of Hakim & Letin. Got her and one other schooner, doing mostly Levantine and East African coast trade. Wish I could have got that cargo. My luck's out."

Without thinking, or observing that at the dock gates there was a watchman, who, at the moment, had his back turned and was in voluble altercation with one of his countrymen, Captain Eli strolled inward. He finally halted, and with hands in pockets stared, suddenly discovering something else that made him curious.

"That's blamed funny!" he thought. "Big cases marked 'Mining machinery,' but a couple of stevedores chuck 'em into the slings as if they were empty. Also cases of merchandise put up like heavy prints that seem just as light, and as— Good Lord! Up there on the bridge! If that ain't Bill Morris, I'm dotty. So he's got a ship out here, eh, after it got too hot for him about everywhere else on salt water! Lost two ships in the Pacific trade, under mighty suspicious circumstances, and had his ticket taken away, last I heard of him. Ummh! Ten or twelve years ago, that was. So he's skipperin' this craft, eh? If him and me hadn't locked spars two or three times, I'd go over and rile him up with a leetle light, airy banter. I guess he's—"

"Hey you! Got any business here? How'd you get past me at the gate?" a voice disturbed him. And although the fellow spoke bastard Greek, Drake, who, with a sailor's facility, had picked up considerable of the tongue, understood, and turned to see the watchman glowering at him.

"Why?" he asked. "Can't anybody come onto your dock? Nothing secret about it, is there?"

The watchman sputtered something about none without a pass from Hakim & Letin being allowed in, and somewhat peremptorily ordered Drake to clear out. Not being accustomed to such treatment, disgruntled, affronted, but recognizing the weakness of his position and the futility of retort, Drake turned and, swearing under his breath, obeyed.

It is possible that the episode might have passed from his mind entirely, but for an encounter that followed some hours later, when, just as he was turning toward the *Malabart*, a man whose face bore the almost indelible stamp of the engine rooms of ships, with grease worked deeply into the pores of the skin, respectfully touched his cap peak and accosted him in fairly good, though accented, English.

"Captain Drake," he said. "Excuse me, sir, for stopping you, but I am a good man out of work, and want a job on your ship, sir."

"Sorry, my man, but we're full up," Captain Eli replied. "Too full," he added, and would have proceeded on his way, had not the applicant insisted.

"I am good man, sir. First-class engineer; but I would take anything in your engine room. Because me, I have big family, and ships are all full now, it seems to me, sir. I lose job when not my fault. Not at all. When I took engines of ship Rhodialim anybody tell you they scrap heap. I make 'em good. And now, without word, since that Captain Bill Morris come, I am fired. He say have his own engineer and—"

"Huh? What's that?" Captain Eli, who had been slowly moving forward with the insistent one at his side, stopped and stared at the man. "Do you happen to know the name of the new engineer?"

"It is Simmons, or Simons, or something like that."

Drake's mouth pursed itself as if to whistle an exclamation, and for a moment he stood absent-mindedly staring at the stones beneath his feet. But his thought ran: "Simmons! Simmons! That was the engineer of the ship that Bill lost last, and he was one of the chief witnesses at the insurance investigation. Something funny about this business!"

He abruptly started away, saying as he did so: "You come on board with me, and I'll learn if there's anything can be done. Let me see your ticket." And then, a moment later: "Beltramo—Giuseppe Beltramo is your name, eh? And your ticket shows a long, clean record. No wonder they didn't want you on that boat. Never mind the questions, now. I'll ask all the questions myself."

136

As a rule the relations between Captain Eli Drake and his chief mate, William Catlin, were of two separate characters, inasmuch as afloat they observed the distinctions in station and Drake brooked no interference; but it was well known that ashore they were more intimate than brothers usually are, and confidants in nearly everything. Hence, when the commander sent for Catlin upon his arrival aboard, and on his entry into the cabin addressed him as "Bill," Catlin thought: "Something's turned up." Aloud he said:

"Landed something, skipper?"

"Landed enough to set me to a heap of thinking, Bill," Drake said. And then he bent forward and in a confidential tone told of his experiences, ending with: "It seems to me there's some sort of a job being put up by Hakim & Letin; and—well, there might be some way for us to make something out of it."

"Sort of an opportunity, eh?" Catlin grinned, remembering that the Cape Cod man had earned the reputation of being an opportunist. "Maybe you can see one, but I can't. Don't mind my thick-headedness. I can get anything when it's explained, all right."

But Drake seemed to have become absorbed in some thought of his own. He stared absently through the cloud of pipe smoke; and finally chuckled, as if he had reached a solution of some problem.

"I think I sort of grab an idea," he said at last, getting to his feet. "You're a hell of a good friend, Bill, but as a helper in working out a puzzle you don't amount to much. Never mind. Think I got it, myself. So just talking it over with you did have some use, after all. You go down and keep that feller I brought aboard interested, while I slip below and see the chief. Most likely be in his cabin, I expect."

They went out together and Drake sought the engineer.

"Forbes," he said to that gray-haired veteran. "Can you find something for an engineer out of a job to do for a few days?"

"Can't find enough to do myself, let alone make work for a new man. If this keeps up— Hold on. While I think of it, that chap Flint, my third, asked me today if I thought there was a chance for him in the navy. Now if he got a month off to go to the nearest place he could pass his examinations and file his application—"

"The sure-enough right thing! Let him take a month, and put this feller on until Flint comes back. Come on up topside and talk to him."

The result of the conversation was that two men, at least, were made happy that evening—Flint, who had got unexpected leave for a month, and Beltramo, who had got a temporary billet.

But Drake was not on the ship when the shift was made. In the roughest suit of clothes he could muster he had gone ashore and made his way to a not too-clean bar, where he knew that pilots were wont to gather. There he patiently waited for the arrival of one he knew. The man came at last, and Captain Eli drew him into a little private room at the rear.

"Christophe," Captain Eli said, "I have done you a favor once or twice, and you're the kind of man that likes to repay. Well, the time has come when you may be of use. Now first, you've got to keep your mouth shut—not one word—not one word to anybody, not even your wife, of what we say here in this room."

The pilot, whose face was seamed with years and sea service, promptly lifted his hand and swore an oath that would have satisfied any band of conspirators that ever existed.

"First, you know this sea as well as any one, I take it?"

"By Heaven! Better than all save one or two. Was I not a fisherman in these waters when old enough to float? I know every foot of it and every reef, and every island and—"

"Good!" Captain Eli interrupted. He leaned across the little table between them and lowered his voice. "Christophe, if you were going to sink a ship that was supposed to be bound eastward—say for Jaffa—where would you do it?"

For a moment the pilot's mouth hung open and his eyes were wide, as if he feared for Drake's sanity.

"But, sir, captain—you—you are not going to sink— You don't mean that—"

"No, of course not! I sink nothing. But you think it over carefully and answer my questions," Drake continued. And the pilot, still wondering, slowly lowered his eyes, shut them as if to ponder such a case, and then asked: "What time of year, captain?"

"This time of year," Drake replied.

And again the weather-beaten old pilot shut his eyes and thought.

"Listen, sir," he said in his quaint but adequate English. "Many things one must think of. If mens want to sink ship, but not drown anybody, they must be not too far from land for open boat, eh? Must be some place where not too much danger big seas for small boats, eh? Must also be some place where nobody see—away from fishermen's boats, or cargo boats, or bigger ships—some place lonely this time year. Plenty places man could scuttle ship, but few where get all these things what want, eh? Well, about now most fishin' boats work"—he got up and walked to a rough map that was tacked on the wall and that was almost solidly smeared with the trails of many fingers across its surface—"works up about here mostly. In some months, here; some months, there; but now, about here. So no good up there." His finger moved as he talked. "No good through here, because big ships go there. No good there, because small ships what do island trade work in and out. So, here best place for all things. Almost only place which fit all I speak between here and Island of Rhodes. Not too far out of the way. Very good place. Deep water—plenty water and not much chance boat ever drift when hit bottom. Yes, captain, sir, that best place anybody can think of—right about there."

His gnarled finger ceased to move—pointed at open water off Nauplia.

They sat down again and, while Christophe eyed him with perplexed looks, the captain reflected.

"That, you think, is a place a man who knew these waters well would select?" he said. "But a man who didn't know them?"

"God knows where!" the pilot exclaimed, lifting his hands and letting them fall to the table again. "It is the place—the place I say—where one who knew would choose in, say—seven times out of ten. As you, sir, know, there are some thousands of islands."

For half an hour Drake continued to catechize, but without stirring the old pilot from his conclusions.

"Well, Christophe," he said at last, arising to go, "I'm going to hire you for a cruise that may never take place; but I'm taking a little gamble on certain things. You begin work tomorrow, always with your mouth shut. Here's what you are to find out: First, when the Rhodialim sails. Second, if she's taking a pilot aboard, and if so, who and what he is. And third, you're to report to me aboard the *Malabart* each evening just after dark. I don't care to have too many notice that you come there. Is it understood? Going wages, of course," he concluded, with Yankee thrift.

"Yes, sir, captain. Very well I understood it, and do what you ask. Maybe some time you tell me why all this, eh?"

"Maybe," said Drake laconically, as he thumped upon the table to pay for his bill. And he left behind him one who was still wondering a little if a certain Captain Drake was all there.

Catlin had a surprise on the following morning, when told that they were going to take on some supplies. And he was still more astonished when Drake asked him to muster the crew and learn whether there was any man aboard who had ever had any experience in diving. Catlin found a stoker who admitted that years before he had worked for a salvage company. Drake told the man to get on shore-going clothes and come with him, and the twain disappeared. The man returned that afternoon accompanied by a truck, which duly unloaded and brought aboard a collection of stuff that made even Catlin scratch his head, and caused conjectures for'ard as to whether The Old Hyena was going into the wrecking business. It consisted of a complete diving outfit—air pumps and all—as well as huge collision mats and handling gear. Drake did not appear until evening, and seemed unusually speechless, and he dined and waited for Christophe.

The latter came at last, grinning with self-satisfaction, and was at once closeted with Drake, who asked: "Well, what did you learn?"

"That Rhodialim, she sail day after tomorrow. She got most her cargo aboard now. But it's funny, captain, sir, she got one man who knew this sea same as me. Long time ago he fisherman, then go away, and been down Smyrna where not got too good name. Good man, when sober, but too much drink, so never get good job. That man I see in saloon. He most full and— You owe me thirty drachmas, I spend on him get him fuller, so he talk. Bymeby he borrow fifty drachmas from me, which also you owes me. He brag some and say pretty soon he pay back. Pretty soon, maybe two weeks, he come back with plenty money in pockets. But he shut up like oyster when I ask how make this so much money, and he say nobody but him ever goin' know that. Now what you wish me make?"

"You go home and keep on keeping your mouth shut. Come aboard at noon tomorrow. We sail tomorrow afternoon." Drake was suddenly decided in his movements.

"How long be gone from my old woman?" Christophe asked.

"Can't tell. Maybe one week, maybe two. Not likely to be longer, I think. But all you've got to do is to come aboard and I'll tell you then where we're bound. I'm going to clear for Smyrna. There will be no secret about that."

On the following morning when Captain Eli went ashore he took with him the chief engineer. The latter returned with two big machine cases and armored, high-pressure hose, together with a case of fittings. Late that afternoon the *Malabart* slipped out and away, so palpably light that other sea captains who observed her shook their heads with understanding. A ship putting to sea in ballast in dull times evokes the sympathy of the seawise. Aboard the *Malabart* there was an air of gloom among the crew.

The captain and owner, walking the bridge, said to Catlin:

"Well, Bill, I'm taking a gamble—thousand to one shot, that's all."

When dusk fell the island of Thermia lay close in to starboard, and the man at the wheel stood ready to port his helm and bring her over from the sou'-east-by-east to an easterly course to round the island,

140

that being the route toward Smyrna; but old Christophe, standing behind him, took the wheel, rang for slow speed and groped in toward the island. It loomed up about them, a rocky point, before he said over his shoulder to Captain Eli:

"Here's where we can lay to, sir. Good anchorage here in this cove, and no risk of wind."

All that night she rocked there, gently; on a sea that was almost without a swell. And when morning came, to the crew's further curiosity, she brought in her hook, swung about, and headed due west, plodding along at slow speed and apparently purposeless. A liner came out of the north and gave her a passing hoot. Christophe, eyeing the other boat, said to Captain Eli:

"She be for Messina way, and now not likely be another ship along here for ten days. That's what those mens know. If I make good guess, that's why they clear Pirzeus today, after big ship go, sir."

"And when will we make that Island of Hydra?" Drake asked, staring to the westward.

"Just about sunset, captain, sir. Then we slip round it and there are small islands between it and mainland, and entrance into Nauplia which so long and so big it is like long gulf. We lay behind them islands, sir, and—see what shall see about midnight, I think, sir."

Drake caught his dry, knowing grin, but did not entirely share his confidence as to the outcome of their strange voyage.

The pilot's prediction as to progress was fulfilled; just as a hazy sunset colored the tips of the high, bleak mountains behind which the day disappeared, they passed the isle with its abandoned and obsolete fortifications, and hove to in waters that seemed to have been deserted since the time of ancient wars. Night fell with a thin, low-lying fog that seemed to sweep down from the great bastions of Nauplia and rest on the still waters. The stars were obscured and a new depression engulfed Drake.

"The weather's against us," he said gloomily, to the storm-beaten old pilot. "They could pass us at a couple of cable lengths and we'd never know it."

"Not if we were out in a small boat, listening," Christophe said. "In small boat hear everything. On ship, no—not so quite well. We must put out boat and get out maybe two three miles and wait. Yes, maybe fog too bad, one way, but very good, other. When they pass we get course then slip quiet, very quiet, same way, with *Malabart*, eh?"

Drake pondered. There seemed no other method. He cursed the fog, but ordered a boat away with Catlin and the pilot aboard, the latter assuring him that he could find his way back to the ship if the night were as black as the pits of Satan. A long wait followed after the boat had disappeared. The gloom of the darkened *Malabart*, the lack of the bell striking the hour, the absolute stillness of the ship, were all upsetting. The very lifelessness of the protected water where she lay was annoying, for there was not the slightest lapping whisper of a wave against her hull. Down in the engine room even the stokers who kept up steam had been cautioned against the clanging of a furnace door or the ring of a shovel. Had one passed the *Malabart* within ten yards he might have thought her the ghost of some long-abandoned ship. Drake listened from the outer wing of the bridge, bending over, sometimes with a hand cupped to his ear, until he was tired. He had about decided that his voyage and expenditure had been born of folly, when he heard a faint creak, followed a minute later by another. Then Catlin's voice below hailed softly, and the boat pulled around to the side ladder, which had been lowered and swung barely above the water.

"All right, sir. She passed so close that she almost ran us down. She had doused her lights and was not doing more than five or six knots. Christophe says there could be no mistake. She was the Rhodialim, all right."

The pilot joined in with: "About a mile and a half out. Long row back."

"It won't do for us to follow too closely on their heels, anyway," Captain Eli said. "But are you certain that you can pick her up again, Christophe, in all this murk?"

"I know the course she will take. I think so, with luck," the pilot said. "They not alter course again. Too much else business think of, I expect. Just keep straight on about five, six miles; then stop. They not want go much farther. Might meet small fishin' boats out of Nauplia. Not take chance of that, eh?"

Captain Eli stood blockily, a dim figure in the darkness, and seemed making mental calculations.

"I don't think we'd best be in too much of a hurry," he said at last. "We've got to take the chances of being too late. If the crew are in on it with the commander, mate and engineer, there'll be no time wasted. If they're not, the boats won't be ready to lower, and besides he'll have to put up a bluff at saving the ship, to fool the crew. We'd best give them at least an hour and a half."

"That crew, captain, sir, are the scum of the water front," Christophe put in.

"But just the same, we don't know that they're in on it," Drake replied. "Bill Morris don't like to cut too many in on his crooked work. Seems to me more likely that he'll try to stampede 'em into the boats after putting up a great show to save the ship. He'll call on his engineer for steam and announce that they must beach her. The engineer will either pretend to start the engines, or swear that he can't turn 'em over. That would stampede the crew, if they're the sort one picks up in these parts. I think we've got to risk it, and give 'em an hour and a half, certain. After that it depends on how quickly we can pick her up. Beltramo tells me that she's fitted with two sea cocks only into her main hold, because her engines are set well aft. So she's not likely to fill within some hours after they're opened, and I've got it doped out from what I know of Morris' work that's the way he'll put her under, if that's what he intends to do; but it's only little things that are queer which makes me think that's what he's up to. Big gamble, but—"

"Must be. If not, why he not go on to east'ard?" the pilot asked. "I'm sure of it, captain, sir."

But Drake was still doubtful when, still in blackness and running at slow speed, the *Malabart* nosed out into the sea with the pilot himself at the wheel and keeping an eye on both time and compass as he took up the trail. To the commander's ears it seemed that with the ship so light that her blades were barely under water the thrash of the slow-turning screw must be audible for miles. He saw the wheel slowly revolving under Christophe's hands and sensed that the pilot was now where he thought they might find the sinking ship.

Captain Eli knew that both Catlin, and the second mate, Giles, and nearly all the crew were forward peering into the dimness ahead, but it seemed impossible to see anything on such a night. It was a matter of luck, and he felt a dawning apprehension that his luck was out. Watching the compass over the pilot's shoulder he saw that the ship had made one complete circle and was now holding dead ahead. The wheel again whirled, and they began another circle, a mile deeper in that huge bay surrounded by high and forbidding mountains, when there came a soft whistle from forward and a pattering of bare feet. Catlin's muffled voice came from below:

"Hold her, sir, hold her. I think we've sighted the Rhodialim about two points off the port quarter."

Drake jumped to the engine tube—it having been arranged that a man was to stand by to obviate the use of bells, inasmuch as the sound of an engine bell might carry far in such stillness—and now the *Malabart* lost way and came to a stop. The boat, which was swinging barely above the water, was lowered, and Drake, Catlin, and two men tumbled in and fell to the oars. They rowed quietly.

"There she is, sir," Catlin whispered.

Exercising still more caution, they drew down on the dim shape that lay inert and heavy on the water. They came alongside and listened for voices, but caught no sound. They found the boat davits hanging idly over the water, and went up the falls noiselessly, and stood on the deck. Together they ran here and there, making a search for any human being. Not until then were they confident that she had been abandoned. Listening down the main cargo hatch they could hear the swirling and gurgling of water and the soft bumping of empty cases and crates.

"Get back to the ship, Bill, and rush across all the men that can be spared; so that if that gang are standing by waiting for the Rhodialim to sink, we can knock 'em overboard. Tell Christophe to bring the *Malabart* alongside twenty minutes after you've gone. That'll give you time to be back here ahead of her; so if we have to repel boarders, we'll have the men to do it. Be as quiet as you can and get a move on."

Catlin slipped away and over the side like a ghost. After he had gone Drake listened attentively for a few minutes, then went back and again bent over the open hatch. Afterward he tried, by leaning far over the rail, to estimate how deeply the scuttled ship had already sunk. It seemed to him that she couldn't last very much longer. Taking an electric torch from his pocket, he went below. She was a fairly deep ship, of good draft, and he was pleased to observe that the cabin floors were not yet damp. He decided that if the sea cocks were of the diameter given by Giuseppe, the former engineer, she had at least an hour and a half longer to float. He knew that her fires must have been drawn, because Morris would not run the risk of the sound of a boiler explosion drawing attention to the spot, if there chanced to be any boat within hearing.

"He knows this business of scuttling ships better than any one I ever heard of," Drake soliloquized. "But if he cleared off this time, without waiting to see her under, he made one hell of a mistake."

He looked at his watch in the light of his torch and meditated: "If Bill moves lively and doesn't lose his way, he should be back here in half an hour from now. If he loses his way in this blamed fog—I'm afraid we cut it pretty short!"

He climbed back to the deck, went to the port side, from which the boat had put off, and listened, prepared to answer a hail, if Catlin returned groping and had to shout to learn his bearings. Then from the opposite side of the ship, he heard a single telltale thump, as if an oar in clumsy hands had slipped from an oarlock and brought up with a bang.

Drake ran across to the starboard rail just in time to hear a muttered imprecation, in colloquial Greek:

"Quiet there, you lubber! If the skipper and those two pets of his are hanging around, we've a fine chance of getting away with anything."

Drake pursed his lips into a silent whistle, and through his mind ran the thought: "It's the crew of this craft come back. Probably suspected something and are trying somehow to double-cross Morris, Simmons and whoever they've let in on it with 'em. I'm a fool. Should have kept at least one man with me for such an emergency."

Quick as was his thought, his action was quicker. He jerked off his boots and threw off his jacket. He ran aft in the direction that he was certain the boat must take to board, and leaned over the rail just as a man started to climb upward.

"Get back into that boat and sheer off," he called down. "This ship is abandoned and is salvage."

The man hesitated, and a voice from below ordered:

"Go on up! We'll talk this over on deck."

"Like hell you will!" Captain Eli declared. "And if any man tries to come on this ship, he's looking for trouble. Sheer off, if you want a talk. If you want a fight, come ahead."

The man holding the boat fall climbed up and got a foothold on the strake. He threw a hand inward and caught a rail stanchion and swung upward, encouraged by muttered comments.

"All right! If you will have it—" Drake growled.

And leaned far over, and struck. In the gloom and darkness he had not struck well, and instead of knocking his man overboard into the boat below, he merely shifted him outward just beyond reach of a second blow. Drake threw himself over the rail and hanging by one hand struck again with the other. It was a body blow, but the man was tenacious, clung to the rope, swayed like a pendulum, and, as he swung back, kicked at Drake with his heavy sea boot. But this time Drake's fist smashed home, and the boarder grunted, loosened his grip on the boat fall, and went slithering down among his companions. Drake climbed back over the rail just in time to feel a stunning smash on the back of his head, and was not until then aware that while he had engaged one assailant, another had climbed up the opposite boat fall with a monkey-like agility, and had come behind him.

Infuriated by the attack, he whirled, seized the man, lifted him as if he were a bundle of waste, and, with a giant's heave, threw him far outward. The man shouted as he fell, but Drake did not hear the splash; for now he found himself fighting desperately with two other dark shapes who charged silently. Even as Drake fought, he recalled what he had overheard, which convinced him that these men also had no wish to recall Morris and his fellow conspirators. Drake grinned at the humor of that situation—a scalawag crew trying to steal aboard the ship they had abandoned, Morris and his fellows somewhere out there in the dark, himself battling for the salvage like a dog for a bone, and all the time, down there in the hold, the sea cocks flooding the sinking ship.

The number of his assailants increased. They were urged on by the leader in a hoarse mutter:

"He's alone. He must be alone, because no one else comes. Down him! Down him, because he's probably got a boat coming!"

Drake fought desperately. Two of his assailants went to the deck and lay there struggling, as they tried to recover their senses. Veteran fighter that he was, the participator in events which had earned for him the sobriquet of The Old Hyena, he used his, head coolly, his fists heavily, and as he moved here and there slipped out of the dangers of being cornered and fought for time.

Then came the accident. Retreating, his heels caught over a coil of rope that had been carelessly left on the deck. He struggled vainly to recover his balance, but they were on him like a pack of wolves. And in a fighting, struggling group came to the deck, where they twisted and turned as he tried to regain his feet, was pulled down, tried again, was struck heavily over his eyes, saw stars, shook his head like an enraged bull, and felt himself pinioned to the deck while one of the men he had previously knocked down arrived in time to kick him in the ribs. He was now roaring with fury, heedless of all alarms and thinking of nothing but revenge. He did not hear the angry shout of Catlin and his men coming on deck. The hold on him suddenly relaxed. He sat up, rubbing his bruised side and clearing the blood from his eyes, heard Bill Catlin's fighting oaths and got to his feet. Both forward and aft shadowy forms of men in flight flitted across the decks. He heard Catlin's shout:

"Don't let 'em get back to their boat! Knock 'em out and hold 'em. They've probably killed the skipper. If Drake is dead, we'll drown the whole damn lot!"

"Yes, don't let 'em get away, Bill," Drake shouted, climbing to his feet and regaining his full senses. "I want 'em. Particularly that fleabitten rat who gave me the boots. Lash 'em up and get 'em together. Quick! The ship may sink under us at any time."

Both he and Catlin ran here and there to bring matters to a conclusion, and within a few minutes there were seven somewhat bruised and battered ruffians thrown into the nearest cabins and, despite their protestations and appeals, locked in. Their leader, who time and again shouted that he was the second mate of the Rhodialim, was the first to whine for mercy. He cried, in comprehensible English:

"You hell of an Ingleeshmans tie us up and put us here to drown. You let us go we make no more of the fights. We go quiet. But capitano, please, sir, not drown us."

"Drown nothing!" Drake growled. "If we see that we can't save the ship, we'll bring you up and turn you loose in your boat, you damn pirates! And listen here! You keep quiet now. We've got no more time to waste on you." He turned to Catlin and said: "Lock 'em in. We've got to fall to, if we want to keep this craft afloat."

They hastily ran out to the deck just in time to hear Giles, the second mate, calling:

"Ship's coming, sir. Shall I flash a light for 'em, or hail?"

Drake himself cupped his hands and called: "*Malabart*, ahoy! This way!" When he got a response, he ran back to where he had fallen, struck a match, found his electric torch that had fallen from his pocket, and with it as a beacon, directed the *Malabart* to come alongside.

He called for Beltramo to come aboard to point out the location of the sea cocks, and for the collision mats to be put across. He set lookouts to guard against the possibility of other boarders, and himself took a hand at the work.

"If the others haven't heard the row, it's not likely they'll come back," he said. "But we'll take no chances; we'll keep as quiet as possible, just to avoid any more risks of interference. Move lively now!"

The men of the *Malabart* ran here and there, their bare feet pattering, and pulled and hauled a huge, unwieldy mat to the outward side. Then they ran its looped lines forward and under the ship's hull. The *Malabart* sheered off to give play, and the men fell to the lines, heaving and tugging, as the mat went over the side and submerged itself at the point indicated by Beltramo. Throughout their work, running, and pulling, and hauling, that same air of noiselessness, of low-spoken orders, was maintained. In the same muffled silence, filled only with sounds of movement, the other mat was fixed on the starboard side and drawn taut, and the officers, listening intently down the hatchway, were encouraged when the sounds of swirling and gurgling were no longer audible.

A huge cable was brought across from the *Malabart*, fixed

through the for'ard bits. The *Malabart's* screw turned, and she slowly moved ahead until she took the strain of the tow and headed back for the shelter of the islands where she had lain in wait. Down on the engine-room steps Captain Eli held his torchlight against a water mark and slowly his face lost its grimness. His eyes twinkled when he saw the ship was no longer taking in an appreciable or dangerous quantity of water. He mentally estimated the time, and muttered: "We'll make it, sure, unless she springs another leak, or the mats fail!"

Neither accident came, and in the dawn the *Malabart* towed her salvage into the sheltered waters, slacked off and came alongside as the Rhodialim's anchors splashed into the sea. Drake, going across to his own ship, where the cook was serving out hot mugs of coffee, gulped one, and eyed the remnants of the two packing cases that Forbes had opened on the *Malabart's* deck. Two centrifugal pumps, stocky and powerful, squatted there in the midst of the confusion, and the engineer was directing the fitting of the steam lines.

"We'll lash the ships alongside. It's safe, I think, and it's so still in these waters they'll not chafe," Drake said to Catlin and the engineer. And that maneuver was quickly effected. The pump suckers were hauled across and splashed into the half-drowned hull of the salvaged ship and a few minutes later two great streams of water were pouring steadily into the sea. When daylight came the diving apparatus was planted on the Rhodialim's deck, and, guided by a water torch, the man who had abandoned diving made a descent, found the sea cocks and closed them. And now the salvage was practically assured.

It was nearly noon when Drake said to Catlin:

"Now we'll go below and get at the bottom of this business. We'll have a little chat with that second mate we've got trussed up."

They brought the man up to the deck. He was sullen, cowed, and palpably frightened. Drake regarded him coldly for a full minute, frowning before he said:

"We brought you up to get at the truth of this. Why did you come back to the ship? Did Morris send you?"

The man started to evade, to stammer, to make palpably false statements until Drake threatened with:

"Stow that guff! The only chance you've got is to come across with a clean yarn. If you do that, you'll get away clean. Now quit your waving the hook, or back below you go, until I can hand you over to the shore police in Pirzeus. If it suits you better to talk Greek— Christophe, come here and tell me what this man says. I want to get it straight."

Christophe came, added his own urgings to overcome the man's reluctance, and then listened with a dry grin to a voluble confession. Now and then he interrupted with a question, and although Drake understood the gist of the mate's words, Christophe finally turned and in his own way told what he had learned.

"Thees man, he think maybe he and these other mens can maybe get lots of little things like chronometers and glasses and such what left behind; so after lost Captain Morris boat in fog, they row back see if she still afloat, and come aboard. He swear he not know anything about how she sink on purpose. Engineer what Morris frien' run on deck, yell she sprung big leak, and Morris make fuss, and then say no hope and mus' take to boats. When these man come aboard and find you, they thinks maybe ship not sink after all, and if they can get her back they make lot of money for save her. So, fight like hell. He swear that all he know. Maybe he spik truth, I think so."

Drake stared at the man for a moment. Then, with apparent irrelevance, he asked Christophe:

"How do people go by land from Nauplia to Pirzeus, and how long does it take?"

"Road over the mountains, sir. Easy go. But take maybe two, three days."

"Telephone, I suppose?"

"Sure, captain, sir. Nauplia fine city. One time capital of Greece and—"

"Good! You tell this man we're going to keep 'em aboard the *Malabart* until we get ready to make it to Piræus, and that nothing will happen to them, unless they try to leave before we get ready for them to go."

The mate of the Rhodialim understood, and broke into profuse promises; but to make certain that they could not escape, Drake had all the boats of the *Malabart* brought around to the salvaged ship, moored, and the oars taken away, before he liberated his battered prisoners and told the cook to feed them.

Catlin was still wondering what Drake had in mind when, a few days later, the Rhodialim was ready to put to sea under her own steam. Then Drake said to his mate:

"Mr. Catlin, you take Beltramo and whatever scratch crew you need for the engine room and ship, and go aboard the Rhodialim and follow us to Piræus; but first have the boat that scum came in brought around, chuck in grub and water enough to take them to Nauplia, then chuck them in after it and tell 'em to go and be damned to 'em."

The mate's wonder ceased on the day when the two ships came to the crowded docks of the Greek seaport, amid the babbling exclamations of those who recognized the salvaged ship. Drake called to Catlin to accompany him, and they walked from the docks to make their official reports.

"We ought to get a neat bit of salvage money out of this trip," Catlin said.

"We'll get that all right. And I'm going to cut it up—half of it, anyhow, among every man that was with us. Christophe ought to get a good chunk, and so should Beltramo."

"But what I can't get is why you held that gang of beach combers until we were ready to come here," Catlin said, observing that The Old Hyena was in high good humor.

"I waited to give Bill Morris and his pals time to get back and swear to their story of how the ship was lost," he said. "It's about time they, as well as Hakim & Letin, were put out of business."

THE LUCKY LITTLE STIFF,
by H.P.S. Greene

Originally published in Adventure, Oct. 1, 1927.

France. Mud. A khaki-clad column of fours slogging along to the rhythm of their own muttered but heart-felt blasphemy—a common enough sight in the winter of 1917-1918.

But in one particular this procession of sufferers was unique. On the shoulders of each performer shone bright silver bars, and their more or less manly chests were spanned by Sam Browne belts. A casual observer would have taken them for officers. But no, on each breast was a pair of silver wings, and their uniforms were of well-fitting but variously designed whipcord. The pot-bellied little person in

151

the indecently short yellow serge blouse who led them was an officer; his followers were flying lieutenants.

They were a part of the personnel-in-training of the great American aviation field of Issy-la-Boue, the advance guard of the ten thousand American bombing planes which publicity agents said were going to blast the Huns out of Berlin.

The column passed between two long barracks, one of which, filled to capacity with double-decker bunks, yawned thru an unfinished open end.

"Squads right!" shrilled the pot-bellied one with the captain's bars in a startling tremolo. "Heh!"

The men behind squads-righted in a dispirited fashion and came to a halt in straggling lines. The squawky voice continued:

"I want to say that you are the most undisciplined body of men I ever saw. That—er—mélée you staged when you were unwittingly marched into—er—contact with a body of enlisted men was the most disgraceful exhibition on the part of officers so-called I ever saw in my life. I—er—want to say you are a disgrace to the service. That's all I want to say. Oh, I—er—believe Lieutenant Crosby has something to say to you."

Flying-Lieutenant Crosby stepped forward and cleared his throat. He was a born Babbitt, a destined getter-together.

"Men," he began, and then hesitated. Perhaps he should have said "officers," but that wouldn't have sounded right either. He rushed on, "I want to remind you that Happy's and Sam's funeral is this afternoon. All flying is called off as usual. There wasn't much of a crowd out for poor old Bill yesterday. I know it's a long walk and all that but we want to get a good crowd out this afternoon. The cadets are going to try to get a good crowd out for their fellow who got bumped, and we want to get a good crowd out too. That's all I wanted to say."

He retired to the ranks. The fat officer shouted "Dismissed!" Then he changed his mind.

"As you were. The commanding officer wanted me to announce that quarantine to the post is on again until the perpetrator of the outrage of stopping the Paris Express has been discovered and punished. Dismissed!"

The half-broken ranks scattered in the direction of their barracks. Toward the one with the unfinished end went three oddly dissimilar figures. They were always together, and of course some one had already thought of calling them "The Three Musketeers."

One was short, dark and slim, with pathetic eyes and a dispirited mustache. Another was tall and lathy, with a long lugubrious countenance. The third was blond and almost corpulent.

"I knew it, Tommy, I knew it," said the tall man. "How come you and 'Fat' to pull such a stunt, anyway? Ain't such a joke now, is it? What're you going to do about it?"

The three entered their barrack and sat down on a bunk near the open end, well away from the crowd huddled around the stove in the middle. The little man gazed sadly before him.

His mustache drooped dolefully. Some observant person had re-marked that he could read Tommy by his mustache. When it was freshly waxed and pert, he was just going on a party. When it was sorry and unkempt, he had just been on one.

"You know we didn't mean any harm," he said. "All that stuff the frogs put out about our trying to wreck the train was a dish of prunes. As if it wasn't bad enough to miss the truck and walk out here twelve miles from town without having all this on top of it. When the quar-antine for the itch was taken off, and Fat and I got those 'thirty-six hours on condition you don't go to Paris' passes, we got by the M. P.'s at the *gare* in Paris all right.

"We went out through the baggage-room. I wasn't in the Ambu-lance for nothing. We came back into the station the same way, and once we got on the train we went right to sleep. They sure do put up a good champagne cocktail at Henry's, and then all those beers at the Follies!

"Well, when I woke up we were at a station. I looked out and the sign on it said Chateauroux. I knew where we were all right be-cause I've flown over the place. We'd passed Issy. So I woke Fat up and pulled him off the train. There was another train standing in the station, and I asked a frog where it went to and he said it was the Paris Express. So I knew it would take us back to Issy again, and we hopped on.

"We got into a third class compartment with a lot of *poilus*, and they had *beaucoup* red wine, and we drank to *la belle France*, and *les-États-Unis*, and when I woke up again the train was just leaving a station, and the sign said Issy-la-Boue. By the time I realized what it all meant we were going too fast to jump off, so I pulled that handle on the wall, and the train stopped.

"When we saw how wrought up the frogs were, we beat it. No wonder we had to come over and help them win the war, if they're all as bum shots as those birds were! Guess they thought we were bandits or spies or something. Well, we had to walk home to keep from being A. W. O. Loose from roll-call this morning, and never got home till four o'clock. Suppose after flying, I'll have to go over and 'fess up to Herman, or you birds will never get any more passes. But I know I'll never get one if I stay here for the duration of the war."

"No pass ain't *nothin'* to what you'll get, boy!" said "Long John." "Shot at sunrise, is my bet. But I admire your self-sacrificin' spirit."

"Never mind, we'll take our medicine, won't we, Fat? And if I don't mention you, maybe he won't say anything about it."

Fat grunted dolefully. Outside a bugle blew. The three rose to go.

"It's me and Tommy to fly the eighteen meters," said Long John. "Where do you go, Fat?"

"Machine-gun," was the answer.

"Hum, too bad. I heard the guy they shot there last week croaked. The bullet went right thru his leg, and the quack dressed the place where it went in all right, but forgot to see if it came out. Gangrene set in and his leg rotted off, and they had to shoot him. Now a feller your build—say, it wouldn't go through at all. Just stay there and fester—"

But his victim was gone.

* * * *

Tommy flew badly that morning. He was all in, his head ached and, besides, he was worrying about that interview with Major Herman Krause. And then he had to practise landings—nervous work at best in an unfamiliar ship. Finally he blew a tire and was bawled out unmercifully by the instructor.

Luckily it was on his tenth and last trip, and he breathed a sigh of relief when the lecture was over and he could go. He went to the barracks and policed up. Shave, shine, but no shampoo. There was hardly enough water for drinking and shaving, and that was brought many miles in tank wagons. Bathing was something one went without at Issy—and felt not much the worse unless the scabbies set in.

Once militarily clean, Tommy dragged himself to headquarters, entirely ruining the new shine so painfully acquired. He entered the presence of the adjutant feeling like a whipped schoolboy. He saluted and stood at attention.

"Sir, Lieutenant Lang to speak to the commanding officer."

The adjutant kept on writing for about five minutes at a desk stacked with piles of reports. Then he looked up savagely and spoke with a slight accent:

"What? Oh, yes. What for?"

"About the Paris Express."

"Go right in. He's waiting."

Tommy went in and stood with trembling knees before the C. O.

He was a large florid man with beetling brows and his manner was not encouraging.

"You? Well? What about it?"

Tommy explained as well as he could, stressing his innocence. He thought his plea must have softened an executioner, but Major Krause was uncompromising in attitude and words.

"Young man," he said, "you are a disgrace, sir! A disgrace to the United States Army!" Tommy thought he had heard those words before. "We have been having considerable trouble with the guard. Those cadets are the worst disciplined body of men I ever saw." Again a familiar note.

"As for you—you seem to have trouble keeping awake. A permanent assignment as commander of the guard ought to give you beneficial practise at it. Of course, after keeping awake all night, you will need to sleep in the day-time. You are therefore relieved from flying duty. Report at guard mount this evening and every evening until further orders. That will do."

Tommy saluted and went out, his heart sinking. There were only three known ways of getting out of Issy-la-Boue. The first was to break your neck. The second was to fly so well that you were graduated. The third was to fly so poorly that you were sent to Blooey for reclassification, probably as an armament officer. Which was generally considered the lowest form of life so far discovered in the air service.

All these methods were dependent on flying. Once a man was taken off flying duty, it took an act of Congress to get him away from the place.

The little man wended his way back to the barracks. His comrades were sitting on their bunks, and he poured his tale of woe into their receptive ears. Being beyond words, they accorded him silent sympathy. Finally Fat spoke:

"Well, I'm lucky to be out of it. Say, did you hear the news? Brock was washed out on the fifteens this morning."

"That makes seven in a week," said Tommy after a pause. "How'd it happen?"

"Same old thing. Wings came off."

A bugle called. Most of the flying lieutenants went outside and, joining others from near-by barracks, formed in line. A few commands, and they were in one of the rivers of mud which served as roads at the field. Presently they were halted behind three long two-wheeled pushcarts; each cart bore a long box covered with an American flag. The mourners stood in the mud for half an hour waiting, and then a dispirited looking band appeared. Its bass drum echoed *boom-boom-boom-boom-boom*, and the procession started.

Through the gate of the camp it went, and out on to the main road, while the drum kept up its sad, hollow sound. Yard after yard, rod after rod, until the cortège had walked two miles. Then it turned into a young but flourishing cemetery, with red, raw mounds in orderly lines.

The men were formed around three fresh graves. A pale-faced Y. M. C. A. man stumbled through the burial service. A red-faced Knight of Columbus did likewise. A Frenchman flew over and dropped some dessicated roses. Then they all marched away again; only the boxes and a small burial party remained behind.

The band struggled with its one tune, a lively quickstep, according to regulations. Two old peasants drew their cart to one side of the road to let them pass.

"*Comme ils sont trists, les 'tits Americains!*" said the woman.

"*Quelle musique!*" answered her spouse.

* * * *

The three chums went back to their bunks.

"Do you birds know anything about being the commander of the guard?" asked Tommy with some concern.

"No," replied Fat.

"Sure," answered Long John. "I was chucked out of the first training camp. First, you have to have a gun."

"A rifle?" asked Tommy.

"No, you little sap. Officers don't carry rifles, or flying lieutenants either. A pistol."

"But I ain't got a pistol."

"Borrow one then. Do you know the general orders?"

"I don't know any generals, orders or debility either."

"Never mind trying to be funny. You may find out it ain't no joke about generals. The Old Boy himself and the Silly Civilian are going to inspect the post tomorrow. I saw the orders over at the operations office for every machine to be up that can get off the ground. I suppose that means a lot more long walks. But it's most time for guard mount; you'd better run along and find a gun."

Tommy disappeared and finally returned with a regulation web belt and holster in one hand, and a .25 caliber automatic in the other.

"What are you going to do with that popgun, you idiot?" asked Long John disgustedly. "Are you going hunting canary birds, or what?"

156

"I couldn't find a regular gun, and a cadet loaned me this. He said officers had taken it before and put a dirty sock or something in the holster so the butt would just show, and got by all right."

"Very well, then, take one of Fat's socks. The smell may keep you awake. Is the blamed thing loaded? Look out you don't shoot yourself. There's the call, now. Put on your belt. You fool! How many belts are you going to wear? What do you think you are, a past grand master of the Holy Jumpers? Take off your Sam Browne. There—get going, now.

"Well, away he goes, and he doesn't know whether Julius Cesar was stabbed or shot off horseback. Did you ever see the like, Fat? But I bet he comes out all right some way, the lucky little stiff. I never knew it to fail. Well, let's go up by the stove."

But Tommy wasn't such a complete fool as he appeared. He knew the old Army advice for shavetails, "Find a good sergeant and stick to him." The sergeant of the guard was a grizzled old sufferer who had been through it all many, many times. He engineered the guard mount and posted the guard. Then Tommy drew him to one side.

"What do I do now, Sergeant?" he asked.

"Well, the lieutenant has to inspect the guard three times, once between midnight and six o'clock in the morning. First ask them for their special orders, and then for their general orders. If they make a mistake, I'll nudge you and you say, 'Correct him, Sergeant,' and I'll fix him up. It's getting dark now. Would the Lieutenant like to make his first inspection before supper?"

Inspection was a hectic affair. The guard was composed of cadets who had joined the Army to fly and remained in it to mount guard, and it was their intention to make it as interesting as possible for all concerned, especially their superiors. But the old sergeant was equal to the occasion. He steered Tommy by the traps planted for him, and then showed him the guardhouse.

There the commander of the guard ate his slum and then returned to his barrack. Long John grabbed him by the arm as he entered.

"That frog was around again today, and he brought a lot of stuff," he whispered. "You're in on it. Doc is goin' to make punch. Be around at nine o'clock."

* * * *

Tommy was there at the appointed time. At the far end a crowd was gathered. Men were perched as closely as possible on the double-deck bunks. In their midst Bacchanalian rites were in progress. "Doc," a stout man with a red, satyr-like countenance, was beating a huge bowl of eggs. Before him within easy reach and frequently applied, was an assorted row of bottles. Tommy read some of the labels—Cherry Brandy, Martell, D. O. M., Absinthe.

"My God," he muttered to himself, "everything but nitroglycerine."

The party was undoubtedly a success. There were songs and dances and stories. Finally it got to the speechmaking stage. An interruption in the form of a volley of shots was welcome to every one except the current performer. A trampling of feet, and then more shots followed. A voice at the other end of the barrack shouted "Attention!" as Major Krause stumbled in. He had evidently been running, but he tried to stalk around in a dignified manner. Somebody whispered—

"Those damn cadets have been shooting off their guns and raising hell again, and he's been trying to catch them."

The major approached the end of the barrack where the party had been in progress. He sniffed suspiciously, but the punch-bowl had been shoved under a bunk and the bottles into boots, and there was no evidence in sight. Finally he asked—

"Are there any guns in this barrack?"

"No," Tommy spoke up. "I know, because I was trying to borrow one this afternoon to mount guard with."

A partially suppressed titter rose and fell again. The C. O. wheeled around furiously.

"So it's you again, is it?" he thundered. "Carousing in here while your superiors attend to your duties. Get out to your guard and put a stop to that indiscriminate shooting. I swear if I see you again tonight I'll prefer charges and have you broke!"

Tommy stumbled out into the darkness and headed in what he thought was the direction of the guardhouse. His head was buzzing painfully. A volley of shots sounded somewhere in front of him. He felt vaguely that he ought to do something about it, and ran in that direction, only to fall over the guy-rope of a hangar and fall heavily. More shots behind him. He got up and staggered on. Suddenly there was a flash and a report right before him. Then a voice yelled—

"Halt."

"Commander of the guard," bawled Tommy.

A dark figure loomed up vaguely in the murk. He struck a match and saw a grinning cadet working the bolt of his rifle and waving the muzzle around dangerously. Suddenly it exploded and Tommy felt mud splatter over him.

"I thought I saw something moving and halted it, and it wouldn't halt, so I fired, but I don't understand this gun very well, sir," said the cadet, still working at the bolt.

The commander of the guard turned and fled. He was getting dizzier every minute. Finally he tripped over another guy-rope and fell, to rise no more.

When he woke, it was with the consciousness of having been annoyed for a long time by a rasping noise which was still going on. He tried to pull himself together and think. He could vaguely discern the bulk of a hangar. There was a queer, unexplained rasping. Filed wires—Wings coming off—Funerals—

The noise stopped, and presently a dark figure crept out through the hangar door and started to steal away. Tommy drew the little automatic from its holster and fired. The next thing he realized was that there were flashlights and men everywhere. The sergeant of the guard. Major Krause. Calls for explanation. Tommy tried to explain. A voice said—

"You fool, you've shot the adjutant!" Strong hands seized him and hustled him away.

* * * *

Next morning, when a detail came to the guardhouse, Tommy was still in a daze. The leader told him to police up, as he was to go before the C. O. He was still confused when he was led into the office at headquarters.

The commanding officer was there, and Captain La Croix, the French officer who advised as to instruction. Also a large, fierce man with stars on his shoulders, and a little civilian with glasses and a trench coat several sizes too large for him. Tommy's legs seemed to be made of butter.

Major Krause was speaking, and strange to say, his voice was not unkind.

"Lieutenant Lang," he said, "I revoke everything I said yesterday. You have done a great service for your country. I regret to say that a small file was found on the body of the adjutant, and that some of the ships were found to have been tampered with—so skillfully that detection was very unlikely. Inspection of the adjutant's papers brought out evidence that he was an Austrian citizen. Tell the general and the secretary how you came to discover what was going on."

"Well," blurted Tommy, "it was this way. I was dizzy and fell down two or three times and finally I decided to go to sleep. Then some guy kept making a filing noise and waking me up, so I shot him."

* * * *

That evening three flying lieutenants were finishing an illicit meal of chicken and champagne at a little French inn about three miles from the field, and the smallest of the trio was finishing a story.

"There was a long argument," he said, "and the general and the major were all for preferring charges, but Captain La Croix stood up for me and said I was a good pilot, and finally they agreed to let him get me transferred to a French observation squadron at the front."

The tall man and the fat one looked at each other and at their little companion. Then they ejaculated as one—

"You lucky little stiff!"

WHEN EVERYBODY KNEW,
by Raymond S. Spears

Originally published in Adventure, July 15, 1928

A swaggering monster of a man, with long, tangled black hair, a cascade of blue steel whiskers and sunken caverns for eyes, thundered on thick soled boots into the Many Moons Barroom where he surged with long and eager strides to the center of the three man width of liquid counter. As he approached, those between him and his apparent point of destination spread swiftly to right and left.

"Set 'er up!" he growled, shaking his head, snorting, and turning from side to side till he had surveyed the whole circumference of the establishment with his sunken, glowing eyes.

He drank what looked to be a ridiculously little drink for so huge a carcass; he wriggled all the way down as the tiny shot burned in his throat. He gurgled and choked, as if the drink were in proportion to him, and after four or five fillings of the barrel shaped little glass he reached tentatively for the outflaring yellow handled revolver which was of a size in proportion to his beef. He gave sidelong glances into the big mirrors behind the bar after three or four false alarms with his gun. And he had a drink after each half completed movement. Then suddenly he pulled and let go a shot. He looked around. The bartenders stood with their hands lifted, like squirrels' paws, and other patrons of the place were skittering without dignity out of the way, drawing toward the front and rear entrances through which the ones who always avoided trouble vanished like mist cloud shadows. The big fellow took some more drinks, and at intervals in a tentative kind of way he let go a booming shot. And presently, when he had reloaded his cylinder twice from loose ammunition in his trousers pockets he threw a pinch of silver on the bar, enough to pay for his drinks, and surged into the square.

There, with his big legs spreading, he weaved and swayed while he looked around. Court House Square of Boxelder was a glow and a sparkle of yellowish lights, with here and there the colors of red, green, blue and sundry hues, the brighter places being saloons, dance halls, gambling places, the most ornate of which had pool and billiard tables imported at enormous cost. Large boxlike buildings were dull—the reputable emporiums of trade, where hardware, food, dry goods and outfits were to be bought.

Swing doors were flashing to the shadows of ingoing or outgoing figures. As he looked around, the big fellow caught flashes of sparkling points, the eyes of humans, shining in the gloom like those of dogs or cats, some green, some golden, some purple.

"I'm Bill of Buck Hill!" the man murmured in his throat, so that it sounded like a growl; and then, louder, "I'm Rearin' Bill of Buck Hill!"

He looked around rather expectantly, and raised his chin higher, throwing back his head.

"I'm Rearin' Bill of Big Buck Hill!" he shouted. "I'm two yards wide and nine feet high—*Woo-who-o! Woo-who-o!*"

At that shout—"*Woo-who-o!*"—men, standing at every bar around the square and all the way down to the Claybank Delight, turned and glanced at one another.

"'Tain't Texas!" One shook his head. "That'd be *e-yeow-w!*"

"'Tain't Prairie—hit'd be *Hi-i-i-i!*"

"'Tain't Rebel—'tain't Yank." An old veteran shook his head.

"'Tain't old Mississip' shanty boat landing whoop er soundin' hail."

"Ner mule skinnin' cowboy—none of them!" another declared.

"That's green timber!" a square shouldered, high headed man remarked as he turned a sheet of a weekly paper in the lobby of Squint

Legere's hotel.

"My lan'! He's bad!" A bystander shook his head. "Y' c'n tell that—the way he growls— My lan'!"

"Who is he?" some one asked, and another raised a warning hand.

"Cyarful, ol' man! He's from Buck Hill. I've been t' Buck Hill. Hit's way yonder in the head of Snake Creek Bad Lands. My land'! I was glad the sun didn't set on me up theh; yes, indeedy! He's Rearin' Bill—my lan'! Don't 'tagonise 'im. He comes from a bad country!"

The hoarse, rumbling growling of the man thus identified came around the square in the middle of the street. Horses hitched along the rails turned their heads to look at the phenomenon going by, twitching their tails and snorting a little under their breaths. A dog ran out in the dark from the sidewalk, wagging its tail, yipping as it pranced. Rearing Bill turned and growled at the vagrant beast, and the dog stood on its hind legs in an enthusiastic invitation to come on and play!

Some one laughed in the gloom of a passageway between two saloons. Rearing Bill threw a bullet into that shadow insult and then slammed two shots which sent the dog squealing in creased terror the other way around the square. A man's yell of alarm rose frantically from the passageway and the clatter of loose boards and the fall of a stack of booming empty kegs reverberated around.

"*Woo-who-o!*" Rearing Bill whooped, and the echoes returned from faces of Bad Land cliffs.

"Lawse, he c'n shore yell!" listeners said in low voices.

As the big fellow shambled nearer, the gamblers around the tables hesitated, the drinkers at the bars held their liquor poised, looking over their shoulders at the front doors; and those with nothing special to divide their attention withdrew to the rear or side entrances. The bartenders, who must perforce stay and take it, wiped their hands on their aprons, their fingers twiddling, all except Flat Face Dink of Squint Legere's liquid annex. Flat Face Dink lifted the corner of his lips; then he gave the long, red, cherry wood bar an extra dry polish.

"My gracious!" the observing Tid Ricks whispered. "Dink don't care f'r anybody in the world! He's all nerve, Dink is! Come the devil himself and Flat Face'd say to him, 'Name yer pisen, old boy—how's hell t'day?' He would, honest! I bet he would."

A heavy footfall out in front of Legere's shook the planks till they boomed and creaked. Rearing Bill of Big Buck Hill surged into the middle of the barroom. Tid Ricks shrank into a corner. Patrons along the bar watched anxiously through the mirror reflections. Flat Face Dink deliberately turned his back and stacked up a pyramid of glasses.

"I want pisen!" the newcomer declared, shambling toward the bar, where they gave him ten feet width according to his size, looks and actions.

Flat Face Dink flipped up a quart bottle, tall, straight sided and long necked, and set up a thick, fluted glass to hold two good liquor drinks. Rearing Bill looked at the glass, picking it up.

"Put 'r thar, mister!" Rearing Bill said, enthusiastically. "You got a measure 'cording to the man here—put 'r thar!"

Flat Face Dink colored happily under that praise, and drank with Rearing Bill, something he never did except with the most distinguished of patrons.

Rearing Bill holstered his gun with the stained ivory handles. He was a gentleman among gentlemen, in Squint Legere's, all on account of the appreciation of Flat Face Dink of the appropriateness of measures for a man, serving glasses according to one's size. Rearing Bill surged forth into the street again, popped away a couple of times and went on his way.

He began to sing:

"I'm Rearing Bill of Big Buck Hill.
  Snake pisen is my cure.
Of human flesh I eat my fill;
  An' I takes my whisky pure."

He ended the verse with a chorus of shots. He aimed at lights, which crashed in broken glass, for he could shoot pretty straight. His gunfire made the horses nervous, and they pranced around. When he was on one side of the square men scurried on the opposite side to remove their mounts, either racing out to the livery barn and corral or down toward Strollers' Campground on the creek bottom.

Rearing Bill's horse was built on his own generous scale, but he had begun to ride it when it was too young; and now the beast, which would have been a good draft horse, was a swayback with a tired look in the lop of its ears. When Rearing Bill came by, however, the animal pranced and shook nervously.

* * * *

Word had been sent to City Marshal Pete Culder, who was out in his home cabin. The messenger said that Rearing Bill from Buck Hill had come to town. At least, the fellow had said he was Rearing Bill and acted as bad as they make them. Culder promised to come right down, but he wasn't seen by any one on that hectic night.

164

After shooting up Court House Square the disturber went into saloons and took tentative shots at bottles and glasses. Keen observers noticed that he shot with accuracy. He held his biggest of revolvers with a free, powerful grip which on the pull landed the lead slugs in whatever he aimed at, whether tin lamp base or peak glass on a pyramid of glasses.

Rearing Bill shambled from saloon to saloon. On each circuit he became more uproarious, more exacting in his demands; and when in the Happy Medium a frightened bartender put out a half size whisky glass instead of a double size according to the fashion set by Flat Face Dink, Rearing Bill with a grizzly-like swipe of the muzzle of his gun knocked the unfortunate liquor clerk senseless. He then stood, amused for an instant by the spectacle of the poor devil sprawled limp on the floor.

"Heh!" Rearing Bill snarled. "Cheat me on m' liquor, eh! Heh!"

He turned, surging to glare from sunken eyes at the white faced onlookers. As he stared at them one by one they all shrank, watchful of the swinging of the carelessly handled revolver, the drunken man's unsteady finger on the trigger, the hammer drawn back at full cock and the big, powerful paw holding the barrel as steady as a mounted cannon.

* * * *

There was in Boxelder a shiftless, shaky, friendless hanger-on known as Odd Jobbing Det Linver, a huddled up, raggedly dressed fellow who was kicked around by every one. There had been an interval of ten or fifteen minutes' quiet when Odd Jobbing Det appeared in Squint Legere's barroom. The man who had been reading the weekly paper in the lobby laid it on the hotel clerk's desk and entered the barroom from the lobby just as Det entered from the rear alley, looking anxiously behind him.

Rearing Bill had catfooted, as softly as a grizzly bear on the sneak, into the front entrance. Flat Face Dink looked up with a genial smile of welcome, so the bully grinned widely as he started for the bar. Thus Odd Jobbing Det backed right into the very big fellow he was scared to meet. It was an abrupt collision.

Rearing Bill grunted. He glanced around, stopped and saw the cringing, shrinking wretch who looked up at him with utterly abject fear. For an instant Rearing Bill stared and glared; then he began to grin as he surged at the victim thus thrown in his way. Odd Jobbing Det backed till he was stopped by the wall. Then Rearing Bill cuffed and kicked, abusing the wretched weakling, who blubbered, whimpered, choked and begged. The more he pleaded for mercy the more the bully slapped and poked him with the big revolver.

"I've a notion to kill you," Rearing Bill suggested tentatively, "'sultin' me thataway. I've a notion to cut yer heart out an' eat it! I've a notion to shoot ye—'sultin' me. Me—bumping into me—walkin' all over me. I've a notion to kill an' eat ye f'r breakfast—'"

The spectators, shrinking along the walls, edging away, froze with expectancy as they saw the tentative suggestion of murder congealing into determination to kill. Rearing Bill had worked himself up to a fury. He was weaving in savage ferocity. He glanced around, covertly from under his bushy brows, taking in the white faces and the fears in the eyes of the beholders.

"Yes, sir, I'm going t' kill you!" he suddenly snarled.

But, like a cat playing with a victim Rearing Bill deliberately delayed. Here was a worthless, terror stricken, utterly helpless and friendless victim. Odd Jobbing Det looked his sorry misery and his voice went up in a shrill breaking wail of hopeless terror, for he felt the drunken brute's determination to "get a man", establishing a reputation as bad, killing to see a victim kick.

The man who had been reading the paper gazed curiously at the spectacle. He had recognized the whoop of Rearing Bill as that of a green timber woodsman, a logger from the pine, spruce or hemlock belt somewhere. Now he saw the big fellow clearly and, staring at him in surprise, recognized him.

"Why, you damned skunk!" he muttered, just like that, and started straight across the barroom, bare handed.

There was a gasp of amazement among the other spectators. Rearing Bill heard or felt the difference in the echo. He froze for an instant as he cunningly turned his eyes to look out of their corners. He discovered the swift approach of the spectator and turned to look.

Rearing Bill's face convulsed. A regular gorilla expression of ugliness and cruelty crossed his features. He had clicked his teeth and shaken his tangled mane, fluffing up his steel black whiskers. At sight of the interrupter he shrank in precisely the same way that Odd Jobbing Det had done, and lines of cruel satisfaction changed to the same quivering of terror and pleading.

"I didn't mean nothing! I didn't mean nothing! I were jes' foolin'!" Rearing Bill's voice rose higher and shriller. "I wa'n't really goin' to hurt 'im, Mister Benson! Hones'—honest!"

"You lie!" the other exclaimed, cuffing the big face backhandedly. Under cover of the stinging blow, Benson snatched the huge revolver from the loose grasp of the bully's hand.

Then with the barrel of the weapon Benson pounded the big fellow across the floor, backward. Rearing Bill yelped, cried out, choked and at last turned to run. Contemptuously, Benson gave him a kick; and then as the bully yelled he fired the big gun at the floor under him so that the huge boots bobbed high and thumped to frantic efforts at escape, crashing out into the night. Outside Rearing Bill raced, plunging to the swayback drayhorse, and he rode furiously away in the dark, heading up Snake Creek.

* * * *

When he was out of hearing, his nervous yelps lost away in the Bad Land distance, the crowd came back into Squint Legere's barroom to see what miracle had changed the echo of Rearing Bill's whoops. They found the other stranger, Benson, unloading Rearing Bill's revolver of the yellow stained ivory handles. Bystanders whispered excitedly at what this fellow had done, barehanded, right after calling Rearing Bill a skunk.

"My lan'!" Tid Ricks gasped. "I never hoped to see anybody brave as that—my, gracious! He just acted like he wa'n't 'fraid of nothing in the world, yes, sir! Why, he slapped that big feller 'fore he even took his gun away! It was the nerviest thing anybody eveh did get to see!"

Squint Legere did the honors. Benson just must take a drink.

"I'll take one," he assented, "and no more."

He meant it. No one urged, or even suggested, a second drink. Benson went to the night clerk for his room key. Legere checked him at the foot of the stairs.

"Excuse me," Legere said. "'Course, I mind my own business—but you knew him?"

"Oh, yes! Went to school together."

"That so! Back East, I expect?"

"Yes, Minnesota."

"That makes me think. You're Benson—Robert Benson," Legere said, "I see by the register."

"Oh, yes!"

"Not—uh—not Patient Bob—uh?"

"Why—" the flicker of a reminiscent smile crossed his face—"I've been called that—"

"Shu-u!" Squint exclaimed, softly. "'Course, I mind my own business, Mister Benson!"

"'Course, know that. Well, goodnight!"

Squint Legere returned to the bar where he was awaited with interest by a curious crowd.

"He's Patient Bob," Squint remarked in a low voice.

"Not— Say, Patient Bob Benson! Shu-u-u-u!" voices gasped.

"An' I seen 'im settin' theh all the ev'ing, reading the paper, cool as you please!" Tid Ricks broke the silence. "Why, he neveh even looked up when that old fourflusher come shootin' by, no, suh! I seen it with my own eyes. I knowed he was *good*. Same time I neveh dreamed he was Patient Bob—but when he got to goin'—'course—"

"'Course!" others assented. "Anybody'd knowed, then, he was *good*!"

THE SOUL OF
HENRY JONES,
by Ray Cummings

Originally published in Argosy—All Story Weekly, Aug. 21, 1920

At the age of thirty-two Henry Jones awoke one brilliant summer morning with the sudden realization that the soul in him was starving. He lay quiet, staring idly at the white ceiling above the bed, his mind groping dully with this abrupt enlightenment. After a moment of mental confusion—for the enormity of the conception stirred him profoundly—he raised himself upon one elbow in bed and looked at his wife who lay sleeping beside him.

He had always thought her pretty in a quiet, unobtrusive sort of way. He did not remember ever having noticed before the wrinkles that were beginning to show around her eyes, but he could see them there now, plainly. And her neck seemed very thin and stringy, and the line of her lean jaw very sharp. That he had never noticed before either. The thin locks of straight black hair that were spread upon her pillow were shot through with gray. The vision of a great soft, fluffy mass of wavy golden tresses flashed into his mind—the crowning glory of no particular woman, but just an abstract picture.

Henry Jones shivered a little and fell to staring at the round white face of the tiny alarm-clock on the bureau. Then, after a time, he found himself thinking that it was unusually early for him to be awake, for the clock hands pointed to half past five.

He slid noiselessly out of bed. For a moment he stood irresolute; then he began to dress swiftly, watching his still sleeping wife with a furtive air and feeling somehow very guilty. When he was fully dressed he caught a glimpse of his reflection in the mirror and paused an instant to view the completed picture.

The mirror showed a short, rotund little man in a light gray suit, with a narrow black leather belt that bulged out prominently in front; a round, pink and white almost cherubic face, with light blue eyes, eyebrows so light they were almost unnoticeable; and sandy hair with a tiny bald spot on top.

But what Henry Jones saw was a pair of sad, wistful eyes with the soul shining out of them—a soul patiently yearning for the satisfaction of its desires.

The little suburban village in which Henry Jones lived and worked was just beginning to awaken into life, as he passed down its streets that early summer morning. He held himself very erect, with his chest expanded, breathing deep of the morning air and walking rapidly.

A girl was coming toward him down the narrow sidewalk of the maple-lined avenue—a trim, buoyant little figure. Henry Jones noticed her slim, silk-clad ankles as she drew closer. And he saw, too, that she wore neat, high-heeled shoes that were very trig and becoming. He watched the ankles and the shoes as they approached. Henry Jones was an expert on the latest styles of shoes, for he was by profession a shoe clerk. But there was in his appraising regard of this particular pair on this particular morning a look that was not wholly impersonally professional.

As the girl passed him, Henry Jones raised his eyes to her face.

She was a very pretty girl, with curving lips and soft, fluffy golden hair blowing low about her ears. He did not remember ever having seen her before, but as he met her eyes he smiled—a frank, friendly, comrady sort of smile he felt it was—and he heard his lips murmuring "Good morning," as his hand went to his hat.

The girl did not pause, but as she passed he thought he saw that she, too, was smiling. And afterward he remembered vividly that the pink of her cheeks had deepened to a sudden red, and that her long lashes had fallen shyly. Henry Jones threw out his chest still farther and strode forward with a song in his heart.

Six years before this important morning to the Jones family, Martha Lewis had married Henry Jones. At the age of twenty-five—one year Henry's junior—she had felt herself in a fair way of being laid upon the shelf of perpetual maidenhood, and so she had married the prosaic, plodding Henry, as the only available eligible unattached young man of her acquaintance.

You are not to imagine Martha Lewis as an acrid, designing young female. She was merely a comparatively unattractive girl according to the standards demanded by the young men of Rosewood. Like many other girls of her type, Martha was blessed, in exchange for physical beauty, with a considerable stock of good common sense. Throughout her years of adolescence she had cherished secretly all the usual dreams and romance of young girlhood. Then, realizing gradually that their fulfilment was beyond her, she had put them resolutely away, and at her father's death, when she was twenty-four, had calmly turned to face the world with the resolution to make the best of existing circumstances.

And so she had married Henry Jones—deliberately, because she wanted to. She was in love with him, of course, just as she knew he was with her. It was not the love of her dreams, but a steadfast, practical, common sense love. Probably it was the better kind, she often told herself; and yet—because she was only human, and especially because she was a woman—there were times when, underneath the prosaic contentment of the daily routine of her married life, she found herself wanting something more. For Henry was neither in looks nor by nature inspiring to the female mind. But he made her a good husband; Martha knew that, and she loved him and was content.

This was Henry Jones's wife—not the woman he knew—but the real woman, as she was on this summer morning when his soul suddenly expanded.

Martha was in the kitchen preparing the meal when he returned. He pecked her upon the cheek, hastily mumbled something about not feeling well, and going out to get the morning air, and then escaped into the dining-room with his morning paper.

During the meal he sat silent, pretending to read.

"Eat your eggs," said his wife abruptly.

Henry Jones came back with a start from the rippling little stream beside which he had been lying, and ate his eggs almost sullenly.

Martha was glancing at the newspaper. "I see the shoe factories are in trouble again. That'll put up your prices at the store."

"Yes," said Henry, and went on eating his eggs.

Martha waited a moment. "How's the new clerk getting on, Hen?" she volunteered again. "Are you going to keep him?"

"Guess so," said Henry. His inner being shuddered at the nick-name his wife used so frequently; but outwardly he felt he was main-taining his composure.

"It must have been that salad last night that upset you," went on Martha after another interval of silence; to which Henry answered nothing.

All that day at the store Henry's work revolted him as nothing had ever revolted him before. He longed for freedom. He wanted to wan-der through dim, cool, mossy woods; or to lie beside babbling brooks upon his back and watch the birds in the trees overhead; or to sit braced against a tree-trunk with a book upon his knee, reading poetry to a pair of blue eyes staring up into his face. Henry had never read much poetry, but he knew now he wanted to.

And she would brush back her straying locks of golden hair and implore him to read more. And then he—

"That hurts my corn," said Henry Jones's customer irritably. "Can't you give me one a little wider at the toe?"

At dinner that evening Henry's malady was unimproved. He ate very little, seemed disinclined to talk, and equally unable to read his evening newspaper. To Martha's anxious questions concerning his health Henry guessed his "liver was out of order"—a surmise that the pink and white of his cheeks and the clearness of his little eyes stout-ly denied.

He would have none of the pills she tried to force upon him, but promised, if he could be allowed to spend the evening at Williams's Billiard Parlor, watching the games, to take it when he came home in the event of his not feeling better by then.

So, immediately after the meal was over, Henry put on his hat and escaped from the oppression of domesticity into the freedom of the great outdoors. But he did not go to Williams's Billiard Parlor. In-stead he turned sharply, as soon as he was out of sight of his home, and headed in exactly the opposite direction.

Now you can readily understand that in this state of mind it was inevitable that sooner or later Henry should meet the other woman. That is in no way peculiar; but it is rather surprising that in Henry's case she came into his life this very first evening.

There is a little lake near Rosewood, which during the summer months is ideal for canoeing. It was toward this lake that Henry bent his steps. The night was warm, but not unpleasantly so, for there was a stiff breeze blowing. Almost a full moon hung overhead, with scudding, low-flying clouds passing swiftly across its face at intervals. Henry jammed his straw hat down firmly on his head and strode forward with rapid steps into the wind.

Not that Henry was particularly interested in canoeing. Mr. and Mrs. Jones had, in fact, never been in a canoe together. Henry had never been in one in his life, for he was an indifferent swimmer in spite of his fleshiness, and the obvious frailty of this form of boat held no appeal for him; and if his wife had ever been in one he did not know it. She had never suggested it except once—soon after they were married—and that he had long since forgotten.

Henry struck the lake near its upper end, where it was wildest. He was glad to find himself quite alone; be laid his hat on the ground and sat down close beside the shore, facing the wind that blew strongly toward him from across the water. The lake was rough, and the sound of its little angry waves beating against the pebbly beach at his feet thrilled him. After a moment the moon came from behind a flying cloud and the water was lighted with silver. Henry sighed rapturously.

For perhaps ten minutes he sat motionless. Then abruptly coming from up the lake he saw a lone canoe. It was hardly more than two hundred feet off shore, and was heading downward, across the wind. Henry could see it plainly in the moonlight—a canoe with a single occupant, a girl, seated in its stern and paddling with a single paddle. The empty bow of the canoe rose high in the air.

Henry watched it with furiously beating heart as it rose and fell on the silvery waves. The girl was paddling desperately, and evidently with waning strength to keep its bow from blowing around toward the shore.

The wind increased with a sudden gust, and all at once the girl stopped paddling. The bow of the canoe, acting almost like a sail, swung rapidly around. The canoe rode more quietly now, but drifted steadily shoreward. After a moment the girl started paddling again, and came slanting across the waves in a direction that Henry realized with a start would land her almost at his feet.

Another gust forced her to increase the force of her strokes, but still she could not hold her own. She was almost opposite Henry, and hardly fifty feet off shore, when she gave up again; this time evidently for good, for she held the paddle idle across her knees.

The canoe blew inshore rapidly. Henry was sitting in the shadow of a tree and knew the girl had not seen him. Another moment passed and the bow of the canoe grated upon the pebbly beach, hardly ten feet from where he sat.

Henry started to his feet. The girl was standing up, gingerly trying to walk shoreward in the rocking little craft. Henry shouted. The girl looked up, startled; and at the same instant a wave struck the stern quarter of the canoe, sluing it around. The girl lost her balance and fell overboard.

Henry leaped forward to the beach. He was not a bit frightened, he told himself afterward; instead, there was joy in his heart—a fierce, reckless joy. For this at last was life!

The canoe, partly filled, rolled sidewise to the waves and grounded. The girl struggled to her feet, knee-deep in the water and soaking wet. Henry ran past the canoe, and without hesitating, waded out and stood facing her.

"I fell overboard," announced the girl.

"Yes, I—I saw you," said Henry. "I was sitting there." He waved his hand vaguely toward the shore. His heart was almost smothering him; yet he felt no surprise, for it seemed only natural and right that she should come to him so unexpectedly and so soon. For Henry at once recognized this girl standing beside him in the lake as the girl he had passed and smiled at that morning.

And then, in a flash, he knew also that it was to her beautiful blue eyes he had been reading poetry all that day, and it was her wayward golden tresses that had floated before him and would not go away, even when the customer was annoyed because a shoe pinched.

"Why, you're all wet," said Henry.

"So are you," rejoined the girl. Then suddenly she laughed—a little silvery peal, like far-off bells at sunset, Henry thought. "How silly of us. Let's go ashore," she added.

"Let's," said Henry. "Let me help you." He put his hand upon her arm; her dress was wet and cold, but the touch made him tremble.

It was only a few steps to the dry beach. The girl shook her skirts and sat down in the grass, shivering a little. Henry took off his coat instantly. It was quite dry, and he wrapped it around her shoulders. The girl smiled at him gratefully.

"What a silly thing! I got down there at the end of the lake, and when the wind came up stronger I couldn't get back. You can't hold it up against the wind when you're alone, you know."

Henry didn't know exactly, but he nodded confidently.

The girl took off her little slippers and emptied the water out of them.

"I live about a mile beyond the point—on this side." She pointed down the lake. "I don't know how I'm going to get home—I'd hate to walk out in the road looking like this." She glanced ruefully at the clinging wetness of her filmy dress. "And I wouldn't want to leave the canoe here anyway."

"You mustn't trust yourself on that water again tonight," said Henry. And something made him add doggedly: "I won't let you do that."

"I couldn't make it alone across that wind," said the girl. "But I could easily if"—she hesitated—"if you'd paddle down with me. Would you mind?"

Henry's heart almost stopped beating.

"It's easy enough for two," the girl went on, "when the bow's not up in the air—and there's an extra paddle. The wind's letting up anyway. If it wouldn't be troubling you too much—it isn't far by water."

"No—I mean yes—of course I will," said Henry.

The girl stood up. "I'm cold—good gracious, look at that canoe; we'll have to empty it out."

Together they lifted the canoe. The water came spilling out of Henry's end, wetting him still more, and they both laughed. Then his coat slipped off her shoulders into the lake, and again they both laughed.

"Dog-gone it, I didn't want that coat to get wet," said Henry ruefully. A wonderful feeling of comradeship had sprung up within him; he almost forgot his apprehensions of the coming canoe ride.

"I'm sorry," laughed the girl, rescuing the coat.

"I mean I wanted to keep it dry so—so you wouldn't be cold," Henry explained.

"Oh," said the girl, and smiled. And again Henry remembered afterward that her lashes had fallen shyly; and he was sure that in the moonlight he had seen the flush that came to her cheeks.

"I'll sit in the bow," said the girl when they were ready.

They pointed the canoe out into the lake. The wind had gone down considerably, and the little waves were perceptibly less high. At the girl's direction Henry steadied the canoe while she climbed its length and sat down on the bow seat with her back to him. Then he drew a long breath and waded recklessly a few steps into the lake, pushing

the canoe in front of him. Then somehow he managed to clamber into it.

The canoe rocked violently, but did not overturn. He sat erect and
rigid upon the stern seat holding his breath, the little paddle gripped
tightly in his hand.

"I'll paddle on the left, if you don't mind," said the girl. "I'm tired
of the other side."

Henry blessed the good fortune that had placed her with her back
toward him. He was surprised that they were still float; and more surprised that they seemed continuing to stay afloat.

The canoe, pointing directly into the wind, rode easily. Henry
found he could put the paddle over the gunwale into the water and
still they did not upset. The girl took a stroke. He held his paddle as
she was holding hers and took a stroke also—awkwardly but nevertheless with some effect.

"We go that way—down the lake," said the girl; and pointed on
his side. Then she paddled harder.

As the canoe swung around broadside to the waves it began to
roll. Henry felt a wild desire to drop his paddle and grip the sides
with his hands.

"It's a beautiful night, isn't it?" the girl remarked.

Henry remembered then that the moon was shining. But he was
afraid to look up; he kept his eyes fixed upon the girl and imitated
her strokes as nearly as he could.

After a moment he suddenly found that he could bend at the waist
with the roll of the canoe, keeping his shoulders level. And paddling
didn't really seem so difficult; and every moment as they approached
the narrower part of the lake the waves were getting less high.

At the end of the fifteen-minute trip, Henry's soul, temporarily
compressed, had expanded again, bigger, freer, more dominant than
ever. They landed on another little beach, almost in still water, in
front of a little cottage. Henry manfully pulled the canoe well up on
shore and stood again facing the girl.

"My name is Elsie Morton," she said. "I'm awfully obliged to
you. Won't you come in a minute and get dry, Mr.—"

"Jones—Henry Jones," said Henry. "No, I think I'd—it's pretty
late; I'd better get on home. I'm glad you're safe."

The girl took the paddle from his hand. "I'm awfully obliged," she
repeated. "It was a silly scrape to get into, wasn't it. I'm sorry you
got wet."

"'Sall right," said Henry. "I'm glad you're safe."

"Stop in and see me, then—soon. Mother will want to thank you."

Henry looked into her eyes earnestly. "I will," he said abruptly. "Good night" He shook her hand swiftly and turned away.

"Good night, Mr. Jones—and thank you," she called after him.

The plight of Henry Jones in facing his astonished wife that evening might well have alarmed a far more expert evader than he. All the way home he planned what he should say to Martha.

He ended by telling part of the literal truth but none of the actual truth: that he had met a friend and gone in a canoe, and they had upset and never, positively never, would he ever go out in a canoe again.

And Martha, when her first shock of surprise was over, had laughed. Henry never knew whether she believed him or not. For she said nothing, but put him to bed at once—without the pill, since he declared earnestly that the evening's exercise had made him feel much better.

After this first rapturous adventure, Henry's soul-malady grew rapidly worse. And with its development came a corresponding ability for dissimulation with his wife. He ate his meals; he discussed with her the petty details of his business, and entered into her own gossip of the neighbors; just as he always had. But underneath it all a seething torrent of emotions possessed him, threatening every moment to tear away the anchor of his life and hurl him adrift. And Henry did not care. He did not have the least idea for what he was headed; he never stopped to reason it out. He only knew he was happy—riotously, wonderfully happy—and free—free in spirit at last.

Now I would not have you believe that all this happened to Henry's soul that first day. It did not. It progressed onward with steady growth over a period of nearly a month.

Henry developed, after that first evening, a sudden passion for billiards; and later for poker, which he told Martha some friends were starting as a twice-a-week little game. And Martha had listened to his swaggering statement that "a man must have some vices," with inscrutable eyes, and let him go. Perhaps now she fathomed—in part at least, for she was wiser far than Henry—the malady with which he was suffering. And so she did nothing, but waited; which you shall see was perhaps the wisest thing she could have done.

Henry called upon Miss Morton some ten times that month—always in the evening. Miss Morton, it appeared, was living with her mother for the summer only, in this tiny cottage which they had rented. They had been in it hardly more than a month, and fortunately, neither during that time nor subsequently during Henry's regular evening visits, had either of them needed to purchase a pair of shoes at Dale's.

About himself Henry was reticent. What he told of his affairs was fictitious but plausible. Miss Morton having few friends in the neighborhood, seemed hospitably to welcome his calls. Upon the occasion of his second visit, he had told her frankly, but with some embarrassment, that he had never been in a canoe before that first evening with her. And he was still more confused, and a little hurt, when he showed not the least surprise at his confession.

"But I want to learn, Miss Morton," he added earnestly. "Won't you teach me?"

Miss Morton would. And so began the series of canoe rides and lessons with which their friendship developed to its climax, and Henry's soul underwent its next and final great change.

You are to picture Henry, then, on this momentous tenth evening, sitting very erect and manly upon the stern seat of Miss Morton's canoe, in his shirt-sleeves, his forearms bared, hatless, and with his hair rumpled and pushed straight back—almost, but not quite, covering his bald spot. Miss Morton herself lay at his feet in the bottom of the canoe on a pile of cushions—her golden hair nestling against one of flaming red, and her baby blue eyes looking up into Henry's face. And Henry was supremely happy—an unreasoning, turbulent happiness—as with long, swift strokes he sent the canoe skimming over the shimmering silver lake.

The moon overhead hung in a cloudless, starry sky; a soft, gentle summer breeze fanned his flushed face. Distant music from a talking machine on one of the cottage porches floated distinct across the lake. Henry looked at the girl's gracefully reclining figure with a heart too full for words.

"I love the sound of music over water, don't you?" asked Miss Morton softly.

Henry let his paddle trail idly in his left hand. A sudden madness possessed him. He leaned down and put his other hand over the girl's as it lay in her lap.

"I love you—Elsie," he said huskily.

Miss Morton gasped; she stared for an instant into Henry's flushed, eager face with its pleading eyes. Then she laughed.

"Why you—you funny little fat man," she cried.

Henry withdrew his hand as though from a red-hot stove.

"No—no, I didn't mean that. Oh, I'm sorry—really, I am, Mr. Jones. I didn't mean to hurt you—really I didn't. But you are funny, you know, when you talk like that." The girl poured out the words swiftly. Her tone was contrite, but the merriment did not die out of her eyes.

Henry sat up very stiff and straight, staring out over the glistening water.

"I didn't know it was funny," he said; the words came hardly above a whisper. "'Sall right, Miss Morton. Only—I didn't know it would be funny."

His eyes, with a dumb, hurt look in them like the look of a wounded dog, fell to hers an instant. Then in silence he turned the canoe and paddled back to her home.

Let us not pry too deeply into Henry's feelings that terrible night. They can be imagined, but they cannot be told. He did not close his eyes until dawn, but sat propped up in bed, staring blankly across the moonlit little bedroom. Once in the middle of the night he became aware that his wife was not asleep, but lying wide awake watching him.

As he turned to face her, she put her hand gently upon his.

"What is it, dear?" she asked softly.

"'Sall right," said Henry. He felt the answering pressure of her hand. In the dim moonlight, her face suffused with love and tenderness, seemed suddenly very beautiful. "'Sall right, Martha. I was just thinking. You go to sleep."

Thus, in the gray light of dawn, in the agony of disillusionment, and with his sleeping wife's hand in his, Henry Jones faced and solved his great problem. The change—for like all the rest it was only a change in him—came gradually. The turbulence of his thoughts slowly calmed; the ache in his heart grew less.

And then, clear and shining as a beacon light this new idea, this new feeling, rose in his mind. He seized it, lingered over it, gazed at it from every aspect. And then came a great sense of rest and peace stealing over him. He sighed, gripped his wife's hand tighter, and fell into a dreamless sleep.

At breakfast next morning Henry was abnormally cheerful. Martha made no reference to his long vigil the night before, nor did he. But his eyes followed her around with a strange light, and his usually pink face was flushed even pinker with excitement.

After breakfast as he started for the store, he kissed her good-bye with extraordinary enthusiasm.

"If it's a good night tonight I've a surprise for you," he said mysteriously. With which cryptic remark he turned abruptly and left the house.

The weather was perfect that evening—a full moon in a cloudless sky, and only a gentle breeze.

Refusing explanation, Henry led his wondering wife immediately after supper directly to the public boat-house at the lower end of the lake, hardly more than a mile from their home.

"I took the morning off," was all he would say. "I bought something for you as a surprise."

Into the boat-house he took her, expectant and thrilled, and there he proudly displayed a tiny green-painted canoe, lying upon a little platform that sloped down into the water.

"For you, Martha," he said. "I bought it for you today."

"Oh, Henry, a canoe for us!"

"I bought it for you—this morning. Don't you see, Martha—that's what I've been doing all these weeks—learning to canoe so I can take you out."

"Oh, Henry—dear!" Martha put her hand timidly upon his arm.

"I'm an expert canoeist, now, Martha—you'll see."

In the dimness of the boat-house he put a sturdy arm about her waist; he could feel she was trembling.

"I'll take you out now," he went on. "Wait—I've got some cushions."

He was back in an instant with his arms full of pillows, which he tossed carelessly into the canoe with the paddles. Then with ostentatious skill he slid it down into the water, and tenderly placed his silent, trembling little wife in the bottom upon the cushions, so that she would be at his feet as he sat in its stern.

Out upon the lake he paddled with lusty strokes, straight into the shining ribbon of moonlight. Martha lay quiet, gazing up at him as he silently bent to his work. Music floated to them over the water. Another canoe passed, with a boy and girl in it—a girl who reclined in the bottom playing a guitar. Henry—with a great consciousness of equality—waved to them in friendly greeting.

Then all at once he shipped his paddle and leaned down to his wife, letting the canoe slip forward unguided. Her eyes were wet and shining; her hand stole upward to meet his.

"Life and—and everything is wonderful, isn't it, dear?" said Henry Jones.

THEN LUCK CAME IN,
by Andrew A. Caffrey

Originally published in Adventure, Nov. 15, 1928.

The sergeant was a much abused man. Wartime flying had not used him any too well; nor had after the war aviation done any better. Now he was nearing the end of his Army career.

The sergeant had wanted to fly. He wanted to go solo and do his own birding. It had always been his one ambition. And it was through no fault of his own that the big desire had never been fully realized. Fact is, along those lines the much abused sergeant was without fault. He had always done his share.

The sergeant was too willing in 1917. Later—too late—he realized this. Had he held off, as the other millions did, and waited for the war to get at good speed, he would have made his way into a ground school and started right. But the sergeant did not know that there were to be such schools. None knew this. So the sergeant enlisted. Willingly the aviation branch of the Signal Corps took him. Oh, yes, of course, they said he would fly.

But the sergeant turned out to be a handy mechanic. Good mechanics were few—and are still—so the sergeant, though he didn't guess it, was never going to get to fly.

On the other side of the pond his bad luck continued. That was when they made him a sergeant, made him a sergeant, chief airplane rigger, while they made flying cadets of the goldbricks in his squadron. That hurt—hurt like—well, it hurt.

"But look here, Sergeant," his commanding officer said in rebuttal, "now let's be reasonable; it takes years to make a good mechanic. And only hours to *lache* a full fledged pilot; and the stuff of which airmen are made need not know anything—or much. See the point? You're important on this field; these other birds going out as cadets are, as a rule, culls we're glad to be rid of. Now get back to your hangar and feel satisfied that you are doing your bit, and a hell of a big bit, Sergeant!"

That line of official chatter did not help the sergeant at all.

"I've heard it before," he told his rigging crews. "Doing my bit! Bit be damned! The effect of my first patriotic drunk has worn off. What I want to do is fly and I'm going to!"

The sergeant did learn to fly; but he "stole" the flying time, begged all the dual control instruction he could mooch and waxed mighty handy on rudder bar and stick. And he learned quickly. You see, like many other mechanics, he really knew how to fly before he ever had a ship in his hands. Once in the air he merely had to gain the feel of the thing. And he got it too. He made a takeoff on the third hop, landed on his fifth.

His job was on a pursuit field—all single seater planes. The ship on which he had learned—a Nieuport 23—was a two place visitor. He was all set to fly alone. Then, that same day, they took the 23 away. The sergeant saw red, and spoke in the same color.

"Cheated again!" he said. "I'm going into town, get all drunked up and take an M.P. apart! Wait and see!"

* * * *

You can not get the sergeant's point of view unless you have loved air and wanted to fly. But if you had loved air and wanted to fly, you would have gone to town with him and helped take a flock of M.P's apart.

Unofficially grabbing flying time wherever and whenever he could get any, the sergeant lived in hopeless hope, if such a thing exists. But our war lasted only a day; and once gone it was gone forever. The sergeant's field did not go directly out of business, with the coming of the Armistice, but his interest in things did. For him it was the end of everything—and nothing.

Then, with the idea of training more pilots for future wars, headquarters sent the sergeant's squadron on to an Avro, two place, training field. The sergeant's interest came back. He stole lots of time, loved Avros and added acrobatics to his straight flying. The war after the war was treating him better.

New made flying cadets came to that field. Lord! Where did they get such dubs? The sergeant wondered. From every orderly room at the center was the answer. It was a dog robbers' holiday.

"I'll get the C.O.'s permission to turn you loose, Sergeant," an instructor said. "You can fly rings round any bird in this group. I'll get papers through for you too; no reason why you shouldn't get a brevet. I understand that they've handed commissions to a few 31st men."

The sergeant said that they had.

For a night, life couldn't be improved upon.

Next morning, February 12, headquarters "washed out" all flying and called in the Avros. They say that the sergeant took a lieutenant of M.P's apart at high noon of the same day in the public square at Issoudun. After that, for him, the world fused.

The sergeant's outfit came back to the States. Air Service wanted to hold some of its best mechanics. At Mitchel Field they promised the sergeant and some of his gang that, were they to reenlist for another stretch, flying would be their dish for sure.

The sergeant took his discharge. Then he was tempted—and fell. He put up his hand for another hitch. And headquarters shipped him to Carlstrom Field, Florida.

* * * *

New classes of cadets came to that field. Even one of the cooks from the sergeant's overseas squadron was among them. They were the worst cadets the sergeant ever saw. But he worked planes for them; and in turn, headquarters never did put the sergeant on flying status. But the much abused one continued to mooch some unofficial airwork. So the months of his one year enlistment dragged by and he came toward the happy end, the end which was going to be so welcome because he did not give a good, bad or indifferent damn. And he told his C.O. as much when that worthy asked him whether he intended to sign up for a third cruise.

"You're not talking to me, Lieutenant," the sergeant said. "For three years I've lived on hope. When I took on this reenlistment, they promised me, on a stack of Bibles, that I'd fly. And have I?"

Any number of ex-overseas men could answer this.

"But this time you will," the lieutenant said. "This school has the ships and men now, and I'll promise you—"

"Tie that outside, Lieutenant," the sergeant answered, "I've heard it all before. By this time next Monday afternoon, America will have one more civilian on her hands. And she's going to collect a mean problem, too. I'm sore, Lieutenant. I've been cheated too often to smile and turn the other cheek. This deal I've had handed me by Air Service smells like a eucalyptus kitty— See that guy climbing into that rear cockpit—" the sergeant pointed to a plane at the deadline—"well, that same jaybird used to be a bum cook in my outfit overseas. Shane's his name. All that feller ever did for American honor was lap up French booze and make trouble. He was our ace of aces at it, too. Shane and me, Lieutenant, have been two different kinds of soldiers, but today he's getting in official flying time and I'm still begging rides like a raw John Recruit. Where's your damn' justice in that? I'll answer—out for lunch with two rags around her eyes! Me, reenlist? In a pig's eye! Wonder what's wrong with that plane."

The plane into which they had watched Cadet Shane climb had started for a takeoff, bounced into the air, fluttered a few rods and dropped again for a hasty landing. It taxied back to where they were standing. It was one of the sergeant's ships. At the deadline the instructor, Lieutenant Black, swung from his front cockpit, removed his goggles and said:

"Wish you'd look this ship over, Sergeant. The controls jam in the air. Bob Watts was flying it this morning and he had the same trouble."

"I'll work her over," the sergeant promised. He looked at his watch. "Four o'clock now," he said. "You won't want to fly any more today, Lieutenant. She'll be jake in the morning."

"That's O.K. with me, Sergeant," Lieutenant Black agreed, and walked away with the sergeant's C.O.

Cadet Shane was sore. He had been robbed of his afternoon period and did not care who knew that he was burned up.

"Damn' funny you guys can't keep ships in condition," he said. "I haven't had two hours' airwork outa this hangar in two weeks."

"Too damn' bad about you, Shane," was all the sympathy the sergeant extended. "If you're as rotten a flyer as you were a cook, the field will be the winner if you never fly."

* * * *

For the next hour the sergeant, with a helper, worked the ship that went wrong in the air. At the end of said time he had located nothing wrong with the controls. Bob Watts came along during operations and told his story. Then, just to be on the safe side, the sergeant sent for the field inspector, Blackie Milander. He came along and demanded—

"Wot's eatin' you, kid?"

"This crate, Blackie, was turned in because her controls froze in the air," the sergeant said. "I've looked her over, and my fair haired helper here has looked her over, and Lieutenant Watts was on hand and had his say and look, and we find nothing wrong. The control cables, all of 'em, are O.K. Not a fray on any of them. The ball socket joint is jake; and the pulleys are free. Now, you give her the expert eye, Blackie, and say what's to be done. Gladly we pass the buck to you and, if failing, you muff the torch thus thrown, well you'll get burnt."

Blackie, working till long after retreat, scratched his head finally and announced:

"Damned if she ain't got me stopped! On the ground here, everything's free. D'you know what I think, Sergeant?"

"If a thought there be, Blackie, shoot before it burns you out. What do you guess?"

"I think that Watts and Black are full of hop! There's nothing wrong with this pile of wreckage, and I'll give her a clear bill. Let me O.K. that flying sheet."

When the hangars opened in the morning the sergeant's C.O. was at hand.

"What did you learn about that plane of Black's?" he wanted to know. "Anything haywire?"

"Not a thing, Lieutenant," the sergeant admitted. "What say if you and I give it a hop right now? See if we can locate any 'bugs' in the air."

"We'll do that little thing," the C.O. agreed. "Got a helmet and goggles I can use?"

While the C.O. waited, and the men started the plane's motor, the squadron clerk came to the hangar for the C.O. They talked for a few minutes, then the C.O. told the sergeant:

"I'll have to call this flight off for now. There're some papers for me to sign. I'll see you later."

Fifteen minutes before the first cadet class reported for the nine o'clock period, Lieutenant Black came to the line. The sergeant told the lieutenant all that he had not learned.

"But I don't want to pass the buck too crudely," the sergeant concluded. "What's the matter with us two going up in the thing and learning what's to be learned?"

What the sergeant wanted was more airwork. He would have taken his flying on the tail end of a rocket were no other means offered. The fact that a ship's action was in question meant nothing to him. More than likely the sergeant was glad that nobody had been able to locate the kink; test flying is always to the liking of a real lover of air. The betting's even that the sergeant had planned this moment during the previous night. As he talked, he talked Black toward the waiting plane. The instructor was adjusting helmet and goggles, and his silence gave consent.

"It's funny," he finally said, as they waited for the motor man to warm the engine, "but those controls did jam. I don't want any of my cadets to get in dutch through mechanical faults. They're bad enough without that. The Lord only knows when I'll be able to turn any of them loose. Such an iron fisted bunch of shovel apprentices I've never met. They wouldn't't've made good K.P.'s. for the wartime *kadets*.

"And these damn Jennies have got to be right, Sergeant. As right as they can be, and if they were twice as right as that, they'd still be all wrong. Climb in and we'll take a turn of the field."

* * * *

While they were adjusting the safety belts, Cadet Shane came running along the line of hangars. He scrambled aboard Black's lower wing and talked into the instructor's left ear. Black throttled his motor low, pushed back his goggles, thought for half a minute, studied his instrument board dials, shook and kicked his controls, then turned to the man in the rear seat and said:

"Sergeant, I'm going to give the cadet his hop. These controls seem to be O.K. Chances are, there was nothing wrong with them.

"Jump out, Sergeant, and I'll let you know how they act. Watch my first turn of the field and see how I'm getting along. Climb in, Shane! Let's get going!"

The sergeant went back to the hangar. He wasn't talking to anybody, for the time being, but he hurled an open can of red paint the length of the big building and said to a few idle privates—

"Clean that up!"

Then, where a group of flying cadets were busily rolling two small cubes on a work bench, the sergeant came down in hot wrath, threw the harmless squares through the skylight and yelled—

"Get to hell out of this hangar and stay out!"

After that the sergeant went out, retrieved the dice and reestablished the game. He told the cadets that he was sore about something but could not recall just what. After sending the privates off to goldbrick in the post exchange, the sergeant mopped up the paint.

Master Sergeant Sciples, in charge of the hangar, came along to start the day. Sciples was spending this enlistment on the construction of certain souvenirs. And at no time did he allow hangar work to cut in on his program. He was an easy boss. Sciples looked at his sergeant rigger and came out in language that lay people erroneously suppose is solely characteristic of the Marine Corps. Here and there, without half trying, Master Sergeant Sciples could extemporize in a manner that would make the Marine Corps' glossary look like a first reader for morons. Sciples' language, to say the least, was able.

"Sergeant," he said, "one look at you, you tells me that you haven't had your morning flight. When will you forget this flying stuff and put your mind on next week's debut into the outer world? Why, you— Snap into it and get wise!"

"But, Sciples," the sergeant said. "It's the same old story. The same thing that I've been up against for three years. And it makes me mad, Sciples. Hell, if I live to be a hundred, I'll never lose this desire to fly. It's different with you, you old decrepit"—the sergeant was never entirely tongue tied himself—"You don't care about flying. The bug's never grazed upon you. You don't know the hell and pain and longing that an egg like me faces, Sciples. Why, Sciples, this thing of giving a right arm for something is nothing. I'd do another stretch in this damn' Army if I really thought that I'd aviate. And that is what I call bravery."

"Crazy as a loon!" Sciples exclaimed. "Why you—you don't know enough to—"

"And this was the most cruel thrust of all, Sciples," the sergeant went on, "this thing that came off half an hour ago, why—" The hangar's telephone rang, and Sciples, with the sergeant still talking, strolled toward the instrument—"why, there I was all set to take off with Black. Had myself nicely planted in the rear seat, and who comes out and robs me but my ex-cook, that rotten cook, Shane, and—" There were tears in the thick voice.

For a minute Sciples talked over the line. In the end he said, "Well that's hell," and hung up.

"What's hell?" the sergeant forgot his own troubles long enough to ask.

"Cadet Shane," Master Sergeant Sciples said, "Shane, the man who unseated you, Shane and Black spun into the ground ten miles from here. They both burned to death."

TOO MUCH PROGRESS FOR PIPEROCK,
by W.C. Tuttle

Originally published in Adventure, April 30, 1922.

I never seen anything like her before—not alive. One time I found a piece of an old fashion magazine, and there was a picture of a female in that—a female that some feller drawed; but I just figured that it was all imagination with him. I take one look at this live female and then I takes off my hat to the artist.

She said she was an artist. What in —— anybody could find to draw in Yaller Rock County—except guns—was more than I could see. Me and "Magpie" Simpkins was down at Paradise, setting in Art Wheeler's stage, when she got on, headed for Piperock.

Art got one look at her and then jackknifed his four horses in trying to turn around and go the wrong direction. Magpie Simpkins never took his eyes off her. Magpie's old enough to know better, but he didn't seem to. Art's eyes don't foller the road much, with the result that he runs a front wheel off Calamity grade and danged near sends us all to our final destination.

She said her name was Henrietta Harrison. Art pulls up for a breathing spell at Cottonwood Crick, and we stops in the shade of a tree. She looks at the big tree and then she says—

> *"Under the greenwood tree*
> *Who loves to lie with me,*
> *And tune his merry note*
> *Unto the sweet bird's throat———"*

"Me," says Magpie, kinda foolish-like.

"You!" snorts Art. "Tune your merry note! Haw! Haw! Haw! You could 'lie———'"

"Mebbe you could!" says Magpie, mean-like. "But your wife wouldn't let yuh."

"Set down, you ancient he buzzards!" I yelps. "Ain't yuh got no sense?"

"I don't understand," says Henrietta.

"Nobody does," says I, consoling her. "If we did, we'd know whether to lynch 'em or send 'em to the loco lodge, ma'am."

"Magpie makes me tired," declares Art. "Any time he wants to tune his note———"

"It's my note, Mister Wheeler. If I want to tune my own note———"

"I was merely quoting Shakespeare," says the lady.

"Giddap, broncs!" says Art Wheeler, and we rocked on into Piperock.

I'll tell you right here and now; beauty ain't even skin deep in Piperock. We've got wimmin folks—that is, some has—but nobody ever kidnaped any of 'em.

If they belonged to me I'd trust 'em with any man.

There's Mrs. "Wick" Smith, who jars the hay-scales to two hundred and seventy-five, and wheezes plentiful. Art Wheeler's better half tasted of life and found it sour, and never got the acid out of her system. Mrs. "Testament" Tilton looks upward for guidance in all matters except when it comes to flattering Testament's head with a skillet. When Mrs. Pete Gonyer is in sight, Pete's voice sinks seventeen inches below a whisper. Somebody remarks one day that Pete's kinda henpecked.

"Henpecked, ——!" says Pete. "Orstrich—if there ain't nothin' bigger what wears feathers."

Mrs. Steele, the wife of our legal light, is six feet two inches tall, and she's always oratin' about the sanctity of the home, whatever that is. One cinch, the prize never hands down any decisions in his own home.

Mrs. Sam Holt goes through life worrying about somebody alienating the affections of old Sam, who can barely hear himself yell, and has to eat his spuds mashed or miss the taste of 'em.

There's the Mudgett sisters, who must 'a' been the originals of the first cartoon of "Miss Democracy." Cupid would have to use a .30-30 if he went to work for them. Scattered around the range is a occasional female, but nothing that you'd bet your money on in a beauty contest. Annie Schmidt is cooking for the Triangle outfit, but the same don't seem to cause any of the other ranches to go short of help.

Henrietta Harrison horns into Piperock. Piperock takes a deep breath. Bad news travels fast, and it ain't long before there's a need of another hitch-rack in Piperock. Sam Holt runs the hotel—or thought he did; but Ma Holt got one look at Henrietta and shut up the book.

"Every room is taken," says she.

"Who by, Ma?" asks old Sam.

"Me!"

"Ma'am," says Magpie, "I reckon mebbe Mrs. Smith will take a boarder."

Wick said she would. Wick locked up his store and took the valise in one hand and Henrietta's elbow in the other, kinda rubbing Magpie and me out. We sat down on the sidewalk intending to speak unkindly to Wick when he came back, but Henrietta came back with him. Wick sets the valise down on the sidewalk.

"Ma said she was goin' to have company, and won't have no room."

"This Summer?" asks Magpie.

"I ain't no hand to argue," says Wick.

Pete Gonyer comes over, and Magpie asks Pete about taking a boarder.

"Y'betcha," says Pete. "Pleasure's all mine. Mrs. Gonyer'd be plumb tickled stiff. Live all your life with us, ma'am."

Pete almost stands on his head, bowing and scraping like a ground-owl; but just then Mrs. Gonyer comes down the sidewalk, but Pete don't see her.

"Pete!" she snaps.

"My ——!" gasps Pete. "The rope broke!"

Mrs. Gonyer looks at Henrietta and then at Pete.

"I run out of horseshoes," says Pete. "I had to come to the store——"

Pete goes on into the store and Mrs. Gonyer follows him inside.

"I must find a place to board," says Henrietta, kinda sad-like.

"Eatin' part's easy," says I; "but it begins to kinda look like yuh might have to hive up under that greenwood tree."

"I'll take her in before I'll let her sleep under a tree," says Magpie.

"You'll take her in?" says I. "You mean, we'll take her in, don't yuh? Half of that cabin is mine."

"It was my idea, Ike."

Just then Testament Tilton and his wife drives into town. Testament is a sanctimonious-looking old pelican. He looks at Henrietta, and his lips move, but I know they don't move in prayer.

"Miss Harrison needs a place to stay," explains Magpie. "Have you folks got any extra room?"

"Brother Magpie, we have," says Testament. "We have."

"Where?" asks Mrs. Tilton.

Testament turns and looks at her kinda queer-like for a moment and then back at us.

"That's the question," says Testament. "I thought we had room, but where is it?"

"Well, get out of the wagon," says Mrs. Tilton, nudging Testament. "Me and you have got to do shoppin'."

"I think it is an insult," says Henrietta. "I've half a notion to leave."

"I've got a —— good notion to leave with yuh," says Magpie.

"Let's make it a trio," says I.

"What are you insulted about?" asks Magpie.

"I ain't so danged particular that I'd mention any one little thing."

"I came here to recuperate," sighs Henrietta. "I escaped from every one and went to one country where they would never expect to find me, and I am not welcome, it seems. I thought I might find a new theme in the wild dances of aboriginal tribes. That sort of thing is new and original, I think."

"I think so too," nods Magpie. "They sure do dance wild around here."

"Often?"

"Every time we can find somebody what can call a quadrille. Round dances don't go very good, 'cause there's always some woman accusin' her husband of huggin' some other man's wife———"

"I don't mean civilized dances."

"Neither do I," agrees Magpie.

Then cometh "Muley" Bowles, "Chuck" Warner, "Telescope" Tolliver and Henry Peck, the four disgraces of the Cross J outfit. Muley, the poet, is too fat to work. Telescope, the tall thin tenor, is too proud to work. Chuck Warner wiggles his flexible ears, lies fluently to every one, and proves an alibi every time "Jay Bird" Whittaker, his boss, tries to make him work. Henry Peck has kind of a dumb way of going through life, and plays a banjo.

They sees us and don't lose no time getting off their broncs and investigating. Muley takes a look at Henrietta and swallers real hard. Telescope stumbles over Chuck's foot and almost falls into her.

"Will you introduce me?" asks Henrietta.

"Well'm," says Magpie, "Miss Harrison, I makes yuh used to Muley, Telescope, Chuck 'n' Hen. They're jist common or ordinary cow-punchers. Cowboys, meet Miss Harrison, a artist."

"T' meetcha," says Telescope. "Mr. Simpkins misinformed yuh, ma'am. My name is Tolliver—one of the Kentucky Tollivers, ma'am."

"Oh!" says she.

"I'm named Bowles," wheezes Muley. "One of the Oklahoma Bowles."

"His paw was a famous man," says Chuck. "He'd 'a' been greater, but the posse roped him just short of the State line. I'm named Warner—a name made great by some doctor who built a patent medicine. Pleased to meetcha."

"Speak up for yourself, Hen," urges Magpie. "Tell the lady about yourself."

"I'm named Peck," says Hen. "I can't think of any smart thing to say today."

"I am Miss Harrison. For a reason," says she, "I am incognito."

"My ——!" gasps Telescope. "Is that so? I used to know a family of that name. They was Eyetalians—or Mexicans. Good family though."

"I detest a *nom de plume*," says she, smiling.

"Me, too," agrees Muley. "I never had one, but the looks of one was a plenty for me."

"The lady can't find a place to live," says Magpie. "Nobody is willin' to sleep her."

They lets this soak in, and then Telescope says—

"What's the matter with her?"

"Nobody got any room."

"My trunks will be here tomorrow," says she.

"Female drummer?" asks Hen.

"I?" says the lady, kinda dignified-like. "I am an arteest."

"Oh—yeah. Kinda like what, ma'am? Do yuh paint?"

"I dance."

"By cripes!" grunts Muley. "We'll give a dance."

"I—I am an interpretive dancer," she explains.

"Oh, yeah," nods Telescope. "I see."

"You're a kindly liar," says Chuck, "because you don't see nothin'. Ma'am, I'm plumb ignorant of the word you used."

"Why—I—er—do nature dances, don't you know?"

"Nature? Oh, yeah."

"Oh, yeah," mimics Hen. "You see just like Telescope did, Chuck."

"I—er—really, I do not believe I can explain it to you," says she. "Unless you have seen one done, it is difficult for the lay mind to grasp——"

"That's a word I've been tryin' to get for years," says Magpie. "Every time I've looked at this Cross J bunch I've tried to think of a word to describe their mentality. I thanks yuh for the word 'lay mind,' ma'am. Them four snake-hunters sure have that kinda minds."

"It ain't the hoochie—" begins Hen.

"It ain't!" yelps Telescope. "The lady never said nothin' about muscles. Henry, your horns are gettin' too long."

"Clip 'em, cowboy," challenges Hen. "Start clippin' and see which one of us gets dehorned first. You've got a pretty fair spread yourself. If the lady don't do that kinda dances it's her lookout, ain't it? Yuh don't need to whoop about it. I noticed yuh down at Silver Bend at the circus——"

"Now have a little sense," advises Magpie. "You pelicans are too danged anxious to show off before the lady. You fellers spillin' lead up and down the street ain't gettin' her a place to lay her head, is it?"

"If she only wants to lay her head—" begins Chuck; but Muley steps on Chuck's ankle and shoves him aside.

"Ma'am, I apologizes for my friends. They mean well, but they ain't got no sense. Now, it appears to me that you are lookin' for a place to sleep."

"It took that idea a long time to appear to you, Muley," says Magpie. "Jist in what shape did you get this here bright vision? I don't think that Piperock needs any assistance from the Cross J cow-outfit

194

when it comes to housin' our guests. I'll take care of Miss Harrison, y'betcha."

"Can't she get a room at Sam Holt's place?" asks Chuck, serious-like.

"Ma Holt," says Magpie, winking at Chuck; "Ma Holt says that every room is full."

Chuck wiggles his ears at Magpie and then looks over toward the hotel. Then he grins and says:

"You wait, will yuh? I *sabe* the cure for that."

Chuck goes over to the hotel, and in a few minutes him and old Sam comes over to us. Old Sam says—

"Ma'am, we've got a vacancy and can sleep yuh fine."

Chuck grabs her valise, and him and the lady and old Sam beats it for the hotel.

"Now, what in —— did Chuck do to cause such a condition?" wonders Magpie.

"Chuck lied," declares Muley. "The son-of-a-gun lied; but what did he lie about?"

Naturally none of us knowed, so we went over to Buck's place and had a drink. We waited around for Chuck, but he didn't show up; so me and Magpie went home. I said "home," but it wasn't home any more. Magpie got dissatisfied right away.

"Hawg-pen," says he. "Anybody could tell that hawgs lived here. Lawd never intended for men to live alone this away."

"You living alone?" I asks.

"You don't count, Ike. A man like me kinda pines for the soft things of life."

"Mush?"

"Mush! Naw-w-w! Always thinkin' of your belly, Ike. A woman don't mean nothin' to you."

"I don't mean nothin' to her, Magpie; so it's fifty-fifty. Have you gone and fell into love again? Why, you danged old gray-backed pack-rat!"

"Age ain't no barrier to happiness, Ike. It ain't kind of you to point out a man's failin's thataway. Love knows no barriers."

"Nor nothin' else, Magpie."

Magpie Simpkins is about six feet and a half in his socks, and he's built on the principle of the thinnest line between two points. He's just got hips enough to hold up his cartridge-belt—if he's careful. His face is long and his mustaches look plumb exhausted from just hanging down past his mouth. His mind is full of odds and ends that never fit into anything.

A ordinary man in love can be handled, but Magpie ain't ordinary. Love is quicksand and no help in sight to that *hombre*. I've herded him past several affairs of the heart, liver, and lungs, but each time the attack is harder. The D. T's are a cinch beside what that pelican suffers when the little fat god of love stings him with a poisoned arrow.

Mostly always I hangs a extra gun to my belt and fills my pockets with rocks. Listen to reason? Say, that feller's ears don't hear nothin' but "love, honor and obey"—that, and the church bells ringing.

I went to bed that night, leaving him setting on the steps, talking to himself about the gentle touch of a woman's hand. I asked him if he remembered the one what "touched" him in Great Falls. There wasn't anything gentle about that one, being as she took his watch and three hundred dollars. That was another case of love at first sight, and then he went blind.

As I said before, bad news travels fast. The next day is Sunday, but that ain't no excuse for every puncher from Silver Bend to Yaller Horse to come to Piperock. I don't think that the Cross J bunch went home Saturday night.

Sam Holt never sold so many breakfasts before in his life. Some of them hair-pant specimens ate two or three times. Muley Bowles comes back to Buck's place with his belt in his hand, and groans when he tells me that he thinks he got ptomaine poisoning for breakfast.

"You done et three orders of ham and aigs," says Hen.

"You say 'ham and aigs' to me again and I'll massacree yuh, Hen."

Magpie comes back from breakfast and acts kinda sad-like.

After everybody is back from breakfast, old Sam Holt shows up. The bunch kinda crowds around him.

"I has to come away," informs Sam. "Ma's goin' t' feed the strange lady, and she won't allow nobody in the dinin'-room."

"Won't allow nobody in the dinin'-room?" parrots Telescope.

"She has her orders," grins Sam. "Only one man is allowed to see her."

"One man?" asks Magpie. "Sam, who is that there man?"

"Why, Chuck Warner, of course."

"Chuck Warner, of course," nods Magpie, like a man talking in his sleep.

"Chuck Warner," wheezes Muley. "Of course."

"Of course," says Telescope. "Chuck Warner."

Then we sets around and looks at each other.

"Chuck Warner?" says Hen, like he was trying to remember somebody by that name.

"Works for the Cross J outfit," says I. "Kind of handsome *hombre*. You must remember him, men."

"Oh-o-o-oh, yeah," nods Telescope, fussing with his gun. "Chuck Warner."

Magpie gets up, yawns and walks slow-like out of the door. Art Miller kinda saunters out, and then Telescope seems to desire fresh air. Muley kinda groans and starts to get up, but them three orders of ham and aigs has sort of depressed him, and he sinks back into his chair.

He takes out a piece of paper and a pencil and begins to write. You've got to hand it to Muley when it comes to poetry. In about fifteen minutes Magpie, Telescope and Art drifts back, and the three of 'em lines up at the bar.

"Here's hopin' he breaks a leg," says Magpie.

"Or splits a hoof," adds Art.

"Who yuh wishin' all such luck to?" asks Hen.

"Chuck Warner," says Telescope. "He's—Ma Holt wouldn't let us in, but we peeked in the winder and seen Chuck dancin' a war-dance for the lady."

"I'll dance for her!" says Muley. "I'll dance Chuck's scalp for her. Why won't Mrs. Holt let anybody in?"

"She's got her orders," says old Sam.

Just then "Scenery" Sims, the sheriff, comes in. Scenery is a squeaky little runt, and suspicious of everything and everybody. Magpie gets right up, takes Scenery by the arm and leads him outside.

"Now," says Telescope, "what kind of a frame-up has Magpie got under his hair?"

We hears Scenery say—

"Aw-w-w, is that a fact, Magpie?"

Magpie nods and jerks his head toward Holt's place. Scenery nods, and they starts for the hotel, with me and Telescope, Art, Muley, Hen, "Half-Mile" Smith, "Doughgod" Smith, "Tellurium" Woods, "Mighty" Jones and Pete Gonyer.

Magpie leads Scenery to a window of the dining-room, and they both peers in. Scenery looks at Magpie, kinda queer-like and nods his head. Then he tries to go in the door, but it's locked. Mrs. Holt comes to the door and scowls at Scenery.

"You can't come in," says she, and starts to shut the door; but Scenery shoves a foot inside and blocks it.

"Mrs. Holt," squeaks Scenery, "yo're defyin' the law. Actin' that-away puts yuh liable for contempt of court."

"Well," says she, kinda dubious-like, "mebbe that's so, Scenery. I'll let you in, but the rest of you snake-hunters'll have to stay outside."

"We bows to superior intelligence, ma'am," says Magpie.

In about a minute here comes Chuck Warner with his hands in the air, and behind him marches Scenery with a gun poked into Chuck's back. Chuck looks at us and says—

"What's the matter with this —— fool?"

"Head for the jail!" squeaks Scenery. "Head for the jail!"

"You're crazy!" wails Chuck.

"All right, all right," squeaks Scenery. "We've both headed th' same way."

Henrietta Harrison comes to the door, but Mrs. Holt shoves her back inside and shuts the door.

"Poor Chuck," says Magpie. "Poor Chuck."

"Poor, ——!" howls Chuck. "I'm goin' to kill somebody for this."

"Gettin' violent, Scenery," says Magpie. "Don't take a chance."

"I'll handle him, Magpie. Point for the jail, you scalp-dancin' id-jit."

Chuck took one look at us, and then headed for the jail, with Scenery trottin' along after him.

We all went back to the saloon. Pretty soon Scenery comes from the jail, and he's got a beautiful black eye where Chuck walloped him. Scenery is peeved. Old Judge Steele shows up, kinda ponderous-like, and Scenery explains the whole thing as far as he knows.

"*Loco parenthesis*," says the judge. "Reverted to sex. I always knowed there was aboriginal corpuscles in his arterial system. He is *non compos mentis*."

"*Lignum vitæ*," nods Magpie.

"Exactly," says the judge. "You stated the case, Magpie. Who is the lady in the case?"

"Name's Incognito," says Telescope. "Incognity, *alias* Harrison."

"Hah!" says the judge, serious-like. "This will need *finesse*. I shall go over to the hotel and have speech with the maid."

I reckon he got in in the name of the law, too, but anyway he got in. Me and Muley went out and sat on the sidewalk, when here comes Mrs. Steele and Mrs. Wick Smith.

"Have you seen anything of the judge?" asks Mrs. Steele.

"Yeah," nods Muley. "He went over to Holt's to see a lady."

"Oh!" says Mrs. Steele, looking at Mrs. Smith.

"Men," says Mrs. Smith, "men are considerable alike, and a judge ain't no different than the rest."

"That old cormorant?" explodes Mrs. Steele. "The only difference is—he's worse."

"We've got to unite," says Mrs. Smith. "A united front must be showed. Let's go and talk to Mrs. Tilton before Testament falls from grace."

They toddles up the street, headed for Tilton's place. But Old Testament wasn't home. I reckon he was kinda snooping around, 'cause he comes out from behind Pete Gonyer's blacksmith shop and walks up to us.

"What was them womin talkin' about, Brother Ike?" he asks.

"They've gone up to hold a war-talk with your wife, Testament. Appears that there's a united conspiracy against the lady what come yesterday. They've gone to warn your wife, I reckon."

"Love's labor's lost," says Testament, sad-like. "She don't need warnin'. Where is said lady?"

"Her and Judge Steele are holdin' a conference over in Holt's place. Yuh might go over and add your spiritual presence, Testament," says Muley.

"I might," nods Testament. "I'm sure ready and willin' to pass spiritual advice. A man of spiritual knowledge is always needed."

Testament's last words were kinda faint, as he was hittin' the trail to Holt's front door.

"Paw," says Muley, sad-like, "Paw wanted me to study for the ministry. Seems like a minister can git into places where a cowpuncher can't."

Mrs. Holt met him at the door and let him in. Pretty soon we sees Mrs. Steele, Mrs. Smith, Mrs. Gonyer, Mrs. Wheeler and Mrs. Tilton. They comes down the sidewalk toward us. Me and Muley starts to go into the saloon, but Mrs. Tilton yelps at us—

"Henry Peck, do you know where my husband is?"

"He—he's givin' spiritual advice to a lady," says Muley.

"I suppose Pete Gonyer is measurin' her for a pair of horseshoes," says Mrs. Gonyer, mean-like.

"And maybe Wick is tryin' to sell her a bill of groceries," says Mrs. Smith.

"I seen Art curryin' his horses," states Mrs. Wheeler. "He ain't curried one of 'em since he owned them four horses—and he greased his boots this mornin'."

"Here comes Mrs. Holt," says Mrs. Steele. "Mebbe she brings news."

Mrs. Holt was all out of breath, and them women didn't seem inclined to let her get any of it back. Magpie and Telescope comes out of the saloon and moves in close.

"I hopes to die!" gasps Mrs. Holt. "I hopes to die!"

"You're got a cinch," says Telescope. "We all have to."

Them females gives Telescope one gosh-awful look, and then surrounds Mrs. Holt, who gasps out her story.

"She—she's dancin' for Testament and the judge—barefooted!"

"No!" declares five female voices at once.

"Yes! Her and the judge has a long talk and I heard 'em. She tells him that Piperock don't appreciate art."

"My Art?" asks Mrs. Wheeler.

"I don't know. Lemme talk, will you? The judge said he longed for the day when Piperock would become the greatest place on earth, and he said she had a good start right now. This here female opines that we're fifty years behind the times. She asks him why folks don't wake up around here. The judge says they're just waitin' for the right person to come along and set the alarm. She says she's the greatest dancer in the world.

"She wants to show off, but the judge says that all Piperock ain't as intelligent as he is and mebbe they'd not see things in the right light.

"Then Testament Tilton comes in. The judge introduces them two, and explains about her bein' the greatest dancer on earth. Testament Tilton says he's originally from Missouri. Then he laughed like a danged hy-e-ner. I don't like to say that about a preacher, but——"

"Speak your mind, sister," says Mrs. Tilton. "I like your description."

"Well," continues Mrs. Holt, "I had to go away for a few minutes, but when I got my eye to the crack of that door again I hears the judge sayin'—

"'Testament, I reckon the rest of the country will kinda set up when we lets 'em know that Piperock is going to exhibit the greatest dancer in the whole danged world, eh?'

"Then Testament says:

"'Brother Steele, you've said a lot in them few lines. Your idea of givin' this under the auspices of my church is goin' to make a hit with the womin folks. That takes the curse off.'

"Just then this here female shows up—barefooted."

Mrs. Holt stops for breath.

"Can she dance? asks Mrs. Smith, wheezin' quite a lot.

"Well—" Mrs. Holt looks around at us, and swallers real

hard—"well—Mrs. Smith, I reckon we better go over to your house to tell the rest of it."

They went across the street like they was afraid they'd get wet.

"I'll never eat another meal in Sam Holt's place again," declares Muley. "I'll get even with her by boycottin' her husband."

"I'm goin' home," says I. "The peace and quiet of Piperock is about null and void, and I need solitary communion with my pet hunch. Somethin' tells me that all is not well. In fact somethin' tells me that all is not only not well, but in danged delicate health."

Nobody can read Piperock's mind, but I've seen disaster come and go, and my personal prognostications are about on a par with a weather man prophesyin' fair and warm in Death Valley.

I'm cookin' supper when Magpie shows up, and the blasted idiot is grinning from ear to ear. He pours coffee over his potatoes and puts sugar on his bacon and then begins to talk.

"The rhythm," says he, "the rhythm of nature is a wonderful thing, Ike."

"Yes," says I. "It must be."

"The breeze of Spring; the waving of the branches of a tree. True poetry, Ike. The human form divine is the only thing capable of ex-pressin' these here e-motions."

I takes out my gun and puts it beside my plate.

"Magpie, there's a curse on you, and you might as well spill it all now. I'm not interested a danged bit, but any old time you starts out bobbin' from flower to flower I knows what's comin'. Spread your hand."

Magpie smiles at me and then shoves back from the table.

"Ike, here's where we jump fifty years ahead of Paradise and Curlew. We has hung to the old order of things too long. We has be-come moth-eaten and stale. Don't yuh know we have?"

"Anything would—hung up for fifty years, Magpie."

"We still dance quadrilles and waltzes, the same of which went out of style with flint-lock muskets. Now, we sheds the scales off our eyes and comes out of our shells into the dawn of a brighter day. Piperock entereth a reign of classical dancing, Ike.

"Miss Harrison is goin' to elevate us, but we have to give her our able assistance. There seems to be a female sentiment against her here; but that's plumb natural, bein' as we're in a rut and don't know no better. Judge Steele and Testament Tilton has seen her dance. Them two are real progressive, Ike, and they sees the possibilities.

"Testament Tilton says it's got anythin' beat he ever seen, and he's had his eyes open for sixty-six years. Miss Harrison says she'll teach

Piperock the rhythm of motion and then give a show for the benefit of the church. She's gotta have a class of five to start with, and after them five has learned all about it they can each take a class of five. See how it's done?"

"Has she picked her class?"

"I picked 'em for her, Ike. She kinda leans on me."

"Might better 'a' picked a fish-pole. Who'd you pick?"

"Me and Pete and Wick Smith and Art Wheeler and you."

"I ain't ripe," says I. "You better put me back on the tree."

"She wanted you, Ike. Mentioned you right off the reel. Said she wanted a representative group. Well, I got 'em, didn't I? Everybody wanted to help, but five was all we could use."

"Is Chuck still in jail?"

"Nope, Chuck's mad. Yuh see, he told Mrs. Holt that him and Miss Harrison was goin' to get married, and he wanted Mrs. Holt to take care of her and see that none of the men came near her. Chuck was showin' her some Injun dances, and it was a good chance to get even with him for lyin' all the time. Mrs. Holt was willin' to take her in, bein' as she was to marry Chuck.

"Testament has talked Mrs. Holt into keepin' her until this here church benefit is over. It's goin' to be a e-leet affair, I'll tell a man. Nothin' like it has ever been thought about before, Ike. This is one time when Piperock shines as a social center and abolishes her rough career."

When it comes to dancing I sure have always shook a wicked hoof, but this kinda stuff had me hoppled. You take two or three little running steps ahead, stop and wave your arms in the air, and kick out behind like a mule. Then you duck to one side, whirl around, lift up your arms again and go hippety-hopping around the place, kinda singing—

"Tra-la-la—, tra-la-la, la, la."

That represents a little zephyr of Spring, you understand. There was five little zephyrs in our Spring. We zephyred around and around. Miss Harrison said we was getting the idea. Then she had us zephyr alone, while the other four little breezes set down and made smart remarks. There was considerable feeling aroused during this lesson.

Five little zephyrs took her back to the hotel, and then one little zephyr went home and packed up his burro. That one little zephyr had a vision of a big blow coming and wanted to get out of the road.

Magpie tried to plead with us, but me and the mule remained firm. Magpie's voice was full of tears, but I shook my head, packed my jassack and went to live a while with "Dirty Shirt" Jones, who lives several miles away from the center of disturbance.

Dirty Shirt ain't neither sane nor sanitary, but he appreciates me a heap. Dirty is cockeyed, but he believes in handing you bokays while you are yet in the land of the living and not waiting until you are ready for your weight of sand.

Dirty squints at me and says:

"I know you'd show up, Ike. It's about time for Piperock to make a fool of itself again. What's itchin' the old town this time?"

"Interpretive dancing."

"Oh yeah. I don't know what in —— that is, Ike; but it sounds like Piperock might adopt it. Magpie's the ring-leader, ain't he? Sure."

Dirty knows Piperock as well as I do. For a week I helped him on a copper prospect, and not a word of Piperock's doings percolated into our happy home.

Then Dirty got dry. When Dirty Shirt gets dry there ain't nothing short of sudden death will stop him this side of Buck Masterson's place.

Therefore we packs our burros and pilgrims to the city of Baal, as Testament calls it every Sunday. Testament has just got two sermons. One is on temperance and the other is on the evils of strong drink.

We has to pass Mighty Jones' place on our way in, and we finds Mighty settin' on his wood-pile, playing with a coyote pup. He squints at us.

"Goin' to Piperock?"

I admits our ultimate destination.

"Better go home. Testament Tilton says that Piperock is goin' to run a dead heat with Sodom and Gomorrah, whatever pair of horses them two is."

"What's the matter with Piperock?" asks Dirty.

Mighty hitches up his pants and spits very expressive-like.

"High-toned. Yessir, Piperock is gettin' uppity—part of 'em, and the rest are packin' two guns per each. Tonight means trouble in that town, y'betcha."

"Tonight? Why tonight, Mighty?"

"Social affair tonight, that's why. Two dollars per ticket, and not a gun allowed into the hall. I've got a ticket, which I'll sell yuh."

"Goin' to save my money for ca'tridges," grunts Dirty, and we pilgrims on.

We went right down the street of Piperock, looking neither to the right nor left, and heads straight for Magpie's cabin. Looking into the open door we sees Magpie bending over the cook-stove, frying meat.

"*Klahowya*," says Dirty.

Magpie drops the pan on the floor and whirls with a gun in each hand.

"Dancing makes you jumpy?" I asks.

Magpie shoves his guns back inside the waistband of his pants, kicks the hunk of meat into the skillet and turns back to the stove.

"How's Miss Harrison?" I asks.

Magpie turns and squints at me.

"She's gone, Ike."

"De-mised?"

"De-parted."

"Kinda busts up the show, don't it, Magpie?"

"Like —— it does!"

"How comes she to de-part thataway?" asks Dirty.

Magpie flops the meat and sets it on the back of the stove. Then he sets down on a bunk and combs his mustache.

"You ain't heard, have yuh, Ike? No. Well, here's the how of it all. You left hereabout the time that all the married womin are faunchin' around, organizin' a vigilance committee to hang their own husbands, didn't yuh? Well, Wick and Pete and Old Testament and Art Wheeler and Judge Steele decides that Piperock and posterity needs 'em more than jealous wives do, so they up and orates that for th' interests of the furtherance of Piperock they're goin' to stick to their original idea of learning the latest thing in dances.

"Them womin combines against such proceedings, and locks their doors against said husbands, with the result that we puts up bunks in the Mint Hall for all them errant husbands. Miss Harrison hangs on to her room at the hotel and Mrs. Holt enlists with the belligerent wives and hives up at Judge Steele's.

"Inside of three days them husbands are plumb anxious to go to their wives, but wifie has nailed the front door shut. Them there dancin' lessons has improved us wonderful, Ike. I gets old Sam Holt to dance in your place.

"Then we finds out somethin'.

"Judge Steele goes sneakin' around home late at night after our lessons, and he peeks under the curtains in his house, and he sees Miss Harrison teachin' them womin to dance, and the judge swears that they ain't got enough clothes on to flag a hand-car.

"The judge so forgets himself that he raps on the window, and he gets a lot of bird-shot sprayed into the seat of his pants.

"Miss Harrison has double-crossed us, and the next night we chides her about it. She gets kinda woolly and informs us that the ladies invited her to teach them so they could do their part in the performance. She was teachin' 'em the 'Dance of the Raindrops.'

"'My——!' grunts Wick. 'My wife ain't no raindrop.'

"'I ain't goin' to permit Mrs. Tilton to appear in no mosquito nettin' and bare feet—not in public,' declares Testament.

"Things got kinda deadlocked, Ike. The tickets are all sold for the performance, and the church realizes over two hundred dollars. Me and the judge goes as a committee to confer with Mrs. Smith and Mrs. Tilton, and they refuses to arbitrate. They opines that what's good enough for their husbands is good enough for them. Mrs. Tilton says:

"If Testament can wear a gee-string and imitate a willer-tree, why can't I wear a porous-knit undershirt and imitate a drop of rain?'

"What could we do? We went back and held a council of war. Pete said he'd be —— if his wife was goin' to be a spectacle. They all declared that they wasn't goin' to let the world at large gaze upon their property in the rough. Miss Harrison declares that it must go through. There yuh are, Ike.

"Miss Harrison was taken to Paradise this morning and was put aboard the train. Art Wheeler drove the stage, and Pete Gonyer, Judge Steele and Testament Tilton acted as shotgun guards. Our premier dancer has went."

"Which busts up the show, eh?" says Dirty.

"Not while Magpie Simpkins roams the plains, it don't. Piperock is goin' to get a look at interpretive dancin', y'betcha. How much civic pride has you two snake-hunters got?"

Me and Dirty don't say a word, being as we don't *sabe* his wauwau. Then he hauls out a jug of pain-killer and we sets down to do homage.

After all danger from drought is a long time past, Magpie points out the duty of a real honest-to-grandma citizen. He orates openly that the future of a city is only as broad as the inhabitants will allow. He asks Dirty Shirt if his views are narrow.

"Wide as the ocean, and beggin' to expand," says Dirty.

"I'm the widest human bein' yuh ever seen, Magpie. Dog-gone me if I ain't wider than anythin' anybody ever seen. How about you, Ike?"

"'I've got you skinned about four ways from the jack," says I, and somehow I believed it.

Magpie got in between us and took Dirty's gun away from him.

"Killin' ain't expansion," explains Magpie. "Piperock has entertained too many times in the interests of the undertaker. Piperock is so far behind the times that the seventeenth generation of Montana's human race has started and finished and we're still runnin' the wrong way of the track."

"Are we that far behind the rest of the world?" asks Dirty, tearful-like.

"Further," assures Magpie.

"Then let's be up and doin'," urges Dirty. "My ——, I never realized that we was runnin' in the dust. How does we start in to speed up the old buggy?"

"I," says Magpie, "I am the little jigger who is goin' to lead Piperock to th' promised land. I am the pelican which is goin' to make Piperock a place of honor and glory and a social center. I has been throwed down by the best citizens, you know it? Puttin' their personal feelin's ahead of the best interests of the city, they has laid down upon their labors, willin' to let poor old Piperock slumber and waller in the dust of decay; but the womin can see what it means to the city, and they're firm as rocks. I have got one of the best dances yuh ever seen, gents.

"The ordinary poetry of motion is the weavin's of a drunken Siwash with a sprained ankle beside this here dance of mine. Miss Harrison said it had anythin' beat she ever seen."

"Do yuh have music for this kind of dancin'?" asks Dirty.

"Well, kinda," assures Magpie. "Frenchy Deschamps' jew's-harp and Bill Thatcher on his wind-pipe. Bill bought it a short time ago. Said that ever time he got a bull-fiddle busted it cost him ten dollars for a new one; so he buys him a wind-pipe. If anybody shoots holes in that thing he can patch it up."

"That's a new instrument on me," says Dirty.

"That's it," says Magpie. "We're so far behind the times, Dirty, that we don't recognize things that the rest of the world has been usin' for years."

"My ——!" wails Dirty. "This is awful, Magpie. I'm grateful to yuh for callin' my attention to same. Ain't you grateful, Ike?"

"Remains to be seen, as the feller said when he dug into a Injun grave."

"Ike's grateful," says Magpie. "Ike's the gratefulest human bein' on earth."

"That ain't no ways true," objects Dirty. "I'm the most gratefulest."

I gets between Magpie and Dirty and makes 'em put up their guns. Then we all took a last look at the inside bottom of the jug of pain-killer.

Piperock appreciates art, there ain't no question about that. There's fellers in town for this social event that ain't been outside their dug-outs since the big blow. Plain and fancy horse-thieves, unsuccessful rustlers, hairy old shepherds that says "Ya-a-a-ss" and "No-o-o-o," just like a sheep, and others too numerous and or'nary to mention.

Scenery Sims is setting in front of the Mint Hall with a sawed-off shotgun on his lap, but he lets us in.

"How does she look, Scenery?" asks Magpie.

"Well," squeaks Scenery, "everythin' is all right so far, but them ex-dancers is all back from Paradise. The women is all up there in the hall now. Bill Thatcher is drunker'n seven hundred dollars, and somebody has hit Frenchy in the mouth and kinda crippled his part of the orchestra. Shouldn't be s'prized if there'd be buzzards circlin' Piperock in the mornin'."

We went up into the hall, which is all fixed up for the social doings. They've got the stage all curtained off and the room is full of chairs. Mrs. Smith, Mrs. Tilton, Mrs. Gonyer, Mrs. Holt, Mrs. Wheeler and Mrs. Steele are there. Magpie leads me and Dirty up to the stage and in behind the curtain.

"My ——!" gasps Dirty. Sheep!"

"There's four sheep tied up back there—all rams."

"Sheep—yes," agrees Magpie. "Them is what Miss Harrison calls 'atmosphere.'"

"At—— Oh, my!" gasps Dirty. "What's she mean, Magpie?"

"Accessories to my dance," explains Magpie. "I'm the star performer in 'The Shepherd's Awakening.'"

"What do we do?" asks Dirty.

"You fellers are fauns."

"I'm the old buck deer—me," declares Dirty. "You're more cockeyed than me, Magpie, if you can see me with four spindle legs and a spotted hide."

"A faun," says Magpie, "a faun is a thing that looks like a human bein', but ain't. It wears skin pants, but from there on up it's plumb nude. On its head is little horns, and it's got a tail like a goat. It plays a tune on a wooden whistle."

Me and Dirty looks at each other, kinda foolish-like.

"I think it's lovely of you two gentlemen to step in the breach," says Mrs. Tilton.

"Step in the—oh—!" croaks Dirty, wild-eyed. "This is terrible!"

"It will be a big thing for Piperock," says Mrs. Gonyer, "and it will teach the male sex that the women are the real progressives. Don't you think so, Mr. Harper?"

"There's goin' to be a lesson taught," says I. "Experience is a great teacher, but I ain't never learned much. I thought I was wise, but I finds that— Well, I ain't never wore a tail like a goat and blowed on a wooden whistle yet."

"I hope that Testament's skin pants will fit Mr. Harper," says Mrs. Tilton. "Mr. Harper is a little wider across than the Reverend."

"Mr. Jones will be a little snug in Sam's," opines Mrs. Holt, "but he don't have to do only one little dance."

Dirty's bad eye rolls a complete circle and then stops with a dead center on the tip of his nose. He grabs me by the arm and flops down in a chair.

"Ike," he gasps, "Ike, shoot me while there is yet time."

"Shoot yourself—you've got a gun," says I.

"I know it, bub—but I'm so nervous I'd miss."

Dirty just sits there and sweats.

"Them sheep—has they been trained?" I asks.

"They've been here two days," says Magpie. "They ought to be used to the stage."

Sudden-like we hears a crash down-stairs, the sound of loud voices raised in anger, and then up the stairs comes Judge Steele, Wick Smith, Pete Gonyer, Art Wheeler and Sam Holt. They've got Scenery Sims in their clutches, and he's squeaking like a rusty gate. They files into the door, and Magpie greets 'em with a gun in each hand.

"Come ye in anger?" asks Magpie.

"Kinda," admits Pete. "This whangdoodle tried to stop us."

"Put your hands up!" snaps Magpie, and the whole gang reach upward. "Take their guns away, Scenery."

"Now," says Magpie, "what's eatin' you backsliders?"

"Ma-a-a," wails Testament. "You ain't aimin' to carry out your threat, are ye?"

"I'm goin' to dance—if that's what you mean," says Mrs. Tilton, mean-like.

"Arabellie, does you mean that you womin—" begins Wick.

"Wick Smith, you started this," says Mrs. Smith. "You told me I was narrer. You said I was fifty years behind the times, didn't you?"

"That —— Magpie Simpkins put them words in my mouth, Arabellie."

"I won't stand for it!" yelps Pete. "No woman of mine can———"

"Pete, you shut your face!" whoops Mrs. Gonyer. "If you don't want to see me imitate a raindrop—vamoose. I sure am goin' to rattle on the roof."

"I'll git out a injunction," says Judge Steele. "By mighty, I'll declare it a public nuisance! I'll stop this here——"

"You'll set down and keep your face shut," says Magpie. "You five pelicans are goin' to set right down and look and listen. Has you all got tickets?"

None of 'em has bought a ticket, and they opines they won't.

"Scenery," says Magpie, "take two dollars from each of 'em."

Them five arose up an yelped like a pack of wolves, but Scenery got ten dollars out of the bunch, and then we made 'em take front seats.

We hears some gosh-awful sounds coming up the stairs, and into the door comes Bill Thatcher. He's got one of them Scotch windpipe instruments and it's wailing like a lost soul. Behind him comes Frenchy Deschamps. Neither of 'em are in any shape to make music for anything except a dog-fight, but they flops down in their chairs at the front of the stage and acts like they meant business.

Scenery recovers his sawed-off shotgun and sets down on the corner of the stage, where he can watch them disgrunted husbands.

Me and Dirty follows Magpie to a place he's got partitioned off for a dressing-room. Through the curtain we can hear Yaller Rock County beginning to come in. Me and Dirty are just sober enough to kinda be indifferent to death or taxation.

Magpie gives us our costumes, which consists of cowhide pants with a tail tied on, and a jigger made like a cap, with yearlin' calf horns sticking out the side. He also gives us each a little whistle made of a willer.

"Where's the shirt?" asks Dirty.

"Fauns don't wear shirts."

"What do you wear, Magpie?"

Magpie holds up a mountain-lion skin and a breech-clout. Dirty looks things over and then says to Magpie:

"If you escape, Magpie, will yuh do me a favor? In my cabin—in a old trunk, is a suit of clothes. I paid sixteen dollars for it the year Bryan run for free silver, but I never wore it. Will yuh see that they lays me out in it? Lawd knows I don't want to be buried in a outfit like this."

From outside we hears "Fog-horn" Foster's voice—

"We-e-e-ll, come on, you mockin'-birds!"

"The house must be full," opines Magpie, fastening his lionskin.

"Full of hootch and ——" sighs Dirty, sliding into his cow skins. "I'm goin' to die like a —— cow, I know that."

"My gosh!" grunts Magpie. "I've plumb forgot we ain't got no announcer since the judge quit. Ike, will you do the announcin'?"

"Then I won't have to dance?"

"Sure you'll have to dance, but all you've got to do, Ike, is to tell 'em what is comin' next. The first thing on the program is a solo dance, which is knowed as 'The Gatherin' Storm,' by Mrs. Smith; and then she gets assisted by the five 'Raindrops,' consistin' of Mrs. Holt, Mrs. Tilton, Mrs. Steele, Mrs. Gonyer and Mrs. Wheeler. Mrs. Smith is doin' the solo in place of the departed champeen dancer of the world. Will yuh do this for me, Ike?"

"Do it for Magpie," urges Dirty. "Do anythin' to get it over."

I went on to the stage, and I got the shock of my life. Them females are out there, and I'm a danged liar if they ain't undressed about as much as possible. I takes one look and staggers for the curtain. I hears one of them women bust out in a "haw! haw!" as I went past, but I never stopped to think that I wasn't wearing any more than the law allows.

I steps out through the curtain and looks around. Never did the old hall hold as many folks. Fog-horn Foster and Half-Mile Smith are settin' in the front row, across the aisle from each other. They stares at me for a moment; then both gets up like they was walking in their sleep, steps for the aisle and bumps together.

Fog-horn hit Half-Mile and Half-Mile hit the floor, after which Fog-Horn went right on up the aisle. Half-Mile got up, looks at me again, and follers Fog-Horn, but he ain't tryin' to catch Fog-Horn—he's tryin' to go past him.

"My ——" gasps "Cinch" Culler, lookin' wild-like around. "Won't somebody please hold me? I won't be responsible——"

"Ladies and gents," says I. "I'm out here to let yuh know what's comin' off."

"Wait a minute," says Abe Mudgett, standing up. "I've got my two sisters here with me, and if anything more's comin' off——"

"Set down!" squeaks Scenery, waving his shotgun at Abe, and Abe sets down.

"Now," says I, "I'm out here to announce that the first thing on the program is Mrs. Smith. She's goin' to imitate a storm comin' up, and then Mrs. Holt, Mrs. Tilton, Mrs. Wheeler, Mrs. Steele and Mrs. Gonyer are goin' to show yuh what raindrops look like. This here——"

"Haw! Haw! Haw!" roars Pete Gonyer, but his laugh don't show that he's tickled so awful much.

"Haw! Haw! Haw! Mrs. Smith is goin' to imitate— Haw! Haw! Haw!"

210

"Haw! Haw!" howls Wick. "My wife looks as much like a storm as yours does like a raindrop, Pete."

"My wife," states the judge, standing up, "my wife ain't goin' to do no —— fool thing of the kind. I'll show her——"

"Set down!" yelps Scenery. "Set down, you old Blackstone blatter! This is once when you don't hand down no decisions."

"Git off the stage and let 'er rain!" howls Telescope Tolliver. "I'll see it through if I have to wear a slicker."

"Ready for us to play?" asks Bill Thatcher, kicking Frenchy to wake him up.

"Use your own judgment, Bill," says I. "I've done all I can, and now I'm goin' to let nature take her course."

I starts to step back through the curtain, when "Polecat" Perkins yells—

"Ike, I was wrong—you're only half-cow."

I gets back inside. Them women are all scared plumb stiff, but Mrs. Smith wheezes—

"Ladies, we've made our bluff—let 'er go!"

Just then Bill Thatcher's instrument begins to wail and wail, shutting off all chances for Frenchy Deschamps to be heard.

"Sweet Marie!" howls Mrs. Smith. "Gee cripes, don't he never learn a new tune?"

I ducks out of sight and the curtain slides back.

If Mrs. Smith knew anything about dancing she forgot every step. She trots out on the stage and starts something like Kid Carson used to call "shadow-boxing." Then she turns around about three times, stubs her toe and falls down. Standing in a line across the stage is the rest of them females, with their hands up in the air like they was being held up by somebody with a gun.

"A-arabellie!" wails Wick. "My ——, woman, git out of sight!"

Mrs. Smith gets to her feet and yelps back at Wick:

"Git out of sight yourself—if you don't like it! I'll teach you to flirt with a dancer. Start the music over again, Bill."

"Em-m-m-i-lee!" shrieks Sam Holt. "Ain'tcha got no modesty? Go put on your shoes and socks!"

Bill Thatcher starts squealing on his instrument again, and Mrs. Smith starts doing some fancy steps.

Wow! Here comes Judge Steele, Art Wheeler, Pete Gonyer, Testament Tilton, Wick Smith and Sam Holt, climbing right over the top of folks.

"Git ba-a-a-ck!" squeaks Scenery, waving his shotgun. "Stop it! Whoa, Blaze!"

"Look at the wild man!" howls somebody, and here comes Magpie across the stage hopping high and handsome.

"Stop 'em, Scenery!" whoops Magpie. "Dog-gone 'em, they can't bust up my show!"

Man, I'll tell all my grandchildren this tale. Them outraged husbands came up on that stage, while Yaller Rock County yelled itself hoarse and made bets on whether it would be an odd or even number of deaths. Magpie hit Pete in the neck and Pete lit with one leg on each side of Bill Thatcher's head. Wick Smith got hold of his wife and them two started a tug of war.

Me and old Sam Holt got to waltzing around and around, which wasn't a-tall pleasant, being as I'm barefooted and Sam ain't. I seen Mrs. Wheeler and Art locked in mortal combat, and just then I hears Dirty Shirt Jones yelp—

"Heavy, heavy hangs over your head—"

I whirls just in time to see what's coming, but I can't escape. Dirty Shirt has turned the atmosphere loose. Them four he-sheep—four ungentlemanly woollies, with corkscrew horns, are buck-jumping across that stage, seeking what they may hit. I swung around to meet the attack, and I reckon the leading sheep hit him a dead center, 'cause I felt the shock plumb to me.

Maybe it hit Sam a little low, because it knocked all four of our feet off the floor, and the next in line picked us in the air and stood us on our heads.

I seen Wick Smith, braced against the edge of the stage, trying to pull his wife over the edge, the same of which is a invitation to a sheep, and the old ram accepted right on the spot. Mrs. Smith grunted audibly and shot into Wick's arms. Scenery Sims starts to skip across the stage, but a ram outsmarted him, and I seen Scenery turn over gracefully in the air and shoot, regardless, with both barrels of that sawed-off shotgun.

Them load of shot hived up in the chandelier, the same of which cut off our visible supply of light.

I heard the crashing of glass, and I figures that the hallway is too crowded for some of the audience. I lays still, being wise, until the noise subsides, and the crowd has escaped. Then I moves slowly to my hands and knees. I feels a hand feeling of my legs, and then a hand taps gently on my horned cap.

"I—I thought," whispers old Sam's voice kinda quavering-like, "I—I thought they was all old ones, but a sheep's a sheep to me."

Bam! Something landed on my head, and I seen more bright lights than there is in a million dollars worth of skyrockets. Then things kinda clear up, and I hears old Sam saying to himself:

"Well, I killed one of the —— things. If I go carefully——"

I can dimly see old Sam sneaking for the front of the stage. I'm mad. I got up and sneaked right after him. No man can mistake me for a sheep and get away with it. I jumps for old Sam's back, and just then he seems to kinda drop away from me. I reckon he forgot about the five-feet drop from the stage, and I know danged well I did. I reckon I sort of lit on my head and shoulders on top of somebody. There comes a squeak from Bill Thatcher's instrument, and then all is quiet.

I wriggled loose and starts to get up, but a strong hand grabs me by the ankle, yanks me off my feet, and I hit my head on a chair. I kinda remember being dragged down them stairs, and then I feels my carcass being dragged over rough ground. It was a long, hard trip, and I reckon I lost about all the skin on the upper half of my body. Finally I bumps over a step, gets yanked inside on to a carpet, and then I hears a voice very dimly—

"Sweetheart, I brought thee home."

Then a light is lit, and I sees Mrs. Smith putting the chimney on a lamp. Without turning she says—

"I reckon you'll confine your love to me after this, eh?"

Then she turns and looks at me, setting there on the floor with my back propped up against a chair. I looks around. Just inside the door, sitting on the floor, is Wick. Mrs. Smith looks at me and then at him. Then she wipes her lips and stares at Wick.

"Sweetheart, eh?" grunts Wick, getting to his feet. "Arabellie, ain't you got no shame? Dancin' up there without nothing on to speak of, and then you has the gall to bring your sweetheart home with yuh."

"Did—did—didn't I—bring you home, Wicksie?"

"You—know—danged—well—you—didn't. I always knowed you was kinda sweet on Ike Harper."

"On that!" She actually yelped, and pointed her finger at me. "Sweet on him?"

I gets to my feet, but my legs ain't very strong. I says:

"Lemme a-alone. I don't want no man's wife's love—especially one what hauls me home by the ankle. When I git married I want a clingin' vine—not a pile driver."

I never did have much sense. A feller in my condition ought to keep his mouth shut and sneak away soft-like. I turns my head toward the door, and just then the weight of the world hit me from behind, and it was a lucky thing for that house that the door was open.

I landed on my hands and knees in the yard, with all the wind knocked out of my system. Wick has got some rose-bushes in his yard. Like a animal wounded unto death, I reckon I tried to crawl around on my hands and knees to find a spot to die in.

All to once I sees one of them ——— sheep. It's only a short distance from me. I know if I move it's going to hit me sure as ——— so I remains still. I'll bet that me and the sheep never moved a muscle for fifteen minutes.

Then all at once the sheep spoke.

"For ———'s sake, if you're goin' to butt—butt and have it over with!"

I got to my feet.

"Get up, Dirty Shirt Jones," says I. "What kind of a way is that to act?"

Dirty weaves to his feet and stumbles over to me.

"Ike, thank the Lord, we're alive!"

"Don't presume too much. Medical science says that a man can live after losin' a certain amount of skin, but I'm bettin' I've passed that certain limit. Let's sneak home and save what life we've got left."

We sneaked around the Mint Hall and Wick's store, and at the corner we stumbles into somebody.

"Who goes there?" asks Dirty.

"Go ———!" wails Magpie Simpkins. "Help me, will yuh? I wrastled all the way down here with one of them ——— sheep and now I'm afraid to let loose."

"You and your———atmosphere!" groans Dirty.

"I'm settin' on it," wails Magpie, "I've got a kink in my neck. Will yuh hold it down until I can get up?"

Just then a voice from under him starts singing very soft and low—

"There's a la-a-a-nd that is fairer than this———"

Magpie gets to his feet and takes a deep breath.

"Testament," says he, "what made yuh blat like a sheep?"

But Testament's mind is not dwelling on sheep—not the kind of sheep that Magpie meant.

Then the three of us starts limping toward home.

"Mebbe," says Magpie, kinda painful-like, "mebbe we progressed too fast. Piperock don't appreciate it, gents, but this night the old town jumped ahead at least fifty years."

"Jumpin'," says Dirty, reflective-like, "Jumpin' don't hurt nobody, but, holy hen-hawks, it sure does hurt to jump that far and light

214

so hard."

We pilgrims along, everybody trying hard to make their legs track. Finally Magpie says—

"Personally, I think that interpretive dancin' has anythin' skinned I ever seen."

"Me too," says I, "and parts I never have seen."

INTO THE BLUE,
by F. Britten Austin

Originally published in The Blue Book, March 1924.

It was in a bitterly pessimistic frame of mind that, having seen my baggage into the hotel, I went for a first walk along the asphalted esplanade of Southbeach. I had no pleasure in the baking sun, in the glittering stretch of the English Channel that veiled itself in a fine-weather mist all around the half-horizon. The exuberant, bold-eyed flappers, promenading in groups of three or four, the vivid polychromatism of their taste in sports-coats, seemed to me merely objectionable. The hordes of worthily respectable middle-class families complete with children—with many children—that blackened the sands and overflowed into the fringe of the water oppressed my soul with their formidable multiplicity.

I thought, in a savage emphasis of contrast, of the neat little yacht that should now be bearing me across the North Sea to the austere perfection of the Norwegian fiords. And I cursed myself for the childish imbecility of exasperation with which—when, at the last moment, with my suitcases all packed, I had received a telegram informing me that the yacht had come off second-best in a collision with a coaltramp—I had picked up Bradshaw and sworn to myself to go to whatever place I should blindly put my finger upon as I opened the page. The oracle had declared for Southbeach—Southbeach in mid-August! I shrugged my shoulders—so be it! My holiday was spoiled anyhow. To Southbeach I would go. And now, as I contemplated it, I was appalled. What was I going to do with myself?

A paddle-wheel excursion-steamer came up to the pier, listing over with the black load aboard of her. Up and down the beach, in five-minute trips, a seaplane went roaring some eight hundred feet above the heads of the gaping crowd. I had done all the flying I wanted in the war, thank you very much. Other potentialities of amusement there were apparently none. If I could not discover a tolerably decent golf-course, I was a lost man.

I am not going to give the chronicle of that first day. It would be a study in sheer boredom. That night, after one of those execrable dinners which are the peculiar production of an English seaside hotel, I had pretty well made up my mind that—oracle or no oracle—I would shake the sand of Southbeach off my feet on the morrow. Sitting over my coffee in the lounge, I was in fact already consulting the time-table for a morning train, when my cogitations were suddenly interrupted by a violent slap on the shoulder.

"Hello, Jimmy!"

I looked up with a start, before my identification of the voice had time to complete itself.

"*Toby!*—Toby Selwyn—by all that's splendid!" It was years since I had seen him, but in this dreary desert of uninteresting people he came like an angel of companionship, and I welcomed him with delight. "Sit down, man. Have a drink!"

* * * *

He did so, ordered a whisky-and-soda from the hovering waiter. I looked at him as one looks at an acquaintance of old times, seeking for changes. I had not seen him since the Armistice, when our squadron of fighting scouts was demobilized and a cheery crowd of daredevil pilots was dispersed to the four quarters of the globe.

He had not greatly altered. His face was a little thinner, more mature. His hair was still the same wild red mop. His eyes—peculiar in that when he opened them upon you, you saw the whites all round the pupil—had still that strange look in them, as though somewhere deep down in them his soul was like a caged animal, supicious and restless, which I so well remembered. The reason for his nickname jumped back into my mind. It was from his little trick of suddenly and disconcertingly going "mad dog," not only when he swooped down, against any sort of odds, upon a covey of Huns, but in the mess. Some one had called him "Mad dog;" it had been affectionately softened to "dog Toby;" and "Toby" he remained.

"And what on earth are you doing here?" I asked.

He smiled grimly.

"Earning my living, old bean. Introducing all the grocers in England to the poetry of flying, at ten bob a head."

"So that was *your* machine I saw going up and down the sea-front today?"

"It was. Five-minute trips—two bob a minute, and cheap at the price. Had to do something, you know. So I hit on this. There are worse things. Put my last cent into buying the machine—ex-Government, of course. She's a topping bus!" His voice freshened suddenly with enthusiasm. "It's almost a shame to use her for hacking up and down like this. You must come and have a look at her."

"Thanks," I replied, "I'd like to, but—"

* * * *

Our conversation was abruptly interrupted. Toby had jumped to his feet. Coming in through the door of the lounge was—miracles never happen singly!—an only-too-familiar, smiling and middle-aged married couple and—*Sylvia*! Toby obscured me from them for an instant as he went eagerly toward them—an instant where I weighed the problem of whether to stay or bolt. The last time Sylvia and I had met she had told me, with a pretty sympathy that ought to have softened the blow, that she would always be glad to have me as a *friend*, but— The problem was resolved for me, before I could decide. Toby was leading the trio up to me.

"I want to introduce an old pal of mine—Jimmy Esdaile."

Mr. and Mrs. Bryant shot a swift smile at each other and then to me as we shook hands. Sylvia almost grinned. I felt a perfect fool. "Good evening, Mr. Esdaile," said Sylvia in her sweetest tones, her gray eyes demurely alight.

Mr. Esdaile! The last time, it had still been "Jimmy." It is true that since I had somewhat boorishly informed her, upon that occasion, that I had no manner of use for being her *friend*, I had scarcely a legitimate grievance if now she chose to be frigid.

"Wont you sit down, all of you?" I suggested. "Mr. Bryant, you'll take a Grand Marnier with your coffee, I know."

"Thanks, Jimmy, I will," said Mr. Bryant, seating himself. I saw Toby stare. His astonishment visibly increased as Mrs. Bryant, having comfortably disposed herself upon the settee, added in her motherly fashion: "And what in the world are *you* doing here, Jimmy?"

"That's what I'm asking myself," I replied. Toby cut me short in what might have been a witty answer had I been allowed to finish it.

"You people know each other, then?" he demanded.

Mr. Bryant smiled.

"Yes. We've met Jimmy before—haven't we, Sylvia?"

"He used to be an acquaintance of ours in London," corroborated Sylvia imperturbably, delicately underlining the word acquaintance.

Toby probed me with a peculiar look, suddenly almost hostile. I could guess that he was asking himself whether I had come to Southbeach in pursuit of Sylvia. One did not need to be a detective to discover his own eager interest in her. It was patent, with no attempt at concealment. Those strange hungry restless eyes of his seemed to devour her. Quite apart from any personal feelings—any time during the last six months I could have assured you, with perfect sincerity, that my heart was stone dead,—I didn't like it. Toby was not the sort of chap—

But I had no opportunity to intervene. Mr. and Mrs. Bryant, with a genuine kindly interest in me and my doings that at any other time I should have appreciated, monopolized me. And Sylvia flirted with him, demurely but outrageously. She called him Toby with the most natural ease in the world. He, poor devil, was awkward in an uncertainty whether she were playing with him, jerkily spasmodic in his answers, devouring her all the time with those strange eyes of his, wherein I recognized that same caged-animal look familiar to me as a preliminary to an outburst of "mad dog" on those nights when there was ragging in the mess. She, I could see, was enjoying herself at playing with fire.

* * * *

At last I could stand it no longer. I switched off from the amiable platitudes I was exchanging with her parents, interrupted her in her markedly exclusive conversation with him.

"I didn't know Toby was a friend of yours, Syl—Miss Bryant," I said.

She turned candid eyes upon me.

"Oh, yes, we have known Toby quite a long time—soon after you dropped us—nearly six months, isn't it, Toby?"

She took, evidently, a malicious pleasure in reiterating his Christian name. I messed up the end of my cigarette before I remembered not to chew it. Toby looked up suspiciously.

"I had no idea, either, that you were a friend of the family, Esdaile," he said. He also had dropped the "Jimmy."

Sylvia answered for me.

"Not exactly a *close* friend," she said sweetly. "Are you, Mr. Esdaile? We had almost forgotten each other's existence."

I could have smacked her.

Toby looked immensely relieved. I could see that, for the moment at least, he definitely put certain doubts out of his mind. He seemed to be trying to make up for his spasm of hostility when next he spoke.

"He's an old pal of mine, anyway, aren't you, Jimmy? It's like old times to see you again. D'you remember that little scrap with a dozen Huns over Charleroi? That was a good finish-up—the day before the Armistice."

I remembered well enough—remembered that after that last fight, at the very end of the war, I had landed by a miracle with my nerve suddenly gone. I had never been in the air since—for a long time could not look at an airplane without a fit of trembling.

Sylvia glanced at me in surprise. The secret humiliation of that finish had made me pretty close about my war-doings.

"Oh, you two knew each other in the war, then?" she said.

"I should rather think we did!" replied Toby. "Jimmy was my squadron-leader—and he's some scientist in the air, let me tell you." His tone of admiration smote me like a bitter irony. "Don't forget you're coming to look over that bus of mine tomorrow morning, Jimmy."

"I don't know that I can," I replied. "I'm off back to town tomorrow." I said this with a glance to Sylvia which found her quite unmoved.

"Are you, really?" she said. "What, on a *Sunday*?" Her eyebrows went up in mocking admiration for my courage.

Confound it! I remembered suddenly that tomorrow *was* Sunday. I can put up with any reasonable amount of hardship, but the prospect of a Sunday train on a South Coast railway!

"*Kamerad!*" I surrendered. "I go back on Monday."

"Good!" said Toby. "The tender conscience of the local munic-ipality does not permit them to allow me to earn my living on the Sabbath. Tomorrow is a *dies non*. We'll spend the morning tinkering about the machine together. It'll be like old times, before we went up for a jolly old scrap with the Hun-bird. She's worth looking at, too—built for a radius of a thousand miles and a ceiling of over twen-ty thousand feet."

"Really!" I said, with a touch old-time professional interest. "But what on earth do you want a machine like that for? She's surely scarcely suitable for giving donkey-rides up and down a beach?"

"She does all right," replied Toby. "And I like to feel that I've got something with power to it. That I could if I wanted to—" His curi-ous restless eyes lost expression, as though the soul behind them no longer saw me, contemplated something remote.

"Could what?" I challenged him.

* * * *

He came back to perception of my presence.

"Eh? Oh, nothing." He looked at me with that familiar sudden sus-piciousness which seemed to accuse one of attemped espionage into the secrets of his soul. I remembered that even in the mess, intimate as we had all been together, he had always been a queer chap. One had never really known what he was thinking or planning. He turned now to Sylvia.

"Miss Bryant has promised me that one day she will let me take her for a flight," he said, banishing the hardness of his eyes with that little smile of his which was so peculiarly attractive when he chose to exert his charm.

"I'll come tomorrow," she replied promptly. "And then you'll have to take me gratis."

"Of course I will!" he answered, clutching at her promise with a flash of eager delight in his eyes. "You didn't imagine I was going to charge you for it, did you? That's settled, then."

Mrs. Bryant interposed in motherly alarm.

"Oh, Sylvia! Don't do any of your madcap tricks!—You *will* be careful, wont you, Mr. Selwyn?" She turned to me. "Are you sure she will be safe with him, Jimmy?"

"My dear Mrs. Bryant," I assured her, "if there is a better pilot in the world than Toby, I don't know him."

Mr. Bryant took the pipe from his mouth and glanced cautiously at his wife.

"I'd rather like to go up too," he said.

But Mrs. Bryant vetoed this volubly and emphatically.

"No, no, no!" she exclaimed. "Not two of you together! Suppose anything happened!"

I smiled at her nervous fears.

"Nothing *will* happen, Mrs. Bryant—make your mind easy. Toby's perfectly safe. And if Mr. Bryant would like a flight, I'm sure Toby would be pleased to take him."

Toby was looking at Sylvia's father with his enigmatic eyes.

"Of course I will," he said. "But I don't want to worry Mrs. Bryant. I will take Mr. Bryant another time."

The conversation drifted off to other topics. At last, Mrs. Bryant rose for bed.

"And mind, Mr. Selwyn," she warned him smilingly as she shook hands with him, "I shall try hard to persuade Sylvia not to go."

"But you wont succeed, Mother!" announced Sylvia radiantly. "Good night, Toby. Good night, *Mr.* Esdaile!" With which parting shot she left us, and the lounge was suddenly horribly empty.

* * * *

We sat there for yet some time, Toby and I, puffing at our pipes in silence. He leaned back on the settee, with his eyes closed. I was thinking—never mind what I was thinking; but my thoughts ranged far into the dreary future of my life. My glance fell on him, scrutinizing him, probing him, weighing him, as he lay there all unconscious of it. About his feelings I had no doubt. Were they reciprocated? I remembered that peculiarly attractive smile of his, the alluring touch of mystery about him—and almost hated him for them. That was the kind of thing which appealed to women, I reflected bitterly.

He opened his eyes.

"'Puro è disposto a salire alle stelle,'" he murmured to himself, staring as at a vision where this somewhat gaudy hotel lounge had no place.

"What's that?" I said, not quite catching his words.

"Eh?" He looked at me as though he had forgotten my presence, was only now reminded of it by my voice. "Oh, that's the last line of the Purgatorio—where Dante, having drunk forgetfulness of the earth from Lethe, is ready to ascend with Beatrice into the stars of the Paradiso.... All right, Jimmy," he added, with a smile of sardonic superiority which irritated me, "don't worry yourself with trying to understand. You wont. You're one of those whose idea of the fit habitation for the divine soul shining through the eyes of your beloved is a bijou residence in a London suburb. After a few years of you, your wife, whoever she is, will be another Mrs. Bryant."

"Many thanks!" I replied, somewhat nettled, and a little puzzled also. This was a new Toby. We were not given to cultivating poetry in our mess. "But since when have you taken to studying Dante in the original?"

"Oh, I've had plenty of time," he answered, his eyes straying away from me evasively. "I've lived pretty much by myself these last few years." He rose to his feet, cutting short the subject. "Let's go for a stroll, shall we? Get a breath of fresh air into our lungs."

* * * *

I assented willingly enough. At the back of my mind was an obscure idea that, in the stimulated sense of comradeship evoked between two friends who walk together under a night sky, he might open himself to some confidence that would help me to a more precise definition of the relationship that subsisted between himself and Sylvia. In this I was disappointed. He walked along the asphalt promenade, now almost deserted, with the sea to our left marked only by an irregular faintly gleaming line of white in the black obscurity, without a word. He did not even respond to my efforts at conversation. Apparently he did not hear them. Overhead, the metallic blue-black heaven was powdered with a multitude of stars, twinkling down upon us from their immense remoteness. He threw his head back to contemplate them as we walked in silence. He baffled me, kept me somehow from my own private thoughts.

Suddenly he switched upon me.

"There can't be nothingness all the way, can there?" he demanded of me with a curious vehemence of interrogation. His hand made an involuntary half-gesture toward the scintillating dome of stars. "There must be *something*!" His manner had the disconcerting intensity of a man who has been brooding overlong in solitude. "At a distance everything melts into the blue. I have seen blank blue sky where on another day there's a range of mountains sharp and clear across the horizon. And they pretend that in all those millions of miles there is nothing—nothing but empty space!" He finished on a note of scorn.

"But surely the astronomers—" I began.

"Pah!" he interrupted me. "What do you or the astronomers know about it? Shut up!"

Shut up, I did. He was evidently not in the mood for reasonable conversation. He also shut up, pursuing in silence thoughts I could not follow. At last he brusquely suggested returning to the hotel.

* * * *

Next morning, when I met him in the breakfast-room, he was quite his old cheery self, and whatever resentment of his last night's rudeness still rankled in me, vanished in the odd charm of his smile. He reminded me of my promise to spend the morning with him tinkering about his seaplane. I acquiesced, for two reasons. First, I had nothing else to do, and I still retained enough of the impress of my old flying days to be genuinely interested in looking over a machine. Secondly, Sylvia would be coming to it for her flight. An uneasy night had not brought me to any satisfying theory of her real attitude toward him.

It was a bright sunshiny morning as we left the hotel, but a southwest breeze ruffled the surface of the sea; and the white isolated clouds that drifted across the blue overhead were evidently the advance-guards of a mass yet invisible beyond the horizon. Within an hour or two the sky would almost certainly be overcast. For the moment it was fine, however, and I enjoyed the fresh clarity of the air as we walked down the pier together. At its extremity, on the leeward side of the steamer landing-stage, the seaplane rode the running waves like a great bird that had alighted with outspread wings, the water splashing and sucking against her floats as she jerked and slackened on her mooring-ropes.

We hauled in on them, clambered down into her. She was, as he explained to me, intended for a super-fighting-scout, with an immense radius, a great capacity for climb, and a second machine-gun. The space where this second machine-gun had been, just behind the pilot, was now filled with four seats, in pairs behind each other, for the passengers, and he had had her landing-wheels replaced by floats. The morning was still young—nine o'clock struck just as we got on board the machine; and for the next two hours we pottered about her, cleaning her powerful motor, tautening the wire stays to her wings, looking into a hundred and one technical details that would have no interest for anyone but the expert. I enjoyed myself, and Toby was almost pathetically delighted to have some one with him who could enter into his enthusiasms. He had, I could guess, been leading a very solitary life for a long while.

Apparently he almost lived on board her. All sorts of gear were stowed away in her. In one of the lockers I found quite a collection of books, including the Dante he had quoted, and a number of others of a distinctly mystical type—odd reading for a flying man. In another, close to the pilot's seat, was a German automatic pistol.

"Souvenir of the great war, Daddy!" he smiled at me as I handled it.

"But do you know it's loaded?" I objected disapprovingly.

"Yes," he replied. "I shoot sea-gulls with it sometimes—chase 'em in the air. It's great sport."

I shrugged my shoulders. Chasing seagulls with a pistol was just one of those mad things I could well imagine Toby doing.

We gave her a dose of oil, filled up her petrol-tank—one of her original pair had been removed to make space for the passengers, but she still had a five-hundred-mile radius, he told me—and looked round for something else to do.

"Would you like to take her up and see how she climbs?" he invited me.

"No, thanks!" I replied hurriedly, uncomfortable in a sudden embarrassment. I had, thanks to the Armistice, managed to conceal my humiliating loss of nerve from the other fellows. "I've given up flying."

His queer eyes rested upon me for a penetrating glance, and I felt pretty sure that he guessed. But he made no comment.

"All right," he said. "I expect Miss Bryant will be along presently. We'll sit here and wait for her."

* * * *

We ensconced ourselves in the passengers' seats and sat there smoking our pipes. The mention of Miss Bryant's name seemed to have killed conversation between us. We sat in a silence that I, at least, felt to be subtly awkward. The intimacy of the morning was destroyed. Each of us withdrew into himself, each perhaps preoccupied with the same problem. Once, certainly, I caught his glance hostile upon me.

As I had expected, heavy clouds had come up from the southwest, and the sky was now almost completely overcast. But immediately overhead there was still a clear patch where, through a wide rift in the gray wrack, one looked into the infinite blue. Leaning back in his seat, he stared up at it with eyes that were dreamy in a peculiar fixity of expression.

"Jimmy," he said suddenly, in a voice that was far away with his thoughts, "in the old days, when you were flying high to drop on a stray Hun,—say, at twenty thousand feet, with the earth miles away out of touch,—didn't you ever feel that if you went a little higher—climbed and climbed—you would come to something—some other place? Didn't it almost seem to you that it would be as easy as going back?"

I glanced at him. Into my mind flitted a memory of his last night's wild talk about the stars. He had always been a little queer. Was he—not quite right?

"I can't say it did," I replied curtly. "I was always jolly glad to get down again."

He looked at me.

"Yes—I suppose so!" he commented. There was almost an insult in his tone.

Before I could decide whether to resent it or to humor him, I saw Sylvia approaching us along the pier, charming in her summer dress, but prudently with a raincoat over her arm.

"Here's Miss Bryant!" I said, glad of this excuse to put an end to the conversation.

He leaped to his feet with a peculiar alacrity.

"At last!" he ejaculated, as though an immeasurable time of waiting was at an end. He quenched a sudden flash of excitement in his eyes as he caught my glance on his face.

She stood above us on the pier, smiling.

"Here I am!" she said. "But it isn't a very nice morning, is it?"

"It will be all right up above," replied Toby. "Come along—down that next flight of steps." He was trembling with eagerness. I wondered suddenly whether I was wise in letting her go up with him. The man's nerves were obviously strung to high pitch. On the other hand, I had the greatest confidence in his skill—and it was only too likely that she would misinterpret any objections from me, would refuse to listen to them.

While I was hesitating, she had already descended to the lower stage, and Toby had helped her along the gangplank into the machine.

"You see I've brought my raincoat," she said. "It'll be cold up there, wont it?"

"That's no use," replied Toby with brutal directness. "Here!" He opened a locker where he kept the flying-coats for his passengers. "Put that on."

* * * *

I helped her with it. She looked more charming than ever in the thick leather coat, the close-fitting leather helmet framing her dainty features. Then I made a step toward the gangplank.

"But aren't you coming too?" she demanded in surprise.

Toby answered for me.

"Esdaile doesn't care for flying," he said with a sardonic smile, looking me straight in the eyes. There was a sort of mocking triumph in that unmistakable sneer.

226

"Oh—but *please*!" Sylvia turned to me pleadingly. "Do come!"

"I'd rather take you up alone," said Toby in a stubborn voice, looking up from the mooring-rope he had bent to untether.

She ignored him, laid a hand upon my arm.

"Wont you?" she asked.

"I should infinitely prefer not to," I replied awkwardly. I cursed myself for my imbecility, but the mere idea of going up in that machine made me feel sick inside, still so powerful was the memory of that moment long ago when, ten thousand feet up with a Hun just below me plunging in flames to destruction, I had felt my nerve suddenly break, my head go dizzy in an awful panic. "Please excuse me."

She could not, of course, guess my reason.

"I sha'n't go without you," she said obstinately. Her eyes seemed to be telling me something I was not intelligent enough to catch. "And I want to go. Please— *Jimmy*!"

I surrendered.

"All right," I said, feeling ghastly. "I'll come."

Toby stopped in the act of pulling on his flying-coat, and looked at me. His face was livid, his eyes almost insanely malignant in a sudden fury of bad temper.

"Don't think you're going to spoil it!" he said, through his teeth. "I'll see to that!"

With that cryptic remark, he swung himself into the pilot's seat and started the engine with a jerk that almost threw me into the water. I slid down to the seat beside Sylvia. Toby had already cast off the one remaining mooring-rope, and with a whirring roar that gave me an odd thrill of old familiarity, the propeller at our nose a dark blur in its initial low-speed revolutions, we commenced to move over the waves.

For a moment we had a slight sensation of their rise and fall as we partly tore through them, partly floated on their lifting crests, and then suddenly the engine note swelled to the deafening intensity of full power; the blur of the propeller disappeared; a fount of white spray, sunlit from a rift in the clouds, sprang up on either hand from the floats beneath us, hung poised like jeweled curtains at our flanks, stung our faces with flying drops. For yet a minute or two we raced through the high-flung water; and then abruptly the glittering foam-curtains vanished. Our nose lifted. We sagged for another splash, lifted again, on a buoyancy that was not the buoyancy of the sea. I glanced over the side, saw the tossing wave-crests already twenty feet below us.

Instinctively I looked round to Sylvia to see how she was taking it. Her eyes were bright, her face ecstatic. I saw her lips move as she smiled. But her words were swallowed in the roar of the engine, and the blast of air that almost choked one, despite the little mica windscreen behind which we crouched. I bent my ear close to her face, just caught her comment as she repeated it.

"It's—wonderful!" she gasped.

Then she clutched my arm in sudden nervousness as the machine banked side-wise. Below us, diminished already, the pier, the long promenade of Southbeach, whirled round dizzily in a complete circle, got yet smaller as they went. Toby was putting the machine to about as steep a spiral as it could stand. As we went round again and yet again, with our nose seeming to point almost vertically up to the gray ceiling of cloud and our bodies heavy against the backs of our seats, I had a spasm of alarm that turned to anger. What was he playing at? It was ridiculous to show off like this! I did not doubt his skill—but it would not be the first airplane to stall at so steep an angle that it slipped back in a fatal tail-spin. I noticed that Sylvia was not strapped in her seat, and promptly rectified the omission. It might be all right, but with an inexperienced lady-passenger, it was as well to take precautions if he was going to play tricks of this sort.

* * * *

Up and up we went in those dizzy spirals, Southbeach—disconcertingly never on the side on which one expected it—miniature below us; and I could not help admiring, despite my sickening nervousness, the masterly audacity with which he piloted his machine on the very limit of the possible. He never turned for a glance at us, but sat, lifted slightly above us by our slant, doggedly crouched at his controls. I could imagine his face, his lips pressed tight together, his queer eyes alight with the boyish exultation of showing us—or perhaps showing *me*?—what he could do. I did not need the demonstration. I had seen him climb often enough like a circling hawk, gaining height in an almost sheer ascent, racing a Hun to that point of superior elevation which meant victory.

There had been a time when I could have beaten him at it. But there was no necessity to play these circus-tricks now—above all, with a lady on board. Why could he not take her for an ordinary safe flight over the sea, gaining, in the usual way, a reasonable margin of height on an angle that would have been almost imperceptible? I quivered to clamber forward and snatch the controls from him as still we rose, perilously high-slanted, in sweep after circular sweep. The gray-black stretch of cloud was now close above us, the rounded modeling of its under-surface like a low roof that seemed to forbid further ascent.

Again Sylvia clutched at my arm, her face alarmed, and I bent my head down to catch the words she shouted against the all-swallowing roar of the engine. They came just audible.

"Is he—going—through this?"

Toby was still holding her nose up, plainly intending to get above the clouds. I saw no sense in making her uneasy. I put my mouth close to her head.

"Blue sky—above!" I shouted.

She nodded, reassured.

The next moment we had plunged into the mass. Except for the sudden twists as we banked, we seemed to be motionless in a dense fog. But the engine still roared, and drops of congealed moisture, collecting on the stays of the upper wings, blew viciously into our faces. The damp cold struck through me to my bones, and I remembered suddenly that I was in my extremely unsuitable ordinary clothes. There was no saying to what height this mad fool might take us—he was still climbing steeply—and I had no mind to catch my death of cold. Hanging on with one hand to the side of the canted-up machine that threatened to fling me out directly I rose from my seat, I managed to reach the locker where he kept the flying-coats for his passengers, wriggled somehow into one of them.

It was only by setting my teeth that I did it, for my head was whirling dizzily and, cursing the day I had strained my nerves beyond breaking-point, I had to fight back desperately an almost overmastering panic that came upon me in gusts from a part of me beyond my will. I could not have achieved it, had it not been for the fog which, blotting out the earth beneath us, obliterated temporarily the sense of height. I was shaking all over as I got back into my seat. I glanced at Sylvia. She was sitting quiet and brave, a little strained, perhaps, staring at the blank fog through which we drove in steadily upward sweeps.

* * * *

Suddenly we emerged into dazzling sunshine, warm despite the cold rush of the air. All above us was an infinite clarity of blue. Sylvia—I guessed rather than heard—shouted something, waved her arm in delighted surprise, pointing around and beneath. Close below us was no longer the earth, but that magical landscape which is only offered by the upper surface of the clouds. We rose for yet a minute or two before we could get the full impression of it. At our first emergence, great swelling banks of sunlit snow overtopped us here and there, blew across us from moment to moment, uncannily unsubstantial as we went through them, in mere fog. Then finally we looked down upon it all, the eye ranging far and wide over a magnificent confusion of multitudinous rounded knolls, of fantastic perilously toppling lofty crags from which streamed wisps of gossamer vapor, of grotesque mountains and tremendous chasms, such as the wildest scenery of earth can never show.

Familiar as it was to me, I could not help admiring anew the immense sublimity of that spectacle which drifts so brilliantly under the blue arch of heaven when the shadowed earth below teems with rain, that spectacle which the eye of earth-bound man never sees. To the extreme limit of vision it stretched, apparently solid, a fairy country gleaming snow-white under the vertical sun, across which our shadow, growing smaller at each instant, flitted like the shadow of a great bird.

I felt Sylvia's hand squeeze me in her delight. My exasperated annoyance with Toby died down, all but vanished. Perhaps he wasn't such a fool, after all. It was worth while to show her this. That was what he had climbed so steeply for. Now he would flatten out, circle once or twice to imprint this fairy scene upon her memory, and then descend. But he did not. He did not even glance round to us. He held the nose of the machine up, climbed still, higher and higher, in those sheer and dizzy spirals.

This was getting beyond a joke. I glanced at my watch, computed the minutes since we had risen from that gray-green sea now out of sight beneath the horizon-filling floor of cloud. We must be already over five thousand feet up. That was surely quite enough. He might lose his direction, cut off from the earth by that great cloud-layer, miss the sea for our return. A forced landing upon hard ground with those water-floats of ours would be a pretty ugly crash. I craned forward, looked over his shoulder at the dial of the barograph. We were *seven thousand*! What on earth—

I shouted at him, but of course he did not hear it in the deafening roar of the engine. I caught hold of his shoulder, shook him hard. I had to shake a second time before his face came round to me. It startled me with its strange set fixity of expression, the wild eyes that glared at me. I gesticulated, pointed downward. He opened his lips in a vicious ugly snarl, shouted something of which only the ugly rebuff of my interference was intelligible, turned again to his controls, lifted the machine again from its momentary sag.

I sank back into my seat, quivering. Sylvia glanced at me inquiringly. I shrugged my shoulders. She had not, I hoped, seen that ugly snarl upon his face. The cloud-floor was now far below us, its crags and chasms flattened to mere corrugations on its gleaming surface. The seaplane rose, circling round and round untiringly, corkscrewing ever up and up into the infinite blue above us.

I was now thoroughly alarmed. What was he playing at? I worried over the memory of his furious face when I had made my gestured expostulation. Surely he could have no serious purpose of any kind in thus climbing so steeply far above any reasonable altitude. There was no serious purpose imaginable. Unless—no, I refused to entertain the sudden sickening doubt of his sanity. He was playing a joke on us, on *me*. Guessing that I had lost my nerve, and angry with me for spoiling a *tête-à-tête* flight with Sylvia, he was maliciously giving me a twisting. Presently he would get tired of the joke, flatten out.

* * * *

But he did not get tired of it. Up and up we went, in turn after turn—rather wider circles now, for the air was getting rare and thin, and sometimes we sideslipped uncomfortably, and the engine flagged, threatening to misfire, until he readjusted the mixture—but still climbing. Far, far below us the cloud-floor was deceptive of our real height in its fallacious similitude to an immense horizon of snow-covered earth.

I glanced at my watch, calculated again our height from the minutes. We must surely now be over twelve thousand feet! I shrank nervously from the mere thought of again moving to look over his shoulder at the barograph. An appalling feeling of vertigo held me in its clutch. That last glance over the side had done it, reawakening all the panic terror which had swept over me that day when—at such a height as this—I had seen that Hun plunge to destruction and had suddenly realized, as though I had but just awakened from a dream, my own high-poised perilous instability. I sat there clutched and trembling, could not have moved to save my life. I would have given anything to have closed my eyes, forgotten where I was, but the horrible fascination of this upward progress held them open as though mesmerized. I tried to compute the stages of our ascent from our circling sweeps. Thirteen thousand—thirteen thousand five hundred—fourteen thousand—fourteen thousand five hundred—fifteen thousand—I gave it up. It was icily cold. My head was dizzy, my ears sizzling with altered blood-pressure. My lungs heaved in this rarefied atmosphere. I glanced at Sylvia. She looked ill; her lips were blue; she was gasping as though about to faint.

She looked at me imploringly, made a gesture with her hand toward Toby's inexorable back. I shrugged my shoulders in sign that I had already protested in vain. But nevertheless I obeyed. Once more I leaned forward and clutched at his shoulder. Once more, after I had shaken him furiously, he turned upon me with that savage snarl, shouted something unintelligible, and switched round again to his controls.

Sylvia and I looked at each other. This time she had seen. In her eyes I read also that doubt of his sanity which was torturing me. She motioned me toward the cockpit, pantomimed my taking over control. It was impossible. I gestured it to her. Even if my nerves had been competent to the task, it was certain that Toby would not voluntarily relinquish his place. To have attempted to take it from him—if he were indeed mad—would have resulted in a savage struggle where the equilibrium of the machine would inevitably have been lost—in about two seconds we should all of us be hurtling down to certain death. The only thing to do was to sit tight—and hope that he would suddenly have enough of this prank, and bring us earthward again. But even if he had suddenly vanished from his place, to clamber over into the cockpit and take charge was more than I could have done at that moment. There was a time when I might have done it. But now I was shaking like a leaf. I could not have pushed a perambulator, let alone pilot an airplane.

And still we climbed, roaring up and up. The yellow canvas of the lower plane, gleaming in the sunshine, seemed curiously motionless against the unchanging blue that was all around us. The earth, the very clouds below us, seemed totally lost. I could not bring myself to venture a glance down to them. We seemed out of contact with everything that was normal life, suspended in the infinite void. And yet the engine roared, and I knew that we still climbed.

* * * *

We must have been somewhere about twenty thousand feet. My head seemed as though it would burst. I was breathing with difficulty. A little higher, and we should need oxygen. Toby's face was of course hidden from me, but he sat steadily at his controls, apparently in no embarrassment. Probably he had recently been practicing flying to great heights—it would be his queer idea of amusing himself—and was more habituated to changes of atmospheric pressure. I looked at Sylvia. She was plainly much distressed—and more than distressed, *frightened*. I cannot describe the anguish which gripped me as I contemplated her. Whatever I had tried to pretend to myself down there on that distant earth in those six dreary months since my pride had been wounded, I knew now, with an atrocious vividness of realization, that I loved her. And I could do nothing—*nothing*—to save her, if that lunatic in front did not come to his senses! The imploring look she fixed upon me was exquisite torture. Speech was impossible in that deafening roar of the engine, but she made me understand—the bitter irony of it!—that it was in me she trusted. I took her hand, pressed it to my lips. If we were to die, she should at least know what I felt for her. And then—oh, miracle!—I felt my hand pulled toward her, taken to her lips. She met my eyes with a wan smile of unmistakable meaning.

And then, just as I was all dizzy with the shock of it, the roar of the engine ceased. There was a sudden silence that was awesome in its completeness. Our nose came down to slightly below the horizontal. Thank heaven, he was tired of the joke, was flattening out, was going to descend! We began, in fact, to circle in a wide, very slightly depressed, slanting curve. Toby twisted round from his seat, one hand still upon the controls. There was a grim little smile on his face as his eyes, curiously glittering, met mine.

"You get out!" he said curtly. His voice sounded strangely toneless, far off, in that rarefied upper atmosphere.

For a moment I had a spasm of alarm, but I could not believe he was serious. It was too fantastic, at twenty thousand feet in the air.

"Don't be a silly ass, Toby! Take us down. The joke has gone far enough." My own voice was thin in my ears.

He ignored my protest.

"This is where you get out!" he repeated stubbornly.

Was the man really mad? I thought it best to humor him, managed to force a little laugh.

"Thanks very much, but I'd rather go back with you," I said.

"We're not going back," he replied with grim simplicity. "But you are—here and now."

This was madness right enough! Our only chance was to get him into conversation, turn the current of his thoughts somehow, coax him back to earth.

"Not going back?" I grinned at him as if he were being really funny. "Where are you going, then?"

"We're going on—Sylvia and I."

* * * *

He smiled at her fondly, nodded as though sure of her assent. She uttered a little cry of alarm, clutched at me. All the time, while we

233

were speaking, he was steering the airplane automatically with one hand, bringing her round and round in wide, flat circles where we lost the minimum of height.

"On?" I said in innocent inquiry, while my brain worked desperately. Curiously enough, in that moment of crisis, I found my head as clear, my nerves as steady, as they had ever been in my life. All my dizzy turmoil had vanished. I forgot that I had ever had a panic in the air. I was merely trying to think of some scheme by which I might be able to replace him at those controls. "On—where?"

He jerked his hand upward.

"Up there! On and on, until we come to—" He stopped himself suddenly, his face diabolically suspicious. "You think I'm going to tell you, don't you? You think you'll be able to follow us? But you wont! You get out—here and now—d'you understand?"

I tried to be cunning.

"But Toby!" I objected. "I think I know the way—better than you do, perhaps. Change places and let me take the machine."

It was a false move.

"What?" he cried. "You think you know the way, do you? You think you know the way beyond the stars?" He burst suddenly into a hideous laugh, thin and cackling in the awesome silence of that upper air. "Then you'll never get there! I'll see to that! Get out!" He gestured over the side, into the blue abyss above which we circled. "*Quick!*"

* * * *

I glanced at Sylvia. She was sitting numbed with horror, incapable of speech. As I looked, she jerked forward in a gesture of wild protest abruptly checked by the straps which held her in her seat. The airplane rocked in its now tender equilibrium just as something went *crack*! past my head. My eyes were back on Toby in the fraction of an instant. Still twisted in his seat, he was leveling that automatic pistol at me. I could see by his eyes that he was in the very act of pressing the trigger for the second time.

Four years' war-service in the air make a man pretty quick. In a flash I had ducked, flung myself upon him over the slight partition between us, wrenched at his wrist. Risky as it was, it was certain death to all of us if this homicidal maniac was not dealt with. His awkward half-turned position put him at a disadvantage, but he fought grimly, with all a maniac's strength, trying to point the muzzle of that pistol at my body. Automatically, of course, he rose to face me, relinquished the controls to use both hands. I felt the machine lurch and plunge dizzily nose downward. I had one lightning-quick thought—thank God, Sylvia was strapped!—and then I tumbled over the partition headfirst into the cockpit.

It was not thought but instinct with which I clutched the steering-stick,—one had not much time for thought when fighting the nimble Fokker,—got into some sort of position on the seat. We were vertically nose down, spinning horribly—but not once but many times in the war I had shammed dead, gone rushing earthward in a realistic twirling spin and then abruptly flattened out of it upside down and come up like a rocket over the pursuing Hun. This was simpler. I had only to pull her out of it—and only when I pulled her out of it, circled her round once for a long steady glide, did I realize that I was alone in that cockpit. There was no Toby!

I glanced back to Sylvia. She sagged in her seat against the straps—fainted. Just as well, I thought grimly. I touched the engine to a momentary activity to test it, shut it off again for a long circling descent toward the cloud-floor far below. An exultation leaped in me, the exultation of old days of peril in the air. I thought of Toby, with whom I had shared so many, with a sudden warming of the heart. Poor old Toby! He had died as after all he perhaps would have wished to die, high up in the infinite blue—dead of shock long before he reached the earth. I thrilled with the old-time sense of mastery over a fine machine, delicately sensitive to the controls, as that massed and pinnacled cloud landscape grew large again beneath me. My one anxiety was whether it hid sea or land. Then, just as we drew near, I saw a deep black gulf riven in its snowy mass—saw down through that gulf a tiny model steamship trailing a long white wake....

The wedding? That was last year.

Printed in Great Britain
by Amazon